P R A I S E   F O R

Far from Here

"Nicole Baart is a writer of immense strength. Her lush, beautiful prose, her finely drawn characters, and especially her quirky women, all made *Far from Here* a book I couldn't put down."

—Sandra Dallas, *New York Times* bestselling
author of *Prayers for Sale* and *The Bride's House*

"*Far from Here* was a rare journey to a place that left me healed and renewed by the end of this beautiful, moving novel. A tribute to love in all its forms—between a man and a wife, between sisters, and among mothers and daughters— my heart ached while I read *Far from Here*, but it ached more when I was done and there were no more pages to turn."

—Nicolle Wallace, *New York Times* bestselling
author of *Eighteen Acres*

"Nicole Baart is a huge talent who has both a big voice and something meaningful to say with it. *Far from Here* is a gorgeous book about resilient people living in a broken world, finding ways to restore hope and even beauty in the pieces."

—Joshilyn Jackson, author of *Gods in Alabama*
and *A Grown-Up Kind of Pretty*

Far from Here

A Novel

NICOLE BAART

H HOWARD BOOKS
A DIVISION OF SIMON & SCHUSTER, INC.

New York Nashville London Toronto Sydney New Delhi

Howard Books
A Division of Simon & Schuster, Inc.
1230 Avenue of the Americas
New York, NY 10020

First Howard Books trade paperback edition February 2012

HOWARD and colophon are trademarks of Simon & Schuster, Inc.

For information about special discounts for bulk purchases,
please contact Simon & Schuster Special Sales at 1-866-506-1949
or business@simonandschuster.com.

The Simon & Schuster Speakers Bureau can bring authors to your live event. For more information or to book an event, contact the
Simon & Schuster Speakers Bureau at 1-866-248-3049 or visit our
website at www.simonspeakers.com.

Designed by Jaime Putorti

Manufactured in the United States of America

10 9 8 7 6 5 4 3 2 1

Library of Congress Cataloging-in-Publication Data

Baart, Nicole.
   Far from here : a novel / Nicole Baart.
       p.   cm.
   1. Air pilots—Fiction.   2. Missing persons—Fiction.   3. Married people—Fiction.   I. Title.
   PS3602.A22F37 2012
   813'.6—dc22   2011026943

ISBN 978-1-4391-9733-2
ISBN 978-1-4391-9735-6 (ebook)

For Aaron, always

Prologue

Danica

The first time he took me up, I thought I was going to die.

It was an accident, really, a stroke of luck or fate or happenstance that lured me into the cockpit that morning. Under normal circumstances I wouldn't have touched with the tip of my little toe the small red-and-white Cessna 180 that Etsell used for teaching rookie pilots. But his lesson had been a no-show. And the plane was fueled up and ready to go, waiting on the runway for takeoff.

I was huddled in the hangar, arms wrapped tight against my chest to ward off the early-spring chill as Hazel yakked on endlessly about her grandson who was in the army. Later, I wondered if it was orchestrated, if she had baited me with a fresh pot of coffee and the pay-attention-to-me slant of her puppy-brown eyes. But at the time, all I could think of was that her steel-wire mop of hair could use a good wash and set.

"My grandson is going to be in the special ops," she said with a grin.

I nodded, though I doubted that those sorts of things were determined in the first week of boot camp.

"He's going to be one of those secret agents. Navy SEAL or something. Imagine that: Special Agent Jansen." Hazel smirked at my halfhearted acknowledgment. Then her eyes slid past me and she tipped her head in the direction of the runway. "I think Etsell is waving at you."

Etsell always waved at me. Or threw me kisses, winked my way, or fixed me in a gaze that made me blush. But I was grateful for the distraction, for the chance to break the eager hold that Hazel had on me. Although she wasn't blood, she was more his mother than the woman who died in a car crash when he was eight. And I owed Hazel a certain deference for bringing up my husband the best way she knew how. It was nearly impossible for me to drop off Ell at the airport and not give Hazel at least a moment of my time, even though I all but counted the minutes. And yet, as I turned, I remember deciding to buy her a gift certificate for the salon. I could fix her hair without begging for the chance to do so. A daughterly gesture, even if I didn't feel much like her daughter.

I raised my arm to flutter my fingers at Etsell, to offer him a quick, perfunctory farewell before he took off down the runway. But when I caught sight of my handsome husband, that blond-headed god who still took my breath away after nearly two years of being his bride, I realized that his gesture was far from routine.

Etsell was waving me toward him. Beckoning, actually, sweeping both arms in the air in wide, engulfing strokes as if he could, by will alone, draw me to him.

I was shaking my head no even as Hazel put her hand on the small of my back and gave me a hearty shove. "Go on," she prodded. "It's about time."

"No." I was cold-palmed at the very thought of climbing into the cockpit of that floating impossibility. If God had wanted us to fly, he would have given us wings.

"Don't be selfish. It would mean so much to him."

"I don't care." But even as I said it, I knew that today

was the day. Why hadn't I realized it before? I should have woken up sensing a fundamental shift in the balance of my personal universe. A me-sized tsunami, an earthquake of Danica proportions. It took Etsell gesturing before me for the world to tilt on its axis.

"My lesson canceled!" he shouted across the distance between us. "Come on!"

Hazel walked me over, her hand still firm against my back, and Etsell watched me come. He beamed, more accurately, and I knew by the twist of his lips that this was nothing short of serendipity for him. A moment of such destiny, such perfection, he hardly knew how to encompass the joy of it.

I think I would have refused him even then.

But when I was within arm's reach, Etsell pulled me to him. His hands slid up my arms, and in the second before he knotted his fingers in my hair and kissed me full on the mouth, I caught the familiar scent of him as if he carried bits of life in his hands. Petrol. Thick, dark oil choked with dust, and above it all, the sharp tang of metal that made my jaw ache until his lips smoothed the sting away.

"Fly with me," he murmured.

How could I say no?

Behind me, I heard Hazel laugh as she walked away.

Etsell had to half lift me into the cockpit, I was trembling so hard. He buckled the tangled straps of my seat belt, reaching around me as if I were a child. And I felt like one, shrinking and terrified as I watched his capable fingers work the shiny clasp. It was cold outside, but he had rolled up the sleeves of his Henley to the elbow, and sun shone off the pale hairs on his forearm. *My golden boy*, I thought, touching the halo of his honeyed head with my fingertips.

He growled and arched his neck to catch my finger in his flawless teeth.

"I bite," he had teased me once, years ago when we were still dating. But I had known that from the very beginning. Just looking at Etsell Greene was a heartbreaking experience, a painful acknowledgment of the obvious truth that he was not, and would never be, tamed.

Thankfully, his bites didn't hurt, not the real ones, and in the end he sucked my finger like a lollipop and kissed the very tip.

"You're going to love this," he assured me. "We'll get matching planes when you fall in love with flying."

I was too scared to shake my head.

Etsell shut my tin-can door and ran around the front of the plane so he could climb into the cockpit beside me. I noticed little things, details like tiny morsels that I plucked between my fingers and swallowed whole in an act of desperation: the orange vest he zipped up in one smooth motion, the weight of the headset when he settled it over my ears, the cracked plaque that nestled between a dizzying array of switches, dials, and round-faced gauges that proclaimed the airplane a No Smoking Zone.

"We're ready to roll." Etsell's voice was detached and hollow conveyed through the static-riddled radio. My eyes flashed to him, anxious for some sort of reassurance, hopeful that if he saw the look in my eyes he'd call the whole thing off and let me keep my feet planted on solid ground. But he was tapping a dial, showing me what instrument would inform us when the engine was sufficiently warmed up. "There are plastic-lined paper bags in the little pocket at your feet," he teased as he started the engine. "Don't mess up my plane."

Within minutes we were taxiing down the runway, steadily picking up speed as we neared the end of the long swath of blacktop. I squeezed my eyes shut, but the motion and the darkness made me dizzy. It was a drunken, spinning feeling, and I fought it until I was afraid I'd throw up before we ever left the ground. As the earth began to thunder beneath me, I opened my eyes in time to see the nose of the little plane point slightly heavenward and take to the sky.

It wasn't quite what I expected. Liftoff. We didn't shoot into the air like a stray bullet or plunge upward with the sort of vicious thrust I imagined necessary if we insisted on defying gravity. It wasn't violent or gut-wrenching or wild. Instead, we rose in the sort of slow ascent that made me think of bubbles in cream, slow and heavy, drifting lazily from the tip of a stirred spoon. The wheels of the plane parted from the ground in a subtle act of departure that left me feeling weightless and detached. For just a moment, between the earth and the sky, it was if I didn't exist.

"Nowhere to go but up," Etsell whispered against my ear.

We were pressed together, arm to arm, hip to hip, leg to leg in a cockpit so tiny my shoulder brushed the door on the other side. I pushed myself against my husband, huddling in the hard line of his body as if I could make myself more a part of him than I already was.

"Don't be afraid," he said.

I had wanted him to say, "There's nothing to be afraid of."

My stomach stayed behind on the tarmac as we flew, but after the almost surreal moment of separation, my heart was agonizingly present. It pounded out a rhythm that seemed to fill the cockpit as Etsell climbed higher and higher over the fields. There was a terrible beauty in the way he tapped dials and spoke softly to Hazel below. He wore his headphones loosely, the small microphone hovering beside his mouth as if waiting for a kiss while he whispered in a language I didn't understand.

I hoped that if I watched him I wouldn't worry about where I was. But turning my head made my stomach roll in concert with the rise of the hills beneath us, and in the end I had no choice but to accept the slant of the world below me as it slow-danced across the horizon line.

Somewhere in the back of my panicked mind I registered that it was a beautiful day. The undulating hills of northwest Iowa made a puffed patchwork quilt that seemed a thousand miles beneath my feet. And the sky was cloudy-bright, filled with canted swaths of light as the sun alternately shone against a periwinkle backdrop and hid behind clouds like bits of pulled cotton. The air was crisp and clean, and before I could grasp how high we had climbed, we were there among them, surrounded by hillocks of white that made me think of heaven. I could have opened the door and gathered a handful of mist. The thought made me shiver.

"Breathe," Etsell scolded me.

I gasped in a mouthful of air that tasted of exhaust.

"It's gorgeous, isn't it?"

I nodded and discovered that once I started I could not stop the steady bob of my head.

Etsell was gentle with me, climbing slowly and drifting down on crosswinds so I could admire the tractors as they disked fields the color of night. It was lovely, all of it: the dark lines in the dirt that shone like fresh ink, the trees softened by buds on the threshold of splitting open, the grid of gravel roads where cars made snaillike progress. And a part of me couldn't help but love it, couldn't help but be thrilled by the change of perspective that made me feel like I was seeing the world for the very first time. Or maybe just through different eyes.

But most of all, I feared it. Feared it and loathed it with the sort of churning agony that made me frantic with the need to feel my feet on solid ground.

When we finally landed and Etsell turned to me triumphant, I could only choke out one word: "Never."

The spark of joy in his eyes dimmed. "What do you mean?"

This time, I managed two words: "Never again."

1

Offerings

They brought things.

Like hopeful penitents or sojourners making the pilgrimage to a holy land filled with story and sorrow, they arrived with gifts. Most offerings were cradled by careful hands, and delivered with the sort of ceremony and circumstance usually reserved for sacraments. Even the serving plates were chosen with intention, exquisite and rarely used pieces that had obviously been rescued from corner curios and china cabinets. Rescued and washed clean, soap and water removing the accumulated dust of weeks or months. Sometimes years.

Dani accepted an oblong, curved platter adorned with impossibly tiny, hand-painted flowers. The artful, black-hearted pansies were dwarfed by still-warm squares of generous walnut brownies, stacked like soft bricks in a fragrant monument to her grief. And there was a stew in a fat soup tureen, a lidded, porcelain rarity that seemed to glow with the almost heady scent of beef roast and caramelized onions. It was thick and unnatural for a warm May day, and Dani held her breath when she placed it on the counter next to the small army of dinnerware that had begun to amass beneath her painted cabinets. Casseroles and baskets of store-bought fruit and cookies, cups of café au lait with heavy cream and raw sugar, just the way she liked it. If she was really lucky, or if her mom came, the caffeine fix was laced with a shot or two of something stronger. But even the Irish coffee was a waste.

People brought things because they didn't know what else to do. Somewhere, below the tingling numbness that trembled against her skin, Dani knew they were trying, and she returned the favor with a reluctant grace, welcoming each well-meaning act of charity with heavy, outstretched arms. She assured every visitor that their gift was perfect. Just what she needed. The only thing she could bring herself to taste. *How did you know?*

The truth was, she didn't want their food or their condolences. After they left, she upended the brownies into the garbage can, abandoning the stack of fudgy sweets to the cupboard under the sink, where they made her entire kitchen smell like a confectionary. With a long-handled spoon, she ladled the hot stew into the garbage disposal. Chunks of potatoes and whole baby carrots and bits of barley floated in the sink like putrid, autumn confetti until she flipped the wall switch and ground it into a sludgy paste that oozed down the drain. It was all she could do not to vomit.

They were an insult, all those filled plates, those ridiculous portions of food and drink. As if she could eat. As if a chicken-broccoli casserole could fill the space where he was supposed to be.

Nothing could touch it.

No amount of filling could ease the echoing ache of the fissure that had split open her heart, her very life, ripped it straight down the middle so that she knew what it was like to fall to pieces. You didn't fall, not really. It wasn't nearly so dramatic or drawn out. One word or two, just a few, and when the paralysis passed you looked down and realized that you were bleeding from a wound that would surely never heal. It didn't hurt until you saw the blood, until you realized that you had been torn and what was taken from you could not be put back. Not without leaving a scar. Worse. There would be much more than a scar. She felt deformed. She knew she always would be.

Dani didn't want another batch of oatmeal-raisin cookies. Or her friends, her sisters, her mother. Not even a funeral could give her closure. And in many ways she longed for exactly that. For the known.

Etsell wasn't dead; he was *gone*.

That, Dani decided, was infinitely worse.

✒

They brought small sacrifices to the altar of her mourning, but the only oblation Dani accepted was the one that Benjamin offered.

He knocked on her door the day after she got the call, almost exactly forty-eight hours after Etsell's plane went missing from the tiny airport in Seward, Alaska. Dani was furious at first because her reclusive neighbor was knocking on her back door, the whitewashed, creaking screen that opened on a little kitchen garden where nothing much deigned to grow. It was her private entrance and her secret escape, the passage through which she quietly ducked when the front doorbell rang with the insistent sound of sympathy that she longed to ignore. But her rage was rash and unfounded, it fizzled out as quickly as it flared, and Dani was left feeling bereft of emotion, of even the will to stand up and answer the door.

At first she tried to pretend that she wasn't at home. She was sitting at the small breakfast table in the kitchen, a round-topped relic that she had refinished in black lacquer with a rubbed metallic glaze. Her hands were on the soft-ridged surface, her fingers following the almost imperceptible dips and whorls that traced the path of the rag she had used to polish the dark wood after she had sanded the corners and blown away the sawdust with her own pursed lips. Etsell had laughed as she labored over the table. He didn't understand the almost sensual way she swept circles over the new, glossy paint or why her eyes narrowed to focus on every detail in the old tabletop.

"It's nothing special," he told her for the hundredth time. "It was cheap when your grandma bought it, and it's no heirloom now."

"I love the shape," Dani muttered, barely registering that he was trying to provoke her. It was good-natured, it always was, and she wasn't in the mood. The table was finally dry and she was lost in the art of unearthing hints of the original wood grain beneath.

"Oh, I know." Etsell moved behind her, formed himself to her body as she bent over the smooth surface with a sheet of three-hundred-grit sandpaper clutched in her hand. "You like the legs," he murmured against her neck. "The twisting lines. The old-world carved details and . . ."

"Ball feet," she supplied in a whisper. The sandpaper was already slipping from her fingers.

"Ball feet," he echoed. "And you're finishing it . . . Art Deco?"

"With a French Provincial slant," Dani agreed, shrugging a little so that the warm skin at the curve between her shoulder and neck rose to meet his lips. His breath was hot, and she stifled a shiver as he parted the curtain of her hair and spilled kisses against the hidden places beneath.

"I love it when you talk furniture to me." Etsell's voice was low and husky, and Dani couldn't help but giggle.

She spun in his arms, ready to push him away and get back to the task at hand, but he caught her around the waist and lifted her onto the table. "I have work to do," Dani protested, but Etsell was already lowering her, laying her back so that the strawberry spill of her long hair shone like burnished gold against the obsidian wood. She didn't fight him. Didn't want to.

When Benjamin knocked, and an instant later when he unnecessarily announced his presence through the open screen, Dani was remembering the afternoon that Etsell proved he listened to every word she said. As he slid her T-shirt over her head, he whispered about the expeditionary decor of the corner bedroom that she had turned into an exotic library retreat with splashes of wicker, bamboo, and an oversized leather chair accented by tarnished brass rivets. And the way she married a more masculine Mission style with shabby chic touches in their tiny master bedroom. The vertical slats of the well-balanced bed were softened by chenille pillows done in snowfall whites and subtle, minty greens that gave off such an impression of newness that the room felt cool and fresh even in the middle of a Midwestern July.

As his hands spanned her waist, Dani realized for the first time that Etsell listened. He knew her, even though he teased her about furniture restorations and groaned when she insisted on hemming curtains while he watched Monday Night Football. Of course she knew her husband loved her, but the understanding that he heard every word she said nearly choked her as she sat at the very table where he covered her body with his own. The words he whispered were more intimate even than the way he moved above her.

And Benjamin's interruption of her solitary reverie was anything but welcome.

So she sat at the table and held her breath, hoping her backyard neighbor would go away. But he knocked again, and called again, using her given name and then one that made her face flush with heat as if the sun suddenly beat down on her cheeks.

"Danica? Mrs. Greene? Are you home?"

She pushed herself up from the table and crossed the kitchen in a few short strides. Though the door was hidden by the half wall where her refrigerator stood sentinel, Dani could see Benjamin nearly as soon as she stood. He filled the narrow doorway, his frame as long and gangly as the narrow pieces of white molding that encased the door. Though he wasn't obscenely tall—all legs and arms and joints that seemed to turn in unusual directions—he did have to bend a little to peer inside the sagging screen of her door. He could have poked his nose through a tiny hole in the screen, Dani realized. It looked like he was about to.

"I'm home," she told him unnecessarily. Her voice was gravelly and unused, and she cleared her throat quietly, ashamed of the evidence that she was alone. "Call me Dani. How many times have I told you to call me Dani?"

"Sorry. May I?" But he was already letting himself in.

She backed away, giving him space to enter her kitchen uninvited, and took stock of the man before her. In many ways, he was the antithesis of her Etsell. It was strange to be looking at Benjamin in the flesh while Etsell already seemed consigned to the mist and magic of her memory. The two men were night and day, light and dark, and seeing her neighbor's wiry frame only made Dani long for the sturdy breadth of her husband's arms.

Benjamin gave his head a little tilt to let his dark hair fall back from his forehead, and offered Dani a slow, measured smile. It surprised her because it didn't seem to Dani that he smiled often, and when he did his straight, white teeth were overshadowed by a neat goatee. It was the sort of carefully groomed mustache and small, pointed beard that were so carefully maintained they looked more like accessories than a part of his facial structure. Much about Benjamin seemed deliberate, and he gave off a faint, esoteric vibe as if he was a brooding poet or maybe a tortured artist. He made Dani feel a bit nervous, he always had. At least, she realized as she studied his charcoal pants and long-sleeved dress shirt, he wasn't wearing his clerical collar. The top two buttons of his shirt were undone and the only thing that adorned his bare neck was the exaggerated line of his collarbone.

They stood there for a moment, just staring at each other. Dani always expected Benjamin to be smooth, the sort of confident, easy-talking pastor who had populated the darkened spiritual corridors of her youth. But the man who lived in the blue bungalow across her backyard didn't fit any stereotypes. In fact, whenever she saw him in his starched, white collar, it seemed mildly offensive to her, as if he were wearing a Halloween costume out of season.

Benjamin shuffled his feet against the stained linoleum of her kitchen floor, and all at once Dani dredged up manners from somewhere deep in her wounded mind. She opened her mouth to offer him something to drink, but before she could utter a word he took a step toward her and thrust out his hands. Her eyes fell to the span of his long fingers, surprised that she hadn't even noticed that he was carrying something.

"I didn't know what to bring," Benjamin said in the same slow, calculated way he said everything. "So I brought asparagus."

It was true. He cradled a thick bundle of fresh-picked spears, the grape clusters of their smooth heads so plump and tight, Dani was sure that she could catch the faintest whiff of the ground from which they came. The stalks were slender and even, the color a crisp balance between olive and moss.

"Where did you find them?"

The corner of Benjamin's lip pulled up conspiratorially when he said, "I have a spot."

Nearly everyone in the small Iowa town of Blackhawk had a spot, and each one was a secret that was carefully guarded and maintained. When the asparagus grew wild in the ditches every spring, people took to the roads and combed the deep grasses for the treasures that lay hidden beneath. Sometimes a lucky hunter would stumble across a trove, but usually finding the sweet spots took patience and planning. Of course, later in the summer, when the plants had gone to seed it was easy to spot where asparagus had grown. Soft-tufted bushes blew like banners in the breeze announcing every missed opportunity. But finding them back in the spring was a challenge, the sort of undertaking that required forethought and planning, surreptitious groundwork that would not come to fruition for many long months while northwest Iowa lay blanketed in snow.

Benjamin's stoic forbearance had obviously paid off because this was the first of the asparagus that Dani had seen. It made her mouth water.

"There was a gentleman in my church who paid his hired hands to dig up the asparagus plants on his property," Benjamin said when her silence stretched on uninterrupted. He seemed nervous, anxious to fill the space between them with words, even if they were meaningless. Dani forced herself to look at her earnest neighbor. "Why would he do that?"

"He was sick of people harvesting in his ditch."

"My grandfather once chopped down an apple tree

because kids kept taking the fruit it cast off," Dani responded without thinking.

Benjamin's eyebrows lifted in wonder. "Imagine that."

"Is that where you got these?" Dani made herself reach for the asparagus.

"What do you mean?"

"From the guy in your church who dug up the plants."

"No," Benjamin turned over his hands and emptied the cool stalks into Dani's palms. "These were a surprise. A gift."

She turned her gaze to the long lines of the vegetables in her palms, and felt a prickle of wonder at the heft of the bundle, the weight of the spears that seemed too willowy to weigh much more than air. "Thank you," she muttered. And for the first time since people began showing up at her door, she meant it.

Benjamin didn't say anything, but Dani looked up in time to see him nod his acknowledgment. He was already leaving, his hand on the door, and though she was grateful to see him go, Dani felt a pang of loneliness stab through her like a subtle knife. Of course, Etsell wouldn't have been coming home tonight anyway, but just knowing that he couldn't, that he was somewhere off the known map, made her feel like she was the last person living in a hollow, futile world.

"Thank you," she said again.

Benjamin responded by closing the screen door with a gentle click.

It was enough. The sound of the latch falling home, the unexpected kindness of a relative stranger, the evidence of life in her hands. When the first sob wracked Dani, she went weak in the knees and sank to the kitchen floor. *Gone*, her low moans seemed to whisper. *Gone*. But that wasn't true, it wasn't for sure. Not yet.

The Civil Air Patrol had told her that Etsell could very

well be making his way back to Seward even as they sent out helicopters to search for him. Planes went down slowly sometimes, they landed in meadows or on the sides of mountains that seemed too craggy for even sure-footed goats. And his emergency transmitter could have been low on batteries or disabled during a bumpy touchdown. There was hope. There was always hope.

Dani didn't feel very hopeful.

But when her tears stopped, when the heaving of her chest became nothing more than the slow shudder of her spent fears, she saw the detritus of green around her and felt a longing so deep it made her shiver. She had dropped the asparagus when she fell, and the stalks lay in geometric designs in her lap and over the cold, gray linoleum of her floor. They made a strange puzzle of discarded produce, clean and new and freshly plucked from the unknowing ground, waiting to be devoured like little promises.

Dani picked one from the pile on her thigh and snapped off the woody end. The spear was delicate, impossibly thin, and she put it to her lips. It was cool and firm, it crunched beneath her teeth with an unexpected juicy pop. She ate it quickly, grabbing the next before she had swallowed the first. It soothed her somehow, Benjamin's gift, and she feasted on his offering until her stomach hurt.

In the absence of all that mattered, it felt good to be filled with something.

Danica

Hazel told me that Etsell wanted to be a pilot from almost the moment he heard that his mother had died.

"Have you heard of the song 'I'll Fly Away'?"

Of course I had. But instead of justifying her question with a response, I blew a bubble with the watermelon gum I was chewing. It popped against my lips and I had to pick the sticky, pink mess off with my fingertips. I was nineteen. Engaged to the man she considered her son.

"I think that's what he wanted to do," Hazel continued, seemingly unperturbed by my obvious disinterest. "To just fly away, far from here, from every reminder of her."

"He had his dad," I reminded her. "It's not like he was completely alone."

Hazel pursed her lips and slid me a reproving look. "Dani, honey, you're young, but you're not stupid. At least, I didn't take you for stupid. Owen Greene was a sorry drunk. There wasn't a mean bone in his body, but he loved the bottle more than he loved his son, and that's a fact. Etsell lost everything when he lost his mom."

Except me, I thought, remembering the first time that he looked my way with eyes so full of intent I didn't have to wonder if he wanted me or not. Love would come later, I reasoned, giving in to daydreams as my naive idealism painted pictures of our future together. They were water-color soft, an impressionist fantasy. How could they not be? Etsell was beautiful. A dark, tortured soul hidden beneath the guise of a handsome, small-town co-ed—the very epitome of every romantic stereotype and cliché.

"Don't get me wrong, I'm glad he has you," Hazel said. Her words startled me. Had I spoken aloud?

I nodded, assured of my own value in Etsell's world.

"It's just a tough situation all around. I think Ell reminds Owen of her too much. Or maybe not enough."

Etsell's father might have been a raging alcoholic, but his illness was a sort of slow suicide. He tried to make sure that he was the only one affected by his addiction, but no action can exist in a vacuum, and Ell grew up in a home that reeked of sorrow and booze. I should have been furious with the man who failed at raising my soon-to-be husband, but it was almost impossible to hate someone as broken as Owen. He was the sort of simple soul that was afforded but one love in life, and his heart belonged exclusively to his dead wife.

I never met Miss Melanie, but she was ubiquitous in Blackhawk, a part of local legend and lore. Everyone called her Miss Melanie because she taught a generation of second graders at the elementary school before she was miraculously blessed with a child of her own. I'm told Etsell was born a charmer, a prince who stole his mother's heart the very moment she first caught a glimpse of his sweet baby fist. But the tiny curl of his chubby hand was the only thing she saw for quite a while, because immediately after delivery Miss Melanie had an eclampsia-induced seizure and slipped into a coma for almost three days.

Owen didn't blame Etsell, not exactly, but apparently he

wasn't much of a father even after Miss Melanie recovered. He was too old, too set in his ways, too comfortable in the life that he had spent a quarter of a century perfecting with his wife. When she was killed, they might as well have buried him with her. He would have preferred it that way.

Hazel sighed heavily and put her hands on her hips with a sort of finality. "I'm glad he has you," she repeated. "But as much as you hate to hear it, you're just a little girl."

I nearly swallowed my gum in a gasp of indignation. Little girl? Etsell and I had been together for three years—a lifetime—and we had weathered much as one. I considered myself his bride, body and spirit, even then. But before I could assure my fiancé's surrogate mom that I was a woman, she gave my shoulder a hard squeeze and walked with purpose out of the hangar. It was only then I realized that Etsell was coming in for a landing, the wings of his aircraft mimicking the perfect plane of the horizon beneath him.

Owen Greene was undeniably lost in a world of his own wretched design, but he had the sense to buy his only son an airplane for his fifteenth birthday. Of course, it was a rusted hunk of junk, and of course, Etsell couldn't fly it alone. But he loved it with the sort of passion some boys reserve for cars or sports or girls. By the time he celebrated fifteen years of life, he had already logged thirty hours with a flight instructor and was well on his way to receiving his student certificate. In just one more year he officially claimed the status of student pilot, and when he turned seventeen he held his very own pilot's license.

I met Etsell the week after he took his pilot's exam and passed the medical evaluation, the final check ride, and the FAA written test without a single definable mistake or insufficiency. He wanted to take me up in his plane. I refused, but he asked me out anyway.

One Friday night in early fall, we went to Pizza Hut and devoured a medium pan-crust supreme. Afterward, when Etsell took me to Blackhawk's tiny airport under the cloak of a deepening night, I let him hold me against the corrugated metal side of the hangar and kiss me until I didn't know where he stopped and I started.

It was the beginning of everything. The moment when we breathed into each other and the rest of our lives sprang forth like a new bud, filled with the potential of all that we could be. At the very genesis of our relationship, we made an unspoken covenant, the sort of binding commitment that lashed his broken heart to mine as if pressing the hurt against my wholeness could only result in healing. He leaned into me and I let him come, wounded child, lover of air and sky, things above.

I was his ground.

"I want to be a bush pilot," Etsell told me after I had officially accepted his proposal. It seemed a difficult admission for him, the sort of confession that ranked up there with a full disclosure of infidelity. He was studying the way our hands twined together, the interlocking weave of his thick fingers twisted through mine. But when I didn't answer immediately he looked up, eyes the color of slate-rimmed sky hidden beneath dark lashes, and gave me a crooked, hopeful smile.

"I know," I said.

His brow wrinkled in confusion.

"Hazel." Her name was clarification enough.

"And you're not mad?"

I shrugged.

"Would you . . . ? Could you see yourself living in Alaska?"

No. Land of the Midnight Sun, of glacier fields and boundless, uncharted territories. Bears. Moose chewed on geraniums in suburban backyards. I had seen the pictures. And I had read the employment guide that Etsell had downloaded from the Alaska Pilot Exchange and conveniently left on the table in his father's immaculate galley kitchen.

The front page of the hefty booklet declared ALASKA BUSH PILOT in bold capitals and featured an uninspired photograph of a float plane in front of a dreary hangar. It made me depressed just to look at it. But I read it anyway because he left it for me to find, and because I wanted to know what I would face as his bride.

It was a terrifying document. After a brief introduction in which the authors explained that some people believed the dangerous days of the bush pilot were relegated to history, they went on to disprove such comforting notions. Modern technology aside, they cited extremely adverse weather conditions, unpredictable hazards, and the need for dead reckoning when equipment failed. I knew that Etsell often flew by wind triangle when he had a route memorized by heart, but the thought of blind navigation over thousands of square miles of mountains and water and tundra filled me with a quiet dread like thick sediment seeping into the spaces between my bones. It was a helpless feeling, the sort of realization that made me certain my future would be shadowy and unpredictable.

I pictured myself a frontier wife, a woman lined with years and worry, clad in steel-toed boots and red flannel. She was almost unrecognizable, the woman I had become, and her eyes were bleak and haunted as she searched the blackened sky for a flight that would never make it home.

But I couldn't say any of that to Etsell. He was looking at me with his lips slightly parted, his gaze hesitant and hopeful, as if I held the key to his happiness in the palm of my hand. He was a child to me, unruly and impetuous, but desperate for my approval all the same. For the soft touch of my validation.

"Why Alaska?" I asked.

Etsell opened his mouth and closed it. Let a stunned breath escape from between his lips. "Because," he murmured. He seemed confused, distracted, like he didn't know how to explain the feel of the wind on his skin to a fish. I was the fish.

"Because it's Alaska, Dani," he finally managed. "Because it's vast and gorgeous and savage."

I cringed a little, but he was too enamored with his subject matter to notice.

"It's where pioneers belong, and entrepreneurs. And thrill-seekers, wanderers, adventurers . . ."

And little boys, I thought. Grown-up little boys with broken hearts.

"We've got nothing tying us here," Etsell whispered, unraveling his fingers from mine so that he could cup my face.

"My mother," I reminded him. "Hazel. My sisters."

"They'll visit. We'll take them salmon fishing."

I could see him for just a moment, a man on the bank of one of the rivers I had read about online. The Kenai, the Yukon, the Koyukuk. The water was bottle-green and ice cold, and we were all lined up on either side of him like wings. Wings of women who would hold him up. Help him rise when he fell.

"Yes," I whispered. But I wasn't saying yes to Alaska, I was saying yes to him. I couldn't cross my fingers as I stretched the meaning of my ambiguous answer, but I considered the long plait of my braided hair, the way my legs intersected at the ankle, the line of one wrist over the other.

I let him kiss me, and as his lips met mine I imagined the dross of every splintered vow anointing our heads like Arctic snow. They were white lies, inconsequential, nothing. But necessary all the same. It was part of the process of coming together, the way we dulled our sharp edges on each other, made promises we had no intent to keep.

We had done it before. Pretended we fit like the hollow of earth beneath a rock that had rested against the same dirt for centuries. Millennia. And when the raw truth of our differences felt harsh and uncompromising, we shifted positions, tried again. It wasn't deceptive, not really. It was who we were.

2

Genesis

When the phone rang after midnight, Dani wasn't asleep. For a moment her heart swelled with hope, but the tinny trill that shattered the silence of her troubled night was coming from the handset that rested on the kitchen counter, not her cell phone. Etsell would never call the landline.

Dani leaped off the couch all the same, and stumbled bleary-eyed and stiff into the kitchen. She yanked the phone off the base and pressed the talk button with a trembling finger. Five days. The thought flashed through her mind like a spark of something so white-hot it left the memory of a burn against her skin. She felt singed knowing that her husband had been missing for five entire days. They were the points of a star, the fingers on her hand, a number that seemed to signify an end, a completion.

"Hello?" she said before the headset was even against her cheek.

There was a pause on the other end of the line. "Hello? Mrs. Greene?"

"Yes, this is Mrs. Greene." Dani fell against the counter as if someone had shoved her. Very deliberately, she placed the palm of her free hand against the smooth edge of the laminate before her and anchored her fingers to the cool, steadying surface.

"Good evening, Mrs. Greene," the gentleman continued in a voice too accustomed to disaster and loss to betray any hint of what he had called to say. "My name is Blair Knopf. I'm with the Civil Air Patrol in Seward, Alaska. I believe you spoke with my colleague Tim Mason yesterday?"

"Yes, sir." Dani exhaled.

"I'm calling this evening to apprise you of our current situation. I'm not calling too late, am I?"

Dani glanced at the clock on the stove, where 12:17 blinked back at her in an eerie, gleaming blue that made her think of moonlight shattering on ice caps and fathomless glacier lakes. "Not too late at all," she muttered, remembering that it was three hours earlier in Seward. Still light as day. No glowing alien pools of darkened frost and snow.

"Good." Blair seemed to waver for a second, to gather himself before spilling the information that Dani could hardly force herself to listen to.

This is it, she thought, digging her fingernails into a counter that wouldn't give.

"Are you alone, Mrs. Greene? Do you have someone with you?"

Dani ignored the quiet hum of the refrigerator and the crisp, uneven slap of her own heart against her chest. She was absolutely alone. But she didn't want to tell him that. He might try to track down a nonexistent pastor to pass along the news or even call the local police station. A gentleman down the street had been informed of his son's fatal car accident that way—a blue cruiser with flashing lights pulled up to the house. Later he confessed that the Grim Reaper had been forever altered in his imagination. Death didn't wear black robes, he wore a starched uniform with a gun and holster.

"I'm not alone," Dani lied.

"I'm glad to hear that," Blair said slowly. "Ma'am, I'm sorry to be the one to tell you this, but as of this evening we are calling off the official search for your husband's plane."

The little gasp that thudded in Dani's throat was born of shock, not horror. "I thought you were calling to tell me he was dead," she whispered.

Blair swallowed audibly on the other end of the line. "I'm so sorry, Mrs. Greene. Truly, I am." It sounded as if he didn't perceive much difference between an abandoned search and an accounted-for corpse.

"But you didn't tell me that he's dead," Dani cried, her desperation finally clawing its way through the numbness that had shrouded her since she first learned of Etsell's disappearance. "He's not dead. I mean, you don't know that. It hasn't even been a week."

"Five days, ma'am. We've followed every protocol. We've had flights in the air almost nonstop. Civilians, volunteers, CAP . . ."

"How can you call off the search?" She wanted to weep, to scream and hurl insults at the seemingly unruffled stranger who called from a world away, but the reservoir of her tears was dry.

"I'm so sorry," Blair said again, "but we've done what we can. Your husband didn't file a flight plan, and we don't even know where to begin. It's like searching for a needle in a haystack."

"What do you mean he didn't file a flight plan?"

"It's advised. Highly suggested," Blair explained patiently. "But pilots aren't required to file a flight plan in Alaska. The Seward airport is just one of six hundred airports and another couple thousand airstrips up here. If Tim hadn't seen your husband before takeoff, we wouldn't have even known he was gone."

Dani's forehead bloomed with a bright burst of pain. She closed her eyes against the Technicolor light of a sudden, bone-deep headache, and forced herself to speak calmly. "You must be mistaken, Mr. Knopf. Etsell wasn't leaving *from* Seward. He was landing *in* Seward. He called me before he left the hunting lodge where he's been working for the last three weeks. He was flying a load of cargo back, spending the night in Seward, and then he was supposed to come home."

"He made the drop," Blair told her. "Safe and sound. We believe Etsell went missing after that."

For a few seconds, Dani couldn't speak around the lump in her throat. "Excuse me?" she finally choked.

"I thought you knew." Blair sounded confused. "He took off out of Seward. About two hours after he landed, as far as we can tell."

"Why? Where was he going?"

"That's what we'd like to know."

⁓

Dani was still leaning against the counter when she heard the unmistakable click of her front door opening. Blackhawk was a small town surrounded by a prairie of Midwestern nowhere, such a well-kept secret that it was hidden on the map between the curling line of the Big Sioux River and the shaded border of a sprawling state park. It was a forgotten place, and it didn't cross Dani's mind to be concerned that someone was sneaking into her home in the middle of the night. It was probably her mom. Or her sister. Katrina often crashed on the sagging couch in the living room when she didn't feel like going home.

"You up?" a smoky voice whispered from the foyer.

Dani answered without thinking. "In the kitchen, Mom." Once the words were out of her mouth, a part of her wished she could snatch them from the air and swallow them whole. She could pretend that she was hidden in the depths of her small Craftsman home, surrendered to the sleep of the drugged. One of the first things Dani's mom had brought over after the news of Etsell's disappearance broke was a half-empty bottle of prescription sleeping pills. Though Dani hadn't availed herself of the narcotics, they would have made the perfect excuse.

But it was too late. There was the sound of shuffling feet—her mother struggling through the shag carpet in her predictable four-inch heels—then Charlene Vis burst through the old-fashioned salon door that separated the kitchen from the rest of the house. She came in on a breeze of cigarette smoke and cheap perfume, something floral and overpowering that she bought half-price at a flea market two summers ago. She blinked a few times, looking for all the world like a startled bird, a waif of little more than brittle bone and tanning-bed brown skin. But it wasn't the recent skin cancer scare and her mother's continued frequent trips to Tan World that set Dani off. It was her hair.

"Throw those damn clearance boxes away and let me color you!" Dani hissed at the sight of Char's teased coif. Her mother's thinning strands were perched on the top of her head like a windblown nest, and though the gray roots were covered, the amber brilliance of her newly dyed locks leaned far more toward crossing guard orange than brunette.

"You know I like to go with the mood of the day," Char quipped. She gave her T-shirt a slight, attention-seeking tug. It was a subconscious gesture, a small act of self-arrangement that was as natural to Char as blinking.

Dani turned her eyes from the sight of her mother's freckled cleavage where it was framed in the deep V-neck of a revealing top. "It looks terrible."

Char ignored the biting comment and stitched up the distance between them with a few quick, staccato steps. Giving her daughter a smacking kiss on the cheek she asked, "Why aren't you in bed?"

"Because I was expecting midnight company."

"Don't be cheeky." Char clucked her tongue. "I gave you sleeping pills. You should be sleeping."

"I don't want to."

"You're being ridiculous. You'll need your energy to nurse Ell back to health when they find him in that godforsaken wasteland. You should have never let him go up there in the first place. He's probably fallen off a cliff or something. You'll have an amputee for a husband." Char's gaze raked over the bare counter, the empty table. "Got anything to eat?"

Dani sighed. "Check the fridge."

"I thought people were supposed to bring you meals."

"I thought waitresses were supposed to get free food at the end of their shifts."

"Half-price," Char humphed. "And if I have to eat another onion ring this week I swear I'll drop dead." She rummaged through the nearly empty fridge and came up with a carton of Boston cream pie yogurt. "Toss me a spoon, will you?"

Dani stifled a groan, but it was too late to tell her mother to leave. Instead of arguing, she stalled for just a moment and read the names and numbers she had copied onto the piece of paper in her hand one last time. Then she painstakingly folded it in half and half again and slid it into the back pocket of her jeans. The soft crinkle of the paper was a consolation of sorts. Some small corner of her soul could draw a shaky breath at the simple assurance that it was there.

Wrenching open the cutlery drawer with more force than necessary, Dani extracted a spoon for her mom and considered throwing it across the kitchen just as she had asked. But the older woman was already sitting cross-legged in a hard-back chair, peeling the foil off the yogurt container with her teeth so that she could preserve the plastic nails she had glued on. She looked to Dani like a little girl instead of a fifty-something woman.

"Here," she said as she handed her mother the utensil and plopped into the chair across from her.

Char scooped out a spoonful with an eager half smile on her face. She closed her eyes for just a second, apparently savoring the texture, the taste, before she made a sound of disgust in the back of her throat and fixed Dani with an accusatory stare. "You don't have anything else?"

"Asparagus."

Char pulled a face. "Asparagus? Where in the world did you get asparagus?"

"From Benjamin."

"Your neighbor? That preacher from the country church?"

"That's the one."

"He's weird."

Dani lifted one shoulder noncommittally and watched as her mother shoveled another bite of the offending yogurt.

"I want to hear all about the search," Char mumbled with a full mouth. "I came here to be a listening ear. A shoulder to cry on. But I need sustenance first." She swallowed. "What do you have to drink?"

"There's a little bit of Crown in the cupboard above the fridge."

"The good stuff," Char hummed. "Coke?"

"Diet Pepsi."

Char grimaced. "It'll have to do."

While her mother mixed herself a strong drink, Dani put her cheek on the cool surface of the table and let her eyes drift closed. The headache that had blossomed as she spoke with Blair from Civil Air Patrol was now a dull wash of angry color that invaded her peripheral vision. She felt sick to her stomach, hot, dizzy. And though she wanted nothing more than to curl up into a ball and die, there was something settling about having Char around. She wasn't a comfort, not exactly, but Dani was grateful for the chatter even if it grated. For the silent thrum of another heartbeat in the house, mingling with the crooked cadence of her own.

Dani startled when Char finally reclaimed her chair and slammed a glass of dark liquid on the table. "Oops." Char hit her seat heavily and licked up the little pool of whiskey like a cat. "Damn heels. My feet are killing me."

"Wear comfortable heels when you work," Dani intoned, but the words were devoid of meaning, rote. She had suggested the same thing to her mother dozens of times. Hundreds. Her advice always fell on deaf ears. As did her not-so-subtle admonitions to lay off the drinking and stop bringing strange men home from the bar. Etsell had assured Dani once that her mother was not an alcoholic—he knew the signs from experience and in his humble opinion Char just enjoyed a slight, permanent buzz. But not even Etsell, Char's only son by birth or marriage and a virtual god in her estimation, dared to comment on her penchant for one-night stands.

"I know, I know," Char moaned, leaning beneath the table to undo the ankle straps of her rhinestoned heels. "You're so sensible, Danica. Sometimes I think you're the mother and I'm the daughter. I should listen to you more often, shouldn't I?"

Dani didn't respond, but she pushed herself up on her forearms and took a few gulps of her mother's drink. It burned going down, but she didn't do it for the taste or even for the soporific effect of the hard liquor. She did it to take a bit off the top. It was obvious this wasn't her mother's first drink of the night.

"Good girl," Char said as if her daughter was eight and

had just taken her cough medicine without complaint. "That feels better, doesn't it?"

Dani cleared her throat. Didn't bother to nod.

"So," Char began after taking her own generous swig. "Update me. When's our boy coming home?"

It was a cruel thing to say, even if Char didn't mean to give her words bite. For a moment Dani tried to picture her husband living off survival-ration bars and freeze-dried camping food pouches. He could dip water from some glacier-fed stream and use his magnesium fire starter to ensure that he would always be warm. Or at least that he wouldn't die of hypothermia. Maybe he was alive somewhere. Maybe he was sending up flares, anxious for rescue, dreaming of her, the same way she couldn't close her eyes without seeing him.

But try as she might, Dani couldn't get the picture to focus. She couldn't see the label on the silver packet of food. He could be eating turkey Tetrazzini or Mexican-style chicken. For all she knew, he could be eating dust. And her imagination refused to fill in the details of the reality she hoped he still existed in—the black-and-white world she tried to conjure faded to a hundred thousand shades of gray at the edges, a blank space to remind her that no matter how hard she wished for it, her daydreams were likely little more than fairy tales.

"I don't know," Dani whispered. She didn't even realize that she had given her mother an answer of sorts. Her comment was an admission to herself. A declaration of failure on a hundred different fronts. There were so many things that she didn't know.

"But you've heard something," Char pressed, her voice almost scolding. "They were going to give you daily updates."

"I spoke with someone from the Civil Air Patrol about a half hour ago," Dani said.

"Who? I thought the army took care of this sort of thing. The air force?" Char worried her bottom lip, leaving a smudged line of cherry-colored lipstick on her bleached teeth. "The cops," she finally declared. "They're in charge of disappearances and such."

"Not in Alaska. At least, not in this case. Not when planes go missing or . . ." Dani shook her head and caught handfuls of her hair in her fingers as if she intended to pull them out by the roots. "Look," she huffed with more force than she intended. "We've been through this all before. Besides, it doesn't matter anymore. They're calling off the search."

Char's response was almost comical. Her mouth was empty for once and she let it drop open, a crooked gash that tore across her face and accentuated the lines that she tried to hide with antiaging makeup and drugstore night creams. "What?"

"What do you mean what?"

"I mean, what does it mean that they're calling off the search? They've found him, or . . ."

"Or nothing. It's over. They've done all they can."

"But it's *Ell*, Dani. You can't just—"

"I know."

"What are you going to do?"

"I don't know." Dani pulled her hands across her head and let her palms slide down her temples to the place where her cheekbones slanted in perfect symmetry. She covered her eyes because she couldn't bring herself to face the decision she had already made. But there were phone numbers in her pocket. People to call, steps to take, plans to be made. She didn't want to do it; she didn't have a choice.

"I'm going," Dani whispered.

"Excuse me? You're going where?"

"To Alaska."

Danica

Etsell left for Anchorage the day after his twenty-seventh birthday. We had been married for over seven years, and together for almost ten—an entire decade of oneness that ensured I could not remember my life without him. There was no me, only us, and in the wake of the announcement that his enduring, childhood dream was about to get a long-awaited test run, I felt for the first time as if I was married to a complete stranger.

After we said, "I do," Etsell and I eased into the sort of comfortable, easy life that can only be classified as desultory. We didn't make plans or try to plot out an exciting future; we simply existed. My husband continued flying, racking up more and more miles as he taught lessons, piloted local businessmen all around the Midwest, and even flew antique planes in small air shows where little boys asked for his autograph.

I went to beauty school because nothing else seemed to make much sense. A college degree had always appealed to me, and I could have followed in my oldest sister Natalie's footsteps and attended a moderately prestigious private school, but getting my BA was a whim, not a necessity.

Besides, I worried that if I seemed too excited about the possibility of school, Etsell would jump on board and suggest I attend the University of Alaska.

It was always there, hovering between us like an invisible saint, the unspoken dream that was as dear as religion to my husband. But I ignored it, and Ell either didn't dare to bring it up or he was carefully biding his time.

Biding his time, I realized when I saw him take a small suitcase out of our attic and place it carefully on the floor beside the dresser in our bedroom. He didn't put anything in it for many days, nor did he deign to tell me why it was there. I didn't ask, but a part of me knew long before he whispered the words as we lay beside each other like corpses one sleepless, loveless night. I didn't say anything then, but I confronted him the next morning.

"It's three weeks," Etsell muttered as he poured himself a cup of coffee from our ancient coffeemaker. It had a hairline crack at the very top of the thin glass carafe, and enough hard-water stains and mineral buildup to make brewing a pot of coffee a forty-five-minute affair. "I thought you were going to buy a new coffeemaker," he complained, sloshing cream on the counter as he gave the contents of his mug a vigorous stir.

"It's on the list," I told him absently. My head was too thick with thoughts of Alaska to worry about our aging kitchen appliance. I vaguely remembered that it had been a wedding gift from Hazel. A cheap one at that. I pressed my fingers to my forehead to clear it. "But I don't want to talk about our coffee-pot right now. I want to talk about you leaving."

"Leaving? You make it sound like I'm walking out on you. Don't be so dramatic, Dani. It's unbecoming."

"Excuse me," I huffed, stung by his casual dismissal. "But I'm not exactly thrilled that you think you can just waltz in here and tell me that you're going away for three weeks. Isn't this the sort of decision that we're supposed to make together? What if I wanted to go with you?"

Etsell snorted in what could have been loosely interpreted as a derisive laugh. "Like you'd sit in a plane for seven hours. We drove to the Black Hills for our honeymoon because you wouldn't put one little toe on an airplane. We could have gone to Tahiti on my inheritance money. *Tahiti,* Danica. The Virgin Islands, a Mediterranean cruise, Paris . . ."

"That's not the point." I gritted my teeth in an effort to control my tongue. "You should have asked me. Given me the chance to make my own decision at least."

"I thought you made all the decisions anyway."

He said it so quietly, I wasn't entirely sure that I had heard him correctly. But the set of my husband's carved jaw was defiant, his eyes smoldering. This was about much more than an opportunity to help a friend. It was about us. Whether he would admit it or not, I knew in that moment that he needed a break. A break from us. From me?

Stunned, I whispered, "I'm sorry."

Etsell softened then, the sort of whole and immediate disarmament that happened at the bitter end of each of our fights. He threw down his weapons and surrendered. I could feel it in all the spaces between us, in the way every part of me that knew every part of him loosened just a bit. Relaxed.

"Danica Reese," he all but purred, abandoning his coffee on the counter so that he could slide his hands around my waist and pull me to him. "You're jealous. You don't have to be jealous."

"I'm not jealous," I protested against his shoulder, even though I could hardly stand the thought of being left behind. "I just wish you would have told me sooner. That we could have made this sort of a big decision together."

"It's not a big decision. And I really didn't have a choice. Russ's wife has just been diagnosed with breast cancer and he really needs someone to take over his flights for a couple of weeks. May is—"

"One of the busiest tourist months in Alaska," I finished. "I know. And Russ is the good friend of a good friend."

I didn't mean to sound accusatory, but Etsell stiffened. "Russ is more than just a friend of a friend. We've met a couple times and I really respect him. I want to do this for him."

How noble, I thought, but instead of picking another fight I took a deep breath. "Refresh my memory," I said. "You'll just be making routine flights of passengers and cargo from Seward to . . . ?"

"A blip on the map in the middle of the Aleutians. And I won't just be landing in Seward. I'll make flights to Anchorage, Kodiak, pretty much anywhere the lodge guests need their fish toted."

"The lodge is called?"

"Midnight Sun."

"And I'll be able to reach you?"

"Whenever you want. They do have cell coverage in Alaska."

I pulled back from Etsell's embrace and gave him a quizzical look. "I'm sure the state is populated by towers."

"Maybe you won't be able to call me twenty-four/seven, but close enough." He kissed my forehead with a decidedly paternal smack. "It's not like I'm going to the moon."

"The last frontier," I quipped.

"No, space is the *final* frontier. Alaska is the last."

It wasn't a very comforting thought. But what could I do? Etsell had passed off all his regular clients to less experienced pilots, booked a flight from Sioux Falls, South Dakota, to

Anchorage, and packed a carry-on bag with long-sleeved T-shirts and jeans. It was set, with or without my approval.

To celebrate his birthday and recognize his impending departure, I bought a fifty-dollar bottle of wine, ordered a shipment of oysters on dry ice, and picked out an enticing set of black lingerie that left absolutely nothing to the imagination. If the ovulation predictor kit I had used could be trusted, the night Etsell and I celebrated his twenty-seven years of life could also be the night that we conceived our first child. By the time he came home from Alaska, I might have a surprise of my own. Apparently we were becoming adept at making decisions without each other.

But it seemed our night together was doomed from the beginning.

The oysters were a complete waste of money. I had arranged them on a white plate, their shells curved in concentric circles and their flesh glistening and almost iridescent in the light of a dozen tapered candles I had arranged around our living room. The guaranteed-fresh seafood smelled briny and a little off, as if it had spent a few too many hours out of the cold ocean before someone thought to package the large shells. And the crushed ice I displayed them on didn't do much to aid the overall appeal. The shards were melting quickly, juices from the oysters mingling in the tepid water to make a salty, grayish puddle.

But Etsell tried one anyway. He came home from work to find me reclining amid a handful of artfully arranged pillows on the floor, the oysters and wine before me and the lingerie like a bow I had tied around my middle. I could have put a tag on the slight ribbon that hugged my waist: For you. He sank to his knees in the carpet and took one sip of the Napa Valley Chardonnay I had paired with my aphrodisiac offering. Then he slurped down one oyster. It was obvious he had a hard time swallowing.

The feast was forgotten after that. He crawled on hands and knees across the floor to me, and caught my bottom lip between his teeth. I had anticipated the moment all day, but Etsell seemed detached.

The night before my husband left for Alaska, we didn't make love. We had sex.

3

All the Broken Pieces

When Char fell asleep on the couch, just as the sun was beginning to rise over Blackhawk, Dani made herself a cup of green tea and went to sit in the garden. Though she hadn't taken one of her mother's pills, Dani felt drugged and drowsy, hemmed in by the kind of exhaustion that made her limbs heavy and her head light. She wanted to sleep, but the swelling crescent of a carmine sun as it ascended the hills that curved around the tiny town she called home ensured rest would be impossible. If vampires inhabited the night, Dani need never fear one. She was made for the day, and as long as the sun shone she could not bring herself to close her eyes.

The garden was shrouded in a thin veil of May mist, a cool fog that swirled around Dani's legs the moment she opened the screen door to step out into the morning. She hugged the hot mug in her hands and tucked her neck a bit deeper into the fleece that she had grabbed off a hook beside the door.

It wasn't cold, not really, but Dani stifled a shiver all the same. Spring was supposed to be gorgeous and green, lush with new grass and tulips that would open their cups to the sun as if waiting to be filled with warm, golden rays like nectar. But her back-door garden had gone untended for weeks—long before Etsell actually went missing and she had a reason to neglect the spindly flowers and herbs that tangled around the stone patio. The truth was, when her husband left for Alaska, Dani simply forgot about the raised planter boxes that lined the little haven. The basket of pansies on the wrought-iron table went unwatered, the clusters of hyacinth and tulips that lined the path to a bench beneath a willow tree spilled petals like narrow formations of wounded, fallen soldiers, and the few seeds that she had planted before Etsell left were snarled masses of yellow-leafed disorder.

In years past, Dani had strung Christmas lights from the branches of the lilac bushes that flanked the outdoor living space, and decorated the low, crumbling stone wall with sturdy, tempered-glass hurricanes that she filled with white candles. But this year, none of those special touches brightened the usually lovely patio. Instead, the garden was downright depressing cloaked in early-morning fog. It seemed a testament to all she had lost.

A little tremor scurried down Dani's spine at the thought that somehow, in some impossible way, she had known. How else could she explain her uncharacteristic neglect of the garden she so loved? What else accounted for the fact that her Christmas lights and hurricanes, the delicate Chinese lanterns with their exquisitely patterned, snow-colored paper and the expensive torches she had ordered from a specialty magazine, had remained untouched in the back shed? Somewhere, deep down, her heart had acknowledged the fact that there was no reason to prepare, no purpose in waiting for Etsell to come home.

All at once Dani's legs felt weak, her bones brittle, about to fracture. She sat down hard on the stone wall and sloshed a few drips of steaming tea onto her jeans. The dark drops looked like blood to her, a smattering of life that anointed her legs with a meaningless pattern of accidental ruin. Her throat closed around the almost overwhelming desire to cry for the heartbreaking randomness of the sudden stains. Of things that could not be undone no matter how much she longed to reverse them.

Dani didn't know how long she sat that way, staring at the splattered denim and wishing that she could turn back the clock. But by the time she blinked and looked up, the sun had crested the trees and hung like one of her paper lanterns in a sky that would soon be perfectly, painfully blue. It was going to be a gorgeous day.

"You're up early this morning."

She wasn't usually the sort to startle easily, but the world felt fragile to Dani, as if it were made of eggshells and on the verge of cracking, exposing edges, sharp corners that cut without intention. His voice in the solitude of her derelict garden made her jump and drop the mug that held every last sip of her untouched tea. It shattered into a hundred pieces on the flagstone pavers.

"Oh!" Benjamin exclaimed from the farthest edge of his backyard. "Oh, I'm so sorry, Mrs. Greene. I didn't mean to startle you."

"Dani," she whispered, watching as he jogged the short distance between them and dropped to his knees at her feet. "Please don't," she said when she realized what he was doing. "It's fine. I'll take care of it."

But Benjamin was already picking up shards of pottery with his fingers and depositing them in the shallow blade of the spade he had been carrying. "It's my fault," he told her simply. "I clean up my own messes."

It was a strange thing to say, as if Benjamin had offered himself up for voluntary subjugation, but he smiled genially as he knelt before her. And though she knew she should bustle him out of the way and do it herself, Dani stayed rooted to the low wall. She inched her feet back slightly, determining to sweep the ceramic dust into the grooves between the stones later.

"I really am sorry," Benjamin said again. "It was a handsome mug."

"Handmade," Dani admitted. "There are four in the set."

"Three." He sounded sad. "We should bury the pieces. A thousand years from now our descendants could dig them up and wonder at our primitive civilization. Butterflies?" Benjamin held up a particularly large piece that was still attached to the curved handle of the broken mug. There was a swath of buttercream yellow fading into the jagged edge.

Dani shook her head. "Nothing so elaborate. Abstract lines. Modern art. Meaningless."

"I doubt it was meaningless to the artist," he mused.

"I was the artist."

Benjamin's eyes lifted to her face. He studied her for a moment and it was as if she could see the mental gymnastics he was performing to account for the source of her unexpected artistry. Dani was used to people being surprised by her creative streak. Most beauticians didn't go through a brief but furious pottery phase or paint patterns on tabletops with their fingertips.

"I just liked the colors," she said. "The way they blended together. I did a few pieces years ago. I haven't touched a wheel in years."

"Well, you have a knack, meaningful or not. It is—it was—beautiful." Benjamin lifted the final piece and then used the palm of his hands to brush the smaller fragments to the edge of the patio. "Don't cut your feet."

Dani looked down and realized for the first time that her feet were bare beneath the straight line of her stiff jeans. Her toes were numb, foreign to her. "I'll be careful," she assured him.

Benjamin stood and carefully lifted the short-handled spade with one hand, making sure that the remnants of the mug remained in the low basin. He hovered for a second, leaning on his heels as if he was on the verge of saying good-bye and going back to whatever chore had brought him out to his garden on a quiet spring morning. But he didn't leave.

There was a long stretch of uncomfortable silence between them, then Benjamin apparently mustered the courage to ask, "Any news?"

"They're calling off the search." Dani's lips could hardly form the words. She stared at the ground as she said them, at the place where the mug had broken.

Benjamin didn't respond right away, and she felt him lean toward her as if he intended to place a sympathetic hand on her shoulder. Dani shrunk back a little and crossed her arms against her chest to discourage his pastorly touch, the well-practiced homily of advice and consolation that he was undoubtedly on the brink of spewing.

But Benjamin didn't touch her. He didn't offer to pray with her or try to explain that it was God's will. Instead, he pushed a hard breath through his lips, a soft sound of frustration and commiseration that ended with the question she least expected. "Are you going after him?"

Dani's eyes jerked to his face. "Do you think I should?"

He tilted his head and gave her an indiscernible look. "Never do what you should do, Dani. Do what you have to do."

✒

Dani knew she couldn't go alone.

Just the thought of navigating the unfamiliar chaos of a major airport, never mind gathering the courage to actually

board a plane was enough to make her break out in a rash—
or at least feel like she was going to. But her options were
slim.

Char was obviously not the right woman for the job. Taking her mother along on a trip of such magnitude was like
inviting a toddler into a china store. Visions of airport bars
and handsome Civil Air Patrol pilots made Dani shudder.
Whether she realized it or not, Char broke things. Promises,
guarantees, relationships. A misplaced attraction to one of
the people who might be able to help could quickly ruin
everything.

As for Dani's sisters, they were too immersed in their
own lives to fly across the continent with the youngest
member of the Vis family. As the baby of three girls and the
final oops for her single mom, Dani had spent most of her
childhood and young adulthood fending for herself. By the
time she hit elementary school, she was the only person in
the house who knew how to fry an egg, and if she didn't
do the laundry, her sisters were forced to go to school in
clothes that bore the faint but unmistakable odor of spoiled
milk. But Dani's story was no Cinderella tale. Though she
grew into the role of caretaker and surrogate mother when
Char was too busy partying to pay much attention to her
daughters, Dani was neither neglected nor abused by her
makeshift family. Quite the opposite. She was appreciated
and adored, and though she was forced to grow up fast,
there was no lack of love among the quartet of women in
the Vis home—even if it was somewhat backward and un-
conventional.

Unfortunately, one of the inescapable side effects of being
the only constant, the only steady and reliable member in a
family of misfits and mavericks, was that everyone else assumed Dani would always be there for them. They didn't

have to be there for her. And, true to form, she didn't blame them. Instead, she made excuses for them.

Even if Natalie, the eldest of the Vis clan, wanted to rise to the occasion and help, she was too busy finishing up her dissertation. It was the final hoop she had to jump through before she could claim those long-anticipated letters behind her name. Dani could already imagine her sister squeezing such necessary information into every introduction and casual conversation. "Hi, I'm Dr. Natalie Vis. Yes. I have my PhD in women's studies."

And Katrina, the middle child, was no more supportive or helpful. Kat was the daughter who had followed most closely in her mother's footsteps, and Dani often worried that her sister's weekend job of bartending at the only gentlemen's club in a fifty-mile radius would soon entice her sister to step out from behind the bar and light up the seedy stage. If it hadn't already happened. Sometimes when Kat crashed on Ell and Dani's couch in the middle of the night, Dani woke to find her sister curled up under the afghan, a glimmer of sparkle makeup still clinging to her pale cheeks.

Kat was beautiful, and sleep made her look much younger than her twenty-eight years. There was something sinister, almost insidious about the purple eye shadow that creased her lids, the tiny line of stick-on rhinestones that arched in a half-moon from the corner of her eye to her cheekbone. But Dani didn't ask. She didn't want to know. Rather than probing, she made buttermilk waffles and woke her sister with a cup of French roast coffee. Strong and black.

Dani loved her sisters. But she didn't trust them. They couldn't come running for her. They wouldn't.

Yet none of her family's insufficiencies erased the fact that Dani simply couldn't go to Alaska alone. Blair had assured her that she was welcome to continue the search on her own, that there were pilots who would happily charter her for weeks on end or even offer their services for free.

"It's part of the community up here," he explained. "Formal searches simply can't go on forever. There are too many people who go missing, and too much ground to cover—especially when there's no flight record to go by. But Alaskans are known for rising to the occasion. We gather around each other. Many downed flights are discovered by volunteer pilots."

It was a ray of hope. A possibility. What choice did she have? Dani was terrified at the thought of finally being forced to face all her fears, but going to Alaska could be the only chance she had to find her husband.

In the end, there was really only one person she could ask.

Dani called Hazel the morning after she got Blair's call. She was prepared to lay out her case meticulously, to beg if necessary, but Hazel answered the phone as if she had been expecting to hear Dani on the other end.

"So?" the older woman barked into the mouthpiece.

"Hazel?"

"Of course it's me, Danica Greene. You called my number, didn't you?"

Pulling the phone away from her ear for a moment, Dani squeezed her eyes shut and said a wingless prayer for patience. Her resolve dropped like a stone at her feet. "Most people say hello when they answer a phone," she muttered into the mouthpiece.

"Most people aren't me." Hazel waited for the span of a quick heartbeat, then spat out a question before Dani could even consider forming her request. "Got news about Etsell?"

Dani sighed. Whether or not she cared deeply for Hazel, she knew that the older woman would be leveled by what she had to say. She tried to soften her tone, to be tender. "It's not easy to hear, Hazel. They've called off the search."

"Oh I already know that. Have you heard anything new today?"

Stunned and more than a little irritated at Hazel's non-chalance, Dani gritted her teeth. "How do you already know that? I just spoke with someone from the Civil Air Patrol last night. Late."

"Blair Knopf? I talked to him too. 'Round suppertime."

Dani fought an urge to throw the telephone across the room. "Suppertime? He called you at suppertime?"

"I called him," Hazel corrected. "Face it, honey, you're in no position to receive that kind of news and process it properly. Someone with a level head needs to know what's going on up there. I've been keeping tabs."

It infuriated Dani to learn that Hazel had circumvented her to gain information about Etsell's whereabouts. *She's not family,* Dani fumed, feeling indignant and self-righteous. *I'm his wife. She's just his . . .*

"I'm the closest thing he has to a parent," Hazel cut in. It was as if she could read Dani's mind, but for once the grizzled old lady was almost gentle in her reprimand. "I had to know what was happening."

Something inside of Dani wanted to bare her teeth and fight, but it felt wrong to scuffle over Etsell like a piece of carrion. Whom did he belong to? *To me,* she thought, but her husband had always been his own man. Still, she couldn't bless Hazel's interference. She held her tongue.

"Why are you calling?" Hazel asked after a long silence. The raw transparency in her voice was uncharacteristic.

Dani thought about saying nothing. About telling the older woman that she merely called to update, to pass along the news that Etsell was little more than a breath on the wind, scattered to the four corners of the earth like so much dust. But even thinking those words was like staring over the edge of a black hole, a bottomless chasm of nothingness that threatened to suck her in and make her fall headlong forever. Forever without him.

She didn't have a choice. "I have to go there," Dani whispered eventually, suffocating beneath the press of the words, their terrifying implications.

"I was hoping you'd say that."

"Will you—"

"We'll go together," Hazel interrupted before Dani could stumble over her feeble request.

Together.

The term seemed stripped of meaning somehow, broken. Etsell had made so many promises, vows that were rendered powerful by bonds that linked them as one: us, together, forever. With his hands he had fashioned a life for Dani, a home where it felt safe to close her eyes because he had bound the two of them in name, in body, in soul. It was wrong to think of herself with anyone but him.

And yet there was some small comfort to be derived from Hazel's assurance. Dani clung to a shard of hope like the yellow-painted remnant of mug that Benjamin had held in his hand. It was jagged, painful to hold.

"Together," Dani finally agreed. And somewhere, along a seam in the depth of her heart, a fault line splintered and she began to slowly, steadily bleed.

Danica

Three years before Etsell left for Alaska and disappeared off the face of the earth, I bought an empty store on the cobblestoned main drag in Blackhawk and set up my own salon. It was a narrow little building that no one else wanted, almost exactly the same length and width as a one-car alley. I wondered, as I stood with the real estate agent in the dank interior of my new shop, if indeed the space had once been a grassy, graveled byway, the sort of place where the butcher from the deli next door would have leaned his bike up against the cool bricks on a warm summer day.

The thought that volunteer lily of the valley may once have graced the shadows where my future salon now stood cheered me considerably, and made me overlook the low-hung ceilings and water-stained hardwood floors. It helped that the afternoon sun was bathing the unused space in the kind of charmed light that seemed laced with fairy dust and magic. I stood in the middle of a patch of honeyed sun and took one slow turn to survey every square inch of the space I already knew would be mine.

The agent eagerly let me sign the purchase agreement on the spot, flourishing a pen from his lapel pocket and graciously tilting his back so I could use it as a makeshift desk while I put my signature on four different lines. And though he all but danced out the glass front door, I felt I was the one who ought to leave a trail of laughter in my wake.

It never occurred to me that I should have talked to Etsell first.

"You bought a building?" he spat out, choking on a warm grape tomato that he had popped whole into his mouth.

"It was cheap," I told him for the second time. "Very cheap. It's been on the market for years. Nobody wanted it."

"There's probably a reason for that."

"It's small," I consented. "But it's perfect for me. I don't need a lot of space."

Etsell sighed and gave his dinner plate a longing look. Then he set his fork down with a sigh and turned to confront me. "Look. I know you wanted your own salon, but I thought we had agreed that you would convert the spare bedroom. You know, try that for a few years before taking this sort of leap."

"I don't want a home salon." My nose crinkled to show my disgust. "Besides, we need that room. And there's no plumbing, no separate entrance, no—"

"Fine," Etsell interrupted. "Fine. I get it. The spare room is not ideal. But you should have talked to me. . . ." He trailed off, thinking. "You didn't sign anything, did you? This was just a verbal agreement, right?"

I shook my head warily.

"No, you didn't sign anything or no, it wasn't a verbal agreement?"

"I signed papers," I mumbled, unable to look my husband in the eye. My own fork was still in my hand, and I carefully spun the tines around a few slender noodles of the angel hair pasta I had uncharacteristically slaved over for supper. It was a minimalist basil and olive oil toss with fresh tomatoes and fine chunks of parmesan that was supposed to keep Etsell's mouth occupied and his mind open. But it didn't work. Before I had a chance to utter another word, he pushed his chair back from the table and left the kitchen. A moment later I heard the front door slam.

Etsell pouted for a few days. He kept his lessons out longer than normal and joined some of his passengers for beers at the Brass Buckle after chartering a few business trips. Twice he missed supper and came home late without bothering to phone me or offer any sort of explanation.

I let him mope. If he expected me to play the part of the slighted, nagging wife, he was sorely disappointed. I knew from experience that a part of him wanted me to complain bitterly, to bitch and moan so that he could be justified in his anger. But instead of provoking him, I was sweet and demure. I waited out his storm with an almost bland disinterest. It worked. Before a week was up, Etsell was smiling again and it was almost as if nothing had ever happened.

In the first couple weeks after I bought the shop on Main Street, I spent my evenings at the kitchen table, poring over design magazines as I dreamed about my modest boutique. Soon Etsell tired of watching TV alone, and he joined my planning sessions, suggesting we move the counter from the east side of the building to the west and advocating that I should instruct the plumbers to install three styling stations in case I decided to hire an assistant or two.

"But this is *my* salon," I reminded him, trying not to sound as petulant as I felt. The truth was, the plans we were drawing felt like the physical extension of my dreams: pencil-and-paper representations of my thoughts and hopes and longings. It was a reality close enough to touch. Mine. And I didn't feel like sharing.

Etsell shrugged. "You might not want to be alone forever."

In the end, we compromised. Two vanities with gilded mirrors and extra-deep shampoo bowls, one diva dryer chair in cherry-berry, and one pedicure spa chair with a dizzying array of massage options. That final purchase was a big splurge, one that we really couldn't afford but that Etsell deemed necessary. "Girls like their toes pretty." As if I didn't know.

We did most of the renovation ourselves, working our regular jobs during daylight hours and happily allocating all our free time to the project that we had both grown to love. The shop had a certain intangible appeal, a feeling of tranquility that stole over us as we sanded floors and patched holes in the crumbling walls. A few hours of manual labor in my soon-to-be salon rendered even the most frustrating day little more than a faint aftertaste, a hint of something unpleasant that was slowly forgotten with each minute we spent unveiling unexpected beauty.

It was my idea to tear off the drywall and expose the brick-and-mortar walls beneath. They lent the perfect rustic charm to the sleek, glossy anchor of the floor that we refinished in a shade of burnt mahogany. And I advocated for a handmade counter, five thick planks of black walnut that we affixed to a heavy iron base. But it was Etsell who decided we should take out the drop ceiling and see what lay above the vinyl-coated panels and modern lines of stark, fluorescent lights.

We expected our exploration to be quick and easy, but it turned out to be a painstaking discovery. When we lifted the first square tile, the true ceiling of my gallerylike building was several feet beyond the ugly metal grid that the previous owners had installed. All we could see was darkness and cobwebs. Even shining a flashlight into the void didn't work.

The blackness swallowed the light and gave us only the faintest impression of a glow in the incalculable distance.

It probably would have been wise to abandon the idea, put the panel back, and simply paint the ceiling fawn as I had intended to do in the first place. But our curiosity was piqued. We peeled away moldy tiles one at a time until a quarter of the low ceiling was gone. Then half. It wasn't until we were three-quarters of the way done that we could finally see what we had unearthed.

"Wow," Etsell breathed.

I was so stunned I couldn't reply.

The original ceiling of my shop was a gleaming patchwork of twenty-four-inch copper tiles. They were stamped with scrollwork and burnished green at the edges, stained by years of water damage that only made them all the more lovely for their age and wear. Best of all, the roof arched an extra six to eight feet above the standard walls that had made my narrow space seem uncommonly small.

"It's gorgeous," I finally managed.

"I think I've just named your salon," Etsell said with a grin.

I spun on him, exultant in our revelation. "You did?"

"I'm not sure you have a choice." He swept his arm at the blue-green ceiling, the soft shimmer of metal that was like a windswept sky swirled with crisscross trails of sepia smoke. "El Cielo," he pronounced.

"The Sky?"

He nodded.

But I wasn't about to name my grown-up daydream after his first love. "It doesn't make any sense," I countered, shaking my head. "Besides, I think I've known the name since the day I first stepped in this building."

"Really." He arched an eyebrow doubtfully, but I ignored his obvious skepticism.

"I'm going to call my shop Salon La Rue."

It was perfect. For the alley it used to be, and for the long road, the journey ahead.

⁓

The day Etsell left for Alaska, Hazel came into La Rue for her routine appointment. She wasn't the sort to fuss with her hair, but after I gave her a gift certificate years before, she just kept coming back. There wasn't much I could do with her wiry mop but keep it neat and trimmed. She had a little natural wave, and her gray was not an altogether horrible color, but our monthly sessions greatly improved when she allowed me to do a regular deep-conditioning and high-gloss treatment. Hazel always left the salon smart and stylish, and came back six weeks later looking as if she had been flying with the cockpit door open.

"Same old?" I asked as she settled into the plush styling chair. I didn't bother to wait for an answer. "We could go a little shorter today. Something cropped and elegant. Or, if you're not in the mood for change, I have a new deep conditioner for dry hair and your normal gloss treatment with a slight violet-based tint."

"Violet? You mean purple?"

"No," I rushed to assure her. "It's soft, very faint. It's just to counteract any yellow tones—"

"Yellow? You mean blond? That's a good thing if I'm looking blond. Back to my natural color."

I paused with my fingers in the coarse nest of her hair. "I think it will look great," I said carefully. *Trust me*, I thought, but I knew that Hazel didn't.

"Just do what you've always done." She coughed, not bothering to cover her mouth even though I hadn't yet draped her in one of my black, embossed capes.

Determined not to roll my eyes, I caught her gaze in the mirror before us and gave a bright smile that I hoped came across as genuine. "Whatever you want, Hazel."

She fixed me with a hard, unreadable look. "Don't you be smart with me, Danica Greene. We're going to need each other with Ell gone."

My husband had left only hours before, and I was taking great solace in the everyday familiarity of my beauty shop. Not much had changed since Etsell and I redesigned it, but there was a well-worn path that lent the space a certain used, homey feel. The caramel-colored line of smoothed floorboards started at the front door and disappeared in the shadow of a display shelf where I kept bottles of glittering nail polish and shampoos that smelled of honeysuckle and coconut. Just walking into La Rue was a calming experience for me. From the jazz music that spilled softly out of Bose speakers to the way the pendant lights cast luminous swaths of gold around my meticulously arranged chairs, everything worked together to give me a sense of place. Of peace. And I wasn't about to let Hazel ruin it.

"Oh"—I waved my hand dismissively—"he won't be gone that long." Spinning her chair with my foot, I reached for a clean cape from the drawer in the chic vanity.

"Not too tight," Hazel warned me.

I fastened the Velcro the same way I always did, but she tugged on it anyway.

"All I'm saying is you never can predict these things," Hazel muttered when I tipped her back and began to slowly rinse her hair in the sink.

"Mm-hmm." I squirted out a generous amount of shampoo and used my strong fingers to my advantage. Maybe if I kept scrubbing, she'd be too preoccupied to bother me with her unwelcome musings.

But Hazel wouldn't be deterred. "I mean, he has a ticket back and all, but he's always wanted to be a pilot in Alaska."

My hands stiffened. "Are you suggesting that Etsell would stay? He has a life here," I snapped. "A wife."

"I know, I know," Hazel assured me.

For the next half hour we hardly said another word to each other. And yet there was something taut and unspoken between us. It was the same thing I felt when Etsell kissed me good-bye. Apparently, she felt it too.

Something about his absence felt permanent.

4

Far Away

The air at thirty thousand feet was clearer somehow, backlit and brilliant as if the entire sky was on display in some heavenly gallery. Danica could admit that it was gorgeous, an impossible work of art that shimmered like a pearl beneath the splash of hot sun a thousand light-years away. But any benevolence she felt toward the thin place between the mountain range of cumulus and the dark edge of space that threatened above was the direct result of antianxiety medication, strong meds that made her feel bleary and muddled, foggy around the edges, as if she was trapped in a warm glass bottle. Her panic was a damp smog around her, but it was capped in, held tight so that she could feel the pressure of it against her skin, waiting to explode.

"How you holding up?" Hazel asked, showing the smallest hint of concern for the very first time since they left Minneapolis hours before.

Danica blinked and ripped her gaze from the window, realizing that she was holding the requisite airline magazine with white knuckles. The pages were creased and torn. "Fine," she said, but it was obvious that she was anything but fine.

"Breathe, girl. You're going to hyperventilate."

Hadn't Etsell said the same thing to her once? Had he told her to breathe, just breathe? As if it were that easy.

"You have a greater chance of dying in a car crash than—"

"I know," Dani interrupted. "I know. I'm not afraid of dying."

"What then?"

But Dani couldn't put words to it. Couldn't describe why the sky was so wholly other, so unnatural and foreign. She tried to tease the heart of her dread from beneath the fog of medication, but it was like clutching at mist. No matter how hard she focused, she came up empty-handed, clammy-palmed, with only the faintest memory of some distant panic clinging to the hollows between her fingers. Giving up, Dani shook her head and forced herself to open the crumpled magazine. There was a two-page spread of a beach in Bali, the sort of place that seemed a universe away, it was so inaccessible to her.

"Half an hour," Hazel said, patting Dani's knee awkwardly. "Can you feel that we're going down?"

"Good Lord," Dani whispered, because as soon as Hazel mentioned it, she could feel that they were descending. There was an empty place beneath her stomach, a black hole where the pull of the earth felt like an inescapable gravity dragging her down.

"Can't you take another pill?"

Dani shook her head and reached for the plastic cup of cheap airline wine that she had emptied an hour ago. She took Hazel's water instead and drank it in one long gulp, filling her mouth with big cubes of ice and crunching them frantically.

Hazel looked at her in bewilderment for a moment, then she abandoned all pretense of concern and laughed. "How in the world did Etsell ever end up with you?"

"I resent that," Danica muttered around a mouthful of chipped ice.

"I could ask it the other way if you prefer: How did you ever end up with Etsell?"

"That's no better. No matter how you say it it sounds like we don't belong together. Like our marriage is some sort of a mistake."

Hazel tipped her head as if seriously considering the implications of Dani's words.

"You think my marriage is a mistake?" Dani hissed before Hazel could speak her mind.

"I never said that. You and Ell are just a bit of an enigma."

Dani leaned back in her seat with a sigh and pressed her fingers to the corners of her eyes. She wanted to tell Hazel that it was none of her business, that she would do well to keep her unwanted opinions to herself, but snapping at the older woman seemed like a self-destructive thing to do. Instead, Dani bit her tongue and hoped that Hazel would go back to reading the crime novel she held open on her lap.

But Hazel dog-eared the corner of a page in her book and closed it with a snap. Turning away from Dani, she laid her forehead against the tiny airplane window and stared down at the peaks of mountains that were just beginning to poke above the clouds. *The Aleutians?* Dani wondered, glancing past Hazel to take in the craggy, unscalable summits. As she watched, the clouds beneath them parted and they were granted a sweeping, undisrupted view of the wild earth below. It was breathtaking and beautiful and terrible.

Dani's stomach lurched, and one word bubbled up from somewhere so deep inside it took a bit of her with it. She moaned, "No."

With her face still turned toward the window, Hazel reached blindly for Dani's hand and held it fast.

"He's out there," Dani said, her voice high and fast. "He's out there somewhere, isn't he? How are we going to find him?"

Hazel didn't answer.

⁓

"I'd like to see a moose," Hazel said when Danica emerged from the terminal restroom. Landing had been a stomach-churning, soul-stirring affair, and as soon as Dani's feet touched the solid ground of the Ted Stevens Anchorage International Airport, her body had rebelled. Vomiting in a public restroom was not her idea of a good time, and capping it off with one of Hazel's ill-timed and insensitive comments didn't do much to improve her already foul mood.

"Go to a zoo." She meant it to sound like a joke, but there was an edge to her voice. Dani forced a placating smile and tightened the shoulder strap of her backpack with a shaking hand. When Hazel ignored her, she raised her eyes to take in the view before her.

Though she hated flying no less after spending five straight hours in the air, she had to admit that the Anchorage airport was one of the most amazing buildings she had ever been in. Instead of a wall, one entire side of the long terminal was made of glass. It framed the mountains surrounding the city in a picture so clear and pixel-perfect it could have been a computer-generated image. Dani fought an urge to touch the vast window to make sure that it was real.

The view was undeniably breathtaking, but it filled her with a sense of disquiet, a feeling of dread that made everything seem somehow sinister. It was nearly midnight, but the sun was still low on the horizon and it painted the sky pink and orange, wetting the tips of the mountains with a rust-colored wash that was surreal in its splendor. She knew that she was being dramatic, that the panoramic vista before her was the sort of scene that inspired painters and poets, prophets and kings. But the jagged edge against the horizon put Danica in mind of a serrated knife. She was exhausted, and nursing a headache. In the long shadows of the mountains, her quest seemed huge and impossible. Foolish.

Doomed.

"I'll bet you ten bucks that we see a moose," Hazel said. Apparently she was unaffected by the scene before them. Or worse, impervious to the task at hand.

But Danica knew that wasn't true. Hazel was trying to distract her. "Ten bucks," she sighed, shaking on it. "Time frame?"

"Tonight. I bet we'll see a moose tonight."

"Make it twenty."

"You've got yourself a deal."

Dani was convinced that Hazel's longing to catch a glimpse of the wildlife would be a wish unfulfilled, but before they had managed to leave airport property, they nearly hit one of the gentle behemoths as it grazed beside the road. The moose lifted its head and stared at them for a moment before he seemed to blink in boredom and returned to the grass at his feet.

Hazel chuckled a little and took one hand off the steering wheel to offer it, palm up, before Dani. The younger woman dug two tens out of her wallet. She didn't mind parting with the money. She figured she owed Hazel a much greater debt than twenty dollars. And paying Etsell's would-be mom in cold, hard cash was easier than attempting to return her generosity with the sort of relationship that she couldn't quite piece together no matter how hard she tried.

Their final destination was Seward, a town on the cusp

of Resurrection Bay that could easily have been reached by one last half-hour flight. But Dani had put her foot down. She simply couldn't stand the thought of another airplane. Hazel hadn't put up much resistance—except to insist that she would be the primary driver—and they ended up booking a hotel partway between Anchorage and Seward, splitting the three-hour trip into two shorter legs.

"Shouldn't we call Blair?" Dani asked when they were on the outskirts of the city. Seward Highway unfolded before them, a long stretch of road that suddenly took a sharp curve and revealed the Cook Inlet in one generous rush.

"Not anymore," Hazel said. "I told him we'd call when we landed if it wasn't too late. But I don't want to wake him now. We'll call in the morning."

Dani glanced at the dashboard clock and realized that it was after one in the morning. It didn't feel that late, and yet her stomach clenched with the faint nausea of exhaustion. "It's unnatural," she complained. "The sun shouldn't shine in the middle of the night."

"I kind of like it." Hazel tapped her brakes and pointed out the passenger window to the steely water beyond. "That's the Turnagain Arm," she narrated. "And that stretch of beach beyond the stones? It's the beginning of the mudflats."

"I had no idea you were so well versed in Alaskan geography," Dani said, easing Hazel's arm out of the way with her fingertips.

"I researched. Google Earth. Travel Alaska. There's more on the Internet than pornography, you know."

If Hazel was trying to get a rise out of her, Dani was too travel-weary to take the bait.

"Buck up, princess." Hazel grinned wide enough to reveal the silver fillings in her teeth, but it looked more like a grimace to Dani. "Imagine we're on a road trip. You've never been this far from home before."

"That's exactly the problem."

Some small part of Danica wished that she had the kind of camaraderie with Hazel that fostered intimacy, or even casual conversation. Everything would be eased a little if only she had someone to share it with. But Hazel irritated Dani. She tried, they both tried in their fumbling, well-intentioned ways, but it seemed impossible for them to hit the mark. They always missed each other.

Hazel stopped attempting to draw Dani out of her miserable silence as they made their way from Anchorage to Girdwood, and the car slowly filled with an awkward tenor of apprehension. It was a one-note chord, the hum of something soft but insistent that settled into the places where they didn't dare to speak. Dani could have screamed from the ache of it, from the continuous refrain of exhaustion and hopelessness that clutched at her chest with phantom fingers.

But she held herself together, for what choice did she have? Her husband was out there somewhere, and the man who would try to help her find him. And while her desperation felt infinite in breadth as it pressed against the doors of the tiny rental car, Dani did her best to rein it in, to ignore the haunting early-morning sunset and the way the mountains concealed mysteries she could not begin to fathom.

They were different, the Alaskan mountains. Different from anything she had seen or experienced, in no way comparable to the Black Hills of South Dakota, where she had taken a late honeymoon with Etsell so many years before.

With a small jolt of surprise, Dani realized that she could remember exactly how she felt when she caught her first glimpse of the hills after driving for hours through nothing but endless prairie flatland. They had gotten married before Christmas, but postponed their honeymoon until the weather was more clement. It was a brilliant day in early June when they left Blackhawk, and the sun had traveled with them from their little home through Mitchell and Chamberlain and past a dozen Wall Drug signs. And though it was nearing suppertime, daylight was still overhead when the blue-green line of limestone peaks and ponderosa pine forests blurred the horizon like a mirage.

Dani didn't mean to be so sentimental—she knew it would make her new husband snicker—but she couldn't help it when her breath caught in her throat. "It's beautiful," she whispered.

Etsell was supposed to disagree, to laugh at least and tell her that they could have seen sights much more grand than the miniature mountains of the prairie. But he smiled instead, and raised their woven fingers to kiss the bones at her wrist. "So beautiful," he agreed. "And sacred. Did you know that the Sioux and the Cheyenne considered the Black Hills the spiritual center of the world? Holy ground."

Religion was like quicksand as far as Etsell was concerned, seductive, deceptive, slow to drag you down. But there wasn't an ounce of sarcasm in his voice when he spoke of the consecrated earth before them. It made Danica feel filled somehow, as if her groom had gifted her with something sweet and heavy and warm. The richness of his words seeped into every dark crevice and made her think, not for the first time, *He is everything.* And she added to that belief, *We are everything. We are holy.*

Dani remembered turning from the mountains then and focusing on the tangle of their hands, the individual peaks and valleys of knuckles and bone. *These are my hands,* she marveled. *And his.* They seemed profound to her.

The mountains that towered over her on the road to Girdwood held none of the sanctification, none of the quiet awe of the pine-covered limestone of the rugged Black Hills. In fact, Danica's memory of the Hills was stripped of its rough-hewn splendor and relegated to something out of a children's fantasy, a black-and-white *Lone Ranger* Western with gentle Indians and a kindhearted cowboy who embodied every good but misguided intention. It was as if in the shadow of the Chugach Mountains she realized for the first time that the Black Hills weren't really mountains at all.

There was no kindness here. Nothing gentle. The wild land around her seemed ripped from the earth in an act of violence that left everything defensive and torn. Danica raised heavy-lidded eyes to the hulking giants that hemmed her in on every side, and suppressed a shudder. Monsters lurked here. Wolves and demons and beasts that were meant to devour and destroy. The rocks were so sheer, the trees so dense that it seemed terrain fit only for claws.

She cupped her hands in her lap and stared at the intersection of lines across her palms. The twin trails that ran parallel to her wrist, the arc that separated her thumb. When she balled her fists, the crests were there. The secret range that she had made with Etsell still existed in part, though her hands were older, her skin dry and cracked from water and chemicals. She tried not to think about it, but there was a question in the lonely lines of her fingers. In spite of her best efforts, she wondered if Etsell's calluses would ever again fit against her palm.

When Hazel's cell phone rang, it seemed otherworldly, detached. Dani watched as Hazel patted herself in an effort to locate the source of the sound, and when she finally produced it from the hip pocket of her Columbia shell, she tossed it at Dani.

"You answer it. I'm driving."

Without looking at the number Danica flipped open the scratched Motorola. "Hazel's phone," she said.

"Hazel?"

"No, it's Danica Greene. Hazel is . . ."

The older woman waved her hand dismissively and kept her gaze on the road before her.

"She's indisposed at the moment. Can I take a message?"

"Hi, Mrs. Greene, it's Blair Knopf calling. Can I assume you've made it safely to Anchorage?"

"Actually, we're halfway to Girdwood. I'm sorry we didn't call. We figured you would be sleeping."

"I was."

Danica wasn't sure what to say, so she said nothing at all. Neither did Blair, and the silence between them stretched so long that she wondered if they had been disconnected. "Mr. Knopf?"

"I'm still here," he said. "Call me Blair."

"Is there something I can do for you?"

The line trembled with a moment of static, but Dani thought she heard Blair sigh all the same.

"Something has come up," he began. "I just got a call that we have another missing person."

Dani's throat tightened. "Does that mean you can't help us?"

"No," Blair said, "nothing like that. It's just . . . I have a question for you."

"Of course."

"Do you know someone by the name of Sam Linden?"

"I've never heard of him."

"Not him," Blair clarified, "*her*. Her real name is Samantha, but she goes by Sam. That name doesn't ring a bell?"

Dani was tired. Tired and confused, and her strange conversation with Blair was only making matters worse. She laid her forehead in her hand and closed her eyes. "No, I've never heard of a Sam, or a Samantha, Linden. Should I have? What does this have to do with Etsell?"

Another silence. Another weighted pause. "We have reason to believe that she may be with him."

"What do you mean?"

"We think they disappeared together."

Danica

I always knew that other women found Etsell handsome, but I didn't realize just how irresistible he was until one morning when Katrina woke up on our couch. It was a snowy Sunday in January, and Kat had snuggled under the tattered afghan even longer than normal. She might have been hungover—it was hard to tell with my sister because she could hold her liquor so well—but I prodded her off the couch anyway and dragged her to the bathroom, where I gave her my terry-cloth robe and a fresh towel from our linen closet.

"I'm making brunch," I told her. "All you have to do is make yourself presentable. Omelets will be on the table in twenty minutes."

It was hard to maintain any sort of routine when my family assumed our home had a revolving door. Romantic nights in front of our potbellied, wood-burning stove were often interrupted by my mother, since her waitressing hours were unpredictable at best and she felt the need to burden us with her presence when she wanted to unwind after a long shift or avoid one of the guys she was sick of stringing along. And Kat seemed to think that married or not, I was still her baby sister and blood trumped wedding vows.

When I was a kid, I half expected her to crawl into my bed at some point every night, it was such a given. I even left a night-light plugged in to the outlet on the opposite wall of my bed just so that Kat could find her way in the dark with minimal drama. I don't think she came because she was scared or upset, it was more of a comfort thing. A way of reaching out in the darkness and resting her fingers against a touchstone, a constant. Me.

Natalie would never have stood for that sort of nonsense, and even though my older sisters shared a room, Kat didn't go to her for solace. They would have had more in common. They could have whispered about their high school crushes and commiserated about the fact that their classmates tried to use them to score alcohol. It was common knowledge that Char was often too lit to realize what came in and out of our house in the form of cheap bottles from the liquor store.

But instead of creating inroads with Natalie, Kat crept across the hallway and opened the door to my room. She always paused for a moment in the narrow crack, her hair fanned out behind her and glowing with light from the streetlamp just outside our living room window. Then she'd slip in quickly and ease the door shut, tiptoeing two steps to the edge of my bed before breathing my name into the stillness.

"Dani? You awake?"

Even if I was, I wouldn't answer. And whether she suspected I was faking or not, she always lifted the edge of the sheet and climbed beneath, curling herself against my body as if she was a very little girl and I her mother.

Kat never tried to talk to me, and she always snuck away before Natalie's alarm was set to go off in the morning. I don't know how she did it, if she lay awake in the darkness and watched the moon keep time as it arced across the sky in the frame of my open window, or if she just had an internal alarm clock that alerted her when Natalie was at risk of discovering her nighttime ritual. But I left room for Kat every night, tucking myself tight against the wall so that there would be room for my leggy sister in my twin bed.

By the time I married Etsell, Kat had other bedfellows to keep her warm at night. However, she must have found them lacking. When Ell and I bought the little house on the edge of town, she started showing up again. I probably should have discouraged her, but I was a new bride and my husband was still tolerant of every caprice. It was charming to him how deeply I loved my messy and often hard-to-love family. So we left the front door unlocked, and draped my grandmother's afghan over the arm of the couch as a sign of our permission if not our outright invitation.

Most mornings after she slept over, Kat accepted one filled-to-the-brim mug of coffee, and then dragged herself back to the double-wide that she still shared with our mother. But we had an implicit understanding that Sundays were different. On Sunday mornings she washed off her makeup and the cloying scent of cheap perfume and joined us for a makeshift family brunch around the table in our kitchen.

On the morning Kat crossed the line, I was making her favorite: cheese omelets with bacon so crisp it was nearly burnt. After years of scrambling eggs for my sisters, I had perfected the art of making fat, fluffy omelets with just the right amount of sharp cheddar melting out of the sides. Ell was partial to sausage and mozzarella, but we both knew that when Kat showed up I would default to preparing whatever she preferred. He didn't complain.

"Kat's in the shower," I told him as I shredded cheddar with just a hint of contrition. There was a round of fresh mozzarella in the meat drawer that would have made delectable omelets.

He peeked at me over the top of the Sunday paper and I could see the corner of his eyes crinkle with amusement.

"Don't look at me like that."

He smirked. "You're such a mother."

"What's that supposed to mean?"

"Good things. It means all sorts of good things. You're a wonderful woman, Danica Greene."

I flipped him the bird. He laughed out loud.

When Kat finally emerged from the shower, pink-cheeked and toweling her long, dark hair, it was finally obvious that she had had too much to drink the night before. Her eyes were glassy and her grin was lopsided; it matched the off-center loop of the belt on her loosely tied robe. She looked like a woman who was clinging to her composure, drawing it around her like a garment that didn't quite fit.

My eyes raked over her, assessing the damage. Then I put down my spatula and tugged the fabric of my pink robe tight around my sister. I cinched the waist snug. "If you're not hungry, I can bring you home." Her car was in our driveway, but I didn't want her driving it. My stomach clenched with worry at the thought that she had driven it only hours before.

"I'm starving," Kat said. She dropped the towel that she had been using to dry her hair on the counter, and pulled out a chair next to Etsell. "Smells amazing in here."

I tried to catch Ell's eye but he was too busy attempting to refold the newspaper. "Dani's a great cook," he said mechanically. He loved Kat, but he didn't like her after she'd been drinking. He went all stiff-necked and quiet, as if her intoxication was an affront to his sensibilities. Which didn't make sense at all. Though his father had been an alcoholic, Etsell wasn't a teetotaler.

"I make eggs," I said, serving them each a thick wedge of omelet. "I make really good eggs and not much else."

"Oh, that's not true." Kat slurred her words only slightly. "You make the best spinach-artichoke dip I've ever had. And no one can touch your cookies."

"They're Toll House."

"Still."

I sat down across from her and watched as she took three bites in quick succession. I half expected her to get nauseous, to excuse herself from the table, but she chased her mouthful of eggs with a big swig of coffee and reached for more.

Kat reminded me so much of our mother it was unsettling. They had the same eyes, the same fine arch of delicate brows that gave them a perpetually curious expression. I had wondered before if that's why men found them so tempting—because when they fixed you with that coquettish, wide-eyed look, it was hard not to imagine that those eyes burned just for you. Kat had the ability to unnerve me with a glance.

But the similarities didn't end with their eyes. Char kept a photograph of herself in high school on the dresser in her bedroom, and I had watched my sister grow into the spitting image of the black-and-white portrait. They were both slender and tall with features that were just a little larger than life: big eyes, full lips, broad shoulders. Beautiful. Beautiful and dangerous.

"So good," she murmured, licking a strand of cheese from her fork. "All it needs is some orange juice. Do you have any orange juice?"

I pushed myself back from the table, but before I could rise, Etsell put his hand on my wrist. "I've got it, honey. Stay put." He gave me a conspiratorial squeeze and I felt myself settle.

Etsell grabbed three glasses from the cupboard beside the sink, then lifted a gallon of orange juice from the refrigerator with his pinky through the handle. He kicked the door closed and made his way back to the table.

I didn't realize that Kat had been watching him until I heard an appreciative sigh escape her lips. It was a muted puff of sound, an exhalation that could have meant a hundred different things. But I knew my sister.

As Etsell passed her, Kat reached out and cupped a hand against the seat of his jeans, giving him a little pinch with far too much relish.

Despite a shocked bounce in his step, Ell ignored her. And I tried for a second to convince myself that it was innocent, that sisters did that sort of thing all the time to their brothers-in-law. But fury billowed up in me despite my best efforts to contain it. My anger was smoky and dark, menacing. "What the hell was that?" I sputtered.

Kat's eyes shot to mine and there was guilt written deep within them. It was a raw, uncharacteristic emotion for her, but she blinked and the moment passed. "He's delicious, don't you think? You are one lucky woman, little sis."

Her nonchalance confused me, and I looked to Etsell for confirmation that I was overreacting. My husband wouldn't meet my gaze, a sure sign that he was just as uncomfortable as I was.

"I don't know what you were thinking, Kat," I fumed, "but that is not okay. Keep your hands off of my husband."

"No harm done." Kat was availing herself of all her charms now. Her lips curled with a mixture of condescension and intrigue, an expression that made me feel indignant and small all at once. Like this was just one big joke and I was too slow to get it. "I never had a father," she purred. "I don't know how to act around men."

"Bullshit." Etsell didn't usually put himself between me and my sisters, but his muttered curse gave me courage.

"I didn't have a father either, and I would know enough to keep my hands off my sister's man."

"I don't have a man."

"That's not the point."

Kat sighed and forked another bite of her omelet. "You're making a big deal out of nothing. Ell's a hunk. I'm sure he gets hit on all the time."

"You were hitting on my husband?"

"You're such a drama queen."

If Kat hadn't been impaired, I seriously think I would have leaned across the table and slapped her. As it was, it took the span of a breath or two for her to realize that she had gone too far. She swallowed carefully, laid her fork down, and stood up.

"I'd better run. I'm meeting a friend at—"

"Go."

It took Kat only a couple of minutes to throw on her dirty clothes from the night before. We could hear her banging around in the bathroom, then footsteps across the floorboards in the hall followed by the slam of the front door. I forgot my reservations about her driving until it was too late—she squealed out of the driveway and down the street before I could even think of stopping her.

When we couldn't hear her car anymore, Ell walked around the table and draped himself over my shoulders. He kissed my temple and sighed. "What was that all about?"

"My sister is crazy."

"I don't think she knew what she was doing."

"Don't try to defend her."

"I'm not defending her," Etsell said.

I twisted in my seat and grabbed my husband's arms. "Has she ever done anything like that to you before?"

The startled look on Etsell's face said it all. "No, of course not."

"Is it true what she said?" I pressed. "Do you get hit on all the time?"

"Well"—he smirked—"not *all* the time."

"I'm being serious."

Etsell crouched in front of me and took my face in his hands. Holding my gaze, he said, "If I do, I don't notice it. You're everything, Danica. You always have been. You always will be."

It was what I wanted to hear so I leaned into him and let him wrap his arms around me.

But the morning stayed with me for a long time, and it must have bothered Kat, too, because our couch was bereft of her midnight company for weeks. When she did finally show up one night it was months later and she left without breakfast or even a cup of coffee. She never apologized, but I didn't expect her to.

In a way, and after I stopped hating her a little, I was grateful. Kat hadn't meant to do it, but she woke me up to the truth about my husband. My marriage.

There are no guarantees.

5

Resurrection Bay

The flags that flanked the long circular driveway leading to the entrance of the Alyeska Resort hung limp in the early-morning calm. Though a bronze brazier with a perennial flame coaxed warmth into the cool air, Danica still stifled a shiver. It was late spring, but there was snow in the shadows between the trees. Not much, and it was really more like slush, gray from traffic and age. But it was perfect for packing into dirty snowballs if Danica felt so inclined. She did not.

It was a breathtaking morning, bright and brisk, uncharacteristically clear, according to the valet who kept her company while she waited outside for Hazel to emerge. He had dark eyes and skin that glowed the color of brushed suede, and his smile was too friendly to be entirely innocent.

"Got plans for the day?" he asked, warming his hands over the fire.

"We're going to Seward," Dani said after a pause. She lifted her eyes to the ring of mountains that hemmed in the resort, hoping he'd pick up her disinterested vibe and leave her alone.

He didn't. "We?"

Danica sighed inwardly, wondering how to explain her relationship with Hazel. "My friend and me," she managed.

"Day trip?"

"No, we'll be there for a while."

"Such a short stay? The forecast is fantastic. You could take the aerial tram to Seven Glaciers. Or you could walk the Nordic trails. Moose Meadows is great, even this time of year."

Danica nodded.

"I didn't convince you, did I?"

"We're going to Seward," she said again.

It sounded significant to her. A declaration of intent. Weighted with possibility like heavy stones hung from the corners of a flagging hope she hardly dared to raise. Seward held mysteries, but she believed every mystery could be solved if only the right questions were asked. If only.

Hazel finally lumbered out the sliding doors fifteen minutes past their agreed-upon meeting time. She had aged overnight, and dark circles bruised the skin beneath her eyes. Danica considered the disheveled woman before her and knew she looked no better. She decided the valet must be pretty hard up if he had stooped to flirting with her.

Blair had stolen their sleep last night with one unnerving phone call. She and Hazel didn't speak much after his late-night interruption, and though Dani assumed that the news couldn't have hit Hazel as hard as it pummeled her, in the telling light of a bright morning it was obvious that Etsell's surrogate mom was starting to bow beneath the weight of it all. For a brief moment, Danica felt a stray wisp of sisterhood bind her to Hazel. She clutched at it, but then the older woman barreled past her without bothering to even say hello. The feeling passed.

Dani stepped off the curb behind Hazel and followed her

across the parking lot to their rental car. Hazel clicked off
the locks and popped the trunk, and the two women lifted
in their carry-on suitcases without saying a word. It wasn't
until they were buckled in and on the road that Hazel broke
her self-imposed silence.

"Have you had breakfast?"

"No."

"Are you hungry?"

"No."

"Me either."

Hazel retraced their path from the night before, blurring
through the tiny town of Girdwood in minutes. There was a
Tesoro gas station on the corner of the Alyeska and Seward
highways and a small strip mall that boasted a pleasant-looking
bakery. Dani caught a glimpse of the racks of muffins and fat,
glossy doughnuts, but instead of enticing her, they turned her
stomach. *Coffee*, she thought for a fleeting moment. *I could go
for some caffeine.* But Hazel aimed the car toward Seward without a backward glance.

They followed the water for several miles before the road
angled inland and the mountains loomed almost celestial in
their height and splendor. There were clouds now, but they
were high-breasted confections, preening whirls of white
that decorated the rugged peaks like dollops of whipped
cream. Dani couldn't help but admire the obvious beauty
of the range that surrounded her, but beneath the grandeur
there was something undeniably sinister. Each pinnacle was
seductive, a Siren luring in unsuspecting hunters and hikers,
pilots. The hills were beautiful and deadly.

Nearly an hour passed before Danica worked up the courage to ripple the stillness between her and Hazel. She could
have made small talk, but she jumped right into the deep
end and asked the question that had been burning her lips

since the moment she hung up with Blair the night before. "Did he ever mention Sam?"

Danica knew she sounded desperate. Hazel would have told her if Etsell had talked about Sam Linden. Wouldn't she? But she couldn't help hoping, believing, that if she phrased it just so, Hazel would remember something. Anything. A detail, a conversation, a feeling she couldn't quite pin down.

Not only had Blair's phone call robbed Danica of sleep and denied her even a moment of peace, it also refined her fears—it distilled everything down to one consuming ache. More than a week had passed since her husband went missing, and though she still longed to find him hale and whole, what Dani really hungered for as their rental car sped down a winding mountain highway was the truth. So she asked. And asked again.

"No," Hazel said.

"What about Samantha?"

"Nope."

"Sami, then."

"Etsell never mentioned a Samantha or a Sam or a Sami. The first time I ever heard her name was when you told me about her last night."

"What about another woman? Maybe he changed her name—"

"Danica, stop." Hazel slammed her hand against the steering wheel. "You have got to let this go. I don't know anything about Samantha Linden, I swear to you. Why would I lie?"

"To spare me the truth?" Dani spoke quietly, dispassionately.

"The truth that Etsell often flew with a woman? A woman who was a hunting guide at the lodge he worked for? A woman who made regular trips from the Midnight Sun to wherever her clients needed her to be?" Hazel speared Dani with a sharp look. "Stop trying to read into things. Sounds perfectly innocent to me. Besides, if I knew something, I'd tell you. When have you ever known me to spare anyone from anything?"

"So you don't know anything," Dani persisted.

"Nothing."

"There was no woman."

"Well, Dani, obviously there was a woman. But that doesn't mean what you think it means."

How do you know?

Dani wanted to break something. Not because she was so hurt or angry or sad. True, her mind was captive to a hundred different scenes, failures and fights, moments that she was suddenly convinced were enough to drive her husband into the arms of another woman. But the thought of Etsell with this stranger, this Samantha Linden, was numbing somehow. Danica turned it over in her mind, studying the sharp, unexpected angles, and thought, *So this is how it ends.*

When she had believed that Etsell went missing on his own, she understood the concept of death by broken heart. But nothing had prepared her for the possibility of this. Of his disappearance being intentional, a premeditated loss of self. A severing of "us." It opened up a place inside her that she didn't know existed, a corner of her soul so new and raw and untouched, she couldn't help but press it and wonder what sort of pain she was capable of feeling.

It changed everything, knowing that Etsell might not have disappeared.

He might have left.

Of course, when Blair called to alter the very fabric of her world, he didn't say that. He merely asked a few benign questions and told Danica that a certain Samantha Linden had been declared missing just that afternoon. They didn't know for sure, but she might have been in the plane with Etsell.

"My husband has been missing for nine days," Dani said, vaguely aware that there was a certain veiled urgency when she uttered "my husband." As if their wedding vows invalidated any insinuation otherwise and bespoke an unassailable proprietorship. "If they're together, why was Ms. Linden only reported missing today?"

"Sam is a skilled hunter and a fine outdoorsman, uh, outdoor*woman*. She's been known to disappear from time to time. She abandoned her car on the Denali Highway once and lived off the land for nearly two weeks."

Blair sounded impressed and Dani muttered, "Good for her," before she could stop herself. *Good for her*, like Samantha's talents should earn her a gold star or something equally inane.

"Anyway, according to Russ Manfred, Sam had taken the week off and was flying to Seward with your husband. We know she got off the plane in Seward—she had lunch at the Yukon Bar—but now we're wondering if she got back on."

"Why?"

"She didn't show up for work."

"Maybe she decided to live off the land again." Dani's comment came off snide, but Blair seemed to take it seriously.

"That's a very likely possibility. But we're investigating every scenario. It seems just a little strange that Etsell and Sam would go missing within a week of each other, don't you think?"

"Why?"

Blair stumbled. "Because they worked together. Because they flew together so much. And just a couple of hours after they landed in Seward, they both went missing."

Dani couldn't help it. As the rental car sped toward Seward, she pictured Etsell and Sam leaning toward each other in the cockpit of her husband's borrowed plane. He had a soft smile on his face, the right corner of his mouth quirking a little as if to point to his one and only dimple. His eyes sparked green and gold, and though she knew every inch of his skin, the scent of his cologne, and words his mouth would form before he even said them, she was stunned by how magnetic he was. Of course Samantha Linden spirited him away. Who could blame her?

As if to agree with her private train of thought, Hazel released a long, low sigh. It was a sad sound. A sound of defeat. But then Hazel shook her head, twisting her neck as if she had long hair and she wished for a ponytail. Dani didn't doubt that Hazel had made that exact movement a thousand times in her life. Ten thousand. There were a handful of faded photos of her with a dark braid that fell halfway down the middle of her back to prove it. And Dani was personally familiar with the look of resolve that settled over Hazel's features; the way she squared her shoulders like a seasoned linebacker and set her jaw as if she expected a fight.

In a rush of awareness, Dani was grateful that Hazel was by her side. Hazel would fight for the truth. She would find Etsell.

"See the water?" Hazel nodded toward Danica's window. "It's Kenai Lake. It means we're getting close to Seward."

Dani's chest seized. Her heart curled in upon itself, tugging the corners close so she wouldn't have to face all that was to come with her soul wide and vulnerable.

It was a move she had perfected.

Blair Knopf was older than Dani had imagined him to be. He had the voice of a thirty-something, but when he held out his hand to shake Dani's, it was wrinkled and as rough as fine-grit sandpaper, the age-spotted skin of a man quickly approaching seventy. And yet he didn't seem old. His hair was thick and boyish somehow—it looked like his wife had cut it, with dubious success—and his eyes were clear and cheerful. If the deep lines arching to his temples could be trusted, he was a man who laughed much.

But he wasn't laughing as he regarded Danica.

"Welcome to Alaska," he said solemnly. "I'm sorry your visit is the result of such sad circumstances. Is this your first time here?"

Dani nodded. "It's beautiful," she told him, because he looked so heartbroken. It struck her in that moment that Blair thought she was in Seward on a fool's errand. As far as he was concerned, Etsell was already gone. Dani could see it in his eyes. "The mountains are stunning," she said, pressing back against his doubt with an attempt at untroubled banter.

"Thank you." Blair seemed to take personal credit for the beauty of the earth around him. "Seward is really spectacular. You should be touring the glacier, taking a boat around Resurrection Bay, sampling the fare at Ray's Waterfront. . . ." He shook his head. "But I suppose you'll have a bird's-eye view of it all, won't you? Nothing like seeing the world from the perspective of God himself."

Dani stole a peek at her surroundings and swallowed down a wave of panic at the sight of the papier-mâché airplanes before her. Blair had insisted on meeting at the Seward airport, and Dani stood bathed in the low shadows of at least a dozen tangible nightmares. They were winged beasts, allegedly large enough and sound enough to carry a precious cargo of life, but to Dani they seemed poised to devour their captives whole.

The Seward airport was a tiny affair about the same size as Blackhawk's own rudimentary airfield. But while Blackhawk's airstrip was frequented by only a smattering of pilots, Blair assured Dani that Seward was a regular Grand Central Station in spite of its size. She could hardly believe it, considering that there was only a single runway and two modest-sized Morton buildings surrounded by a chain-link fence. There was also what Dani considered to be a sort of airplane parking lot, and it was here that Blair made his introductions.

Here, Dani thought, her fingers tingling from fear and anticipation. *He was here.*

As Hazel stepped forward and presented herself to their Civil Air Patrol savior, Dani felt herself inexorably pulled toward Blair's plane. It reminded her of Etsell's, but it was older and obviously had more life experience. She lifted her hand to trace the white numbers against the midnight-blue paint, to touch the hard scales of the monster. The metal was cold, the rivets and bolts protruding like keloid scars. She stifled a shiver and backed away, thrusting her balled hands into the pockets of her coat.

"How?" she whispered, not even knowing what she asked. How do you stay afloat? How did he go missing? How will I ever find him again?

"She's a beaut, isn't she?" Blair asked, coming up behind Dani and putting a comforting hand on her shoulder. It was a brief, fatherly touch and Dani leaned into the light pressure for a moment before he pulled away. The absence of his hand left her feeling unbalanced, dizzy.

"Etsell had many affairs throughout the course of our marriage, but they were all with airplanes," Dani said wryly. She didn't add that Sam Linden loomed in her mind as the one person who could change all that. Who could tear Et-sell's perfect record into bits of bitter confetti. "I'm sure he would have loved your plane."

Blair didn't ask her if she agreed, and Dani was grateful for that. She hadn't bothered to tell him about her fear of flying, about her downright loathing of anything with metal wings. Her husband was missing, and her resolve was iron. Never mind the fact that she had a pocketful of pills that were sup-posed to carry her through. She fingered the plastic bottle, feeling the tumble of tiny tablets.

"I was thinking we'd just get an overview of the area this morning. I'll take you around the bay, and then we'll get a taste for the fjords. I could show you Exit Glacier and the Harding Icefield. . . ." Blair shrugged a little self-consciously. "I know that sounds kind of touristy, but I thought you might like to get your bearings up there a bit before we start really looking. Tomorrow it will be all business and binoculars."

"This morning?" Dani all but whimpered at the same mo-ment that Hazel said, "Sounds good."

Blair looked between the two of them, a wrinkle between his eyes creasing even deeper as he considered the unlikely pair. "If you had something else in mind—"

"No," Hazel interrupted before he could finish his thought. "We're not here to waste time. We're here to find Etsell."

Blair started to say something, but thought better of it and offered the two women a wan smile. "We'll do the best we can."

As Blair readied the plane, doing a preflight check on the flaps, the weights beneath the wings, and every other minus-cule wire, attachment, and connection, Hazel pulled Dani aside.

"Are you going to be okay?"

"Fine," Dani muttered between clenched teeth. "I just wasn't prepared for—"

"Flying today. I know. Is it too late to take your meds?"

Dani gave Hazel a dour look.

"Do you want to stay back? I can go with Blair today and you can join us tomorrow," Hazel said.

But Blair was already calling in the flight plan on his cell phone. Dani could hear him giving his plane ID number, the amount of fuel, estimated travel time, route, and number of passengers. Three. Any misgivings she had were buried beneath a sense of obligation. It was her duty to get on that plane.

Blair helped Hazel into the narrow backseat of his Cessna 172, then locked the passenger seat into place for Dani. "I imagine you know your way around one of these," he said with a knowing wink. "Do you fly much with Etsell?"

"Not much," she said. It didn't seem like a lie to her. She might not have been present in the cockpit, but she was with him every time he flew.

Dani buckled herself in, using logic to guide her as she fussed with the straps. Breathing shallowly around the boulder that seemed poised to crush her chest, she reached for the set of headphones on her side of the cockpit and settled them over her ears with a sense of finality.

"Can you hear me?" Blair's voice crackled.

"Yes." It was all she could do to make herself respond.

"Hazel?"

"Loud and clear."

When they taxied down the runway, Dani's skin pricked with the knowledge that nine days earlier her husband had taken off from this very runway. For a moment she could feel the stir of his excitement, the burst of adrenaline that must have washed over him every time he took to the air in this place that had been the object of his longing. Etsell had wanted this so much. He idealized it and planned for it and bound it with the woven strands of his wishes into private definitions of *success* and *contentment* and *home*. Dani didn't understand, but as the Cessna picked up speed, she tried.

And in the mayhem of noise around her, the roar of the engine and the rumble of the lightweight plane as it parted the wind like water, Etsell hovered near. He whispered words in her ear. Words that were too soft to discern but impossible to ignore. Insistent phrases, demanding tones, that could have been declarations of love and commitment or the final shout of his frustration, of his pain over a marriage gone bad without her even knowing that it soured a little more every day.

"Did you leave me?" Dani whispered.

"What was that?" Blair asked, darting her a quick look at the exact moment that they lifted off the ground.

But Dani couldn't begin to explain. And as the airplane gained altitude and shot like an arrow out over a rocky beach toward Resurrection Bay, she was seized with a dread so suffocating, she actually put her hands to her throat and tried to claw it away.

"Resurrection Bay is nine hundred feet at its deepest, so it's one of the northernmost ice-free bays. It's accessible even in winter."

Blair was talking, but to Dani his voice was merely cacophonous nonsense, nothing more than white noise that throbbed against her head.

"Many planes have gone down here, and they are quickly swept out to sea. Not much chance of uncovering anything that has crashed in the bay."

Dani didn't mean to look down, but her eyes were drawn to a sparkle below, a slash of sunlight that glowed on the water like an open window. There were boats under her feet, and dark shapes that loomed far beneath the surface of the steel-colored bay. The wind rolled over the wings of the plane and rocked it, shiplike and slow. Some fragmented corner of her mind acknowledged that it was stunning, all of it, but Dani hated and feared it with a ferocity that left her gasping.

"Are you okay?" Blair asked, turning to regard her as she struggled for air.

Dani couldn't answer.

"Danica?"

The blackness started in the corners of her eyes and slipped steadily inward. Dani could hear Blair call her name, and Hazel join the chorus to make it a frantic duet. The cockpit was hot, but Dani was frozen, trembling uncontrollably as they flew on the cusp of a world she never wanted to know. Gulping, crying, she finally managed to scream, "I can't do this!"

She pressed her face to the icy window, weeping as she scraped the glass with her fingernails, trying to force her way out.

Danica

The first time I dreamed about Etsell's disappearance was the night after my complete breakdown in Blair's plane.

There were a few minutes of absolute mayhem in the sky, of shouting and turbulence and fear before Hazel leaned around my seat and caught my arms from behind. She held me in an iron embrace, her headset bumping against mine as Blair banked hard toward the water and turned us around. I think she whispered something, a faint hum of words tickled the back of my mind, but I was too hysterical to focus on the meaning.

When we were grounded and I had escaped the confines of the pocket-sized cockpit, I came to my senses so quickly, it was as if I had been doused in ice water. The air was cool and clean, the breeze a soft reminder that my nightmares were irrational. I was so humiliated I couldn't bring myself to face Blair. "I'm sorry" played over and over in my head, a chorus without end, since my lips seemed incapable even of tracing the syllables of my apology.

As Blair shut the doors of his airplane and repositioned yellow blocks around the wheels, I stood at a distance, hugging a dark cloud of shame to myself with arms wrapped tight against my chest. I would have simply left, but Hazel had the keys to the car, and she was stuck so close to Blair's side they seemed to move as one. I could see her mouth moving nonstop. He held his tongue and nodded, keeping time with the long stream of her monologue.

It took only a few minutes for Blair to set everything right. Then he faced Hazel full-on, smiled politely, and left her in the middle of a sentence. She stopped with her mouth wide open, and I watched in horror as Blair headed straight for me. I held his gaze for a second, but it was too hard to look him in the eye and I dropped my head before he had crossed the space between us. I braced myself, preparing for the verbal lashing that I sorely deserved.

But when I could see Blair's sneaker come toe-to-toe with mine, he didn't say a word. Instead, he reached out and folded me to him, resting his cheek on the top of my head. He smelled of oil and exhaust, a scent so familiar and comforting I had to close my eyes against a barrage of memories.

"You okay?" he asked after a moment.

I nodded against his shoulder.

"I shouldn't have done that to you," Blair said in a bizarre twist on the apology that I had been mustering up the courage to offer. "It wasn't fair of me to just assume you were ready for all that. You just got here."

"It's not that." I pulled away, and we stood there awkwardly for a moment before I took a step back and offered: "I hate flying. I'm terrified of it. I thought I could handle it, but . . ."

"Ground work," Blair said with a casual shrug. "We'll keep you busy on land while Hazel and I take to the air."

I battled a quick burst of jealousy—it didn't seem fair that Hazel and this relative stranger were the ones who would continue the hunt—but it was short-lived. Blair's suggestion was more than I could have asked for. I figured I would be useless if I couldn't join them in the plane, but with one thoughtful suggestion Blair gave me a place in the search. My role was relegated to little more than paperwork and prayer, and yet it was something. The corner of my mouth tweaked. "Thank you."

"No thanks required."

Before Hazel and I left to check in at the Holiday Inn Express, Blair retrieved a file folder from his car and handed it to me with a look of determination. "I saved everything," he said. "I know it's a macabre souvenir, but I thought you would like to have it all the same."

The folder was about half an inch thick, and as I thumbed through the contents I suppressed a shudder. There were newspaper clippings with headlines that gave voice to the fears that gathered like a sinister fog inside my head: "Pilot Missing"; "Plane Vanishes Out of Seward. Search Continues"; "No Sign of Pilot Who Disappeared on Sunday. Weather Slows Searchers." The titles became steadily bleaker. And among the newsprint were photocopies of flight plans, memos from the Alaskan Air Command Rescue Coordination Center in Anchorage, and a handwritten note that contained one cryptic line: Remind volunteers not to crowd the sky.

Blair reached for that scrap of paper and lifted it out of the file. "Sorry. Don't know how that got in there."

"Volunteers are crowding the sky? Looking for Etsell?"

He nodded. "They were."

Were. But not anymore.

That night, bolstered by a half-dozen flat hotel pillows, I flew. The sky was filled with planes, peppered with multi-colored aircraft like sprinkles on sun-blue icing. I squinted at the brightness of it, and felt a thrill of hope that all these people, all these planes had cluttered up the sky just to find my Ell. How could they fail? Every square inch of the wild earth below was charted by some intrepid pilot. I could taste their success; I could almost hear the moment when someone cackled into the radio, "I found him."

But the heavens were too crowded, and when the first collision erupted in a ball of fire and smoke, my expectations were stripped away in an act of sudden violence. All at once it was happening everywhere, the sky full of faithful volunteers was awash in the angry orange of burning jet fuel, the sun was obscured by vapors of toxic fumes. I could hear the scream of frantic descent, an unearthly wail as metal dropped from the sky like hail.

It was then that I remembered I was flying. *Flying.*

I wasn't in a plane. I had wings. And they were singed and smoking; I felt the burn as if each feather was made of skin.

When I fell it was from an unfathomable height. There was no end to my descent as I plummeted past all those planes, those rescuers who were in need of rescue. But instead of crying out to me, each pilot sighed as I passed.

They shook their heads in defeat. And though they didn't say it, I could see it in their eyes. *We're sorry. We're so sorry. We couldn't find him.*

⁓

When I was young, I dedicated months of my life to finding my unnamed father. Char's definitions of "mother" and "father" were loosely held, and even when I was very small I rarely called her Mom because she found the title too matronly. So it stood to reason that the identity of my dad would be a thing of little consequence to her. But it was huge to me. Monumental.

I don't remember the moment that I realized families

were meant to include a dad, a man who smelled of after-shave and sawdust and sweat, and who would undoubtedly grip me under the arms and swing me up high to perch on his shoulders like I had seen my friend Courtney's father do. My longing for the sound of a deep voice in our home was something that didn't happen all at once—it materialized, slow and pervasive like steam filling a room, until everything was obscured by the haze of my want.

In kindergarten I drew pictures of our family and included a father figure that I had never known. He was taller than the stick drawing of my mother by half, and the blaze of his crayon-red beard—a characteristic I had borrowed from Courtney's teddy bear of a dad—lit up my square of parchment paper like a flame.

"Does your mommy have a new boyfriend?" my kindergarten teacher asked. If she was being derisive, I was too innocent to notice.

"No," I told her, "this is my daddy."

Though I could never recall her name, for years to come I could see the look on her face as clearly as if I captured her expression in a photograph. Her eyebrows arched and drew together to form a dark cloud across her forehead, and her lips pulled into a tight line that reminded me of a pair of limp earthworms. "Your daddy?" she repeated. "Really."

Even at five I could hear the disbelief in her voice.

After that I stopped drawing my imaginary dad into pictures. But I harbored a secret passion for him, a yearning so acute I sometimes lined pillows behind my back when I slept so I could pretend that he had read me bedtime stories and dozed off in the middle of *Horton Hears a Who*. It was a childish fantasy that I gave up in middle school when Kat started coming into my room at night.

We talked about him sometimes, Kat and I. Char insisted

that all three of her daughters were "gifts" from different fathers, but Kat and I were convinced that we bore a resemblance too distinct to be accidental. It was something in the way that we walked, an athletic, almost masculine gait, and our mouths, which were wide and generous, filled with teeth so straight and perfect and big Char called us her pony girls. Natalie was different altogether, shorter and darker, the prisoner of painful-looking braces from ages thirteen to sixteen. She hated them at the time, but Char was working as a secretary at one of the insurance companies in town and they offered dental coverage in her medical package. She quit the week after Natalie's braces were taken off.

Lying in bed at night, Kat and I would catalog the ways we were dissimilar to our older sister. We would put our hands together, tracing our fingers and wondering at the parallel loops of our fingerprints. Maybe, just maybe, they had been fashioned from the same template. And maybe, just maybe, we could find the man who inspired them if we tried.

We weren't very good detectives, but we watched men at the grocery store and on the street. No one was excluded from our narrow-eyed analysis, not even men who wore wedding rings or held the hands of other little girls. Char wasn't very discriminating. Why should we be?

Once at a Fourth of July parade in Blackhawk we were sure that we caught a glimpse of him. Kat and I were perched in front of the bakery, sitting with our backs against one of the old-fashioned streetlamps that still graced a single block of Main. The road was paved with bricks for this one short stretch, and though they were sunken and cracked, they possessed a certain provincial charm that I was aware of even at the age of eleven.

Char was waitressing, and Natalie was working as a summer intern at the library in town, so Kat and I were left to our own devices for celebrating the humid holiday. We had been fishing in the river for most of the morning, but when the mosquitoes got too bad we went back to Char's trailer, sprawled in front of the window air conditioner, and sucked on grape freeze-pops until our lips turned purple.

The parade started at four, but we walked downtown at three so that we could get prime seats—streetlamp seats, where we could lean against the wide wrought-iron base and stick our feet into the road. It was no secret that the Blackhawk Fourth of July parade sucked. But it was also no secret that everyone threw ludicrous amounts of penny candy to make up for it. Kat and I had stuffed plastic grocery bags into our jean-shorts pockets to carry the booty home. I loved the mini Tootsie Rolls. Kat came for the butterscotch candies, even though they were usually cracked from their journey across the bricks before they skidded to a stop at the curb.

For the entire hour before the parade started, I stole glances at my sister out of the corner of my eye, trying to preserve the afternoon in amber so that I could revisit it for years to come. I counted Kat's presence beside me as a stroke of pure luck, a gift that I would not take for granted, because my fourteen-year-old sister had lately become too mature to hang out with the baby of the family. She spent hours on the phone with boys from her class, and preferred painting and repainting her toenails to helping me work on the tree house that the Vis girls had cobbled out of scrap lumber the year Natalie turned twelve. I was well aware that the only reason Kat had deigned to spend the Fourth with me was that Char forced her to. I half suspected there was money involved.

But that didn't bother me. It wouldn't have been the first time Char bribed one of her girls. Besides, Kat was beside me whether she wanted to be or not.

The parade started the way it always did, with the local Corn Queen sitting beside the mayor in the cab of a brand-new John Deere combine. I always thought it was silly the way the prom-dress-clad princess roosted on the jump seat like an exotic bird, waving her hand in a motion so practiced I could actually mouth "elbow, elbow, wrist, wrist" in time as she twisted her arm. She looked downright comical next to the mayor, a man with a shock of snow-white hair who was plump as a Weeble and just as cheerful. The farm machinery was his idea, and he made the most of his imagined small-town appeal by wearing overalls and a Dekalb baseball cap. It was ridiculous, and I knew it. But that didn't stop my heart from skipping a beat as I heard the brass of the high school marching band blare the first few notes of the fight song.

When Kat spun on me with that look on her face, I was sure she was going to yell at me for dragging her to the parade. I opened my mouth to remind her of the candy, of the fact that she didn't really have a choice, but the intent in her eyes stopped me short. She wasn't angry, she was excited.

Leaning over, Kat pressed her lips against my ear and said, "He's here."

Even with her mouth tickling my skin, I couldn't quite make out her words. Or maybe I just didn't understand them.

"He's here!" she said again, louder. "I think it might be . . . *him*."

There was a weight in her voice that sent a tremor down my spine. Him. There was only one him in our life, even if he wasn't really in it. "Where?"

She pointed across the street in the direction of the fabric store, where a wide, checked awning in the red-and-white of a faded picnic blanket trembled under a light breeze. It was a favorite spot for viewing the parade because it afforded an ample swatch of shade on even the hottest afternoon. As could be expected, a crowd was gathered beneath, and I scanned the riot of faces furiously.

"Next to the woman with the white sunglasses," Kat coached me. "By the guy with the sleeping baby."

And just like that I found him.

He was shorter than I had imagined, and balder. His hairline had retreated from his forehead in a lopsided formation, but though his coif left much to be desired, there was something in his eyes I loved. He had an open face, happy. And as I watched him, he grinned at the duo of clowns on a tandem bicycle in the street before him and raised his hands above his head to catch the candy that they threw.

I was surprised when he caught it, when his face sparked with the brief joy of triumph, and I found myself smiling back at him, warm with a wondering that seeped through my bones like a drug. *Is it you?*

"Let's go!" I shouted to Kat. I was already standing up, jerking her by the arm with a latent enthusiasm that had been revived at the delight of our shared intrigue.

But there was a semi in between us and the man with the million-dollar smile. It had a brand-new cattle carrier hitched to the back, and there was a small army of children inside pelting the crowd with water guns. I laughed, turning my face toward the spray, and exalted in the perfect and fragile blend of my life in that moment: the scent of cold water on hot bricks, Kat at my side, and him across from me, his mouth pulled into a grin that I recognized from the mirror.

I didn't realize that Kat was still planted on the curb until the semi had passed and a pickup truck with a sandwich board in the bed bearing an ad for a local bar had taken its place.

"Come on," I urged, yanking on her arm with a giggle.

Kat sliced me with a look. "It's not him," she said, and though I could barely hear her words over the din, I could read her lips.

I sat down hard beside her. "But—"

"But nothing." She shook her head. "I shouldn't have . . . It's ridiculous to think that we could find him."

"He's—"

"Just some guy," she finished.

I wanted to argue with her, to yank her to her feet and run across the crowded street to meet him face-to-face.

And say what? I think you're my dad?

Of course he wasn't. Kat was right; he was just some guy. The magic of the moment popped like a soap bubble—all that was left was the thin film of a hope that I was too old to nurse. All at once I knew that it was pathetic, really, downright sad how I reacted like a child at the sight of a man who on second glance could not have been more different from Kat and me if his skin was the color of the lamppost I leaned against.

I tried to shrug it off, the intimacy of our shared and brief conviction, and watched the remainder of the parade with the same cool detachment as my soon-to-be gorgeous sister. She rested the fine line of her chin on the back of a long-fingered hand, and I envied her wisdom, her age. Her ability to so easily let go of something that proved to still hold me in a powerful grip.

Kat never mentioned him again.

But the night of the parade was the first night that she ever cracked the door to my room and crawled into bed beside me.

6

Tightly Held

The Holiday Inn Express of Seward was a squat, three-story building that overlooked the small-boat harbor in Resurrection Bay. Every room boasted a view, whether it was of the mountains that safeguarded the bay city or a picturesque vista of a mismatched collection of sailboats against a backdrop of snowy glacier fields. Beautiful as it was, to Dani the poignancy of it all was sensory overload. There was unfamiliar birdsong in the trees, notes that flew high and true and rang clean against the crisp-cool edge of spring air. And unfurled masts that stood taut in expectation, waiting for the inevitable chance to test the wind over the water. The trees were sharp-edged and perfect, the breeze scented with pine and salt and earth that was slowly being warmed by a brilliant sun. Everything was bright and angled and new. Dani felt as if she had to shield herself from the promise of it.

"I love it here," Hazel said with a mouthful of scrambled eggs. The hotel had an extensive breakfast, and the room where they gathered plates heaped with Danish pastries and hot reindeer sausage was resplendent with light from the floor-to-ceiling vaulted window.

Dani didn't know if she was talking about Alaska or the hotel.

"You could stay here all day and watch the boats sailing in the harbor."

As if Danica had the time or inclination to waste her day watching the water bob with miniature vessels like corks in a bathtub. All the same, her gaze drifted out the window and followed a blue jeans–clad sailor as he ran a loving hand over the hull of a red-and-white sailboat. A name had been painted on the side in billowy, black script, and Dani squinted to make it out. *Pride & Joy.*

"What are you going to do today?" Hazel lifted a link of grainy sausage to her lips. "Have you tried this yet? It's pretty amazing."

"No." Dani stifled a shudder at the red-orange meat. She forked a corner of her cheese Danish but left the bite un-eaten on her plate. "I'll be busy," she said. "Blair gave me that file, you know."

Hazel slanted a purse-lipped look Dani's way. "I don't know if you should be wallowing in that."

"Wallowing? I am not wallowing."

"Well, you're not going to learn anything from those newspaper articles. It's not like they'll offer some sort of hint about Ell's whereabouts."

"I want to read them," Dani said in a tone that slammed the door on further discussion. "And then I'm going to call Russ. He said that he'd fly up to Seward as soon as we were here and settled."

"Good." Hazel nodded once at Dani's admission. She seemed pleased that the younger woman was finally going to initiate contact with Etsell's friend and employer. Russ had been trying to get hold of her since Ell went missing, but Dani resolutely screened his calls. She just didn't know if she blamed Russ Manfred or if she feared hearing what he had to say.

"Would you like me to be here when he comes?" Hazel asked.

Dani blinked in surprise as Hazel worried her bottom lip. "Thanks for the offer," Dani said, "but I'll be fine. I don't want you and Blair to cut anything short."

Hazel popped the last of her sausage into her mouth and gave Dani a thin smile. "Keep your cell phone on you. We'll call if anything comes up." Then she pushed back from the table and gathered up the remnants of her breakfast. Without another word, she crammed everything into the garbage can at the entrance to the breakfast room and disappeared down the hallway.

Dani was thankful to be left alone. She held up her Styrofoam coffee cup in both hands and breathed in the bitter steam. It was terrible coffee, metallic-tasting and oily, but at least it was strong. She couldn't see past the greasy film of the dark surface, and that suited her just fine.

Hazel was hardly the ideal companion, but Dani was grateful that she had accompanied her all the same. There was something calming in the candor of her no-nonsense presence, and though her abrupt departures and awkward silences were sometimes unnerving, Dani was accustomed to the older woman's eccentricities. While Hazel's every quirk and personality flaw was obnoxious in Blackhawk, here Dani found them strangely comforting. Ell loved Hazel. He thought her gruff demeanor was charming, and though it was hard for Dani to agree, Alaska seemed to require a strong measure of Hazel's implacability.

"Use it," Dani whispered, stirring the soft cloud of steam that hovered above her coffee cup. "Use that iron will and find Ell." But even before the words faded, she questioned their worth. She felt like a die-hard fan cheering for a win even as the clock wound down to the final minute.

When her coffee had been drained and her plate was a graveyard for picked-apart pieces of uneaten pastry, Dani finally heaved a sigh and tore her gaze from the view before her. Her legs felt leaden, stiff and heavy with the hopelessness that seeped into her bones like a sickness. She placed her hand over the unopened file, pinning it against the table as if she could press it into submission and make it tell her the story she wanted to hear. But she knew what awaited her in the manila folder. Press clippings and quick summaries, journalistic entries that would catalog the facts and fail to record all the emotion that clung mistlike to the contours of Etsell Greene's disappearance.

She didn't have the strength for it this morning. Instead of cracking open the file, Dani tucked it under her arm and left the breakfast room through a glass door that opened onto a boardwalk of sorts. The wharf was directly below her, and to her right the walkway stretched past a collection of shops and eateries straight into the historic heart of Seward. It was bustling with people, even at such an early hour. What had Ell always told her? Spring was tourist season in Alaska.

Dani didn't feel anything like a tourist.

And yet, as her tennis shoes smoothed an already well-worn path, she found herself wandering with all the aimless abandon of a relaxed vacationer. Dani stopped to survey a bulletin board stapled with flyers for heli-tours and snow-shoeing expeditions, but the words blurred together. She paused in the doorway of a narrow restaurant where the warm aroma of fresh-baked bread draped the air with sweetness, but she barely registered the mouthwatering fragrance. It wasn't until she had nearly tripped down the gangplank to the long rows of boat docks that Dani came to herself.

Here, with her feet mere inches from the ice-blue water of the bay, Dani realized with shallow-breathed desperation that she was looking for something. Her chest felt hollow, and against the echoing walls her heart beat a jarring rhythm. *Where?* she thought, her eyes darting from boat to boat as if she were bound to catch a glimpse of Etsell hiding inside one of the low cabins. In her mind Sam was beside him. She flushed to life as a woman swept past Dani on the pier and disappeared onto the dock of a wooden boat. It didn't take much imagination for Sam to fill out in the contours that Dani had just seen: willowy and bright-eyed, crowned with an abundance of hair like chocolate silk.

Jealousy brought Dani to walk slowly past the unknown woman's boat, to steal peeks out of the corner of her eye for a sign, any sign, that Etsell was anywhere but broken across the ridgeback of some unnamed mountain. She didn't know if the thought was comforting or horrifying. But in the end there was nothing to see. The woman was alone, and older than Dani had first presumed. She smiled and waved when she caught Danica studying her from beneath a fringe of long bangs.

"Beautiful day, isn't it?" the woman called.

What could Dani do but nod?

Though her steps were steady, it felt to Dani as if she stumbled to the end of the dock. There was a long beam laid across the final plank, a short seat that welcomed the weight of her sudden fall. Dani felt the weathered lumber beneath her, the splintered concern of world-weary wood against her hands, and repressed an almost irresistible desire to scream. It wasn't fair that Hazel and Blair were thousands of feet above her, doing the one thing she should have mustered the strength to endure. And it wasn't fair that Etsell had defied her every wish and taken off for Alaska like some child on an adventure. He had risked everything the day he decided to leave her and live out his dream.

He had ruined her life.

Fury and despair spun a slow dance in the place where Dani's heart should have been. But they were empty emotions, wrung dry of any meaning from the moment Civil Air Patrol had first informed her that Etsell was missing.

He's gone, she thought almost dispassionately, as the words tumbled through her mind. *He's gone.*

When she glanced over the side of the dock, she could see the sky reflected in the panel of gunmetal water. There was a feathered fringe of clouds speared through with the tall spires of sailboat masts that seemed to prick the heavens. And framed in the middle of it all, she could see her own pale face, the incredulous, wide-eyed stare of a woman stunned, her mouth open as if to utter "Oh." As if her life had taken her completely by surprise.

Russ seemed relieved to hear Dani's voice when she finally called him midmorning. He assured her that the flight from the Midnight Sun would take less than an hour—plenty of time for him to gather up the things he would need for the trip and take her out for lunch in Seward. They agreed to meet at a restaurant off the water, a little roadhouse called Alaska Nellie's.

Dani went back to her hotel room and dropped the unread file of newspaper clippings and other paraphernalia on her bed. Then she ran a brush through her wind-tossed hair and pulled it into a loose ponytail at the nape of her neck. She was about to walk out the door, but something niggled at the back of her mind, a strange impulse to smooth her lips with some plum-pink gloss and brush a little color into her cheeks.

As she tucked a stray curl behind her ear, it struck her that she was afraid to meet Russ. Sure, he was the man who had more or less convinced Etsell to abandon his life and fly to Alaska. But he was also the one person who could help her understand her husband's relationship—or lack thereof—with Samantha Linden. She wondered if Russ would compare her with the intrepid Sam and find her small-town, Midwestern ways lacking.

Alaska Nellie's was an unobtrusive restaurant a block and a half down from the Alaska Sea Life Center. Dani paused with her hand on the door handle and watched the families congregating in front of the blue-gray campus of the indoor aquarium and research facility. She had flipped through the Sea Life Center brochure in her hotel welcome binder, and in spite of the circumstances of her trip to Seward, she briefly wished that she could enjoy the harbor seal display.

When she was seven, Dani had rescued a stuffed seal pup from the secondhand store in Blackhawk. She never named him, but her seal's pebbled fur had been loved smooth in a decade of nighttime cuddling. Before she happened across the sleek pup, Dani hadn't known that she fostered an enduring affection for animals who could live on land and sea, effortlessly part of two wholly different worlds. She would have loved to see a seal in real life; to touch the glass where water and air were divided in half in perfect cross section.

But Dani wasn't in Seward for frivolous indulgences, and she leaned into the door of Alaska Nellie's, setting off a trill of silver bells.

"Good morning!" someone called from the back. "Go ahead and seat yourself."

Dani was early, and not just for her lunch rendezvous with Russ. The restaurant was conspicuously empty. Knotty blond floorboards looked polished and meticulously clean, almost as if no one had yet stepped foot in Nellie's, even though a trifold on the nearest table claimed that they had the best breakfast in Seward. Dani stood inert for a moment, lost between the fading echo of her own footsteps. She glanced at her watch. Quarter to twelve. Maybe it would be best to walk around for a few more minutes.

Before she could make a quick retreat, the bells above the door sang a second time. Dani spun around, surprised by the sound in the still restaurant, and came face-to-face with a man who looked like nothing so much as a pool cue. He was tall and narrow, clad in varying shades of brown, and the top of his bald head was covered with a canvas newsboy cap the color of St. Patrick's Day.

He looked startled for a moment, then a knowing smile bloomed across his face. It bore a certain sad edge; a shadow swept across his brow as if his eyes knew something that his mouth did not. He reached out his hand. "Danica Greene," he said with conviction. "I'm Russ Manfred."

Dani wasn't quite sure what to make of the man before her, but she held out her hand and let him shake it. "You're early," she told him, backing away when he leaned in a bit. Russ seemed to be on the verge of pulling her into an embrace.

"So are you." Russ shrugged. "I was hoping to be here a bit early. To—"

"Gather yourself," Dani finished. "Yeah, me too."

They stared at each other for a few uncomfortable seconds, sizing each other up with the sort of candor that can last only a heartbeat or two. Dani was trying to convince herself that Russ and his cancer-stricken wife were worth the loss of her husband. She wondered what he thought of her.

"Do you have a table?" Russ asked.

"We might have to wait," Dani joked dryly, and was surprised when Russ laughed.

"How about something out of the way?"

Dani followed him to a table in the back section, kitty-corner from the door. There was a half wall along one side of the table and they could clearly see the kitchen on the other side. Like the rest of the diner, it was immaculately clean but seemed empty. Dani craned her neck, looking for the woman who had invited her to seat herself.

"They have good fish and chips here," Russ offered. "If you like that sort of thing. It's kind of an Alaskan specialty."

Dani nodded.

"And reindeer sausage. Have you tried that yet?"

"It's on the breakfast buffet at our hotel."

"Another Alaskan treat," Russ said lamely.

When the waitress finally emerged, breathless and grinning, to bring them glasses of water and menus, Dani wished that she could feign illness and leave Russ to his own devices. Why had she agreed to meet him? The air between them was full of things they couldn't say. Of accusations and apologies that might never be voiced. How could you say such things to someone you'd just met? Besides, it was obvious that Russ felt guilty for strong-arming Etsell into taking over his flights for a couple of weeks. *As well he should,* Dani thought. For all she knew, a handful of routine escorts had turned into something that ensured her life would never be the same.

They were silent while they studied the single-page menu, and when the waitress returned a few minutes later, they both ordered the fish and chips. "Our tartar sauce is homemade," she assured them with a wink. "You're gonna love it."

More patrons were finding their way into Nellie's, and when there was a soft buzz of conversation around them Russ removed his hat and ran his hands through nonexistent hair. The skin-smooth feel of his own pate seemed to shock him because his eyes went wide.

"I shaved it when Kim lost her hair. One round of chemotherapy and poof, it was gone. Sometimes I just forget mine is gone too."

Dani wondered if she should tell him that it was a nice gesture, that he certainly seemed to be a loving husband. But the words stuck in her throat.

"Look," Russ said, picking up the conversational slack, "this is a lot harder than I thought it was going to be. Etsell was a good friend, Danica. I've always looked forward to meeting his wife. I just never imagined it would be under these circumstances."

"Me either." Dani studied the man across from her and realized that his distress seemed entirely genuine. It was bizarre to her how Ell could have formed a bond with someone whom he only connected with online and at yearly National Business Aviation Association conferences, and yet Russ's agony was so real it was palpable. Apparently the odd NBAA event and sporadic emails had been enough to cement her husband's relationship with a man who was more or less a complete stranger to her.

"If I could take it back, I would. If I could erase that telephone conversation and somehow make it that Etsell never felt obligated to help me out, I'd do it in a heartbeat. You have no idea how much I blame myself."

Dani didn't have to guess. It was written all over his face. She sighed. "It's not your fault," she said, even though she felt that in some small way it was. But it was her fault too. Maybe if she and Ell had been in a better place he wouldn't have been so eager to go.

"It's just one of those things." Russ appeared to cling to her absolution. "Even the best pilots get confused up here. The weather is so unpredictable . . . who knows what could have happened?"

"So you believe that . . ." Dani hedged, with her breath lodged firmly in her throat, waiting for Russ to fill in the blank.

The man across the table stared at her like he was the target at a firing range. "I don't know, Danica," he whispered. "I wish I did."

"But you think his plane went down."

"Well," Russ fumbled, "that makes the most sense. I mean—"

"What about Samantha Linden? Do you think she disappeared with him?"

Russ was quiet for a second as he contemplated Dani's words. Then understanding hit him with a slap of unsavory implications, and he put up his hands as if to ward off Dani's suspicions. "If Sam is with Etsell it's accidental. I mean, they're together for purely coincidental reasons. You can't think that, Danica."

"Think what?"

At that moment the waitress appeared with their meals, and Russ turned his attention to her with undisguised relief. He busied himself with the ketchup bottle and then painstakingly unrolled the napkin tucked around his cutlery. But Dani wasn't about to let him off so easily.

"What can you tell me about Samantha?"

Russ popped a couple of crinkle fries in his mouth and regarded Dani with a wary gaze.

"I'm not going anywhere until you tell me about her."

He sighed. "I know what you think, and it's not true. Sam's a wild card. I'm sure she's off having the time of her life somewhere and she just forgot to call the lodge and let us know. She's done it before."

Dani just stared at him.

"They're not together."

"Fine. I just want to know about her. Did she fly with Et-sell often? Did they spend a lot of time together?"

Russ seemed resigned that Dani wasn't going to let up in her line of questioning. "Yes," he said, only thinly disguising his reticence. "But it's not like they had a choice. My wife didn't like it much when Sam joined the Midnight Sun team and I had to fly her all over creation either. But Kim got used to it."

As soon as the words were out of his mouth, Russ real-ized his mistake. He tried to backpedal, but it was too late. Dani knew Etsell's type and she pictured Sam as leggy and well endowed. Maybe with sultry brown eyes. Whatever she looked like, Dani was sure that Sam had the sort of earthy self-confidence that she herself was lacking.

"I really should be going," Dani muttered, ignoring her untouched plate of beer-battered cod. She grabbed Blair's file and tried to slip out of the booth without meeting Russ's distressed gaze. He reached for her arm but stopped himself.

"Don't go. Please. You don't understand about Sam. Be-sides, Etsell had only been here for three weeks. Do you re-ally think he would leave you for a woman he's known for less than a month? It's irrational."

And maybe it was. But Dani didn't tell Russ that Ell had sworn his love for her on their second date.

Her husband was the sort of man who flew high and fell hard.

Danica

I didn't know that Etsell was thinking of proposing to me until Natalie came home from work one afternoon and told me that she had spotted my boyfriend in the jewelry store. Natalie was on summer break, working overtime at the library to put a small dent in the loan she had acquired to pay for room and board at Vassar, and complaining vociferously about the lack of amenities in our little town of three thousand. My sister considered herself practically a New Yorker, though I knew that she could hardly rub two pennies together, and would never be able to afford the trips to Manhattan that she regularly alluded to. She was stuck in Poughkeepsie, and more than likely married to her books, but whenever she came home she loved nothing more than to lord her superiority over us. I was stunned that she even knew I had a boyfriend.

"Ell?" I cocked the spatula I was holding in disbelief. "You saw my Etsell in the jewelry store? Do you even know what he looks like?"

Natalie raised her hand a couple of inches above her forehead. "Blond, 'bout this tall, sort of looks like Apollo in a T-shirt and ripped jeans?"

"That's the one." I turned back to my attempt at risotto and was disappointed to find it sticking to the bottom of the pot. "You just made me ruin supper."

"Order a pizza." Natalie knocked on the counter to get my attention. "Didn't you hear me? I just told you that your paramour is about to pop the question."

"Doubtful. I'm eighteen. I graduated from high school two weeks ago."

"Exactly. *Exactly.*" Natalie huffed, as if that explained everything. "So what was he doing at Elizabeth's poring over the engagement ring display?"

I dug out a bite of the risotto with the end of my wooden spoon and tasted it. "Plaster," I groaned. "It tastes like plaster." Scooping the contents of my failed dish into the garbage can, I tried to focus on why Natalie was so upset. "I guess I don't see what the big deal is," I finally admitted.

"Are you daft? It's a huge deal! Enormous." Natalie crossed the kitchen and grabbed the pot from my hands. She deposited it with a clang in the sink, then took my chin in her hand like she used to do when I was little. The gesture seemed to surprise her. Letting go of my face with a sigh, she stuck her fists on her hips. "Dani, we gotta talk."

"Isn't that what we're doing?"

Natalie rolled her eyes. "You're not taking this seriously."

"Not really. So you saw Ell in the jewelry store. So what?"

"So it's going to be hard for you to leave this place if he proposes."

"Leave?"

"Hello? Iowa State? This fall?"

"Yeah, about that . . ." I backed away from Natalie and yanked open the refrigerator door. "Risotto was a bust. How do you feel about wraps? We have leftover chicken—"

"Do not change the subject on me, Danica Reese. You got

a great scholarship. You are not throwing that away for some farm boy in a pair of too-tight Wranglers."

"He's not a farm boy. He wouldn't know the first thing about tractors or crops or—"

"That's not the point, Dani. He's just some guy. You're leaving this place, remember?"

"This place isn't so bad."

Natalie released a frustrated breath. "You're being ridiculous. We're different, you and me. We aren't like Char and Kat."

"What's that supposed to mean?"

"You know exactly what that means."

My arms were filled with cheese, lettuce, pesto tortilla shells, a pair of fresh tomatoes, and a bulging Tupperware container stuffed with day-old drumsticks. I deposited everything on the counter and took my own indignant stance. Folding my arms tight against my chest, I looked my sister full in the face for the first time since she stomped into the kitchen.

"It's my life, Natalie. *My life.*"

Her eyes went big and round, and she stepped toward me as if she was about to take me by the shoulders and shake. "You're kidding me. You are absolutely kidding me. You're going to stay, aren't you?"

"College is *your* dream," I said, trying not to be cowed by her shock.

"I thought it was yours too."

My shoulders inched toward my ears in an act of self-protection. "I thought so. Once. But I don't know anymore. Maybe I just want to stay in Blackhawk. Mom and Kat need me. . . ."

"I think they're capable of making their own wraps," Natalie growled between clenched teeth.

"It's more than that."

"You're going to marry that guy."

"Etsell Greene."

"What kind of a name is Etsell, anyway?"

"It's his mother's maiden name," I all but whispered.

Natalie leveled me with a look that was so filled with disappointment, I could almost feel myself shrink beneath her gaze. "That's the stupidest thing I've ever heard," she muttered. Then she spun on her heel and slammed out the door of our double-wide, leaving the screen to slap feebly against the crooked frame.

Etsell proposed a week later and we set the date for Christmas, just a few weeks after my nineteenth birthday.

⁓

I was a little girl when I married Etsell, a baby, really. What did I know at nineteen? I may have believed that I had it all figured out, but lying on top of my bed at the Holiday Inn Express of Seward I knew beyond a shadow of a doubt that I had been so naive it was almost tragic.

"You need a man in your life," Ell had told me at the beginning of one of our very first dates. Char had invited him into our little trailer when he came to pick me up for a football game, and he took one sweeping glance at our run-down home and came to a decision. I could feel it in the way he pulled himself up beside me, straightening his back, lifting his chin as if he had discerned a problem and just happened to have the solution tucked in his back pocket. As the words crossed his lips, I knew he considered himself the man for the job. "A little testosterone would go a long way in this place."

"I think we're doing just fine," I told him.

"Whatever. You need a guy. Someone to fix the screen in the kitchen window with more than just duct tape."

"You mean a dad? We're a little lacking in the father department, in case you hadn't noticed."

"I'll be your daddy." Etsell laughed, leaning over to nibble the high arch of my ear, which I had just pierced with a single diamond stud.

I yanked away from him. "That's disgusting."

"The kiss?"

"The implication. I'm doing just fine, thank you very much. We're doing just fine."

"Who takes care of the money?" Etsell demanded.

"I do."

"What would happen if Char's car broke down?"

"We'd take it to the shop."

"Do you lock your doors at night? Wait, ignore that question. Anyone could kick down one of your walls if they wanted to get in. I'll huff and I'll puff and I'll—"

"You're a chauvinist," I said, incredulous. "You act like this really fantastic, understanding guy, but underneath it all you're a pig."

"Oink." Etsell grinned.

"You think the Vis girls are doomed without a man in our lives."

"Oink-oink."

I wanted to be offended, but he was making me laugh. He slipped his hands around my waist and I pushed him away halfheartedly, muttering under my breath, "You and your porcine sensibilities can take a hike, Etsell Greene. I don't need you."

But I did.

For all my bravado, I stayed with Ell. He reached out his

hand and I took it, tentatively at first, without really even grasping what I was doing. But he was seductive that way, capable of pulling me in so slowly that I didn't even realize I had entered his orbit until there was simply no way out. My life circled his with the inevitable magnitude of personal gravity. The only thing that made my utter dependence on Etsell tolerable was the fact that he appeared to be equally as addicted to me.

"You're all I know," he told me once, and I knew exactly what he meant.

It didn't occur to me until nearly ten years and four thousand miles later that maybe I wasn't all he wanted to know. Curling onto my side, I blinked dry eyes and looked out the window at the postcard-perfect view. Etsell had come here, without me. He had picked at a loose corner of our life and unraveled a strand for himself, a thread that he wove into something that I didn't understand and wasn't a part of. As I lay with my head in the pillow of my bent arm, I considered the possibility that my husband was a stranger.

How well did we know each other, really? I could predict that Char would continue wearing suicidal shoes and sleep with losers she met at the bar even if they looked for all the world like they had every communicable disease known to man. And Natalie would never come home again, never condescend to bless us with her significant presence, her self-perceived otherworldly wisdom. Kat would keep on being Kat, smart in ways that Natalie would never accept, but downright brain-dead when it came to making wise and lasting choices for her life. I thought I knew them, but I had never stopped to wonder why Char was the way she was. Why Natalie ran across the country and Kat ran into seedy corners. I thought I knew my husband, but here he was, a runaway too. And I had no idea why he had run.

Never mind the mysterious Samantha Linden. Even without the threat of her presence looming at the fringes of my darkest fears, I had to admit that Etsell was lost long before he ever took off from the landing strip in Seward.

He wasn't the only one.

7

Prodigal

A week in Seward disappeared like a hot stone falling through cold water. The passage was quick and almost violent, sending up ripples that bubbled and fizzed in frantic ascent, only to dissipate like so much steam. Dani clutched at experiences and people and leads that turned out to be nothing more than a red backpack abandoned on the slope of a solitary mountain, a rock that reflected water like light, a whisper of activity swirling into nothing more than the echo of forgotten ghosts. The searchers had left nothing to chance. Every avalanche, hole in the ice, sun glint, and unexplained shadow had been explored.

But there was nothing. They were chasing an impossibility.

Even Blair and Hazel looked defeated by the end of the fourth day. They had logged more hours in Blair's plane than Dani ever thought possible, and although there was a desperate, hopeless slant in their eyes, she encouraged them through two more days of searching. When Hazel mentioned something about the cost of fuel, the thought skittered through Danica's mind that Etsell had a sizable life insurance policy. She could afford a few more days of gas. But as the words *life insurance* impressed themselves on the place in her heart where Etsell's disappearance was still a fresh wound, she felt branded by something poker-hot.

"I can't afford more fuel," she said as if saying it would somehow make it real. As if she could pretend her way back to a normal life—one where her husband's life insurance policy wasn't likely to be cashed anytime soon.

Hazel nodded once, her chin falling to her chest and staying there until she heaved a sigh that seemed to come from the very marrow of her bones. "Okay," she said. "Okay."

And that was that. The Civil Air Patrol had searched. The Rescue Coordination Center had recorded nearly six hundred hours of flying time, covering an area larger than the state of Iowa. The search for Etsell, and presumably Sam, had left little to chance. And it was officially and unofficially over.

Blair dropped Hazel off at the hotel by late afternoon on their final day of searching. There was something almost ceremonial in the acknowledgment that his plane would not go up for Etsell again, and Hazel had called ahead to tell Dani it was over. Dani threw on her coat and waited for her husband's surrogate mother in the lobby, but when the older woman slouched out of Blair's car and made her way hunch-shouldered through the glass doors, she barely gave Dani a second glance.

"I'm going to my room," she announced.

"Supper?" Dani blurted out. She didn't want Hazel to leave, even though she wasn't remotely hungry.

"Maybe. I'll call you later."

Dani felt as if there was more to say. Like she should press Hazel for details, information from their final day of flight that might spark some latent glimmer of hope. Surely there were clues that Blair and Hazel had misread. A reason to try one more day. But even as she longed to find something worth clinging to, Dani knew deep down that she was too tired to try. So was Hazel. So was Blair. The fine art of continuing to clutch at hope had proved to be an exhausting endeavor. Dani let Hazel disappear into the stairwell without another word.

There was a defeated pallor in the air, a gray mist that had followed Hazel and now hung sad and discarded about the room. It was raining outside, but Dani couldn't handle the damp inside so she turned up the hood of her coat and made her way to the back door. There were clouds over the bay, dark and thin like bits of pulled cotton that had been put to some secret, dirty use. Dani eyed them warily, but the rain was needle-fine and assaulted her cheeks with such tenacity she eventually lowered her head and watched the slow progress of her feet along the slick boardwalk.

Seward seemed abandoned in the dim shadows of the waning afternoon. It was as if everyone had made a collective decision to shutter themselves in where it was warm and light and dry. Even the shops and tour companies that Dani passed seemed unusually empty. The odd clerk sat lonely behind a high counter, nursing a half-empty bottle of organic juice and staring into the unnatural twilight that Dani inhabited.

When she ran out of boardwalk, Dani turned away from the water and paced backstreets until she was so cold that her fingers were numb. As the rain drove at her with a new intensity, she looked up and wondered exactly where she was. Too far from the hotel to seek refuge in her room, she decided.

The golden-flecked light from a dozen stores and restaurants beckoned her to take shelter, but Dani wasn't interested until she spotted a long, empty bar in a seedy-looking pub. Warm air breathed over her as she stepped inside, a sigh against her skin that left her fingertips tingling. She pushed back her hood and tried to shake the dampness from her jacket, but it was insistently wet and determined to stick to her sweater. Instead, she unzipped it and peeled off her cold outer layer, hooking it unceremoniously over a wrought-iron coatrack that stood near the door.

There was a couple in one corner of the pub; each was holding a tall glass of beer the color of liquid amber and they were talking in hushed tones. The only other person in the place was the bartender, a middle-aged Native man with a heavy brow. He didn't look up as Dani entered, and he didn't pay her any attention as she took a stool at the bar. She had been hoping for a quiet understanding, for a drink to magically appear in front of her from a sage, tight-lipped barkeep who could appreciate how much she needed it. But the man before her was going to offer no such small comfort.

"Something warm," Dani said, tapping the counter with her palms as if she were patting it into place. "It's freezing out there."

The barman didn't look up, but he went for a pot of coffee that had just finished brewing.

"Something stronger."

He didn't pause in his pour, but he left a good inch of space in the glass mug and unscrewed the cap on a bottle of Jameson Irish whiskey. "Cream?"

"No."

The steam coming off the drink was so fragrant, Dani had to repress a desire to lick it. It was bitter and sweet, sharp and smooth like a momentary oblivion, a place where she could forget. She took a long swallow, relishing the way it burned her tongue and left a scorching path all the way through her chest.

The Irish coffee was gone before Dani realized she had

drank it down to the very last drop. It hummed in the tips of her fingers and radiated warmth all the way down to her feet. Everything felt soft and slightly blurred, and she raised her head to ask for another, but before she could voice her request, the bartender placed a fresh drink in front of her. "You look cold," he said as if to offer an explanation.

"I am," Dani admitted. "Cold and miserable. I'd like to swear a blue streak."

For the first time since she entered the pub, the bartender looked her in the eye. A faint smile lifted the corner of his mouth, and Dani saw the silver line of a scar kiss his lip like a bolt of lightning. "You can do that here," he said. "Use every word in the book. I won't tell a soul."

"Thanks. But it's not my style."

"I didn't think so."

"I could throw something."

He glanced at the neat rows of glasses hanging behind him. "Might not be such a good idea."

"It would make a terrific mess. Don't tell me you haven't thought about it yourself."

"All the time. But I'd like to keep my job." He measured coffee grinds into the filter of a second coffeepot and filled the carafe with cold water from a blue-handled hose. "You're not from around here." It was a statement, not a question, and open-ended enough that Dani could ignore it if she wanted to.

She didn't. "I'm from Iowa."

"Long ways from home."

"Not by choice."

He gave her a hard, unreadable look. It sent something cool and slippery straight through her.

"My husband is missing," Dani said. She wasn't sure why she wanted to tell him this, but all at once the truth was rising inside of her, a high tide swallowing everything in its wake. "He took off from Seward Airport and . . ."

"Disappeared," the bartender finished. "Funny name, right? Elson? Elton?"

"Etsell."

"Sorry about that."

Dani didn't know if he was sorry about Etsell's disappearance or his name. "I've never . . ." She fumbled. "I don't know what to do with it. I should feel something, you know? Something deep inside of me should just know that he's alive. That we need to keep looking."

"Or that you need to stop."

He said it dispassionately and Dani found herself searching his face for understanding, for answers. There were none to be found. "I don't feel anything," she admitted.

The bartender picked up a rag that was draped over a little prep sink and turned it over in his hands. There was nothing to wipe, no surface in the pub that hadn't been fastidiously cleaned, and he held it for a moment in his fist before folding it in a perfect square and laying it on the counter. Dani blinked and looked around, noticing that her first impression had been dead wrong. She hadn't stumbled into a seedy bar at all. It was snug and tidy, a study in crisp right angles and warm light that pooled on dark tables and made the liquor bottles shimmer as if they contained crushed gems. For just a moment Dani felt as if something had settled over her shoulders, a hand-knit blanket that fell on her softly and made her want to close her eyes.

"I really am sorry," the bartender finally said.

Me too, Dani thought. *For so many things.*

"Blame the Alaskan Triangle," he said. "The Kushtaka. God. Fate."

Dani's list of culprits wasn't nearly so lofty—Russ to a

certain extent, maybe Sam, definitely herself and Ell—but when he took out two small glasses and extracted a small, diamond-cut bottle from somewhere beneath the counter, gratefulness shot through her. "Thank you," she whispered. Not because he was pouring, but because he understood.

At the moment Dani's fingers brushed the smooth glass, her cell phone rang in her pocket. It was an unexpected sound in the close stillness of the pub, and she nearly startled right off her seat. Hazel's name and phone number blinked at her on the screen and she flipped the phone open with her thumb.

"Hi, Hazel."

"They found her."

Dani's heart stumbled. "What?" She gulped a breath and tried again. "Who? Who did they find?"

There was a low hiss on the other end of the line, then Hazel said, "Samantha Linden."

Sam defied every preconceived notion that Dani had carefully constructed around her—one furious tap of her hiking boot–clad foot and she crushed the imaginary facade to rubble.

Dani had pictured her tall and fierce, the sort of woman who was all stunning angles and sharp edges. Eyes like fire, Amazonian cheekbones, skin flushed from inside with something wild and maybe just a little dangerous. The kind of woman men either worshipped or secretly feared.

But the real Samantha Linden was a pixie. She stood an entire head shorter than Danica, and probably weighed less than a hundred pounds soaking wet. But that didn't mean she didn't cut an impressive silhouette. Sam exuded a sort of richness, a sumptuous quality that went beyond her trim curves and the exquisite obsidian gleam of her almond-shaped eyes. Her hair was a cropped frame around her face, and her lips were so full, Danica wondered if they were injected. But they were real; they had to be. Nothing about Sam suggested artifice. She didn't wear a stitch of makeup, her clothes were old and torn in places, and she obviously hadn't showered in a week. Maybe more.

Dani couldn't stop staring at her, even though the diminutive woman kept throwing her razor-sharp looks.

"This is ridiculous," Sam finally said, throwing up her hands. They were all clustered in a small conference room at the Holiday Inn—Blair, Hazel, Dani, Sam, and a pair of uniformed policemen—and after an hour of questioning, the formerly missing woman seemed beyond anxious to leave. "I've told you a hundred times. I visited a friend for a couple of days and then I went hiking. I would have been back in time except that I slipped down a ravine in the dark and twisted my frickin' ankle."

The officers had wanted to see her injured ankle, and even Dani was impressed that Sam had made it out of the bush with her leg swollen like a loaf of bread spilling over its pan. It wasn't broken, or at least, Sam told them it wasn't, but the explosion of purple and green and black behind the loose laces of her boot was enough to make Dani cringe.

"And when exactly was the last time you saw Etsell Greene?"

Sam rolled her eyes and light glinted off the dark irises like mica. Her hand leapt out and she yanked a notebook out of the officer's hand.

"Hey!" he shouted.

She narrowed her eyes at him. "It says right here that the last time I saw him was on Saturday, when he dropped me off. Would you like me to underline it?"

The officer snatched his notebook away from her.

"Sam, honey, you have to understand, we've been look-ing for Etsell—and you—for a very long time." Blair patted Sam's arm with a tender hand.

Dani thought it was strange that Blair would call that wildcat honey, but Sam seemed to gentle beneath his touch.

"Look," she said, attempting patience, "I'm sorry that Et-sell Greene is missing, but I don't know anything about it. He wasn't with me, I swear it. We parted ways at the airport over two weeks ago."

Miraculously, Danica believed her. And apparently, so did everyone else.

"You'd better call the Midnight Sun," one of the officers suggested. "They've been worried sick about you."

"More like they've been losing money over me. Who else can lead the hunting tours?"

"You're the best," Blair assured her with a wink.

The room exhaled, a collective murmur of relief at the prodigal daughter returned. But something buzzed at the back of Danica's mind, an insistent whir that grew in inten-sity until blood pounded in her ears and surged florid behind her eyes. Sam's appearance was a simple solution that cast Ell's disappearance in an entirely new light. Dani's role had flickered like a broken compass, swinging from hopeful wife to scorned spouse to lost lover in a matter of days. And now where was she? Standing in a hotel room that smelled faintly of smoke and the memory of cheap banquet food with a woman who was more concerned about taking a shower than the fact that she had been the object of so much specu-lation and fear that psychology books could have been writ-ten about her. Or rather, about the response she was able to elicit simply by going on an unannounced hike.

The prodigal daughter had returned relatively unscathed. But what about the prodigal son?

Dani fought down an urge to scream, to throw herself at the calm, collected men who were so willing and able to simply walk away from Etsell's disappearance without a backward glance. They had tried, she knew that, and yet, didn't they realize that Ell was her husband? Her best friend? Her life? No amount of searching could be enough. No amount of subtle remorse could return to her what had been lost.

Sam had been unofficially released and Blair was offering to drive her to the airport when something inside Dani snapped. "You can't go!" she all but shouted, lunging for Sam as if she was going to scoop her up and take her hostage. But Dani got hold of herself and stopped short of touching the strange woman. "Please," she begged. "I would like a minute alone with you."

The relief that had saturated the room at the eventual acceptance of Sam's return faded as quickly as it had come.

"I think that would be a good idea," Blair said, taking charge after a brief, shocked pause. He steered the two officers out of the room with a fatherly hand. Hazel gave Dani a long look, but she eventually left, too, closing the door behind her with a definitive click.

Only when they were gone did Dani turn to the woman she had vilified a dozen different ways. Sam was so real standing there, her hair mussed and stringy, thrust behind her ears where it was long enough to tuck, and sticking up everywhere else in half-curled bunches like damp weeds. Her shirt was stained, her boots caked in mud and ornamented with broken tufts of purple grasses that were as exotic to Dani as moon rocks. Sam seemed bright to Dani. Bright and tangible, almost shockingly real.

The inescapable truth of Sam's nearness—of her presence and Etsell's absence—was like the fine slice of a knife, a cut that separated him from her with one irrevocable slash. And yet Dani couldn't stop herself from pressing them together, from trying to make the pieces fit so that Ell could go on existing. Even if his existence was relegated to a nebulous somewhere. Somehow. With someone else.

Sam was studying her with a wary, guarded eye, and Dani considered that she didn't have much time. The waif of wild woman before her would run before too long.

There was silence for a few seconds, nothing more than the disharmonious shuffle of their uneven breathing. Then Dani gathered herself and said, "What do you know about my husband's disappearance?"

Sam's gaze turned steely. "How should I know where Ell is?"

The sound of his name on the strange woman's tongue sent something small and black-winged fluttering in Dani's chest. "I know you flew with him almost every time he went up."

"So?"

"So you had to have talked. You'd know if he had a favorite route, somewhere he liked to fly or a vista he enjoyed. . . ."

"I went over this with Blair and the police."

"You haven't gone over it with me."

Sam crossed her arms against her chest. She looked fierce standing there, fierce and foreign, and Dani had to reevaluate her first impression. Sam *was* an Amazon, a petite Joan of Arc, a spark like a fresh-struck match. And she seemed poised to fly—one breath and she'd blow out of Dani's life forever.

Dani changed her tactic. "Please." She took one tentative step forward, battling a desire to grab hold of Sam by the arms and not let go until she extinguished every last question that burned her tongue. "Please, it might not seem like much to you, but if there is anything—however small—that you remember, that might help . . ." She trailed off helplessly.

Sam bit her bottom lip, leaving a line of even marks that looked as if her skin had been carefully stitched. Then she exhaled heavily and said, "Nothing. I'm sorry, there's absolutely nothing I can tell you. Ell loved to fly up here and it wasn't at all uncommon for him to go for a joyride."

"You think it was a joyride?" Dani narrowed her eyes, scrutinizing the other woman for even the slightest hint that she had accompanied Etsell on any one of those rides, for clues that she was anything more than a coworker.

Sam shrugged. "Who knows? Listen, I know this probably sounds cold to you, but this is Alaska. Do you know how many people went missing in 2007 alone? Two thousand, eight hundred thirty-three. I know, because that's the year I started working at the Midnight Sun. We had just lost a group of hikers. They were found three days later, dehydrated and hysterical, but just as often, people aren't found."

"But Etsell is *my* people."

Something flickered through Sam's eyes, the silver flash of a fish in shallow water, but before Dani could discern the emotion it passed.

"I'm sorry," Sam said again.

Those futile words were quenching. All at once, Dani felt cavernous, hollow and empty, as if everything inside her had been scooped out and she had no more strength to stand. *I'm sorry.* What else was there to say? "Do you know what I thought?" she said almost to herself. "When I heard that you were missing, too, I thought that you were together."

"Together," Sam echoed quietly. The weight of the word was not lost on either of them, but she did not bother to deny the unspoken allegation.

"Who was he?" Dani asked suddenly. "I mean, here. Who was Etsell here? Did you know that there was . . . me?"

Sam tilted her head like a curious bird, but she seemed to take Dani's question seriously. She thought for a long moment, then a trace of a smile whispered across her lips and she said, "Of course I knew about you."

Something went out of the room, a tension, a taut line of strain that had been wrenching ever tighter between them. There was an inaudible snap in the air, a moment of clarity, and then Sam turned on her heel and left. No good-bye, no good luck.

It wasn't until Dani watched Sam walk away that she realized they had both spoken about Etsell in the past tense. The finality of it buckled her legs.

Hazel found her like that: in the middle of the conference room, cross-legged on the floor, staring blankly at the wall.

"You okay?" Hazel whispered, sinking to her knees beside Dani. "Did that little witch say something? Did she—"

"I want to go," Dani cut in. "Right now. I want to go home."

Danica

The world shifted while I was in Alaska. It was the soft thud of a bolt falling home, a fresh picture of something familiar that had gone grainy and haloed around the edges, almost ethereal. Nothing had changed, and yet everything was different. Ghosts inhabited my halls, memories of a life with Ell that were frozen in time until they could be buried forever or resurrected from the bay of ice and water where I was secretly sure my husband sank.

When I arrived home after midnight in the middle of a warm June night, I tiptoed through the rooms barefoot, hoping to catch a glimpse of the quiet phantoms that suffused the air with a scent like ether. Sweet and volatile. Ready to explode. But there was nothing to see, no words inscribed on humid windowpanes in whispers that would echo across whatever divide my husband had crossed. No moments of transcendence, no thin places where his spirit crossed mine in an act of divine comfort. Nothing.

It was a hollow feeling. Brittle, delicate, with edges as fine and deadly as blades. I cut myself on them as I turned on the lights in every room, and finally perched on a corner of our carefully made bed, bleeding, waiting. But there was nothing to wait for.

Five weeks had passed since Etsell had last curled up beside me beneath the sheets I sat upon. Just over a month, a small, defined span of time on a calendar of days that would continue to fade into oblivion with each orbit of the distant moon. It was less than a sliver outside my window, the moon, a whisper of nothing more than the faintest reminder that the hours would continue to slip by. Without him.

I remembered the first time we stepped foot in this house, the real estate agent's hesitancy even to show us the white Craftsman with a sinking porch on the very edge of town.

People think that the South has soul, but I know that the North does too. It's different, maybe. Cooler, more restrained. But Blackhawk is a rare gem of town, a family heirloom that sparkles still beneath well over a century of history that has accumulated like so much dust over our collective memory. There are the cobbled bricks of Main Street, a tiny graveyard with hand-carved headstones from the eighteen hundreds, and the oak that stands proud beside the library; it would take six grown men holding hands to encircle the prodigious girth of it. Most visibly there are old homes, houses with character and stories to tell.

Etsell and I fell in love with our home even before we were married. Blackhawk spills out from the center like an ornamental fan and slowly loses momentum as it spins toward the edges of town. The streets are frayed at the outskirts, with dandelions poking through cracks in the concrete and a scatter of forgotten houses that are one small step up from the trailer park where I grew up. But Ell and I weren't aiming high.

We used to walk the streets of Blackhawk when I couldn't stand another moment in the trailer and his dad was passed out on the living room couch. The weather didn't matter.

If it was cold we wound thick scarves around our necks and stuffed our fingers into fat mittens. And when the sun scorched and the humidity topped the charts at over ninety percent, we followed back roads to the river.

The Big Sioux was a shallow, muddy river, but it was wet, and that was enough to entice us to pick our way over a fallen log and let our feet dangle in the slow drag of the water. It wasn't far from town, maybe a quarter mile on gravel past the spot where Thirteenth Street disintegrated into dust. And it was on that corner—the final mark of civilization between Blackhawk and the innocuous bramble of a thin prairie forest—that our dream house stood.

It was a single-story, post–World War I tribute to the unbalanced prosperity and hope of a country emerging from a cloud of disillusionment. There was a cautious optimism about it, the low double arch of the gabled roof and the generous porch spread out in welcome seemed cheerful somehow. But according to the deed, the house had enjoyed only two short years of contentment until the stock market crashed and the Great Depression caught Blackhawk in a strangling grip. You could almost see the effects on the sweet little house.

"It looks sad," I said the first time we walked past. And the twin gables did indeed look like a pair of hooded eyes.

"It could be a great home." Etsell stopped with his fists on his hips and studied the whitewashed structure before him. "It's got a great porch."

"Squirrels've probably built nests all over it." I giggled. "I don't think anyone has lived there for years."

"We'll fix it up," Ell said, a grin in his voice. He came behind me and draped his arms around my shoulders, pressing his cheek to mine so that we saw the house from a matched perspective. "What color should we paint it?"

"Yellow. The color of winter wheat and linen."

And that's exactly what we did.

✒

It didn't feel like home without him. The wind hissed through the eaves in warning and every familiar sigh of settling wood seemed strange. I didn't know this place. I didn't know how to exist in it alone.

But after a few minutes of feeling sorry for myself, I put both hands on the bedspread beside me and took one last self-pitying breath. It was a long inhalation, a gulp of air that nearly ended in a sob, but I broke it off by clearing my throat. Then I pushed myself up, straightened my shirt with a deft tug, and went to work.

Etsell and I had closets across the room from each other, tiny square compartments with narrow doors and glass handles that hung a little loose. His was propped open, always, because there was a full-length mirror on the back. But it hurt to look at his clothes, to walk past and catch the faintest whiff of the crisp cotton scent of his dress shirts as it mingled with the musk of his skin. There was a lone tie dangling from the edge of the mirror—his only tie—and a pair of jeans that I had allowed to rest in a crumpled heap on the floor. I should have thrown them in the wash, but my dismissal of his abandoned laundry had been a gauntlet, a petty way to remind him when he got home that I hadn't just been waiting on pins and needles for his eventual return. Now the faded pair of pants seemed an indictment.

I bent to pick up the jeans and shook them out with one hard flick of my wrists. Then I folded them carefully, smoothing the fabric flat, and placed them on top of neat pile of pants on a low shelf. I straightened everything, separating the hangers that held his shirts and tidying a stack of sweaters he never wore. When the closet was in order, I backed out—careful not to catch a glimpse of my pale face in the mirror—and shut the door.

The room seemed strange with Etsell's closet shut. The door was a white portal, a place that held secrets and memories and wishes that I felt I would never again dare to voice. But one small thing had been done, and it pricked with the double-edged sting of guilt and relief. There was much more that I needed to do.

In the living room, random stacks of Etsell's magazines loitered, poised for his return and the brief moment when they would be thumbed through and just as quickly discarded. Sometimes Ell pored over *Aviation Week* and *Plane & Pilot*, but *Golf Digest* only took up valuable space in the already overcrowded room. Either way, the glossy covers were visual land mines. I shuffled them together and dug an empty cardboard box out of the recycling bin in the garage. It was probably foolish to keep them, but I couldn't bring myself to throw his subscriptions away either. I stuffed the box on a shelf in the entryway and shut the door a little harder than necessary.

Remnants of him lingered everywhere, details that had made our house a home and that now caused me so much pain I felt breathless from the ache of it. The bathroom was the worst. His towel beside mine, stiff from the dryer and unused because I had done a load of whites before I left for Alaska. I wished I hadn't. I wished I could press the white terry to my face and take him in. His shampoo was gone from the shower, and his toothbrush from the drawer. The only thing that held a trace of him was a thin disk of hard soap, a graying cake that he kept beside the sink for washing his hands and face before bed each night. I hadn't touched it in the weeks that he was gone because I hadn't really even noticed it was there. It was a part of the landscape, a fixture in our narrow bathroom.

But I saw it as I stood between the bathtub and the corner sink, and the feeling it evoked in me was visceral.

It was the only thing of Etsell's that I threw away. And in the moment before I clicked off the light in the bathroom, I saw that it landed right on top of the used pregnancy test in the garbage can.

8

Sacrifice

Danica slept on the couch because she couldn't bear to crawl into bed alone. She had slept alone before, but it felt permanent now, like wet concrete slowly setting, and she was afraid that if she conceded defeat on this one small front, her life would slowly harden along severe and lonely lines.

It was the perfect time of year for sleeping with the windows open, and she slid the double-hung panes as high as they would go to let in the night breeze. The air teased her, breathing soft kisses against the edges of the lightweight curtains before suddenly exhaling hard enough to make the wind chimes that hung just outside the front door play a string of chords *presto e forte*. Her first night home was made from the stuff of fever dreams and dark fantasy. Dani didn't really sleep, she rested—with one half-dreaming ear open for the sound of a car in her driveway or footfalls on the steps of her porch.

But no one came until the sun was already bathing the corner where she slept in buttery morning light. The second she opened her eyes, the windy night was less than a memory, and Dani rolled off the couch feeling weighted and strange. She rubbed her face hard, then swept the afghan around her bare shoulders and stepped out into the day clad only in a pair of Etsell's old boxer shorts and a tank top. She didn't bother trying to hide a yawn when she realized it was Katrina who would be the first to welcome her home from Alaska.

"I'm not too early, am I?" Kat called. She lifted a pair of paper grocery bags out of the backseat of her car and slammed the door with her hip.

"Have you been out all night?" Dani asked, taking in her sister's ripped jeans and the sparkly, sleeveless shirt that played back the morning sun like a disco ball. Hardly weekday-morning attire.

"I snagged a few hours at the trailer." Kat jogged sure-footed across the dewy grass and took the porch steps two at a time. "But I haven't showered yet. I was saving that for your house. You have better water pressure."

"And expensive shampoo."

"That too." Kat shuffled the grocery bags to one arm and pulled Danica into a lopsided embrace. "You look like hell."

"Thanks."

"Like death warmed over." Kat dropped a kiss on Dani's cheek and pulled the end of her sister's loose braid. "But we're going to take care of that. I come bringing libations."

Dani stepped back, barefoot on the porch, and studied Kat with a critical eye. "It's seven o'clock in the morning. You brought booze to cheer me up?"

Kat's nose crinkled. "Booze?"

"Libations."

"Is that what that means? I meant supplies. You know, food and drink."

"Provisions."

Kat snapped her fingers and grinned. "Exactly. Provisions. I've taken the next two days off and I'm not leaving your side."

"I don't know whether to laugh or cry."

"Maybe a bit of both. Could you get the door for me? I'm a second or two away from dropping these bags on your porch."

Dani swung the screen door open for Katrina and followed her inside. The living room looked windswept and disgruntled; pillows were tossed on the floor, knickknacks were tipped over on the end table, and one of Etsell and Dani's wedding portraits hung askew.

"Tough night?" Kat asked, toeing a pillow out of the way.

"The wind, I guess." Dani swung the afghan off her shoulders and folded it neatly. She arranged the pillows on the couch and righted the trinkets on the coffee table, but when she reached for the photograph she couldn't bring herself to touch it. "I suppose some of that stuff needs to be refrigerated?" She stole a look at Kat and caught her staring. There was an indecipherable look in her eyes, but she blinked and smiled, dispelling the awkward moment.

"Yeah. I picked up eggs and juice, bread. . . ." Kat peered inside her bags with a curious grin, as if she were seeing the contents for the first time. "Who knows what else? I just grabbed stuff that looked good."

Dani unpacked the bags while Kat scrubbed the coffeepot. There was indeed an eclectic sampling of grocery-store fare, everything from high-pulp orange juice to dried cherries in dark chocolate and a bottle of rum.

"Libations," Dani said, holding up the bottle.

"Arr, matey!" Kat winked and saluted.

There was a squat, shiny green pepper and a little box of button mushrooms with bits of earth still clinging to the stems. Dani knew that Kat hadn't learned to cook in her short absence, so she settled her sister at the table with a week-old copy of the local paper and set to work cleaning and chopping the vegetables for an omelet. Only hours ago she had wanted to crawl into a hole and die, but there was something soothing about the soft snick of her knife on the cutting board and the scent of fresh coffee in the kitchen. The hint of a smile graced Dani's lips, but it came bearing the burden of a sharp and sudden guilt. She bit the insides of her cheeks.

Kat didn't mention Alaska, and it shadowed the air between them, growing in size and clarity until Dani's failed quest sat like an unscalable mountain in the middle of the room. Her own personal Everest. When the eggs were just beginning to bubble, Dani sighed and turned to face her sister. She hated always being the strong one, but if Kat wasn't going to mention Alaska, she had to.

"It really sucked," Dani said, answering the unspoken question. "I tried to fly and couldn't. Hazel was . . . well, Hazel. And there were a couple of days when I thought, when I *believed* that Etsell had disappeared with another woman."

"What?" Kat snapped the newspaper shut and slapped it on the table with both her hands covering a photo of a farmer straddling infant rows of tiny corn. "Another woman? Ell?"

"Well, no." Dani's hands felt useless and unfamiliar, like they were a part of someone else's body. She looked at her open palms, then placed them very deliberately on her hips and opened her mouth to reassure her sister. But Kat was already on her feet, eyes shining with fury and fists at her side.

"I didn't dare to ask," she fumed. "I was going to just let you bring up Alaska when you felt good and ready. But I can't believe this. I mean, Etsell? Seriously? Another woman? I'd like to get my hands on him and—"

"Katrina. There wasn't another woman. It was a weird

coincidence. Nothing, really." Dani shrugged, tried to look nonchalant, but her arms were stiff. "I'm just trying to tell you about it. To tell someone what it was like to be there. I mean, in Alaska with the mountains and the water . . . It's like a different world." Dani shook her head. "It felt like winter but they said it was spring. And I could picture Ell there, you know? It smelled like him, even though I've never been to Alaska, and before a few weeks ago he hadn't either. . . ."

Kat didn't say anything. She stood there and waited, and, like a tap being primed, Dani kept talking. First in spurts, then louder and longer, her voice tight with the power of all the emotions behind the words.

"I spent an entire week wandering the streets of Seward and looking for him. Which is stupid, I know, but I couldn't fly—I tried, believe me, I tried—and there was nothing else to do but sit and worry. And I kept looking for him in the most impossible places—in bars, on boats, beneath the water of the bay as if he had crashed in the ocean and I expected his body to float to the surface in front of me."

"Dani, don't. That's just . . . Please. Don't."

"When I wasn't picturing him dead, I saw my husband with her. This other woman who didn't have a face and who just walked into the middle of a decade—a *decade*—and unraveled all our history in a couple of weeks. How can that happen?"

"It didn't happen," Kat said. She seemed to come to her senses and crossed the kitchen in a few quick strides. Taking Dani by the shoulders, she squeezed tight. "You said so yourself. It didn't happen."

"But it was like a nightmare—not knowing and thinking the worst. And then she came back and he didn't, and I didn't know if I should be happy or devastated."

Kat put her arms around Dani and fit her chin against her

sister's rigid shoulder. "It's not over yet, honey. Just because you didn't find him doesn't mean he's not still out there—"

"Stop, Kat." Dani pulled away and regarded her sister with a cold glare. "Just stop. We both know he's not coming back."

The air in the kitchen was warm, but ice formed in dark corners and seemed to spin fragile webs on the windowpanes like a swift summer frost. The air felt ready to crack and shatter, but then Dani sighed and softened, and the spell was broken as quickly as it was cast. "Oh, God," she breathed. Just that: a name, an incantation, nothing more.

"I know," Kat whispered. They stood there for a moment, less than an arm's breadth away, and regarded each other as if they were strangers though they could both close their eyes and paint the other sister's face from memory. But it was different now. Etsell haunted the room, an echo that hovered beside Dani like the silhouette of a nearly transparent shadow, little more than a ripple in the air.

"The eggs." Dani spun around and knocked the frying pan off the burner, but it was too late. They were burned, and all at once the kitchen seemed heavy with the odor of scorched butter and blackened mushrooms.

"I wasn't hungry anyway," Kat said.

～

They drank coffee in the garden, silent and thoughtful, with only the sound of a summer morning between them. The backyard seemed savage somehow, thick with early-summer growth and clearly untended. The grass was long and the trees were almost ostentatious in robes of lightest green, a color that would soon darken in the sun as Dani's skin would glow with a sprinkling of freckles in the passing of warm weeks ahead. But for a little while, even the untamed tangle of her generous yard would be lovely simply because it was alive. It grew and thrived, and while it would gradually brown at the edges, the early-June splendor of a forgotten garden was still a sight to behold.

When the sisters were jittery and high-strung from too much caffeine, Kat stood and reached to pull Dani to her feet. "Put on some clothes. We're going for a hike."

"A hike?" Dani gave Kat's outfit a skeptical look. "Looks like you better put on some clothes too."

"Got a T-shirt I can borrow?"

Under normal circumstances Dani would be exasperated. Kat's version of help was never very helpful, and often resulted in more work for Dani instead of less. A few years ago, when Etsell and Dani had both come down with influenza A, Kat arrived on the scene to make chicken soup and take care of them. But she didn't know how to make soup, and Dani ended up chopping vegetables in her bathrobe—and spoon-feeding it to Kat when she got the flu too.

Kat had arrived less than an hour earlier, and already Dani was cooking, providing emotional support, and furnishing an appropriate wardrobe for her older sister. But there was something comforting about a familiar routine. Dani knew this role by heart, and though Kat's presumptuousness would have bothered her a month ago, she found it almost endearing now.

"Sure, I've got a T-shirt," Dani said. "And a pair of shorts that won't show your booty too."

"I like my booty."

"Maybe a little too much."

Dani dug jean shorts and T-shirts out of her dresser drawer, then pulled her hair into a ponytail and splashed her face with cold water. Brushing her teeth was an almost religious experience—when she rinsed her mouth she was struck by the bite of peppermint on her tongue and the feeling that some things never changed, no matter what happened. Life went on, even when you didn't necessarily want it to.

Stepping out of the bathroom Dani came face-to-face with her reflection: Kat in her clothes, hair long and loose around her shoulders—the way Dani wore hers when she wanted to feel pretty—looking for all the world like Dani's fraternal twin. Kat was a handspan taller, and her hair was several shades darker, but they had the same upswept nose, narrow legs, long arms. Without thinking, Dani crossed the space between them and wrapped her arms around her sister's slender waist. Kat held her tight.

"Thanks for coming. I didn't think . . ." But Dani didn't finish. She couldn't bring herself to admit that she thought she would have to face this alone.

As Dani laced up her tennis shoes on the steps of the front porch, she lamented the fact that her feet were a full size smaller than Kat's. "You're stuck with a big pair of Etsell's flip-flops, a little pair of mine, or those ridiculous heeled things you came in. Where exactly are we going?"

"Not far." A secret smile slid across Kat's features. "But I have a surprise for you when we get there."

"So we're not actually hiking per se."

"Nah, it's more of a walk. I'll take your flip-flops."

Standing in the shadow of her detached garage, Dani could pretend that she lived out in the middle of nowhere. The yellow house sat on one of the last corners in town, a square edge of concrete where Thirteenth Street met Ridge Road. If she turned down Ridge, the first house she ran into would be Benjamin's. There were a few more houses before a bend hid the rest of the blacktop from sight, but she wasn't familiar with those far-flung neighbors. And if she headed back into town on Thirteenth, she would have to cross an empty lot before reaching Mrs. Kamp's peeling-paint home.

Across the road was a cornfield, and where the concrete of Thirteenth ended, a gravel path to nowhere began.

Kat crossed the empty street and headed down the gravel road with a bounce in her step. "Coming?" She threw a wink over her shoulder, and Dani jogged to catch up. Her chest suddenly felt tight—history crunched beneath her feet as she followed her sister down a trail that belonged to her and Etsell.

"Are we going to the river?" Dani asked, trying to keep the strain out of her voice.

"Surprise!" Kat threw up her arms in mock excitement. "Seriously. Where did you think we were going?"

Dani fumbled. "I don't know, Kat. I don't feel like walking to the river right now. I have a headache. Let's just—"

"Come on." Kat grabbed her sister's hand briefly, squeezed. "Walk with me. The fresh air will be good for you."

"I got plenty of fresh air in Alaska. And it didn't smell like manure."

"The scent of money, baby." Kat wiggled her eyebrows. "See? I'm a good little rural girl."

Dani grunted, but she followed Kat all the same. If she had felt even a little optimistic in the garden, all that hope fizzled away beneath the glare of the rising sun. She felt incapable of turning around, of challenging Kat's will. So she bowed her head and watched the sun-speckled dust rise beneath her feet as the trees around her began to thicken.

It wasn't long before the sigh of the river whispered through the leaves. Though light penetrated the patchy canopy of the hardwood forest, just the knowledge of water lent a certain coolness to the air that brushed fingertips against Dani's skin and raised a little shiver. How many times had she walked this path with Etsell? They had spotted a red fox once, and a mother raccoon with a lone kit. And there was a secret place around an S-bend curve in the river where teen-agers came to drink beer and smoke pot—they had found the empty bottles and blackened joints on more than one occa-sion, and came back with garbage bags to dispose of the waste.

Walking with Kat was different. She bounced and chat-tered, scaring away any wildlife that might otherwise have been caught unawares. And instead of appreciating the quiet hum of the river, she complained about the murky water, the shallow places where sandbars peeked through the surface in uneven swaths of sticky mud and debris.

"You couldn't pay me to swim in there," Kat said when the stood on the damp bank. The water swirled and eddied before them, hiding a world of secrets beneath a silent cloak of coffee-colored opacity.

Dani didn't tell her that she and Etsell had dipped into the river countless times. That they loved the feel of the water on their skin and the knowledge that it had come from distant places when snow melted in spring and rain soaked the ground. Instead, she asked a question. "Why are we here?"

Kat held up one finger to silence her, and thrust her other hand into the pocket of her shorts. After a moment she emerged triumphant and held out her closed fist to Dani. "Here."

When she peeled back her fingers, there was a Swiss Army Knife in the palm of her hand. It was a slim cylinder, painted pink for breast cancer awareness and bearing a tiny white ribbon. Kat had started carrying it around when she began working at the gentlemen's club. Dani wished that her sister would pack Mace instead, or, better yet, find another job. But Kat insisted that the knife was discreet, and that it offered a small amount of security. Dani was glad that her sister had something.

"Are you sure?"

"Yes."

"How short?" Dani asked.

Tugging her chestnut waves into a low ponytail at the nape of her neck, Kat turned around. "This short. Cut it above the elastic."

"That's pretty short."

"It'll be dramatic. A memorial."

The unexpected word stopped them both short, and for the span of a few ragged breaths they stood in complete silence. Then Kat nodded once, a command of sorts, and Dani thumbed out the knife. The blade sprung with a muted click.

"You're sure?" Dani whispered.

"For shit's sake, Danica Greene, just do it!"

At first the blade merely glanced off the shiny breadth of Kat's dark hair. But then Dani wound the length of it around her hand and pulled the ponytail taut. The next slice carved a chunk from the thick rope of hair.

Kat shrieked. "That hurts like hell!" she howled. "Do it fast! Just get it over with!"

Dani worked quickly after that, moving the blade in clean, even strokes. When it was over, Dani held the weight of her sister's gorgeous hair in her hand and felt a grief so profound it almost leveled her.

Kat touched the naked plane of her slender neck, combing strands of hair with her fingernails. She didn't turn around right away, didn't face Dani, and in the interim there was a silence between them that seemed charged with things unspoken. Dani felt an apology bubble inside her, a regret that rose until it threatened to spill from her lips in a torrent of repentance. *I did this to you,* she mourned.

But then Kat turned and regarded her with a look so pure it made Dani feel sorry for all the times she had doubted her sister, all the times she was sure Kat was on a path fraught with failure and destruction.

"I look hot, don't I?" Kat asked, trying out a seductive stare. She pouted her lips. "Glamorous. Sexy."

Dani attempted a smile, but it wisped away long before it formed.

Kat didn't seem to mind. She took the length of hair from her sister's hands and studied it with narrowed eyes. Then she flung it, overhand, into the water. It sailed out over the river before landing with a tiny splash. "Here's to new beginnings," she whispered.

Dani wanted to echo Kat's sentiments, to let the breeze off the water baptize her in the sort of hope that had the strength to believe in a fresh start. But the words stuck in her throat, and try as she might, she couldn't tear her gaze from the place where her sister's offering had sunk. It felt futile. An unseen sacrifice.

Beauty given in vain.

Danica

We walked straight to the salon from the river, stopping for just a minute or two at the house so I could grab my keys. While I rummaged through the kitchen junk drawer to locate my key chain, Kat studied her hair in the side mirror of her car, smoothing it one way and then another, and experimenting with different parts. Keys in my pocket, I stood for a few seconds behind the screen door and watched her as she styled and tugged. I was looking for some sign that she regretted our mutilation, but either she was a good actress, or she really didn't mind what I had done to her. The only expression on her face was one of mild amusement.

It felt strange to fit my key in the front door of La Rue. And even stranger to stand in the middle of my salon and absorb the way the sun played off the copper ceiling and bathed the shop in golden light that rose like fairy dust in the still air. It was a second homecoming, and in some ways this one hit me harder than even those first few moments in the house I had shared with Ell. This was my life. This would be my return to normalcy. And somehow that thought slashed at my chest and left me panting.

But I couldn't let Kat see how my shop affected me. I flicked on the lights, dispelling the lovely, dancing dust, and settled my sister into a chair without giving my surroundings another thought. I spun a black cape around her and secured it tight against her neck. When she yanked at it a bit with her fingers, I slapped her hand away. "You'll itch like crazy if any of those tiny hairs get under your shirt."

"I've never had to worry about tiny hairs before." Kat wiggled her shoulders as if this was a delicious dilemma. "Are you going to use the clippers on me?"

"Maybe a bit in the back."

She shivered again, and I couldn't tell if it was from anticipation or dread.

I spent nearly ten minutes massaging Kat's scalp with shampoo that smelled of a beach in the summertime. Then I rinsed and conditioned, and dedicated the next half hour to shaping a long pixie cut that framed her delicate face. There were sweeping strands that curved along her cheekbones, and a fringe of bangs brushed to one side that accented her eyes. The back was boy-short, but I notched it a bit so she could tease it out if she wanted to.

When I finally spun her around to face the mirror, even I was shocked by the result. Kat looked amazing—sophisticated and elegant, like she should be modeling couture instead of serving up Miller Lite on tap at the disgusting hole in the wall where she worked.

"You're going to have to get a different job," I said. It was a risky pronouncement; Kat hated it when I nagged her about bartending. But I felt bold. I had just transformed my sister into Audrey Hepburn circa *Sabrina*.

Kat angled her chin, studying the cut from every angle she could. She grazed her fingers along her forehead and blended a stray hair back into place. "Everything else is changing," she mused. "I just might."

I suppressed the urge to clap and instead plucked the broom and dustpan from beside the counter where it stood in wait. There wasn't much to clean up, but I swept the curling tendrils of my sister's fallen hair for a very long time.

～

Kat stayed with me for two uninterrupted days, and although the thought of her constant presence had filled me with anxiety at first, by the time she had to go back to work, I wondered what I would do without her. For almost forty-eight hours we existed in a time between, an interim from the real world where I didn't have to deal with the fallout from my husband's disappearance, or even think about the fact that he was gone.

We didn't do much. Sometimes we cooked extravagant meals together only to discover we had no appetite for them. And then at midnight we met each other in the kitchen and warmed up the homemade crab cakes with sweet chili sauce and curls of green onions so peppery and strong we almost couldn't eat them.

For the most part, we reverted to our childhood. Kat painted her toenails blue, but didn't like the way the color made her feet look anemic, so she repainted them green. I opted for something in an iridescent mauve, a shade so discreet it was almost as if I weren't wearing polish. We smeared on Kermit-green facial masks. And we watched movies. Some obnoxious new release, and then *My Fair Lady* because Kat had put me in mind of Audrey Hepburn and it was the only one of her movies we could find in all of Blackhawk.

On the second morning, Char showed up, and for a few hours the Vis girls were almost complete. I felt a brief stab of longing for Natalie, but I quashed it quickly because I could only imagine what would happen if they all gathered around me. A return to life before Ell and a hint of what it would be like after him. It terrified me.

But having Natalie join our ranks would have been preferable to dealing with Char on my own.

My mother arrived sober and subdued, dressed in a pair of plain blue jeans and a crew-neck T-shirt that for once didn't hug every curve. Her hair was somewhat faded and held back with two clips that made her look younger than her fifty-five years. But the thing that surprised me most about her sudden appearance on my doorstep was not the very un-Char-like veneer. It was the look in her eyes.

"Hi, honey," she said, forgoing the pot of coffee on the counter and coming across the kitchen to stand before the chair where I was sitting. At first I didn't know what she wanted from me, but then she put her arms out awkwardly and I realized she expected a hug. I rose and acquiesced, a one-armed embrace that was halfhearted and laced with all the disappointment I harbored because she hadn't bothered to come and see me sooner. Shouldn't my own mother have been waiting for my defeated return? I had been home for thirty-six hours before she bothered to come and see me.

"How are you girls doing?" Char asked, sinking into a chair between us. The question was directed at both of us, but she didn't take her eyes off me.

"Fine," I said a little too brightly. "I cut Kat's hair."

Char blinked at me for a moment before she turned her head slowly to my sister. "Oh!" Her jaw dropped a little. "Wow, Katrina. I don't know what to say."

"Say it's gorgeous," Kat instructed. She drowned the last gulp of her coffee and rose to dump her mug in the sink.

"It's gorgeous," Char repeated obediently.

"I'm going to shower." Kat departed the kitchen without a backward glance, and I was left to wonder if something had happened between her and our mother, or if she was just as tired and sleep-deprived as I was.

"She looks really different," Char said when Kat was gone. "I love it."

Char just nodded.

We sat in silence, and I took several deep, steadying breaths as I contemplated bringing up her absence and my failed trek to Alaska. I wanted to hold her accountable for her actions—or lack thereof—but I didn't want to do this with everyone. To rehash my sad narrative until the words were sucked dry of all meaning. But I decided it was expected. I opened my mouth to give her some truncated version of my story of heartache and loss.

I didn't get the chance to say anything before Char burst into tears.

It was so shocking to see my mother cry that I sat stock-still for a minute or so as she sobbed messily and tried without success to speak through snot bubbles. Then Char moaned, a heartbroken little sigh, and I came to my senses. There was a box of tissues on the counter, and I grabbed them and placed them on the table before her. While she tried to sop up her tears, I poured her a glass of water from the pitcher in the refrigerator and tapped out two ibuprofen into my palm for good measure.

"Here," I said, handing her the cool glass and the small, white tablets. "Take these. Crying always gives me a headache."

"Me too," she mumbled.

We sat in silence for a few awkward moments, and I wondered if I should do something to console her. Pat her back maybe, or offer some words of comfort. But I didn't know how to handle Char in such an atypical state, and instead of feeling a sense of connection with my grieving mom, the distance between us seemed only to widen.

"Do you know what I've been thinking about all night?" Char asked finally, raising her swollen eyes to mine. She gifted me with the faint impression of a crooked smile, but then her lip trembled and she heaved a heavy sigh. "I've been thinking about the afternoon that Etsell asked me for your hand in marriage."

Her words were like a blow, but I squared my shoulders and placed my hands on my thighs to steady myself. "Oh," I said.

"Do you remember that?"

Of course I remembered. But I studied my lap and held my tongue. Maybe if I acted disinterested she'd abandon her obvious attempt to break my heart.

"I thought it was so weird," Char said, oblivious to my distress. "Ell called me up and asked if he could come over for coffee. Can you imagine? That earnest little boy treated me just like a lady. Of course, he was nineteen and hardly a boy anymore, but all I could think about was how young he looked. How childlike. And though he'd seen me in robe and rollers, there he was all formal and trying to act grown-up, pretending like we were practically strangers."

I didn't know that Etsell was going to ask my mother for permission to marry me, but she loved to tell the story after the fact. How he showed up when I was at work and sat across from Char in the tiny dine-in kitchen of our double-wide with his hands folded on the table like a gentleman.

"He sat there like a churchman. Remember those visits

we used to have when you were a little girl? When two men in black suits would come to the house and inquire after the state of our sorry souls?" Char laughed a little, though the memory of those visits was no laughing matter to me. I could still feel the lead in the pit of my stomach as those grave men bored holes into my forehead with their eyes and condemned my silence.

"Ell wasn't like that," I murmured.

"No, of course not. But he was so serious. He said all these sweet things about how much he loved you and how he wanted to spend the rest of his life with you. . . ."

I would have asked her to stop, but my throat was filled with something molten. I couldn't even open my mouth.

"And do you know what I said?" Char shook her head as if she couldn't believe it even now. "I asked if you were pregnant. I told him, 'I'm too young to be a grandma. Ain't no way some baby is gonna call me grandma yet.'"

She couldn't have any idea how deeply her words pierced me, how they mined a deep well of emotions and came up bloody-fingered from the raw wound of my ruined hopes.

Ell had wanted kids right from the start. He loved the idea of rubbing my pregnant feet and pushing back strands of sticky hair from my face as I delivered a houseful of giggling, apple-cheeked babies. But I refused. At first I said we were too young—we weren't ready for the responsibility of kids. And it was true. For a while, at least. When he brought it up a couple of years later and begged that I go off birth control, "just to see what happens," I pretended to agree, but didn't stop popping those tiny pink pills every morning. I hid them in the pocket of a jacket I never wore that hung in the very back of my closet.

I don't know exactly why I was so terrified of having children. It had nothing to do with Etsell; I knew that he would be an amazing father. But just the thought of bringing another person into the world gripped me with the sort of fear that left me short of breath and clammy. Maybe it was because I didn't know what it looked like to be a mother. Or I couldn't envision, no matter how hard I tried, the careful harmony of a family tuned to the mysterious song of a complete and happy parental unit. Neither could Etsell. What did we know about raising children? What did we know about functional families?

"It just . . ." Char fumbled for words. "It just kills me. How could I say that to him? How could I know?"

But there was no way anyone could have predicted it. No way we could have parted the curtain and peeked at all that was to come, the eventual softening that would cause me one day to stop taking the pills, to actually watch the calendar and hope. And there was no way I could have prepared myself for the fact that just when I started to long for the same thing as Etsell, the possibility would be forever snatched away.

A part of me wanted to tell Char that now she'd never be a grandma. She'd never have to hear that dreaded word cross the cherubic lips of a child who bore our mingled DNA. But it was too cruel. So I didn't say anything at all, and we brooded in the weighted stillness of a taut, uncertain morning. Brooded, and mourned for something that we both would never know.

9

A Simple Kindness

For the first ten days after Danica returned home from Alaska, she lived like a hermit. When Kat left to resume her normal life, Dani circled in on herself, cocooning the edges of her existence around her so that she could pretend to forget that the world was going on as if nothing had ever happened. Sometimes she showered twice in a day. And once she went three days without stepping into the bathroom to do anything other than relieve herself. She dreamed about Etsell when she closed her eyes at night, and when the sun dazzled Blackhawk with warmth, she had visions of mountains and a vast, bottomless ocean. Of Alaska.

The clouds on the edge of the horizon were the hunched shoulders of the Aleutians, the darkening sky behind ascended to mark the Kenai Peninsula. The air shimmered when she blinked, revealing impenetrable forests and water frothed with ice as cold and snow-white as winter itself. It was madness, and she knew it. But Danica couldn't stop. She kept looking for him.

She knew what they were thinking. All of them. It was time to bury Etsell. But there was nothing to put in the ground, no remains to tether him to the earth and give her a constant—a place where she could litter flowers upon his memory like the tears she couldn't cry. How could she bury an empty casket? For some reason, a hollow grave was worse than none at all.

Char visited a few times, but Dani was short with her and distant, so after a couple of days her mother decided to leave her alone. And the phone rang infrequently—Hazel tried, and Natalie too—but when Dani didn't answer, even the calls thinned and then stopped altogether. Presumably there was a backlog of messages on her machine at La Rue, but Dani didn't really care if she lost her clients. She wasn't even sure that she wanted to go back to her salon, to that place where Etsell was imprinted on the framework like an indelible watermark. All she really wanted to do was follow her husband. To disappear.

She was doing a pretty good job of it until Benjamin rapped on her back door late one afternoon.

There was no point acting like she wasn't home. Dani was standing at the counter, staring at an apple in her hand and coming to the sad realization that she hadn't eaten all day. Her stomach rumbled at the heft of the fruit in her palm—a sign of life—but the mottled bronze-red flesh was wrinkled and soft. She was so disappointed, she could hardly bring herself to acknowledge Benjamin's presence.

"Hello, Danica," he said through the screen. "That apple doesn't look so good anymore."

She nodded and dumped it in the garbage can under the sink without so much as glancing at her neighbor.

When it became apparent that Dani wasn't about to respond to him, Benjamin pushed the door open cautiously and took a single step into the kitchen. He stopped just over the threshold. "I don't mean to disturb you," he said. "I've been trying to decide if I should come over at all."

Dani turned her gaze to the man before her, but her eyes held a faraway look. She still didn't say anything.

"It's just that I'm mowing my lawn, and I was wondering if you'd like me to cut yours too." The request was almost hesitant, but Benjamin's gaze was steady, direct. "It's getting kind of long."

One look out the back door was proof that Benjamin's tiptoe-soft personality made him prone to understatement. Dani's backyard was a wild, weedy wonderland populated by grass so long that it fell down on itself in coils of defeat. Etsell would have been appalled. His yard didn't have to be perfect, but he liked it tidy.

"Actually, I should have mowed it a long time ago, but I didn't dare to do it until I could ask you in person. I mean, what if you didn't want me to?" Benjamin cupped the back of his neck, and although it was obvious he was uncomfortable, he resolutely stood his ground. "I'd like to do this for you, Danica. All you have to do is say yes."

Dani blinked hard a few times, trying to disentangle her gaze from Benjamin's direct stare. She noticed for the first time that his eyes were an unusual green—the color of pond water and smooth stones and the line of narrow trees that topped the mountains she had flown over in Alaska. It was disconcerting. His eyes were as beautiful and unusual in his face as his pale arms in a battered football T-shirt. He didn't look ecclesiastical; he looked sweaty.

"Yes," Dani said softly. "Of course. I mean, please. It would be great if you'd mow."

Benjamin's smile was quick and brilliant. "Do you care if I park my truck in your driveway? I'm going to have to bag it since it's so long, and it would take me double the time to trek back and forth to my house."

"Okay." Something about the ordinary, everyday nature

of Benjamin's simple kindness made Danica feel off-center. Had he even mentioned Etsell? Her trip to Alaska? Of course he knew about it. The whole town did. The local paper had even featured a short column about her so-called heroic efforts to locate her missing husband. But Benjamin wasn't looking at her like she was a candidate for the mental health ward. He seemed concerned only with her lawn. It was sweet. Uncomplicated.

Dani brushed her palms together as if wiping them clean of some invisible contagion, then dropped them carefully to her sides. Some latent civility inside of her yawned a little, giving her manners a drowsy nudge. She asked, "Can I help?"

For a second it looked like Benjamin would decline, but he appeared to think better of it. "It's pretty warm out there," he told her. "But I know better than to argue."

Dani was taken aback that he would accept her feeble offer, but now that the words were out of her mouth, and he had so guilelessly consented, she didn't see any way to back out. "It's been a while since I've mowed," she fumbled.

"Oh, it's easy. Like riding a bike." Benjamin smiled again, a small tweak of the corner of his mouth that conveyed much more than she would have thought possible. He seemed inordinately pleased. "Many hands make light work."

"Is that in the Bible?" The moment Dani spoke, she wished she wouldn't have. She hoped she didn't sound sarcastic.

But Benjamin didn't seem upset. "Nah. The book of Nana Sue. My grandmother put everyone around her to work so that she could play at the end of the day."

The whole conversation felt surreal to Dani, surreal and impossible. Yard work and overused clichés and Benjamin's nana. "I should change," she said absently, glancing down at the pair of cut-off sweatpants she had been wearing for two days straight.

"Good idea. I'll meet you outside." Benjamin turned to leave, but he paused with one hand in the air. A thoughtful look clouded his features and tilted his chin a little. "You know, Danica, I've been meaning to ask you something."

Suddenly her blood ran icy. Finally. All Benjamin's normalcy was a prelude to this. Was he going to offer his professional services? Maybe a few sessions of counseling or a memorial in honor of Etsell? Dani knew the things they said at those somber funerals, those so-called celebrations of life. They didn't feel like celebrations at all. Instead, the pastor always read the same sad passage, the elegy about dust and ashes that was supposed to make those mourning feel as if death was not only inevitable, it was somehow poetic. Dust to dust . . . She wondered if Benjamin realized that someone as golden as Etsell bespoke the breath of God infinitely more than the ash of the earth. She opened her mouth to tell him so, but it was too late.

"I don't know if you'd be interested or not, but I'm digging up a few plants behind my house to make room for a new patio. If you'd like, I can transplant them somewhere in your yard. I mean, I don't really even know what they are, but they're pretty, and it seems a waste to just throw them away."

Dani hoped the relief she felt wasn't too obvious. "That would be nice," she managed. "Maybe beside the garden wall. I don't think my hydrangea made it."

"It didn't." Benjamin winked. Hooking a thumb over his shoulder he said, "Hey, why don't you move a few of those plants while I mow?" Dani shrugged and he appeared to take her neutrality as consent. "I have some dug up already. Take what you like."

"All right."

"I'll just pull the truck around. Meet me outside?"

Dani watched Benjamin leave, his long, loping stride stretching into a light jog as he crossed her backyard. Then she shuffled to her bedroom to put on a pair of jeans and socks. She felt slow and foggy, but she knew she couldn't do yard work barefoot and bare-legged. Her only intent in changing clothes was to protect herself from flying debris, and yet once she was in the bedroom she hazarded a quick peek in the mirror over her chest of drawers. The woman she saw there was pale and gaunt, hollow-cheeked and almost frightened-looking. Her eyes were wide and haunted, her skin gray. She hardly recognized herself.

Passing her hands over her face, Dani leaned in closer to the mirror and studied the fine lines that had bloomed around her mouth. Were her lips so downturned as of late to accomplish this subtle aging in such a short time? The thought made her smile sadly at the unfamiliar reflection. A part of her wanted to stay here, to commiserate with the lonely girl in the mirror. But she had told Benjamin that she would help, and even now he was pulling the lawn mower to her house, expecting her to work alongside him until they both smelled of sweat and fresh-cut grass. It felt strangely intimate.

It was hotter outside than Dani expected it would be. Her house was shaded by two enormous sugar maples that glowed like embers in the fall and cast shadows over the small rooms of her home during the summer. There was a light, constant breeze that whispered through her windows, but standing in the middle of the yard Dani realized that it was a strong wind. A stiff, hot blast of air beneath a fierce sun that was gloating in anticipation of midsummer. It would be a banner season, off the charts—Dani could feel it in the air, the promise of blistering weeks to come.

Benjamin was already mowing, and since he couldn't take

his hands off the machine to wave to her, he merely inclined his head and gave Dani the same insufferable smile that had flickered across his face in the kitchen. Then he went back to his work as if everything was right in the world, like there was nothing more meaningful for him to do in this one moment than cut her grass and allow her—brokenhearted and abandoned as she was—to help him dispose of a row of withering perennials.

Danica picked her way through the long grass and cut across Benjamin's oversized lawn. There was a pair of gnarled apple trees in the very corner of their lots, angled in such a way that it was impossible to know whose trees they really were. By unspoken agreement, they had always shared the produce, picking only off the side that bordered their respective yards. One year, in a rush of domesticity, Dani had decided to make applesauce of the knobby fruit, and Benjamin had happened upon her filling a five-gallon bucket. They weren't even particularly special apples, but she felt caught in the act of committing a heinous crime against her neighbor—she was taking far more than her share. But apparently Benjamin wasn't concerned with her lack of scruples because he pulled down branches for her, picking everything he could reach and filling her bucket to overflowing.

Etsell had loved that applesauce. It was pink because Dani had been too lazy to peel the apples before she cooked them, and when she pressed the soft fruit through a sieve, the flesh was stained the color of wild roses. It tasted like fresh air and the sleepy sunshine of a warm and lingering fall. Dani had meant to bring a jar to Benjamin, but she forgot. She wished for a moment that she had something to give him, something she could place in his hands for a change.

There were four plants dug up beside the house, their root balls moist and sprouting slim, white rhizomes like strands of overstarched yarn. As far as Dani could tell, Benjamin had extracted a pair of impressive hostas with variegated leaves, a bleeding heart that was done blooming, and a twisted mass of creeping phlox that would take over her yard if she let it. She decided to leave the phlox.

It had been a long time since Dani had stuck her fingers in the earth, but when she stole a peek at Benjamin and saw sweat darkening his shirt, she felt the least she could do was try. The hydrangea that hadn't survived the winter was brittle and dry as dust, but the roots were gnarled and woody. It took her fifteen minutes of hacking with the spade just to rend the bulk of it from the ground, but the soil still bubbled with buried threads. Dani dropped to her knees and attacked the roots with a trowel and hedge clippers. By the time she had cleared a space, her forehead glistened. It was with a certain satisfaction that she leaned back and surveyed the earth she had prepared.

Dani was no gardener, and though the extraction had been a sort of frantic labor of love, she more or less plunked the exiled plants into the ground and smoothed dirt over the top. She found a bag of potting soil in the shed and sprinkled that over all, then finished off her project with a hefty scoop of molding Miracle-Gro and a generous dousing from the hose. Benjamin was done with the backyard, and she was grateful that he wasn't around to see her being so careless. It had felt good to be outside for a while, to forget that grief still cloaked her in a fever dream. But the spell was wearing off. Dani had a headache. She wanted to go inside. To be alone.

The neighborhood was quiet when Dani put the last of her gardening tools in the shed. The lawn mower was silent, and Benjamin was obviously done with his altruistic chore. Dani wondered if she was beholden to make a pitcher of lemonade or resurrect a can of pop from the unused recesses of her refrigerator. Would he expect a few minutes of her company? Small talk?

Dani gathered a steadying breath and tried to soldier her remaining decorum. Somewhere inside was the beauty shop owner, the woman who laughed easily and actually enjoyed listening to people's stories. At the very least, she should be able to muster some genuine gratitude.

Their voices were apparent even before Dani crossed around the side of the house. Benjamin said something indistinct but cheerful, and a woman responded less enthusiastically and with a bit more volume. At first Dani suspected that Char had stopped by, but then the woman snorted and her identity was obvious even though she was still out of sight.

"I'm going to hire someone," Hazel was saying when Dani stepped onto the driveway. "I've told you that, haven't I?" She shot a hard look at Dani, expecting her to confirm whatever she was saying but not waiting for a response. "It's true, Danica needs someone to take care of a few things around here. But it's not your responsibility, Pastor."

"It's not a responsibility." Benjamin smiled. "It's a privilege. And you can call me Benjamin."

Hazel narrowed one eye and studied Benjamin like she was appraising a bull. "I've been to your church, Pastor." It sounded like an accusation.

"I remember you. You wear a blue dress and sit in the back. It's nice to finally meet you properly." His hand appeared before her like magic. It seemed to Dani that it had always been there, waiting, outstretched, reaching for Hazel as if he truly did mean what he said.

After a moment the older woman took Benjamin's hand and gave it a good, hard shake. The sort of shake that was meant to intimidate. "Fine," she said. "But you don't need to be mowing Etsell's lawn. We'll take care of it."

"Just trying to help." If Hazel's prickly reception bothered Benjamin, he did a remarkable job of hiding it. He appeared more amused than put out, and Dani couldn't help but notice that he seemed almost relaxed around the obviously antagonistic Hazel.

"Hello." Dani waved her hand unnecessarily—there was no way either of them could have missed her presence. "Thanks for doing the lawn," she told Benjamin, ignoring Hazel. "Would you like something to drink?" It almost hurt to ask—she was so afraid he'd say yes—but she had practiced the line on the walk over and she dashed it out before she could change her mind.

Thankfully, Benjamin was shaking his head no before she even finished talking. "I've got a meeting tonight, and I'd better get going. You got the plants?"

She nodded. "Three of them."

"Let me know if you want more."

"Thanks."

Benjamin dipped his head toward Dani, and then again to Hazel. It was a slight, almost chivalrous bow that left Dani fearing for his safety. Hazel didn't go for that sort of thing, for anything that smacked of pretension, and she was downright rabid when she caught a whiff of duplicity. But Benjamin's gesture didn't seem pretentious to Dani; it fit somehow.

She watched him lift the lawn mower into the back of his truck and didn't move from her spot as he drove away, because she didn't want to face Hazel. It was tough enough for Danica to spend any amount of time with Etsell's surrogate mother after their failed trek to Alaska, but she feared that Benjamin's assistance had grated on the other woman for some inexplicable reason. She didn't feel like explaining, and she certainly didn't feel like defending.

But Hazel didn't give her a choice. "What was he doing here?"

Dani sighed. "Mowing my lawn. Isn't it obvious?"

"You don't need him to mow your lawn."

"I wasn't doing it."

"I can do it. We can hire someone."

"He was being nice. It's what neighbors do. It's what pastors do, apparently. You know, good works and all that stuff."

Hazel grunted. "That man wasn't interested in good works. Not this afternoon."

At any other time, Dani would be utterly bemused by this sullen interpretation of Benjamin's simple act of charity. But Hazel seemed genuinely upset. "He cut my grass, for pity's sake. Why are you being so weird about it?"

Hazel's gaze traveled the path that Benjamin's truck had taken only a minute ago. She stared at the spot as if discerning his intentions in the final wisps of exhaust smoke. "I saw it," she said finally. "When you came walking up. I saw the way he looked at you."

Danica

They say that men are prone to infidelity. That the ubiquitous seven-year itch is simply a part of married life. But Etsell didn't cheat on me. I cheated on him.

It wasn't a physical affair—in fact, it had nothing to do with sex or even attraction. Instead, my adultery was purely emotional, an interlude that made me feel desired again. The saddest part was, I never meant for it to happen. Etsell and I were doing fine, but suddenly *fine* didn't feel good enough. There was something stirring just beneath the surface, a swirl of emotion that flickered like mercury—slippery and elusive, impossible to pin down. I didn't even realize that we were sinking in quicksand—that I was unhappy—until I opened my eyes one day and saw a stranger smiling at me. He wasn't even handsome, not really. But it was obvious that he thought I was.

After the fact, I tried not even to think of his name, because it was a touchstone of sorts, a way to conjure up all the times Etsell and I failed each other. All the times we fell short. A few brief weeks in my life contained all the guilt and condemnation of the places where my marriage crumbled beneath the mundane weight of the everyday. It was a laundry list of all the small things—the way we started to take each other for granted, the sharp words, the nights we forgot to touch, even if it was only for a moment—but they added up to more than I could have imagined.

It was such a simple thing. I walked into the hardware store and he smiled at me. But it was more than that too: a burst of recognition, a look full of so many things I almost felt affronted by the force of it. I paused in the doorway beneath the fading jingle of the welcome bells and prickled at the surprise of him standing there, watching me like I was more than myself. He drank me in. It was a fleeting touch, a first kiss, the hint of a promise. It didn't hold the same mystery and wonder as the first time I saw Etsell, but that had happened so long ago, I could hardly be asked to compare.

The look passed as quickly as it flitted across his face, and then he called to me across the empty store. "What can I help you with?" He was new to Blackhawk, I had never seen him before, and it seemed odd to me that he didn't know what I wanted. Didn't everyone know what I did in the hardware store? The sheets of sandpaper, the glosses and stains and squat cans of varnish? They seemed an extension of me.

"I need a high-lacquer gloss," I said, gathering myself. "Not much. A spray can should do."

"Working on a project?" he asked. His hands were busy with a stack of papers that he was straightening and re-straightening, but his gaze was trained on me and the corner of his lip seemed to twitch in delight. I *delighted* him. My hair was in a sagging ballerina's bun, my jeans were stiff with dried paint, and I was sure I wore the evidence of my project somewhere on my face, but he looked at me as if I were a mirage, an oasis in the middle of a scorching desert.

"Birdhouses, actually." They were Christmas presents for

everyone on my list, three-tiered beauties that I had stained mahogany and topped with a gabled roof painted a deep brick-red. The gloss was to make the roof shine, but it was hard to remember that small detail with him staring at me.

He raised an eyebrow. "You made 'em?"

Was he flirting? So openly? "All six of them. I am surprisingly capable of swinging a hammer."

He laughed. "You don't look the type."

I wanted to ask him what "the type" looked like, but all at once I was flustered. A warm chill raced through me and my palms went damp. "I know where it is," I told him, taking off for the paint section. I thought he would stay put behind the counter, but he followed me, keeping a modest distance until I stopped in front of the spray cans.

"I'd use this," he suggested, reaching past my arm. He didn't brush against me—didn't even come close—but a jolt of electricity snapped through me at his proximity all the same.

Everything was very ordinary after that. He charged my account for the lacquer and thanked me for stopping in. I left with a nod, feeling contrite and just a little frightened that a complete stranger could disarm me with a smile. But I went back.

We never touched, but we talked. And when his face became familiar, I felt comfortable enough to lean up against the counter and linger a little longer than I should. Just long enough to let his veiled interest infuse me with a sense of confidence, a calm assurance that even if Etsell had grown tired of his wife, I was still an attractive woman. The sort of woman who could make a stranger light up.

I thought it was a harmless flirtation. But one day as I was wasting time in the hardware store, elbows on the counter and laughing at something he had said, the door swung open to let in the cold of a March snowstorm. I didn't bother to turn around, because he was in the middle of a story, something unlikely and almost certainly constructed for my pleasure alone. I was rapt. There was the sound of someone stomping the snow off their boots, then the quick snip of a zipper being yanked down a little, but I ignored it. In the back of my mind I registered a heavy exhalation, rhythmic footfalls, and then, from a distance, the pressure of a hand on my shoulder.

"Just what do you think you're doing?" Hazel barked in my ear.

I spun to face her, and in the second it took me to take in her expression, I felt shame darken my cheeks. She was smiling at me with nothing more sinister than a greeting in her brown eyes, but before I could recover, I watched her absorb my guilty glance. Hazel looked between me and the man who made me feel pretty, her forehead creased in concentration. Suddenly, something clicked. Her face clouded.

"What are you working on now?" she asked me, her voice forced and unnatural.

"A desk," I said, pushing away from the counter and thrusting my hands deep into the pockets of my coat. "It's an heirloom I picked up at . . ."

But Hazel wandered away mid-sentence. "I need a grain shovel," she said as she stomped toward the back of the store. "The head came off mine this morning."

He hurried to help her, avoiding my gaze as doggedly as I avoided his. We were caught. In the act of doing what? Talking? But we both knew it was more. Even if we never did anything more than convey smiles across the hardware store counter, our interactions were laced with land mines. Slip-ups that could destroy everything. Hazel knew that.

I buttoned up my coat and pulled my gloves from the

pockets. If I hurried, I could make it to the parking lot and be long gone before Hazel ever had a chance to pay for her purchase and confront me. But she must have abandoned her quest for a shovel, because well before I reached my car door, I felt her take me by the arm and spin me around.

"Just what do you think you're doing?"

"Getting supplies," I said, but as soon as the words were out of my mouth I realized that my hands were empty. Snow swirled around my head and I pulled my shoulders up to my ears, trying to stay warm, but also trying to hide from Hazel. She looked ready to flay me.

Hazel leaned into me, and though she was shorter than I was, I couldn't help being cowed by the intensity of her stare. "You listen to me, little girl. You don't . . . I have no idea . . . You can't possibly know . . ." she sputtered, her lips struggling to keep up with whatever was going on inside her head. Finally she squeezed my arm so tight it hurt, and said, "Don't be stupid, Danica Greene. Just don't be stupid."

I never saw him again. Well, once or twice from a distance, but I started getting my supplies at the co-op on the edge of town. And though I nearly died of embarrassment every time I thought of Hazel's confrontation, there was a part of me that was grateful that she had come into the hardware store that day. It was like a slap to the face, an unexpected blow that brought me to my senses. I didn't have any feelings for him. He was an ego-boost. Nothing more.

But while I was secretly grateful for Hazel's intervention with my hardware store fling, I resented her assessment of Benjamin. *I saw the way he looked at you.*

"That's absurd," I told her after my neighbor was long out of sight. "He has been our neighbor since the day we moved in. He's Ell's friend." But that wasn't entirely true. They didn't dislike each other, but they didn't have much in common either. "They respect one another," I amended.

"Good for them," Hazel snapped. "But I have eyes in my head. I know what I saw."

A minute ago, I had been too weary to fight her, but the thought of what she was implying stoked me into a swift rage. I bristled. "What are you saying? Etsell's been gone for a month. Do you think Benjamin . . . Do you think I . . . ?"

Hazel looked startled. "No. No, of course not." She pursed her lips for a moment, considering me. Then she closed the space between us and gave me a clumsy hug, thumping my back with one awkward hand. "That look is reserved for Etsell. It took me by surprise, that's all."

I backed out of her embrace and rubbed my temple with the heel of my hand. "Fine, Hazel, whatever. Look, I'm really tired. I'm going to go lay down for a while, okay? Thanks for stopping by."

It occurred to me that I didn't even know why she had come, but my back was already turned and I simply didn't have the grace to stick around and be polite.

"No problem," Hazel said from behind me. "I understand. But I have something for you and I was wondering if you could spare two minutes to help me unload it from my truck."

She sounded apologetic, but even if she had demanded my help, it would have been hard for me to just walk away. Hazel had something for me? Something that required both of us to move it? I paused, but she had already counted on my cooperation. "It's a bit heavy, but even skinny as you are, I think you can manage it. We don't have to transport it far."

I was already looping back to the driveway when I saw Hazel hop up in the bed of the rusty pickup truck that typically held down a forgotten corner of earth at the airstrip. It belonged to the Blackhawk airport, but Hazel left the keys in the ignition and anyone who needed it could use it for hauling leaves or helping a friend on moving day. The truck wasn't worth much, but it accomplished the job, and as I moved around it to survey Hazel's treasure, I found myself indebted to whoever thought it would be a wise purchase.

"Where did you find that?" I breathed. Upside down in the bed of the pickup was an antique trestle table. It was at least seven feet long and featured two bowed iron supports that were green with age. "Is that a French farmhouse? Is it original?"

"Eighteen sixties, give or take a bit." Hazel looked like she was very pleased with herself. "Or at least that's what the auctioneer said. Now, don't get too excited. Someone took it upon themselves to paint it blue at some point in time, but it's still in really nice condition."

I passed my hand over the flaking paint, heartsick that someone had painted the wood robin's-egg blue. But the tabletop was a single pane—oak, I guessed—and therefore not an imitation trestle made from someone's old floorboards. My chest felt alive with butterflies, living things that rose and fell inside of me in spite of my earlier irritation.

"It's gorgeous," I whispered. "It must have cost you a fortune."

Hazel knocked one of the legs with her fist. "More than I should have paid for it, but much less than it will be worth once you restore it."

"You want me to restore it?" I asked. "Are you going to resell it?"

Hazel wrinkled her lips. "It's yours, Dani. I bought it for you."

I dropped my hand from the table and forced myself to take a step away from the truck. "I can't accept this," I said. "It's too much. Even with the blue paint . . ."

But Hazel was already waving away my protestations. "Too bad. It's a done deal. The table is yours and you'd better do something with it or I'm going to be really ticked."

A shocked gasp choked out of me before I could stop it. "You're serious."

"Of course I'm serious. What would I want with a monstrosity of a table like this?"

It was sobering to hear her say that. What would *I* do with such an enormous table? My situation was no different from hers. I was single—the thought sent a shudder through my bones—and childless. Hazel's husband had died of cancer years ago, but she had children, two grown sons, and grandchildren. Maybe I could finish the table and give it back as a gift. Beautiful as it was, I certainly had no use for it.

Hazel seemed to read my mind. "It's for you," she said simply, cementing the offering between us.

"But . . ." My eyes clouded, and I couldn't finish.

"Don't worry. You'll fill it," Hazel said. She was matter-of-fact. Working at the bungee cords she had used to secure the table to the truck, she said it again, a wish. A prophecy. "You'll find a way to fill it. I'm sure of it."

10

Fidelity

After Dani helped Hazel lift the table off the back of the truck—a daunting endeavor that left them both stiff and aching—they were at a bit of a loss about what to do with it. The long table was far too big to fit into Dani's small kitchen, but it was too valuable to store outside. Hazel looked utterly deflated for a moment, and the expression was so out of place against her harsh features that Dani scrambled to find a solution. In the end, they backed Dani's car out of the detached garage and settled the blue trestle table in there.

First Dani insisted on giving the floor a quick sweep and knocking the latticework of spiderwebs from the corner where the table would sit. It seemed wrong somehow simply to abandon the gorgeous piece of furniture in such a dusty, dingy place. And yet, when they stepped back to survey their handiwork, the table looked as if it had been dozing in that particular sun-drenched corner forever. There was a large window presiding over the table that offered a smudged view of the newly tidied backyard, and a red door off to one side that opened onto the patio. Dani imagined sewing white curtains for the window and buying an oversized sisal rug to cover the broken concrete floor.

She smiled wryly at the thought of eating by herself in a garage-turned-dining room.

"It actually looks kind of nice there," Hazel said, affirming what Dani was already thinking. "That chipped paint goes well with the cracked windowpane."

"At least I won't have to worry about making a mess out here."

Hazel laid her hand on the top of the table and picked at a curling flake of paint with her blunt fingernail. "What are you going to do?"

"Well, I don't think I'll have to strip the paint. Looks like I can sand it off. Then, depending on what I find underneath, I'll decide if I want to restore or refinish." Dani glanced up at Hazel and found the older woman chewing on the inside of her cheek. "Oh," she said. "You weren't talking about the table."

Hazel shook her head.

"I don't know," Dani finally sighed. "I don't know how I can go on like this—not knowing. Doesn't it kill you?"

"Of course it does. But I'm not sure we have much of a choice."

"But what if . . . ?" She let the question hang in the air between them, infusing the space with hope that flickered weakly before it was extinguished by the sobering reality of Etsell's loss.

"He wouldn't want this for you," Hazel said. Her voice rasped but her eyes were gentle.

"What's 'this'?" Dani asked, trying to straighten her shoulders. To appear stronger than she felt.

"This is withdrawal. You haven't returned any of my calls, and your mom said that you hardly look at her when she comes to visit."

"You've been talking to Char?"

"She called me."

Suddenly everything clicked. Dani crossed her arms over her chest and gave Hazel her best defiant glare. "She told you to check up on me, didn't she? You're here on an errand for my mother. Well, guess what? I don't need either of you to babysit me."

Hazel didn't shrivel under Dani's accusation; it seemed to brace her. "Nobody is babysitting you, Danica. In fact, it seems to me that we're doing a pretty good job of leaving you the hell alone. Isn't that what you want?"

"That's exactly what I want."

"So you can do what? Curl up in a corner and die?"

"Maybe that's exactly what I want to do."

Hazel snorted angrily. "That's the most selfish thing I've ever heard. I miss Ell, too, you know. But losing you isn't going to make anything better."

Dani's retort caught in her throat. Hazel was worried about losing her?

"I know this is hard," Hazel said. "I think I've cried more tears over Etsell than I shed for my own husband. But it seems to me we aren't honoring"—she paused—"we aren't honoring his memory if we get bitter."

"I'm not bitter."

"You're getting there."

It was true and Dani knew it. She could feel brittle edges sharpening around the place where Etsell was supposed to be.

"You've got to go back to work." Hazel raised an eyebrow and indicated Dani's disheveled appearance with an irritated flick of her wrist. "You've got to start washing your hair."

A part of Danica was furious, downright livid that Hazel

dared to confront her. To tell her how to live—or how not to live—with Etsell's disappearance. "You have no idea what it's like."

But that wasn't a fair thing to say, and Dani could see the hurt splinter in Hazel's eyes. They were quiet for a minute, each tortured by her own memories and the ghosts of shattered dreams. It was a helpless, anguished feeling to know that the future they had planned was an impossible hope.

"Do you remember that movie," Dani finally asked into the silence, "where the guy is trapped on a deserted island for years? He came back in the end. He came back, and the woman he loved had moved on."

"This isn't a movie," Hazel said.

"I know."

"I don't want . . . ." But it seemed that there were too many ways to finish that particular sentence. Hazel didn't even try. She shook her head, as if trying to dislodge some errant thought, and gave the tabletop a good, hard knock. "Hey, I look forward to seeing what you can do with this." She gave Dani's arm a squeeze as she left.

But Dani didn't even touch the table again for nearly two months.

Instead, she woke up the next morning at six thirty without an alarm clock, and knew deep in her bones that it was time to get up.

Dani showered and dressed in clean clothes. Then she made a pot of coffee and put on makeup while it brewed. A dab of concealer hid the dark lines under her eyes, and a touch of mascara made her look more alert than she felt. After towel-drying her hair and setting it with a few sprays of straightening serum, she surveyed herself in the mirror and decided that a different person was staring back at her.

She didn't look like the woman that Etsell had loved, or the grieving wife who had littered the halls of her empty home. It was disconcerting, but the truth was, she couldn't handle herself anymore. She couldn't stand the waiting and the wishing and the despair. The loneliness. Hazel was right. Her life wasn't some Hollywood movie. She really had only one viable choice: she had to go on.

It had been a month since Dani had given a thought to her shop. Except for her brief visit to fix Kat's hacked hair, La Rue had stood empty all that time, shuttered and sleeping. Now that the world felt slightly less unbalanced beneath her feet, Dani wondered if she even had a business to come back to.

When she stepped over the threshold at five to eight, the very first thing she did was walk straight to the answering machine and delete every message. Dani wanted to make a clean break, to tear off those missing weeks from her history with one decisive rip—even if it left the jagged edge of a raw wound. Maybe no one would call. Maybe they had all given up on her already. Somehow, that thought didn't terrify Dani. Getting back to life as normal wasn't so much a chance to start over as it was a way to forget. To layer days and weeks over the hole in her life until it was buried beneath the high gloss of time. If she had to find other ways to anesthetize herself, she would. But this was as good a place as any to start.

As it turned out, Dani didn't have to worry about people forgetting about her. After wandering around aimlessly for nearly half an hour, she rallied herself and came up with a short list of a few things that she could bring herself to do. She clicked on the Open sign, propped open the door to air out the place, and settled down to clean. But before she had a chance to even finish dusting off the shelves that had grown fur in her absence, the front door squeaked open. Eve, the owner of the bakery next door, bustled in.

"You're back." Eve's smile was tentative, but she hurried to Dani and gave her a quick, enthusiastic hug. "I saw your sign." She hitched a finger over her shoulder to indicate the discreet neon invitation hanging in the window.

Dani nodded. "If I have anything to come back to."

"Oh, you do." Eve's eyes glinted. "Is your morning booked?"

Dani's laugh was brief but genuine. "Not exactly."

"Then you have to squeeze me in. I ran into Kat at the gas station and saw what you did to her. I think I'm ready to go short."

"Don't you have to be at the bakery?"

"Mark's there. He'll manage."

It was hard at first for Dani to settle into the persona that her clients expected of her. The weather, local gossip, and Eve's ongoing complaint about the grocery store's new bakery line were topics of conversation that seemed as complicated to Dani as debating the fine points of foreign policy. But the routine was old and familiar, and her hands worked instinctively. Her mind slowly followed.

As she cut Eve's hair, the phone began to ring. Dani got so sick of running back and forth from the styling station to the front desk that she ended up propping her scheduling book on the counter beside her. Her days began to take a patchwork shape, minutes and hours filling in with work for her hands and people to distract her mind. Her heart.

"I love it," Eve said when Dani was done. Then she tipped her double the amount she usually did, pressing the folded money into her palm and closing her fingers tight around them both. "We miss Etsell so much, honey. But we've missed you too. Welcome back."

July evaporated in a humid haze of mundanity. It was a season of tedium for Dani, of remembering details and forcing herself to function and determinedly placing one foot in front of the other. Because Dani felt obliged to follow Hazel's lead, she did her best to pick up the pieces of her life, but the motions were rote. She considered herself little more than an automaton, a well-oiled machine that was capable of performing her daily routine with almost seamless precision—and with only the occasional hiccup. But it was a two-dimensional life, the existence of a paper doll.

Two weeks after Dani picked herself up, a thunderstorm rolled across the prairie sky and dumped nearly two inches of water on Blackhawk. The day was dark as night and the roads rushed with water that ran gray from the rich topsoil of surrounding fields. It was oppressive to Dani, heavy and thick with the suggestion of things unseen, of power and fear and loss, pinning her to her bed until the storm broke by midafternoon and the sun poked tentative fingers through the clouds.

She didn't go to work that day. Didn't even bother to call her appointments and reschedule. The first few people came and found La Rue locked tight, but word spread quickly and the rest of her clients didn't show up. No one ever mentioned that an entire day had slipped through Dani's hands unnoticed. They simply phoned in later and set new dates for their highlights and perms, their French manicures and foils.

"You're different," Char told her one night over Mexican.

Dani glanced up from her *carne asada* tacos, but she couldn't tell if Char thought different was good or bad. She shrugged, peeled a corner off one of her corn tortillas, and popped it in her mouth. "Does that make you happy?"

"Does that make *you* happy?"

Dani didn't know how to respond. Happy? Was that even a possibility anymore? "I'm fine," she said, so that Char would stop looking at her like that.

But Dani's mother didn't seem impressed by her answer. "Fine?" Char balled her napkin in her fist. "You can't be fine, Danica. I'm fine. Natalie and Kat are fine. You're . . . you're more than fine. You have to be."

"What in the world is that supposed to mean?"

Char's eyes were tortured, her fingers stiff as she worried the paper napkin until bits of fiber and dust crumbled onto her half-eaten plate. She looked haggard, old. Dani wasn't used to seeing her mother fall so tragically short of the sensuous, engaging woman she always tried so hard to portray. Her roots were showing again, and she had applied powder to her cheeks with a heavy hand—there were deep crevices around her eyes where the makeup had caked.

"Mom," Dani said—using a designation she rarely used with Char—"I just lost my husband. I'm a . . ." she was going to say "widow," but the word got stuck in her throat. "I think I'm doing okay, considering."

"But I don't want you to be okay." Char shook her head. "You have to be better than okay. You're the only one who got out intact."

It was the first time Dani ever heard her mother express anything other than a sort of defiant pride for the way their lives had unfolded. Char was the tough single mom who managed to raise three equally tough girls. Girls who weren't drug addicts or incarcerated, but who dealt with their own issues all the same. There was Natalie, who ran away from everything: her family, her past, even men. Kat, who embraced her mother's life because it was all she knew. And Dani had never stopped to wonder where she fit, but looking at her life through Char's eyes, she realized that as the baby of the family, she was also the only one who seemed to escape the sad legacy the Vis girls were doomed to accept. A successful business, a loving husband, surely children on the way. And now where was she? Broken, alone. Just another cog on the wheel of a family that was bound to cycle around, spinning toward ever more heartache.

"It's all right," Dani said, reaching across the table. She took her mother's hand in her own, extracted the ruined paper napkin. There were a dozen things she could have said to ease Char's distress. But they were lies, every one of them. The truth was, Dani didn't know if it would ever be okay; if there would come a day in some far-flung future when she could think of her life with anything other than regret. And yet, it was her job to smooth the way. To brew coffee and make eggs, to clean up the messes her sister made and make sure her mother didn't miss physical therapy when the stilettos she wore aggravated the slipped disk in her back. They needed her. They needed her to live a charmed life. So Dani said the only thing she could force out. "Everything is going to be all right."

It tasted like a lie on her tongue.

Danica

When I was nine, I knew beyond a shadow of a doubt that Emmi was the biggest liar I had ever met.

I had spent most of my childhood taking care of myself, or being half watched by my older sisters. But when Natalie let me burn my hand trying to boil milk for hot chocolate, Char mustered up a little motherly responsibility and secured the services of our elderly next-door neighbor. The first time I went to Emmi's house, my hand was bound too tightly in an Ace bandage, and the throbbing was so intense I was sure I was seeing double—double chins drooping beneath Emmi's crepe-paper cheeks. Double folds of powder-soft skin when she reached out trembling arms to take me from my mother. She looked as if her skin had been loosely draped over a frame too tiny to bear it—as if a stiff wind could fill her up and pull all the wrinkles tight like a breeze shaking out a sail.

"We'll have a lovely afternoon," she said in a voice that sounded like it was a day or two away from wearing out completely. "I've made tea."

Char gave her a grateful smile and squeezed Emmi's bony hand. Then she patted me on the head like I was a lapdog and scooted down the front steps before I could utter a single protest. Of course, this was the last place on earth I wanted to be—babysat by some woman who was old enough to remember the Flood. Though she lived next door, I had seen her only a handful of times, and the scarce sightings I had been afforded did not give me much hope for my new afternoon routine. Emmi used a walker when she left the confines of her run-down home—the only framed house in our little trailer community—and the prominent curve in her back put me in mind of a storybook hag, the sort of witch who haunted dark forests and preyed on unsuspecting little children.

But I suspected. I suspected a lot. And I was careful to keep my eyes wide and my coat on as Emmi closed the door behind us.

The old woman led me wordlessly into her kitchen and offered me a seat at the table by pressing her hand on my shoulder until I dropped into a chair. It creaked beneath my weight and I couldn't help but wonder how long it had been since someone besides Emmi had bellied up to her damask-covered table.

The tablecloth had been recently starched and the curving folds that almost touched my lap were scratchy-stiff. From what I could see, her house was so clean it was almost sterile. The only thing that seemed even slightly out of order was a neat stack of mail in the middle of the round table—crisp, white envelopes addressed in the lovely, indecipherable scrawl of a foreign language and smudged in the very corner by a postage stamp that featured a tiny blue-and-white flag. Other than that, the table was empty save for a porcelain cup that held something dark and tepid.

"Do you like tea?" Emmi asked, indicating the flowered cup. I gave it a sniff and was reminded of the scent my feet kicked up when I went thrashing through the undergrowth near the river.

"Not so much?" There was a smile in her sandpaper voice.

I hazarded a peek and found Emmi regarding me with warm, hazel eyes. They were pale and a little milky, like hot cocoa that needed a good stir. But the way they crinkled in the corners made me think for a moment that maybe my reclusive neighbor was not so frightening as I had first imagined.

As it turned out, Emmi was a ninety-two-year-old sprite, a little girl trapped in a dying woman's body. After the first time, when she met me at the door, Emmi merely hollered from the kitchen when I arrived. I could hear the faint, "Don't just stand there—come in!" through the poorly sealed door. She was always waiting for me, queen of her cushioned chair as she presided over a pot of coffee so dark it was almost espresso. When she learned that I hated tea, she took to making me coffee so hot and stiff I could practically stand a spoon up in it. But she brought down the temperature with ice-cold cream she poured from a yellow-handled pot, and softened the bitter bite with as many sugar cubes as I wanted.

As we drank our coffee, she regaled me with tales from the old country, stories of a childhood in Finland that I knew were far too spectacular to be real. Of Shrove Tuesday and the bonfires of Christmas trees that they would burn on sea ice just off the shore. And trading pussy willows for treats on Easter, partying all night during summer solstice.

The most far-fetched stories were also my favorite, a deliciously inappropriate collection of tales that centered around the wood-fired sauna Emmi's father made with his own hands. She tried to convince me that clothes weren't allowed in the sauna. But I knew that couldn't possibly be true. Nor was it likely that Emmi and her siblings ran from the steam of the little wooden hut to jump in snowbanks as high as my head. She raised her hand to show me how deep, and I took a sip of my coffee so I could hide my disbelief.

For the most part, my afternoons with Emmi were quiet. Sometimes I read to her, but more often than not I did homework while she wrote letters that always began the same way: *Rakas sisko* . . .

It wasn't until I had been going to Emmi's house for over a month that she finally opened more of her home to me. I slumped at the table one afternoon, tired and out of sorts because Char hadn't come home the night before and I had stayed up with one ear pricked toward the door, listening for her. When Emmi put an extra sugar cube in my coffee and asked me what was wrong, I burst into uncharacteristic tears.

"Oh, *kultaseni*," she murmured. She never asked me what was wrong, or even why I was crying, but she fluttered her hands around me until I got to my feet. Then she herded me through the kitchen and down the hallway, past the bathroom to the dark paneled door at the farthest corner of her little house. When she reached past me and turned the knob, my tears dried up as quickly as they had come.

Stepping into Emmi's bedroom was like entering another world. The walls were covered with peeling paper, and the floor was an extension of the same gray carpet that stretched throughout the rest of the house, but I barely noticed those things. Instead, my eyes were riveted to Emmi's bed—or what I assumed was her bed. In the very center of the room there was a piece of furniture the color of black walnuts that rose nearly to the ceiling. Two low steps led up to a high platform that was covered in rich cloth the color of crown jewels. There were side walls on the fairy-tale bed, and an arching top that was adorned with brocade curtains drawn back by knotted gold cords. On the arching frontispiece I could see beautiful curved whorls carved into the glossy wood. The whole thing reminded me of a puppet theater, a glorious, shining absurdity that had been snatched from some ancient dream.

But I hardly had time to take any of this in, because Emmi ushered me across the floor and shooed me into the magnificent bed. She laid her palsied fingers on my cheek, pressing my head on a pillow that smelled of rosewater, then pulled a whisper-soft blanket over me. Her hand was light as a mother's touch on my back, rubbing in a pattern that smoothed me to a deep and dreamless sleep before I could even realize how exhausted I was. I drowned in that bed, comforted in a sanctuary where I felt wholly protected, utterly safe. There was nothing to worry about in Emmi's hiding place.

When I woke, the curtains had been drawn around me and I was secreted away in a niche so magical, I wouldn't have been the least bit surprised if I peeled back the heavy drapes to find a unicorn nosing for clover in Emmi's bedroom.

"Thank you," I told her when I emerged, bleary-eyed and still shaking off the soporific effect of the extraordinary slumber.

Emmi smiled over her letter and motioned to the chair across from her with a flick of her fingers. "I brought that bed with me from Finland. I've been sleeping in it ever since I was a little girl."

"It's beautiful," I said.

"It's a bed for a princess. Only a princess can see the carvings. Did you see them?"

I thought of the swirls on the wood, the intricately worked twists and spirals that were cut in images of doughnuts and biscuits and fat loaves of dark bread.

"Did a baker carve it?" I asked.

"No." She smiled. "No, *prinsessa*."

But that was probably the worst lie Emmi ever told. I was no princess.

⚈

Etsell called me princess too, but he did it only in fun. "Buck up, princess," when he thought I was being a wimp. Or "Don't hurt yourself, princess," if I did something unforgivably clumsy that nearly ended in an emergency room visit. But it never bothered me. What Emmi didn't know about me was that I never wanted to be a princess.

Emmi gifted me with nicknames, a love for coffee, and a safe place to land for almost two years of afternoons while Char was off working an assortment of dead-end jobs. But when Emmi died in her sleep just before I turned eleven, the greatest legacy she left me with was a deep love for her—and a deep love for the bed where she allowed me to find rest.

On the afternoons when she could tell that I needed it, Emmi would take me to the bedroom and let me crawl into her bed. Sometimes I would sleep, but sometimes I would lie in the slanted light from her wooden blinds and watch the way it cast shadows on the smooth carvings in the wood. I thought about the hands that made it, the tools that he must have wielded as he translated pictures from his mind to the wood grain of the bed that he so obviously adored. Why else would he cut with such grace? Such tenderness?

I wanted the bed, but I knew that I would never get it. Emmi had a *sisko* in Finland, and a niece who had moved to New York to go to college. A generation had passed, and now there were great-nieces and -nephews and even great-great relatives that polka-dotted a map of the United States. They had never come to visit Emmi in the time that I knew her, but someone came for her treasures all the same. It was a woman about Char's age with creamy skin and eyes like Emmi's, and she ignored me when I said hello.

Of course I mourned Emmi. But I mourned her bed too. The comfort it was, and the history. The life that it encompassed, all the many things and places it had seen. I thought of it often when I lay in my own bed at night, and sometimes when I caught my knee on the exposed metal corner, I would curse the machine that made my frame in a factory. It seemed wrong to me that something I lived so much life in could be made by a taciturn, impersonal piece of machinery.

It was no wonder I fell in love with restoration, with old relics of forgotten furniture that other people resigned to the junkyard. I loved mending what was broken. Taking something that had been cast aside and making it new.

I thought of Emmi when I finally worked up the courage to go back to the garage in the beginning of August. It had been almost three months, twelve weeks to the day, since my telephone had rung with the sound of my world falling apart. I still felt like it was lying in pieces around me, but the debris of my life was something I merely ignored. Something I trampled underfoot every single morning when I got up to go on as normal, to face the routine of my days with none of the passion I had known before.

If left to my own devices, I would have never changed a thing. I would have kept doing exactly what I was doing—living a shadow life. But Char worried about me. She cried, which was something I had rarely seen her do in the quarter century I had known her as my mother. It was horrifying. Thankfully, Kat swung the opposite way in her concern and did her level best to regale me with stories and glitter that more often than not left me a little queasy for my sister. She was all punch and laughter, hard drinks and distraction.

And my family members weren't the only ones who took it upon themselves to make sure I did more than mope my life away. Benjamin came by once a week to drag me outside with his subtle implications and force me to put my hands in the earth while he mowed the lawn. Worst of all was Hazel. After she gave me the trestle table, she never mentioned it again. But whenever I saw her, whenever she stopped by my house or bumped into me around town, I couldn't shake the feeling that she was looking over my shoulder. That she expected something of me that I had not yet accomplished. Her disappointment was almost palpable.

She would have been dismayed by the weeks of dust that had accumulated on the antique table. I resolved never to tell her how long it took me to fully inspect her gift as I ran my finger in the grit, tracing letters at random. Or, at least I thought I was writing at random. It wasn't until I stepped back that I realized I had spelled out my name. My full name—Danica Reese Greene—as if I were claiming the huge trestle as my own.

It seemed a birthright of sorts, the table. A heritage that had come hard-earned on the back of my husband's disappearance and my own apparent loneliness. I procured it through my suffering, just as the shortcomings of my childhood earned me a spot in Emmi's chimera bed. A part of me wanted to walk away from it again, to ignore the fumbling ministrations of the people who hated to see me hollow. But it was a beautiful table.

I could imagine what might have been. Etsell working beside me, laughing as I agonized over the process of purification. The way he would look at me across the long, flat board, and the bench that he would make with his own two hands while I stained the wood a color to perfectly match the original finish. I could see us around it, Etsell and me, and the contours of a family that would never be—mere shadows of a longing that I couldn't even begin to articulate.

It was excruciating to lift my hand to the surface of the table, to push away the dust and examine what lay beneath. My fingertips trembled. But it wasn't entirely the result of my diffidence.

I was no princess, and I would never know a happily ever after. And yet there was satisfaction in this. A certain quiet joy that could be found in reclamation.

In resurrecting the lost.

11

These Days

"Tell me again why you're doing this." Kat leaned back on the old steamer trunk and tucked her legs beneath her so that she was sitting cross-legged. Then she situated a cardboard bucket of popcorn chicken in the pretzel of her calves, and took a long drag on the straw of her jumbo-sized Mountain Dew. "You've got to explain it again, 'cause I can't imagine what you're going to do with that thing."

"It's a table," Dani smirked. "Strange as it sounds, I intend to eat off it."

"But where are you going to put it? It won't fit in your house."

"Maybe I'll leave it here."

"In the garage? Don't invite me over."

Dani didn't look up from her sanding. "I didn't."

"Ouch!" Kat's mouth was full of fried chicken, but she talked around it. "I'm keeping you company, Sis. What would you do without me?"

"I might finish sanding this table." Dani straightened up, wiping her hands together to get rid of the fine film of sawdust and flakes of paint. The top of the trestle table was nearly bare, and it gave her an unparalleled thrill to see the original honey-colored veneer shine through. It was a warm, beautiful color, but she could tell that it would need to be stripped and refinished. Too much wear and tear—and a double coat of obnoxious, undoubtedly lead-based paint—had caused it to fade and lift off in places. She had her work cut out for her, and Dani secretly wondered if she should pass the job off to someone else—someone more qualified to work with such a special piece.

The only thing of any value that Dani had ever restored was an antique secretary's desk with arching legs that had been lathed in twists like sheaves of winter wheat. It was a painstaking process, made all the more tedious by the fact that each carved groove required special attention. Since she didn't have the proper tools, Dani ended up digging a slim nutcracker pick from her messy utensils drawer and using the sharp side to clean each running furrow. By the time she was done, her hands were cracked and raw, and she was sure she needed glasses to correct the squint she had developed. But the table fetched a nice price, and Dani used the money she earned to splurge on a long weekend in Minneapolis with Etsell. It was a second honeymoon of sorts.

Romantic trips and extra cash were the last thing on Dani's mind when she laid the first sheet of sandpaper against the trestle table. This project had an entirely different feel, an undeniable weight because it was the first restoration she attempted *after*. After her trek to Alaska.

After Ell.

As she buffed away the blue paint, rubbing her hand in tiny, light sweeps that left loops of sawdust on the wood, Dani allowed herself to think about all of it. Of the abrupt way that Etsell left and the fears she nursed while he was gone. Then Blair's telephone call and her subsequent exodus to a part of the world she never thought she would see. And finally the slow beat of her days without, the gentle plodding of her life that continued as steady as the tick of a metronome. It wasn't what she wanted. It was so, so far from what she wanted.

But though Dani wished she were finishing the table for a family—for the eventual return of her husband, who wasn't gone, only missing—she couldn't force herself to hope anymore. She didn't have the strength. Instead, with each minute arabesque her hand made over the wood, she polished away the chaff of a shattered life. It was impossible to see what was to come, impossible even to wonder at what she wished for, but there was a sense of starting over in each simple action. Of erasing all that had come before. Or at least, trying to.

That very first night, Danica worked until the moon glowed outside the garage window. It was full and firm, a golden fruit that she could have plucked and placed like an offering in the center of her table—a feast for herself and no one else, for who was there to share it with?

When Kat slipped into the garage after Dani had logged a week's worth of spare time on the table, Dani complained, but it was a facade that she knew Kat would see through immediately. It was obvious even to Dani that the ambitious project had her in a melancholy grip, and so Kat hunkered down with her gas station supper and parried her sister's barbed remarks with amiable sass.

"You should sell it," Kat said. "Paint it black and distress it. That's all the rage, you know."

"Black?" Dani threw a tack rag at her sister. It hit her square in the chest. "Are you kidding me? I would never defile this table by painting it black."

Kat laughed. "Defile? Did you just use the word *defile* in reference to a piece of furniture? I suppose the people who painted it blue *ravished* it. . . ."

Dani rolled her eyes. "I never asked for your opinion."

"It comes free with the company." Kat held out the bucket of chicken. "Have you had anything to eat? I swear, you look skinnier every day. If you keep losing weight I won't be able to borrow your clothes anymore."

"My clothes aren't your style," Dani muttered, but she brushed her hands against her jeans and grabbed a handful of chicken pieces from the bucket. "I can't believe you eat this stuff."

"Deep-fried." Kat winked, popping a piece into her mouth. "As long as I've got the metabolism, I'm going to make the most of it. Apparently it'll all go to crap when I hit thirty anyway."

Dani maneuvered to the opposite side of the steamer trunk and sat next to her sister. They surveyed her handiwork in silence for a few moments, taking in the little piles of blue sawdust and the flat, long plank of wood that had supported well over a century of plates and bowls and elbows. It had undoubtedly seen feast, and famine. Days when the wood seemed bowed by the heft of plenty and the dreams of generations gathered around it. And maybe someone had laid her head on that table and cried. Someone other than Dani.

"It's pretty, isn't it?" she asked. She tried not to sound so needy, but her voice was pleading.

"It's beyond pretty," Kat said. "It's gorgeous. Even half-done and speckled blue." She leaned into Dani, bumped her shoulder conspiratorially. "I think it's good for you to have something to do."

"I have lots to do. I've been working overtime at the salon, and there's so much to take care of around the house. . . ." She trailed off, aware that she was toeing the very edge of an abyss filled with all the grief she tried to keep buried. The house, the yard, the bills, the random letters that came cheerfully addressed to a man who would never receive them . . . there were a hundred reminders every day of her loss.

"But this is different," Kat said, indicating the table. "You love doing it. Your face looks different when you're working on it."

Dani didn't know what to do with that statement. Everyone kept nagging her about changing, and she was getting sick of it. But before she could allow Kat's comment to depress her, Kat stuck her tongue between her teeth in parody and scrunched up her eyes.

"This is your look when you're thinking. And this"—she exaggerated the expression, crinkling up her nose and rounding her shoulders—"is what you look like when you're working on the table. Different looks entirely. I hardly recognize you."

"You can be so obnoxious."

"Oh, I'm so much more than that."

Dani heaved a weary sigh and tossed her uneaten popcorn chicken back in the bucket.

"Hey!" Kat complained. But she plucked another piece out anyway.

The sound of a car outside made them both look up. Danica lived on a quiet corner and the thrum of an engine so close could only mean that it was pulling into her driveway. A moment later there was the heavy thud of a car door being shut and a slow volley of footsteps on concrete.

"Heels." Danica guessed. "Must be Char." She turned back to the table, angling the yellow work lamp that she had dragged from the shed to illuminate an untouched corner. Dropping to her haunches, she laid her hand against the angle, moving the sandpaper over the thick veneer of paint with the greatest care.

"You're off early," Dani said when a figure filled the doorway. The overhead garage door was shut because the wind was whipping up a dust storm outside, but the little side door was propped open with a rock. Dani hadn't realized how much she appreciated the airflow until it was blocked. "My fridge is empty, but Kat's got chicken."

"I already ate."

Dani froze. The voice was not Char's, but it was almost painfully familiar in spite of how little she actually heard it. "Natalie?"

"Hey, stranger."

It was shocking how quickly those two innocuous words disarmed Dani. The sandpaper in her hand fluttered to the floor, and she stood slowly, half afraid that if she moved too quickly the woman across the room would disappear into thin air. But there Natalie was, little changed from the last time Dani had seen her, and yet downright startling in the mere fact that she was standing there—neat and trim as always, and looking like she had stepped off the page from the Work Casual section of a J. Jill catalog and straight into Dani's crumbling world.

Natalie smiled a little, and raised one slender hand to tuck her chestnut hair behind her ear. It wasn't a self-conscious gesture; instead it had a calculated feel: Natalie perceived something out of place and promptly took care of it in the most efficient manner possible. "It's nice to see you, Danica."

Nice to see you? After all that she had been through? But it didn't really matter what Natalie said. A sob tore from Dani before she could stop it, and then she was stumbling across the floor, reaching for her big sister.

Dani clung to Natalie, ignoring the fact that her sister was rather rigid and unresponsive. Four years separated them, but as far as Dani was concerned, it could have been a decade.

More. Natalie was stable and wise and unflappable. She filled a part of the gaping hole where a strong and level-headed mother was supposed to be. Char and Kat and even Hazel all took their own part, but Dani hadn't realized how much she missed Natalie until she was hanging on to her for dear life.

"He's gone!" Dani choked, the cry coming from so deep inside it left her feeling eviscerated. "He left me, and he's not coming back!"

"Shhh," Natalie murmured awkwardly. She patted Dani's back once or twice, then tried to pull away. But something inside Dani had split open, a ripe fruit rending its flesh, and she couldn't let go.

"I can't do it! I can't do it alone!"

Dani's tears spiraled out of control so quickly, it was as if she was being sucked down a dark drain. When the balance tipped and Dani began to hyperventilate, Natalie steered her toward the chest and waved Kat out of the way. Dani's sisters each took one of her arms and lowered her to the improvised bench.

"Come on," Natalie said. "Get a grip, Dani. You're not going to solve anything by sobbing about it."

Dani looked up sharply. "I'm not trying to solve anything," she gasped. "I'm grieving!"

Kat elbowed Natalie out of the way and took Dani's face in her hands. She wiped her sister's tears with her thumbs, a tender gesture that seemed incongruent with her words. "Ignore that cold bitch," Kat said. "You can cry your heart out if you want to. I think it's good for you."

"Sure." Natalie snorted. "All she needs is a good cry. That'll make everything better."

"She lost her husband!" Kat was on her feet in less than a second, finger in Natalie's face as implacable as a weapon. "She can cry if she wants to! Besides, I'm not sure you have a right to determine how she mourns. It's not like you've been here—"

"It's not like I had a choice." Natalie's blue eyes glinted like ice. Leaving Blackhawk had come with a very steep price, and though she had earned more than her fair share of scholarships and grants for undergrad and beyond, she was up to her eyeballs in debt. Kat knew that. Everyone knew that. And everyone knew that it was a source of deep and quiet shame. Natalie raised her chin a little and glared at her sister. "I taught two classes this summer—classes I couldn't get out of. Classes I had to finish—"

"Classes you had to finish because your degree is more important than your family. Etsell was your brother."

"In-law."

"As if that makes a difference!"

"You think this isn't affecting me? You think I haven't agonized over this—"

"Oh, I'm sure." Kat glared. "I'm sure this has been hard for you. I can't imagine how you're coping."

"And what have you done?" Natalie flung an arm in the direction of the bucket of chicken. "Fed her junk food? Thrown her pity parties? Gotten her drunk? Really helpful, Kat."

"Nice. I love how you just assume the worst of me. It's always like that with you. Kat's the bad girl. Kat couldn't possibly do anything right."

"Well, there's certainly a precedent."

Dani didn't realize that the iron band around her chest had sprung loose until a giggle escaped her lips. She put a hand to her mouth, pressing back both the tears and the snicker that seemed so out of place as she watched her sisters turn their attention to the source of their argument. "Some things never change," Dani whispered.

"Looks like you're feeling better." Natalie smoothed her

khaki skirt and arranged her shoulders as if shrugging off the residue of the angry words she had exchanged with Kat. "I'm sorry if I surprised you."

"It's a nice surprise," Dani managed, taking a shaky breath. "I'm glad to see you. And I'm sorry if I ruined your shirt." She nodded at the damp spot on Natalie's shoulder, the place where her tears had wet the white linen of her sister's crisp blouse.

Natalie sighed. "No problem."

Kat glanced between the two of them, a frown creasing her forehead. It seemed that all was forgiven and forgotten, but Kat wasn't quite ready to let go. "If I had known that you were going to be such a bag . . ." she muttered, trailing off.

"You knew about this?" Dani asked. "You knew that Natalie was coming and you didn't tell me?"

Kat zipped her thumb and forefinger across her lips, then threw away the imaginary key. Her pantomime said that she kept a good secret, but her eyes revealed that she regretted it. "You were supposed to be happy. Not dissolve in tears."

"Sorry to disappoint."

"Don't be ridiculous," Natalie said, effectively taking the reins. She turned her head a little so that her chin-length hair fell back from her face. "I would have come sooner if I could. But now that I'm here, I don't want to waste time arguing."

"Right." Kat bent and rescued her bucket of popcorn chicken from the floor. "I'll see you soon, Dani. Natalie, welcome home." She didn't sound very sincere.

Dani thought about calling her back, asking her to stay so that the three of them could spend some time together, but she knew that her sisters functioned better when they saw less of each other. Later, she told herself. After I've had Natalie to myself for a while. She watched wordlessly as Kat slipped out of the garage.

"It really is good to see you," Dani said when Kat was gone.

"You too." Natalie's smile was thin but genuine. "And I want to hear everything. But first I need to work out the kinks from flying all day. I'm dying for a run."

"You still run?"

"Every day. Don't you?"

Dani couldn't remember the last time. "It's been a while."

"Well, sounds to me like you could use a little direction. A few good disciplines. Let's get changed; you're coming with me."

"I am?"

"I'll take it easy on you."

Going for a late-night run sounded like a mild form of torture, but Dani followed her sister obediently. Natalie made benign small talk as she lifted her suitcase out of the trunk of the rental car. Then she led the way into Dani's house as if she owned the place. When she disappeared down the hallway in the direction of the spare room, Dani knew she should have felt annoyed. The last thing she needed was her big sister bossing her around.

But for some reason, it was exactly what she wanted.

Danica

Char used to say that Natalie was born prickly, all elbows and knees, angles and corners that made her hard to get close to even as a baby. She didn't like to cuddle, and instead of squalling like other infants, she would fix Char with a peeved little stare when she was hungry—a look so condescending and so mature beyond her years, Char loved to tell people that the somber child frightened her. When I was old enough to wonder at the strange relationship between my mother and her eldest, I found myself taking turns blaming Natalie's personality flaws on nature and nurture. The pendulum swung one way and I was convinced my sister was indeed born perspicacious, and then it tilted back and I knew my mother had shaped her as surely as hands form clay.

But whatever twist of fate blessed my mother with a child as different from her as night is from day, growing up in the long shadow of Char's irresponsibility, I came to love Natalie's immutable strength. And never did I appreciate it more than the day I split open my chin.

I was six years old when Char's boyfriend of the week invited us to Wild Water West in Sioux Falls. The brochure promised water slides, a wave pool, and a lazy river that looked to me like something straight out of a summertime dream—waterfalls and kids pink-cheeked with laughter and big rubber tubes the color of cartoon ducklings. I couldn't have imagined a destination more awe-inspiring, and even though I hated Maxwell, the grinning idiot who drove a gold SUV and called my mom "baby," I thought of nothing but our water park excursion for days before the red-circled date on the calendar.

When we finally pulled into the jam-packed parking lot and joined the hundreds of people already crowding the turnstiles, I didn't even mind that it was free admission day. Or that I would have to wait in line for a half hour to take one slow spin down the curving water slide. Or even that we had to spread our towels on the hard-packed dirt ground near the chain-link fence because all the loungers were taken. But it was a good thing I didn't know that long before I ever dipped one little toe in the water of the slide, I would be pushed from behind by a group of rowdy teenage boys and fall face-first onto the concrete steps of the giant tower.

I don't remember if I cried out or not. It was over so quickly, and my heart was pumping so much adrenaline, that I didn't realize I was bleeding until Kat screamed. And it wasn't until I brushed a finger against the spot where the line of my jawbone had split a deep ridge in my chin that I felt the first blinding stab of pain. After that I could hardly stand. A lifeguard had to carry me back to the spot where we had left Char and Maxwell tanning.

The emergency room was ice cold, and I shivered in my white terry cover-up, trying not to notice the way blood had made a crimson flower bloom on the puckered bodice. Char was apologizing to Maxwell, and Kat was crying softly, but while I trembled in the plastic seat and tried not to pass out from the throbbing that had spread all the way to my temples, Natalie stood beside me and held her balled-up T-shirt against my chin. She wasn't the sort to offer words of comfort, but it was enough that she was there.

I don't know when I started singing or why, but at some point as we waited I began to whisper the words to "Jesus Loves Me." We went to church because Char thought it was an admirable thing to do, a way maybe to atone for all the ways she had screwed up. At the very least, our somewhat sporadic attendance provided a way for her to feel like we were covering all our bases. But she also religiously read her horoscope in the Sunday paper—just to make sure that everything evened out.

Though Natalie and Kat merely tolerated church, I actually liked it. But then, I didn't have to sit through the entire, boring service. Just before the stern-looking pastor took his place behind an equally imposing dais, the kids in first grade and younger were ushered out by a group of dewy teenagers who brought us to the Sunday-school rooms for our own version of church. We sat on carpet squares and lit a candle when the Bible story was read. Then there was singing and a time of solemn prayer when we all held hands and recited one-line supplications like, "Please be with Cameron's aunt Ethel." It was all a bit baffling, but I loved the songs.

And for some reason as I sat in the emergency room waiting my turn, "Jesus Loves Me" slipped out. I wasn't even sure that I had the words right, but when the song was over I sang it again. And again. And again. No one stopped me. In fact, no one so much as breathed a word about it until the homeless-looking man who was slumped across from me half lurched out of his seat and shouted, "Shut up!"

He was dressed in a shabby sport coat that smelled of mothballs and urine, and his hair hung in greasy hanks halfway down his back. His bushy gray eyebrows were downright terrifying, and it was only when he screamed at me—a sudden, furious explosion from less than six feet away—that I began to cry.

I wasn't wailing or anything, but my muted sniffling only made him angrier. "Shut up!" he bellowed again. "Shut up! Shut up!"

The poor man was probably hungover and my song was like a stab to the brain. But Natalie wasn't feeling an ounce of forbearance. I could sense it in the way she tensed beside me, in the thick aura of indignation that emanated from her and filled the small waiting room with static. "Keep singing," she told me, though I couldn't have squeaked out another note if my life depended on it. "Keep singing," she hissed again, and that only made me cry harder.

When the hobo across the narrow aisle leaned forward to yell yet again, Natalie erased the distance between us in the blink of an eye. She was ten, far too old for the sort of impulses that usually got me and Kat in trouble, and not the sort to act rashly in any situation. But as she pulled back her leg, I could see the determination swathed across her shoulders like a scarlet mantle. I felt a rush of deep tenderness for my sister, a firm understanding that though she may not be affectionate, she was bound to me by blood.

And then she kicked him in the shin with every ounce of strength her little-girl body could muster.

I got six stitches that day, a thin line of careful crosses that would mark the place where I had fallen for the rest of my life. But the pink crescent was never a reminder of our failed trip to Wild Water West or even of the man who shouted at a little girl in an emergency room. From then on, my scar was a testament to the loyalty of my sister. And the sound of her toe cracking against that stranger's shinbone was Natalie's version of *I love you.*

Etsell adored my scar. He traced it with his fingertips or brushed his bottom lip against it in a prelude to a kiss. The doctor who stitched me up told Char that I would likely need plastic surgery, that as I grew the scar would scale my cheek like a mountain climber and leave an ugly, puckered path. But it didn't. Instead, the small ridge of cicatrix tucked itself neatly below my jawline, a hidden imperfection that was visible only to someone who had reason to tip back my head or touch the spot where the evidence of my childhood injury was secreted away.

It was sensitive, always, and when Etsell would trail a knuckle along the contours of my face, I would hold myself very still and wait for the moment when he skimmed over the scar. I'm sure the nerves were damaged, possibly even severed completely and capable of sending only scrambled messages through the delicate filaments of my nervous system. But the slight tingle was a reminder to me, a lodestone that pointed like a compass back to where I began. Back to the place where I was a little girl in the middle of a storm I couldn't hope to understand.

As I ran now beside Natalie, trying to keep pace with her shorter but unimaginably stronger legs, I felt that same strange pull, that magnetic thrum that seemed tuned to evoke every mixed emotion of my youth. Love and fear and hope and regret all mingled together in a past that felt almost preternaturally concocted to prepare me for this day—for these days alone, these days between. The only difference was, back then I believed that I would find my way out. And I had. I just didn't know if I would be so blessed a second time.

"All the way to the top?" Natalie asked when we rounded

the final corner through the twisting labyrinth of the state park. It was a route we had jogged dozens of times when we were both in cross-country the one year we overlapped in high school. I had taken up the sport only because Natalie was a cross-country star and I could tell she wanted me to follow in her footsteps. I quit the year she left for college.

"Sure," I huffed. "Why not?" I had managed the three-mile run through the hills above the river without collapsing. What was another seventy-five steps?

The lookout tower rose above us in the shadows, an angular steeple that gleamed in the light of a full moon. During the day we would have been able to see into three states— Iowa, Minnesota, and South Dakota—but the only thing the climb would afford us tonight would be a spectacular view of a starry sky. I wished for a moment that the moon was waning, but we wouldn't have come this far if the light hadn't allowed us to leave the road.

Natalie hit the bottom step at a jog, but before she rounded the first corner, she had slowed to a steady pace. I counted the steps on my way up—fifteen per flight, five stories in all—just the way I had every time before. If I reached my hand out on step sixty-two and pressed my fingers into the support beam at eye level, I could feel the place where Etsell had carved our initials in the weathered wood. E loves D. It could have been anyone, Ellen loves David or Eric loves Danielle, but I was there when he took his pocketknife and added our legacy to the thousands of others that decorated the tower with declarations of forever. It was indelible for me, an emblem on the wood as permanent as the scar on my chin.

But as I followed Natalie up the winding path, I kept my hands by my sides. I didn't want to feel the grooves that traced his profession of love as deeply as an oath. A broken promise.

"I forgot how hard it is to run in this humidity," Natalie said when I finally joined her at the apex. I was comforted to hear the slight wheeze in her voice.

"It's not humid in New York?"

"Not like this. Nothing is like this."

"That sounds like an indictment," I said, putting my forearms on the railing as if to get a better view of the stars. All I really wanted was to catch my breath.

Natalie leaned on the railing beside me and threw her head back. "It is. I hate it here."

"Why?" I had asked her that question more times than I could remember, but her answers were always vague. I didn't expect anything different now.

But she surprised me. "Because I have a lot of bad memories."

"Of what?" I asked, stunned. "I know Char wasn't always the most present mother, but—"

Natalie's unattractive snort drew me up short. "Char was a terrible mother," she said. "Wait, Char *is* a terrible mother. You know that, don't you? That we grew up different from most kids?"

"Well, yeah, but . . ."

"But nothing, Danica. You were little. We tried to protect you as much as we could—and I guess we succeeded. But for Kat and me, growing up a Vis girl was far from easy."

The moonlight was casting pearls on Natalie's face, highlighting the tip of her nose, the crest of each cheekbone, the place where she would have had a small dimple if she ever smiled big enough to crease it. Her eyes were hard as stones in the otherworldly light, smooth and reflective like pools of dark water where the spitfire of distant stars fizzled and sank. Suddenly I felt like I was standing next to a stranger.

"Char tries," I said haltingly. "I know she's far from perfect, but she loves us, Natalie. She tries."

My sister pushed a hard breath through her nose. "Char has grown up. We all have. But if you could rewind the clock twenty years, you'd understand."

"What's that supposed to mean?"

"Did you know my specialty is sociology of women? Particularly victim advocacy and abuse awareness?"

I was grateful that it was too dark for Natalie to see me rolling my eyes. "Are you trying to tell me Char abused you?"

"Not directly."

All at once my blood turned to ice. "Are you trying to tell me *someone* abused you? One of her boyfriends or—?"

"Your definition is too narrow," Natalie cut in before I could rush to more damaging conclusions. "Traditionally speaking, we were all neglected to varying degrees. But there was also a constant parade of people in and out of our home that inflicted different forms of verbal, psychological, and even physical abuse."

"What are you talking about?"

"Were you ever spanked by one of Char's boyfriends?"

I didn't have to think hard to answer that question with a resounding no. But once I dwelled on it for a minute I realized that I had a very vivid memory of someone slapping Kat. I didn't remember who he was, but I could hear Kat cuss at the man on our couch and feel the back of his hand as if he had whipped it across my own cheek. She had swept me out of the house, assuring me that it didn't hurt, that he had only grazed her. But even then I knew better.

"I'm sorry," I said, because I didn't know what else to say. "I'm so sorry. I always thought that I took care of you. . . . The cooking and the cleaning . . ."

"You did," Natalie assured me, placing a hand on my

shoulder for the span of a split second. She removed it before visions of tight-knit, gossipy sisters could dance in my head. "We all took care of each other in different ways."

We were quiet for several minutes, lost in our own thoughts or maybe trying not to think. I felt we had bridged some immeasurable gap, some chasm that had separated us for years. But in spite of the tenuous connection, I didn't feel any closer to Natalie.

"I understand why you left," I finally said. "I don't blame you for going."

"I understand why you stayed," she countered. "And, Danica? I'm so sorry about Ell."

The sound of his nickname on her lips made my throat seize. "Oh, God," I breathed. "You have no idea, Natalie. How much I miss him . . . How much I failed him . . ." I wanted her to console me, to say that I hadn't failed my husband. But Natalie wasn't given to meaningless sentimentality.

"What do you mean?" she asked.

I swallowed, wondered for a moment if I could tell her about the weight that threatened to bury me beneath a lifetime of remorse and insufficiency. But before I could consider the implications for too long, it all started to come out. "Everybody thought we were the perfect couple," I said. "But nothing was perfect. We fought, we were cruel to each other in small, everyday ways. . . . I was so selfish. So absorbed with what I wanted and so willing to ignore the man that I promised to love forever. I don't even know where to start," I almost shrieked, vertiginous from the climb or the trickle of truth, I couldn't tell.

"Start at the beginning," Natalie said.

So I did. "It started so small," I breathed. "It was easy in the beginning to put him first, to think about us instead of me. But then he wanted kids and I wasn't ready, so I told him I stopped taking my birth control even though I didn't. And then we'd go days without touching and I didn't think anything of it. When he had a chance to live his dream, I resented it. I let him go but it was so grudging. . . ." I didn't realize I was mangling the railing until I could feel splinters in the old wood pierce my skin. "No wonder he left," I choked out. "No wonder I lost him."

"Is that all?" Natalie asked. "For heaven's sake, you've just described every relationship under the sun. We're selfish, miserable people. It's a wonder we exist in relationship at all."

I blinked at my sister, trying to comprehend why she was belittling my confession.

"Seriously, Danica. That's what we do—fail each other; put ourselves first. It's the human condition." Natalie sighed a little. "Etsell knew you loved him. You loved each other better than anyone I've ever known. You didn't fail him."

I knew she was wrong, but somehow my shortcomings didn't seem quite as terrible as they had felt only minutes before.

"We fail each other," Natalie repeated. "Every day in a million different ways."

She meant it as an accusation, proof that the world was a dark and lonely place populated by people whose greatest ambition was to look out for number one. But for some reason in the glow of the moon with my sister beside me I didn't see it that way.

I saw how Etsell cared for his dad in spite of his sickness, and how Kat still laughed with Char about the little things. I thought about my husband and all he did to hurt me—intentional and accidental—and I realized that even now I loved him so fiercely it took my breath away. And Natalie, who had left me to grieve for nearly an entire summer without the balm of her presence, had once avenged me with a well-timed kick. My cynical, fatalistic sister was here. Didn't that say something? She didn't have to come, but she did.

Natalie was right: We fail each other. But sometimes we come through for one another. Sometimes we forgive.

12

Gravity Fades

Natalie acted as if her trip to Iowa—the first in almost three years—was a huge inconvenience. But Dani was convinced of her sister's love, even if Natalie couldn't bring herself to say it and didn't know how to show it. What Dani thought would be a quick, weekend visit expanded into a monthlong stay. At first Natalie talked a lot about her upcoming residency and the research grant that her team had been given for a two-year field study on the effect of domestic violence in immigrant populations. But it wasn't slated to begin until the middle of September, and as the days wore on, Natalie simply stayed.

The first few nights she slept at Dani's house, but Kat kept showing up and then slinking away when she found Natalie sleeping on the couch. So one morning, Natalie got up and moved her things back into Char's trailer, and without so much as discussing the arrangement, Kat packed up her stuff, too, and established a more permanent camp at Dani's.

"I don't know how I feel about this," Dani said as she watched Kat hang a few of her more dressy shirts in the hall closet. "You never asked me if you could move in."

"Is that what you think I'm doing?" Kat laughed. "If only you were so lucky. I'm not moving in, I'm squatting. Just for a little while. Just while Natalie is here."

"How long is she staying?"

"Beats me." Kat shut the closet door with a flourish and spun to face Dani. She was grinning.

"You love it!" Dani said. "You're thrilled that Natalie is back. Here I thought it would drive you nuts. You two are regularly at each other's throats."

"I guess absence makes the heart grow fonder. She's still a pain in the ass, but I kind of missed her."

Dani dropped her jaw in exaggerated shock. "Did you just admit that you miss Natalie?"

"Everyone needs a reality check now and then. Life can't be all sunshine and roses. Our big sister is a good reminder of that."

"Whatever." Dani slid her feet into a pair of sandals and let herself out the front door. Just before the screen slammed she called, "You just like to fight."

Kat's laughter trailed her all the way to the garage.

Sunday nights became an impromptu gathering time. It started with Char making an uncharacteristic declaration that they should take advantage of Natalie's extended visit—it would be gone in the blink of an eye. They needed to spend some time together. Family time. At first Dani balked at it, but it was like trying to hold back the pull of the tide. The Vis girls were nothing if not strong-headed, and even Dani's stubbornness didn't stand a chance against the eclipse of Char, Natalie, and Kat all aligned with the same fierce vision.

In the end, Dani had to admit that there was something undeniably sweet about having everyone in the same room.

Of course, the effect was laced with bitterness, too, for the one person who meant more to her than anyone in the world was conspicuously absent. But somehow the contours of Etsell's memory were sharpened by the women in the room. Each woman carried different tokens of Ell, distinct talismans that they brought with them even if they didn't realize they were pocketing memories like pieces of gold.

Dani could feel her husband in the empty space, in the silences between words and the glances they exchanged when they thought she wasn't looking. They were holding her up, Dani knew that. Just as she had once imagined them flanking Ell—the women in his life shoring him up against a past he'd rather forget and a future he couldn't quite bring into focus—they stood shoulder to shoulder and supported the quiet weight of her grief.

Not that they ever really spoke about it. Instead Natalie bored them with talk of her upcoming research project, and Kat spread local gossip like a thick layer of jam on toast. Char said ridiculous things, made inane observations that she obviously thought were poignant but that were actually ill-timed and, more often than not, meaningless. They grated against Dani, particles of sand that scraped her skin and left her feeling flushed and irritated, but it was obvious that Char was doing everything she could to be a help—to be a mother. It was simply a role she had never gotten good at playing. Dani tried not to hold it against her.

They played canasta around the kitchen table, Dani paired with Kat and Natalie endured Char because that was the only way that they could team up and maintain a fragile peace. Sometimes Dani set out bowls of chips and Chex Mix, and sometimes they ordered a pizza—half supreme and half cheese—and laughed at Kat as she picked off the green olives and ate them with her fingers.

The night Hazel joined them was also the night that Benjamin poked his head in the back door. It seemed odd that they would both stumble into the kitchen within a half hour of each other, serendipitous somehow, because the game had been interrupted when Hazel showed up and it could not go on until the numbers were even again.

Hazel had stopped by with a pair of mismatched chairs, two high-backed relics that she thought would go nicely with the trestle table.

"You could paint them different colors. I think I've seen that in a magazine before," Hazel offered. "It would be eclectic."

"Thanks." Dani smiled. One of the chairs was a stern-looking ladder chair with a flat seat and right angles that were downright puritan in their severity. The other chair arched gracefully, a Queen Anne replica with armrests and moth-eaten fabric on the seat that would have to be replaced. The fabric was rose, the wood a faded ruby, a feminine confection that seemed almost indecent next to the more masculine ladder-backed. Neither was an antique, and Dani imagined painting them in an incongruous palette—a winsome yellow for the ladder-back and a bottomless navy blue for the Queen Anne.

"Would you like a slice of pizza?" Kat offered before Hazel could hop back in her truck and disappear. Kat had always had a soft spot for Etsell's thorny stand-in mom, and as she invited Hazel to stay, Dani wondered if her sister's affection had anything to do with the similarities between Natalie and Hazel.

"I've already eaten," Hazel assured them, but she didn't turn to go.

"Come in anyway," Dani said because she felt like she had to. She had no idea how to navigate an evening surrounded by such a mismatch of women, but asking Hazel to come inside was the right thing to do. It layered one more act of benevolence on the uneven surface of their slowly solidifying friendship.

When they made their way back inside, five decks of shuffled cards were spread across the table as evidence of their interrupted game. Hazel saw them, and immediately tried to slip back out the door, telling Dani that she had some paperwork at the airport she really needed to get working on. Dani was about to let her off the hook, to encourage her to head for home when Kat cut in.

"Paperwork? On a Sunday night?" Kat raised one eyebrow quizzically. "Every party needs a pooper, Hazel. That's why we invited you. You have to stay."

Hazel glowered at Kat, but her eyes were glinting and she couldn't quite repress the smile that played at her lips.

"Besides, now that he's here, we have three pairs. We can all play."

"He?" Dani asked.

Kat pointed one perfectly manicured fingernail at the back door where Benjamin was haloed in the glow of the dim outdoor light. His eyes were round and startled as if he had been caught in the act of doing something illegal. But his shocked expression seemed out of place against the backdrop of his dark, heavy suit. As they watched, he tugged at the collar of his dress shirt. He looked unbearably hot and even more uncomfortable.

"Benjamin!" Dani said. "What are you doing here?"

He looked like he wanted nothing more than to sneak away and pretend that he had never approached her door. But instead of fleeing, Benjamin straightened the hem of his suit coat and said, "I was wondering about landscaping ties. For the strawberry patch you wanted to plant? Lowe's has a sale starting tomorrow and I'm going to pick up a few things. . . ."

"Oh," Dani seemed startled. "Yeah, that would be great. How much do we need again?"

"Forty linear feet, if I remember correctly. That'll make an eight-by-five bed. But you wanted it raised, right? So we'll need at least eighty feet."

"Sounds good," Dani said, shifting her weight and trying not to look as awkward as she felt. "Thank you."

"No problem."

Benjamin turned to go, but before he could vanish in the long shadows surrounding the patio, Natalie clipped across the kitchen floor and threw open the screen. "Why don't you join us?" she called after him. "We're playing canasta and we have an uneven number. We need one more person."

Dani thought he would decline, but Natalie cut a pretty convincing, if not intimidating, profile silhouetted in the warm light of the kitchen. Her mouth was a severe line in her already stern face. Dani couldn't tell if she was asking him or commanding him.

Benjamin appeared taken aback, but he smiled sheepishly as he stepped into the room and surveyed the women around him. "I'm a bit outnumbered, aren't I?"

"That's not the only way you stand out," Kat winked, indicating his tailored suit, the starched white shirt and ice-blue tie.

Dani was startled to realize that her neighbor looked handsome all dressed up. Handsome and out of place. "I suppose you just came from church."

"About twenty people attend the evening service. I'm actually here to recruit," Benjamin said, offering a rare, self-conscious grin.

Char grunted. "Been there, done that. Made my peace with God a long time ago."

Dani and her sister's exchanged a dubious, three-way look.

"Really." Natalie sounded unconvinced.

"We're not terribly religious," Dani cut in before a full-fledged debate could ensue. She could feel Natalie angling for it, and Hazel gathering tired, old axioms around her like lines of defense. "I mean, we believe in God and all, but—"

Natalie cleared her throat.

"Where's your collar?" Dani interrupted, pointing at Benjamin's shirt. She busied herself with gathering up the scattered playing cards and hoped that everyone would take the hint.

In spite of the crackle of emotion in the room, Benjamin seemed to be thoroughly enjoying himself. "I don't wear it all the time," he said. "The older people in my congregation like it, but the younger set finds it antiquated. I like to mix things up, keep everyone guessing."

Dani bent over the cards, hiding a smile. If Char thought her neighbor was weird before, she could only imagine the conclusions her mother was drawing now.

"I don't think we've met," Natalie finally said, offering Benjamin her hand. "I'm Natalie, Dani's older sister. You must be . . . ?"

"Benjamin Miller." He closed her hand in his own. "Dani's neighbor." He turned a reserved eye to Hazel and then Char. "You both look familiar. Hazel, if I'm not mistaken, and Charlene? Dani's mother?"

Char nodded, her eyes sliding from his in an uncharacteristic display of timidity.

"And everyone knows me," Kat quipped, shattering the strange spell in the room. "Enough with the intros. Dani, you and Benjamin are going to have to pair up, and Natalie and I will take on the two young ladies."

After a few clumsy starts, it was surprisingly easy to get lost in the game. It was as if everyone wanted to smooth the jagged corners, erase the first few moments when it seemed as if a collection of such dissimilar people was unquestionably doomed. Against all odds, Dani found herself actually enjoying the company of the people gathered around her table. And if she held herself very still and let the sound of their voices wash over her, she could pretend that nothing existed beyond the warm circle of their laughter. It was oddly comforting.

Hazel seemed a bit baffled by it all, and Natalie worked hard to keep everything flowing smoothly, but Char and Kat were their unvarnished selves. As for Benjamin, he came alive amid the chaos of the kitchen. At some point he shrugged off his suit coat and loosened his tie, and when they paused between games, he slid the noose off his neck entirely and undid the top two buttons of his shirt. He was rolling up his sleeves when Char made a comment that stilled the room.

"You are without a doubt the strangest pastor I've ever met."

Benjamin gave her a calculated look, tipped his head as he considered her words, and then said, "Thank you. I take that as a compliment."

"I meant it as one." Char slapped the tabletop and laughed as if it was the funniest thing she had ever heard.

When the doorbell rang, Dani almost missed it. The off-white grate of the 1940s mechanical chime was situated just inside the door, and could barely be heard above the din in the kitchen. But somehow it filtered through to Dani, and though it took her a moment to realize what she was hearing, she stumbled into the living room before whoever was standing at the door could ring it a third time.

Dani glanced at her wristwatch and was surprised to note that someone was at her door after ten on a Sunday night. It seemed curious that her house should be so full on a random August evening—that someone else would be anxious to join the unusual camaraderie of the hodgepodge of people in her kitchen. But she was brimming with a sort of delicate benevolence, a feeling she couldn't quite pin down but that made her wonder if maybe her world wasn't as war-torn as she imagined it to be. There was a hint of a smile on her face as she turned the handle, a muted optimism that was ready to welcome whoever stood on her porch.

Except for the one person who stood there.

Danica

I tried to tell Etsell early on in our relationship that I hated surprises. That they felt more like an ambush than an expression of affection, an onslaught intended to shock by attacking an unsuspecting victim when she least expected it. When she was least prepared for it. Even as a little girl I couldn't stand the thought of being caught unawares. What if I was so stunned that I said or did something even I wasn't ready for? What if the girl I kept secreted inside scaled the annihilated wall of my defenses and slipped out for all to see?

Ell laughed. "Everyone loves surprises."

"Not me."

"Oh, come on. You just haven't had the right sort of surprise."

But even though he tried to regale me with little things, moments that were meant to delight and astonish, I never warmed to even the smallest tokens of his sudden affection. He brought me flowers at school, but they made me feel conspicuous, and a bit helpless. I didn't know what to do with them. I didn't have a vase or anywhere to store the bouquet of wildflowers except in the dark recesses of my stuffy locker. By the end of the day they had littered the metal floor with petals like whispered apologies, faded beauty that shriveled slowly in accusation. I felt like a failure.

And once, in the very beginning, Ell tried to blindfold me and lure me into his plane. I caught on to his plan long before he was able to lift me into the cockpit, but just the thought of his admittedly well-intentioned subterfuge left my stomach so knotted I felt mildly nauseous.

I tried to explain my aversion to surprises in a dozen different ways, but it wasn't until my twenty-first birthday that my husband came to fully grasp the desperation with which I avoided the unexpected.

The worst of it was, I didn't suspect a thing. I had begged Ell to forgo a big party, and as far as I knew, he had graciously acquiesced. We were supposed to go out for supper with a couple of friends, then come back to our place to play games and have a few drinks. Quiet. Laid-back. Exactly the way I thought the perfect birthday should be.

When we got to the restaurant, we were running a little late. I was flushed from the cold of a particularly frigid February night, and I was laughing at something that Etsell had said in the moment before we swung through the doors. There was a quick inhalation as we stepped into the room, a moment when the whole world seemed to hold its breath in anticipation. But I was only aware of it after the fact, when there was nothing for me to do but regret that I hadn't guessed he would try to do something spectacular. As it was, I just had time to feel a flicker of unease tumble across my skin before the air erupted around me with the sound of a hundred voices screaming, "Surprise!"

In actuality, it was more like fifty voices, but to me it could have been a thousand.

My jaw should have dropped in astonishment. I should have squealed and kissed my husband and giggled over the fact that he had kept such a marvelous secret, but I didn't do any of those things. Instead, to my eternal embarrassment, I screamed. And then, when everyone stood gaping at my peculiar reaction, I burst into tears.

"I'm so sorry," Etsell told me in the coatroom. He cupped my face, smoothed my cheeks with his fingers, tried to erase the shock of what he had done. His eyes were so anguished, it hurt me to look at him.

"I told you, I don't like surprises," I choked out.

"I know. I get that now, and I'm so sorry. I would have never done it if I thought for a second that you would react this way. I just wanted your birthday to be special."

It was far too late for me to pretend that everything was fine, and as my husband studied my face, I felt the weight of what I had done to him splinter across my shoulders. The understanding that I had devastated him broke my heart. I dropped my head to his chest and moaned, "I don't deserve you."

"Don't be silly."

"I'm bossy and boring," I confessed. "I'm a control freak. You try to do something nice for me and I ruin it—"

"You're being ridiculous." Ell hugged me so tight that I couldn't breathe for a moment. "You're none of those things. You're stable. You're strong."

I shook my head against him, but he continued. "Dani, you're fascinating and smart and funny. You keep me grounded."

"And that's a good thing?" I huffed. "Keeping a pilot grounded is a good thing?"

Ell pushed me away from him and held me at arm's length. I didn't want to meet his gaze but he pressed my forehead back with his lips, forced me to look at him. "You are my center," he said. "When I want to run away from everything, to slip off the face of the known world, you call me back."

"Maybe I should follow you," I said. "Maybe the best thing for us would be to leave all of this behind. Go somewhere else. Start over."

Ell was already shaking his head. "Everyone thinks that life begins far from here, in some place where everything is different and new and you can reinvent yourself. But I don't want to be someone I'm not. You know me, and you stay. It doesn't matter where we are or what we do, Dani. You are my home."

I was twenty-one years old. Too young to realize what he was saying to me. Too naive to know that gravity fades. That it dissipates with distance, sometimes becoming a link so weak and tenuous it's a wonder we continue to orbit each other at all. Etsell and I treated love like a state of being, a law of physics that would exist simply because it always had. I didn't learn until much later that love is actually a choice. The sort of choice that we have to make every minute of every day, even when we don't feel like it. Even when all we want is to be anywhere but where we find ourselves.

Because when home is a person, it will always be a moving target.

❦

I never did learn to appreciate a good surprise, and when I saw her standing in a square of dingy light from the picture window in my living room, it was all I could do not to slam the door in her face.

"What are you doing here?" I gasped.

Samantha Linden rocked back on her heels, eyes flashing as if she expected a fight. "I've come a long way," she said. "I really don't need you all up in my face right now."

I swallowed hard and squeezed my eyes shut, trying to get a grip on myself. "I'm sorry," I forced myself to say. "I'm just surprised to see you here. No," I amended, "I'm *shocked* to see you here. I don't understand."

Her dark eyes were haggard and rimmed with blue, and Sam seemed poised on the edge of flight. She glanced at me and then stole a quick peek over her shoulder at the rental car that I realized was parked, running, in my driveway. It seemed to me that she regarded it longingly. Somewhere deep in my mind I registered the thought that I should be more welcoming, that she had indeed come a very long way. But it was so surreal to find her standing on my porch that I simply couldn't gather myself. I stood gaping at her, and she fidgeted closer and closer to the stairs, a bird that was about to dart out of my life and leave me without an answer to why she had alighted in my forgotten corner of creation.

I didn't even realize that I had taken a step closer to her until she put up her hand as if to ward me off. I stopped. We stared for a few moments, silent, scrutinizing each other with a thinly veiled and obviously mutual distrust. And then the reality of her presence on my porch hit me with a final, staggering force.

"Ell," I whispered. "You know something about Ell! Did they find him? Did they find his plane? Is he—"

"No," Sam said, bringing me up short. "There's no news about his plane. Nobody has found anything."

I didn't know whether I should feel relief or despair. But I did know that I was rapidly losing patience with the intolerable woman across from me. Confusion made me blunt. "Then why are you here? I don't even know you. We've met once and it was pretty obvious there was no love lost between us."

Instead of answering my questions, Sam looked toward the house. "You having a party?"

"Excuse me?" I shook my head in disbelief. "I don't really see how that's any of your business."

Something menacing darted across her face, and in the blink of an eye, Sam had skipped down the porch steps, her feet hardly making a sound on the aged wood. "I shouldn't have come," she said over her shoulder. I barely caught the words.

"Wait!" I hit only two of the five stairs, and caught hold of her arm before I could think better of it. Sam shrugged me off angrily. We stood panting, glaring at each other in the dim light that poured through every window in my small house, at a loss for where to go and how to get there.

"Let's start over," I finally said. I really didn't want her anywhere near me, but I also couldn't let her leave without hearing some explanation of why she had come. Alaska was a world away from Iowa, a place that seemed relegated to a dark and shadowy past that I wanted nothing more than to forget. But for some reason Samantha was standing before me, a flesh-and-blood reminder that Etsell was gone and that for a brief time I had feared he had left me in more ways than one.

I put my hand to my forehead and rubbed hard. "Look, why don't you come in. You must be exhausted." I waited for her to acquiesce, but she soundlessly stood her ground. "Have you been traveling all day?" I asked, fumbling. "Maybe some water?"

"Who's in there?" Sam asked, and it felt to me that there was something akin to fear in her voice.

"Uh . . ." for some reason it was hard for me to think back to the minutes before I found her standing outside my door, to the time that I had spent around the table forgetting—even if only for a moment—that my life as I knew it was over. "My mom," I eventually managed. "My sisters. My neighbor. Hazel."

"Hazel? The woman who was with you in Alaska?"

"Yeah." I squinted at her, trying to make out Sam's expression in the dark. It struck me that she tensed at the mention of Hazel.

"No," she said. "I don't want to come in. I just want a quiet place to talk to you."

"We could sit on the porch," I offered. "Or in the backyard? I have some chairs out there."

Sam seemed ready to follow me somewhere, and I nursed a tenuous hope that I would finally get to the bottom of her alarming appearance on my doorstep. "Why don't you shut off your car and head around back?" I said. "I'll get us each a glass of water. Something stronger?"

She shook her head.

"Water then. Can you manage?" I asked, pointing toward the side of the house.

Sam nodded and took off in the dark. I watched her for a few seconds, and when her small form blended with the shadows, I ran back up the porch steps.

"What's going on?" Natalie asked when I burst into the kitchen.

"Nothing," I said, my voice so tight it sounded cold.

"Is someone at the door?" Hazel was out of her seat, on her way into the living room, when I stopped her with an iron grip just above her elbow.

"There's something I have to take care of."

The room went almost icy in the wake of my words. Char laid her cards down. Kat was uncharacteristically speechless. Even Natalie didn't know how to respond to my abrupt change of mood. It was Benjamin who quietly slipped out of his chair and touched my arm in an act of brief comfort. His hand was gone before I could even register that his warm fingertips had rested against my skin.

"Is there something I can do?" he asked.

"No." I took two glasses down from the cupboard and began to fill them from the tap in the sink. No time for the filtered stuff; I could hardly stand watching the seconds tick away as a thin stream trickled into each glass. I tried to paste on a smile but it wouldn't stick. "I'm fine. Really."

"Who's here?" Kat asked.

"No one."

She nodded at the two glasses in my hand.

"Oh." I gave my head a little shake as if to clear it. "No one you know."

"You're acting really strange," Char said, finally pushing herself up from the table. She moved toward me, her bare feet slapping lightly on the wavy hardwood floor, but she ran out of steam long before she made it to me. She stalled in the middle of the kitchen, looking every bit as disoriented and helpless as I felt.

"I'm fine," I said. This time I made my lips hold a placating smile. "I'll be back in a few minutes. Continue your game. Please. Someone else can play my hand."

I made myself walk out of the kitchen without a backward glance, praying that no one would try to follow me, because I was certain I didn't have the strength to stop them. But everyone stayed exactly where they were; I could feel their eyes boring into my back as I swung through the salon door and disappeared into the living room.

I padded quickly across the carpet and used my hip to open the screen. I had told Sam to go around back, but I didn't want to slip out the kitchen door and alert everyone to where I was headed. My plan was to duck around the house and then lead Samantha away from the back patio—I hadn't been thinking when I encouraged her to go there. It was too close to the kitchen. Too close to prying eyes. To ears that would likely strain to catch every whispered word.

But I never made it past the front sidewalk.

Just as I turned toward the side of the house, the sound of a car door slamming spun me around. Sam was illuminated for a split second in the interior light of her car, then she threw the transmission in reverse and the bulb blinked out. She started to back down the driveway.

"Wait!" I screamed. The glasses fell from my hands. One landed on the grass; the other shattered on the sidewalk into bits of sparkling diamond at my feet. "Wait!"

I ran across the lawn, sliding on the late-night dew that was already leaving droplets on the grass. Sam's gaze was glued to the rearview mirror, but in the glow of the dashboard lights, I could see her eyes dart to me. I ran faster.

"Stop," I wheezed, slamming into the side of the car. Her window was open and I reached for the steering wheel. "You have to stop!"

"You're insane!" Sam screeched. She stomped on the brakes and I nearly tripped, banging my head on the roof of the car. "What do you think you're doing?"

"What do you think *you're* doing?" I shouted back. "You can't just show up here and then leave without any explanation. What are you trying to do to me?" I was trembling, I could see the frantic dance of my hand as it tried to gain purchase on her steering wheel. It was so disconcerting to see myself so far out of control that I shoved away from the car and stood in the middle of the road, gasping.

"I shouldn't have come," Sam said. She seemed to be talking to herself.

I wasn't even sure if she was aware of my presence

anymore—she seemed lost in her own private thoughts—but I didn't care about whatever personal demon had taken up residence beside her. I had to ask the question one more time. "What are you doing here?" I struggled to make my voice flinty, demanding, and I could see the effect it had on her by the way she suppressed a shudder.

Samantha lifted her head as if coming out of a trance, and fixed me with a look so hard and unreadable, I recoiled. Her mouth was a violent slash in the pale skin of her drawn face. It hardly moved when she said, "I'm pregnant."

13

Forgive Me

For just a moment, everything stopped. The breeze paused in a suspended waltz, the leaves on a hundred trees pressed cheek-to-cheek. And the night sounds stilled, if only for a second, while a fine tear rent the fabric of Danica's life and tore it end to end. The destruction was so sudden and so complete, that at first she stood there in the middle of the road and wondered what had happened. Why the world was so quiet and heavy. Why her heart was arrested in her chest.

Then Sam put the car in drive and eased away, disappearing down the street toward town while Dani just watched her go.

There should have been more, and Dani leaned toward the taillights of the unfamiliar car as if drawn to a magnet, but it was too late. Sam was gone, and there was no way to know if she would ever bring herself to tell more of the story that had brought her to Blackhawk in the first place. But for once, Dani didn't care. She was numb from head to toe, temporarily anesthetized against the full meaning of what Sam had come to say, until the shrill cry of a distant train split the night, and the fine web of incredulity that had held the truth suspended far above her shattered.

It fell on her hard, the implication of Sam's claim. And yet Dani didn't question it—didn't even think to dispute the veracity of the two words that made her life seem little more than a pathetic parody, a sad and sorry tale that left her bereft of every promise, every hope she had clung to and claimed. Why would Samantha make something like that up? Why would she fly across the world to destroy Dani unless there was an indisputable truth in the telling?

If Samantha was pregnant, Etsell was the father.

Etsell was the father.

The rush of the train as it sped down winding tracks matched the growing thrum in Dani's head. Suddenly she felt everything—the pain of Samantha's words like a razor on her skin, the warm lick of a night wind that seemed sinister—and she longed for nothing more complicated than the ability to crawl outside of her own skin.

When she hit the river path she was blind and running, stumbling through the dark by memory alone. There were brambles off the narrow track, poison ivy and stinging nettle and a host of other nuisances that lay in wait like dirty little secrets. But Dani didn't care. In fact, she welcomed the burn of torn skin, the thin lines where leaves sliced shallow paths along her legs. It was a definable pain, something she could focus on. Something she could soothe with cool water and salve from her medicine cabinet. Nothing like the pain that Samantha had inflicted.

Dani lost all semblance of time as she made her way to the river, but at some point her shin banged against the springy bark of a fallen log. It was the same decaying tree where she and Etsell had often sat, and where she had cut Kat's hair and watched her sister throw the severed ponytail into the water like a sacrifice to the gods. She sank onto the log, pulling her feet up beneath her and resting her chin on her trembling knees. Dani hadn't realized it as she ran, but her whole body was shaking; her teeth were chattering as if she was in danger of hypothermia in spite of the humid summer night.

She could have sat there all night and long into the days that were to come. Dani felt as if she could stay there forever, petrify slowly beneath the canopy of intertwining branches and remain as a warning for generations to come. A prophecy to dissect and examine, a reminder that bore a specific poignancy for each individual observer. *She was betrayed. She lost someone. She lost herself.*

All of the above.

But there were voices in the trees, whispers of a word that slipped between the leaves and hung from crooked boughs like wisps of mist. It took Dani a long time to realize that the word was her name and that the voice that spoke it was only steps away.

"Danica?" Benjamin was fumbling through the undergrowth and making so much noise, it was startling that Dani hadn't heard him well before he was twenty feet from her hiding spot. "Danica? Is that you? I can hardly see you. You're nothing but a shadow."

She lifted her head and saw the outline of her neighbor as he approached the river, arms outstretched. Even if she could have summoned the will to speak, it would have been unnecessary for her to call out because just then a cloud trailed across the sky, and Benjamin and Dani found themselves staring at each other in the otherworldly light of a gibbous moon.

"Beautiful night," Benjamin said, stopping a few feet away from the spot where she huddled on the fallen log. He put his hands in his pockets and gave her a soft smile, as if to prove that he meant her no harm—that he had no intention of interrogating her about her sudden disappearance.

They stayed like that for a few minutes, Dani incapable of speech, and Benjamin holding his peace because he apparently didn't know how to proceed. But they couldn't remain frozen like that forever, and Benjamin finally held out his arms as if to encompass the warm air, the scent of damp earth, Dani. He seemed poised for an embrace, but then he shrugged a little and let his hands drop awkwardly to his sides of their own accord. "Everyone is looking for you," he said. "When you didn't come back we all split up. Guess I found you."

Dani didn't want to be found. Or maybe she did. It was impossible to pin down even her own motivations in escaping to the bank of the river. She felt like a child who had tried to run away, only to make it to the edge of her world and discover that she couldn't bring herself to cross that invisible line into the unknown. So she bunkered down where it was familiar, half hiding, half yearning for the moment when she would be retrieved.

She didn't expect Benjamin to be the one to lead her home. Dani waited warily for him to say something stupid. To ask her if she was okay or if there was anything that he could do for her—to startle her with the gross insufficiency of his sympathy, or worse, his blatant pity. But Benjamin didn't say much of anything. He simply remained across from her, patient and calm, emanating the sort of quiet comfort that eventually made her let go of the death grip she had on her legs and slide to the ground.

"Do you take the trail much?" Benjamin asked, turning to lead her back the way they had come.

When Dani didn't answer, he filled the space between them with small talk, innocuous chatter that she expected to find annoying. But it was a distraction, something that Dani could focus on to keep her mind off of what Samantha had told her.

"You know the old train bridge?" Benjamin continued, but he didn't wait for an answer. "If you cross it and take a sharp left on the far side of the river, about fifty feet down you'll find a deer trail that will take you straight into the state park. It makes for really good snowshoeing in the winter. I've even thought it would be fun to try cross-country skiing."

Benjamin glanced back at Dani, but her lips were pressed tight, her eyes determinedly fixed on the ground at her feet.

"Sometimes," he said, "when I get to the top of the ridge, I wonder what it would feel like to just keep walking. To put one foot in front of the other until I couldn't do it anymore. Sometimes I think it would be really great to do something totally out of character. To just let go."

In spite of herself, Dani wondered what the mysterious Benjamin Miller wanted to let go of. She didn't ask.

"But you know what?" he continued. "I'm not nearly brave enough."

Dani nodded once, even though his back was turned and he would never see her assent. It didn't matter. She knew exactly what he meant. She wasn't brave enough either.

When Danica got home she went straight to her room and locked the door behind her. There was a hum of voices coming from the living room, punctuated by louder exclamations as everyone grilled Benjamin about her whereabouts and why she had disappeared in the first place. She could just imagine the conversation—Char's confusion, Natalie's self-righteous indignation, Kat's fierce protective streak that would undoubtedly be stoked to life—and she wanted nothing to do with it. She feared, briefly, that Hazel had seen Samantha and would somehow discern what had happened by patching together the few fragments of what she knew about the girl and her relationship with Ell.

The thought made Dani sick.

More than anything she wanted to pretend that Sam had never rung her doorbell. She stood numbly in the middle of the bedroom, unable to sit on the bed she had shared with Etsell, and clutched her arms against her chest as if she couldn't get warm. Dani made a desperate attempt to erase the truth from her mind. It was easy enough—to make herself go blank—but there was a problem in the cavity of her chest. Her heart was gasping, given to fits and starts that assured her the wound could not be ignored.

The voices gradually faded from the living room, each withdrawal punctuated by the slap of the screen door. It was nearly midnight by the time the house was quiet, and Dani was surprised to find herself still standing in the very middle of the dark bedroom. Her lower back ached for some reason, and she was suddenly so parched that she felt sure she was in danger of dehydration. She knew that Kat was lurking somewhere in the recesses of her home, but her longing for water outweighed her desire to avoid her sister.

Kat was leaning against the counter when Danica stumbled into the bright light of the kitchen. The cards were abandoned on the table, three neat rows of matching denominations marking the place where each set of partners had raced to make books. Dani and Benjamin had been winning; they were only a couple of cards away from declaring canasta. But the game felt like it had happened in another life. The interlude of her evening was less than a memory—it was as if it had never happened. The cards, the conversation, the brief respite of the night was a scene in a story that she could only vaguely remember reading.

"What the hell was that all about?" Kat demanded as Dani blinked in the brightness. "What are you? Twelve? You can't just run away like that."

Dani looked at her sister out of the corner of her eye. Kat's words were harsh, but her face bore the unmistakable signs of worry. Her skin was drawn and pale, and her forehead was creased with anxiety and more than a little frustration. Dani wanted to say something that would erase the ugly lines from her sister's beautiful mouth, but her tongue felt leaden. Immobile.

Without a word, Dani carefully took a glass from the cabinet beside the sink. She had a vague recollection of performing the exact same action not long before. Had it been only a couple of hours ago? But she couldn't think about that. She remembered instead the smash of glass on concrete and hoped that no one had cut their feet as they left.

"There's glass on the sidewalk," Dani said, her voice less than a whisper. She cleared her throat and tried again. "I need to sweep it up."

"Ben did it."

"Ben?"

"Benjamin. Your neighbor?"

Dani nodded. "Okay."

Kat snatched the glass out of Dani's hand and slammed it on the counter behind her. "Don't play all zombie with me. Do you have any idea how terrified we were? Damn it, Danica. We thought you had done something stupid."

"What?" Dani shook her head, trying to understand what her sister was saying.

"Do I have to spell it out for you? We've all been watching you. You know, for signs that you might want to hurt yourself or something."

Danica laughed, but there was no humor in the harsh sound. "You can't be serious."

"Of course I'm serious." Kat sighed, and as the breath eased from her chest she seemed to deflate. The glittering girl faded, the sparkle in her eyes dulled in a single blink. "You lost your husband, Dani. Something like that can really mess a person up."

It should have been a blow for Dani to hear Kat talk about Ell that way, as if the only thing that mattered anymore was how his absence affected everyone else. But her mind flashed to her late father-in-law, and she realized that Kat's words were true. Sometimes people tripped off an invisible ledge and fell headlong, clutching at air and broken promises as they waited to hit bottom. Is that what she was doing? Waiting for impact?

"I'm not going to hurt myself," Dani said finally. "It's not my style."

"I know." Kat picked up the glass of water that she had taken from Dani and handed it to her. "But you can't just slip away like that. It's not fair."

"I'm sorry," Dani said.

Kat nodded, then she turned on her heel and shuffled out of the room, her shoulders rounded and her steps heavy. Just before she disappeared through the salon door, she paused, back rigid, head bent. "We love you, you know."

"What?"

"We all do, Dani. In different ways and for different reasons. But we all miss you. We want you back. You probably don't want to hear that right now, but I thought you should know."

Dani didn't sleep at all that night, and when the sun rose over Blackhawk she was waiting on the porch for it. It was a vermilion dawn, the sort of morning that heralded thunderstorms and wind. The air was moist and thick with warning, but Dani welcomed it. When a warm gust lifted the dust at her feet and spun it in a brief and crazy dance, it seemed an act of sympathy—a moment of consolation that echoed every bit of the confusion she felt.

The last thing Dani wanted to do was the only option available to her. Though she realized it was probably too late, as the night wore on she couldn't stand the thought of letting Sam vanish without an explanation. In the long, pink shadows of a new day it was almost possible to believe that she had imagined the whole thing. That Sam's appearance and the two words of her barbed confession were nothing more than fragments of a quickly fading nightmare. But something inside Dani felt broken beyond repair, and she knew deep down that even the most cunning bad dream could never touch the certainty with which she had clung to Etsell's love. Surely there was proof of this betrayal. And maybe she was still lingering in Blackhawk.

There was a motel at the edge of town, a dilapidated little motor inn that had preened in chartreuse glory in the seventies. But nobody had touched it since, and in the intervening years the shag carpet and burnt orange bedspreads had seen too much life to be considered anything less than mildly repulsive. An aura of neglect clutched at the lopsided shutters, and even the trees that had been planted to shade a small picnic area just beyond the parking lot looked glum, their heavy heads hanging aslant over peeling-paint tables.

It was as good a place as any to look for Sam, and even

before she pulled into the parking lot, Dani knew that she had found what she was looking for. There was one car at the forgotten motel, and it had rental plates. Dani hadn't paid any attention to what Sam was driving, but the car in question was straddling two parking spaces, tires crooked and opaque windows reflecting light as if they had much to hide.

Dani parked a few spaces down and wondered which door she should knock on. There were two rooms directly in front of the rental car, one marked with a drooping 2 and the other conspicuously blank. But as she considered the possibilities, one of the doors swung open and Samantha Linden stepped out into the hostile day. She glanced at the sky and ducked her head against a growing wind, then hurried to her car, popped open the trunk, and threw a backpack into the dark recesses.

In the light of morning, Dani could see that Samantha had changed much since they had first met. The woman seemed diminished somehow. Her cheeks had been hollowed, the fine bones of her face protruding in angles that rendered her features stern and uncompromising. Even her arms looked severe, like sharp-cornered borders that moved in unconscious formation to protect the slight curve of her narrow abdomen. And it was there, an almost imperceptible softening at her center, a hint of evidence that what she had told Dani was true.

"Stop," Dani said, getting out of her car. She hadn't known if she would be able to go through with it, but her door was open and she was already standing on the cracked pavement before she had time to consider what she was doing.

Sam whirled around, the shock of seeing Dani again evident in the wide disbelief of her eyes. But she laid a hand against the roof of her car, collected herself. "I'm flying standby," she said. "I need to get to the airport."

Dani ignored her. Forced herself to cross the space between them and put both of her palms on the opposite side of Sam's car as if she could hold it in place with her fingers. With her will. "Is it true?" she asked.

Sam didn't answer. She didn't have to. "Look." she sighed. "I shouldn't have come. I don't know why I did."

"It's too late for that now. I know. And I think you owe me an explanation. It's why you came, isn't it?" Dani didn't even bother to mask the bitterness in her voice. It fell from her lips thick and vicious, a toxic scent that poisoned the air between them.

Anyone else would have cowered beneath the weight of Dani's fury. But Sam merely nodded once and drew herself up, straightening her back as if it would take every ounce of her strength to survive what was to come. She didn't shirk away from it; she seemed to welcome it. "I have a few minutes," she said.

"How far along are you?"

"Fifteen weeks."

"How long have you known?"

Sam's lip pulled up in a parody of a smile. "Fifteen weeks," she said.

"What is that supposed to mean?" Dani spat out, unaccountably furious.

"It was a mistake." Sam spoke words of admission, but she jutted her chin in defiance. "Mistakes of that magnitude can only come with consequences to match. I knew we'd pay for it."

It. Dani's mind flashed through sickening scenarios—her husband tracing his lips against the jawline of the woman before her, his hands spanning her tiny waist, worse. She shivered violently and was mortified to feel herself choke on an unexpected sob. "I hate you," she whispered. "*I hate you.*"

"I know."

"Why are you here?" Dani begged. "Why did you do this to me? I would have never known . . ."

Sam squeezed her eyes shut as if she wished herself away. Her forehead pleated along agonized lines, her shoulders tensed, her head bowed. When she looked up, there was something infinitely sad in her face. But she fought it and came up swinging. Ignoring Dani's question, she said coldly, "He was really upset. I figured we could pretend it never happened, but he wanted to tell you."

It was so hard for Dani to think of Etsell in those terms. To imagine her husband, little more than a stranger, arguing with a woman Dani hadn't even known to fear. Was there guilt? Regret? Could he begin to foresee how something like this would forever alter the course of their lives? A part of her loathed him for wanting to inflict the sort of damage that knowledge would impart. And yet she knew that if he had returned—this sin a land mine between them—things would never have been the same anyway. Dani felt sure she would have seen his betrayal written on the page of his skin, felt it in the marred intimacy of his touch.

"We fought," Sam continued, her emotionless narrative blunt and unvarnished. "And he left."

She didn't have to explain what she meant. They fought, and Etsell flew off the face of the earth. Crashed in the mountains. Sank in the sea. Offered himself up as a sacrifice to primitive gods that still haunted corners of the North no human eye had ever seen. There was someone to blame: Samantha. But there was more to it, and even as Dani longed to pin everything on the adulteress across from her, she had to admit that Etsell was culpable too. And as her mind flitted to the moments before he left for Alaska, her own betrayals and insufficiencies, she realized that there was more than enough blame to go around.

"You left too," Dani said, remembering Sam's own disappearance.

Samantha lifted one shoulder, nodded. "I know you think I'm the devil incarnate, and frankly, if I were you I'd probably claw my eyes out. But it wasn't easy for me either. It isn't easy."

Dani made an angry, guttural sound in the back of her throat. "You expect me to feel sorry for you?"

They stood there for a long minute, glaring at each other as thunder began to roll in the distance and the earth exhaled a hot, pent-up breath.

Finally, Sam threw up her hands in surrender, and said, "I'm sorry." The words came out wooden. Rehearsed. Dani had the fleeting suspicion that Samantha Linden had not apologized for much in her life. But even that hard-won proclamation did nothing to soften the impact of all she had just heard.

"That's not enough," Dani hissed. "That will never be enough."

Sam shrugged a little, and moved to get in the rental car. A handful of dissatisfying phrases—tidbits that left Dani wanting alternately more and less—and she was ready to leave.

"Wait!" Dani lunged across the hood, reaching for her in an act of desperation. "You didn't tell me why you came."

For just a moment Sam's eyes betrayed a hint of vulnerability. Of something that looked like carefully veiled torment—an expression as out of place in her unforgiving face as the thickening around her middle seemed incongruous against the lines of her narrow body. "I can't keep this baby," she said when Dani had given up hope that she'd speak at all. "And I wanted to . . . before . . ."

"What?" Dani exhaled.

Sam stalled, swallowed hard. "It's Etsell's baby too."

Danica

"Etsell's gone." For a second I wondered who had spoken, but I was alone with Sam in the parking lot. I had said it. And in the hollow that those words created, I heard the echo of my own assent. My husband wasn't coming back. If I longed for rescue, for the moment when he would step from the shadows to assure me that Samantha Linden was a liar and reclaim all that we had lost, those final clinging hopes were dashed against the strident angles of the woman before me. It was over. All of it. Finally and simply and with all the sad inelegance of a parking lot confession, a morning heavy with the promise of rain.

Samantha nodded once, a quick, perfunctory gesture that seemed to sever any remaining sense of obligation she felt. In one jarring movement she swung herself into the car and started the engine. What else was there to say?

I backed away from the vehicle, almost frantic to watch her go, to assure myself that once she drove out of my life she would stay out of it forever. The implications of her sudden arrival and all she had to confess were already beginning to bind me, to weave themselves around my life with a tenacity that would make all that had happened difficult to extract. Impossible to forget. But before I could face any of that, I needed to be alone.

Alone. The finality of that word was enough to make me light-headed, and I reached for the car to steady myself. My hand grazed the passenger window, and as my fingertips touched glass, the pane began to sink into the door.

"Here," Sam said through the open window. She thrust a piece of paper at me, a wrinkled square of lined loose-leaf that bore the signs of much abuse. It was reflex to take it, to open my palm to her offering, but once I held the mysterious note, I found I wanted nothing to do with it. I tried to hand it back to her, but the car was already past me. I watched as Sam put it in drive and faded from sight beyond the row of trees that blocked the motel from the open road.

I wondered where she was going. Decided I didn't care.

The first drop of rain hit me at the same moment the sun vanished behind a bank of dark clouds. It had been bright and otherworldly only a heartbeat before, but when the angry, orange rays of light were swallowed by the sleight of some unseen magician's hand, the morning was recast in green and blue. Everything turned hazy and indistinct, an underwater landscape, and even before the sky unleashed a summer deluge, I felt like I was drowning.

The rain poured down the windshield of my car, obscuring everything but the quicksilver pattern of water on glass. I sat there for a very long time, breathing in the damp air and turning Sam's piece of paper over and over between my trembling fingers. There was writing all over it—I could feel the etched pattern of words written in a heavy hand, the raised letters traced in reverse like the scrawled code to some forgotten language.

But it was nothing as mysterious as all that, and in the end

I carefully unfolded the paper and spread it flat against the steering wheel.

I wasn't prepared for the familiar script, for my own name scrawled like an invocation across the top. *Dani*, he had written, the final letter topped with a hurried slash that leaned toward a future we would never know. He always wrote my name like that, and it seemed such a hopeful rendering to me, an implicit wish for all that was to come. But it hurt to see the desperation in the slant of his letters, the messy scribble of the two words that covered the page from top to bottom: *Forgive me.*

Over and over again—*forgive me, forgive me, forgive me*—as if it was as simple as that. As if I could say, *I forgive you*, and erase everything that had happened. There was nowhere to start fresh. There was no one left to forgive. Etsell was gone and I had been abandoned to a life of dealing with the consequences of actions I didn't take.

I couldn't forget. And I couldn't walk forward from this day without making a choice. Samantha had made sure of that.

At the very bottom of the paper, there was a string of numbers written in the thick line of a permanent marker. They obscured Etsell's never-ending plea, and shot off the page as if demanding to know what I intended to do about them. There was no explanation, no identifying information at all. Just the ten digits and the instant knowledge that Sam had left me a bridge in the form of her telephone number.

~

Etsell once told me that the few memories he had of his mother were little more than fading snapshots, moments frozen in time that offered up scenes and emotions in flat, uncompromising color just a shade or two shy of reality. He admitted that he often didn't know what he remembered and what he had constructed from borrowed memories, events that people recalled for his benefit and that he unknowingly folded between the pages of his own history. She had left him too soon, and his eight-year-old self hadn't been preoccupied with preserving the scent of her perfume or the way her hair fell against her cheek. It wasn't until after she was gone that he longed for those things. But by then it was too late.

Though he regretted the insouciance of his early years, the nonchalant way he let her slip through his fingers, there was one experience that Etsell could replay with crystal clarity. That day remained in his mind as fresh and unspoiled as the first few flakes of snow in the palm of his own cold hand: six-spired and sharp, with lines so clean and new it almost hurt to look at their carefully carved perfection.

He didn't share the memory with me until the day he told me that he wanted to be a dad, and I didn't understand it. Didn't really even try to. But for some reason, as I wasted half the morning in the prison of my own car, I thought about Ell's mother and the story he clutched like a diamond in his fist.

The summer before Melanie died, she bought an annual pass to Lake Cetan, a little freshwater pond that cut a shallow horseshoe around the tallest hill in the county. It wasn't much of a lake, but the bottom was rocky instead of layered with silt, and it was too small for any type of watercraft, so the water was unusually clear. Even when you were standing waist-deep you could count the stones at your feet. Rimmed by shade trees, and supplied with a small team of rather incompetent lifeguards, it was the best lazy-summer-day destination within a thirty-mile radius.

I didn't go to Cetan when I was a little girl, or at least, it didn't stand out as anything special if I did. But to Etsell, the weeks he spent there with his mother swelled into the fondest memory of his youth. They rose and expanded as one, and gave off the homey-sweet scent of baking bread and wind-tossed sheets and childhood itself.

Though they presumably passed endless languid days dipping their toes in the cool water, the afternoon that shimmered with significance for Ell was the day Melanie finally convinced him to jump off the high dive.

There was a platform in the middle of the lake that had been erected too many years ago for anyone to recall with any accuracy who had been behind its construction. It was a monstrosity, a tangle of metal and concrete that arched out of the water like an artifact from some savage civilization best confined to rumor and imagination. Two diving boards slanted off perpendicularly from a tilting stage, a centerpiece from which everyone on the beach could watch exactly who was in line for the low board, and who had the guts to brave the ladder to the high dive. The fifteen rungs to the towering high board were a rite of passage, a ritual of sorts that separated the proverbial men from the boys and served as the object of many a dare.

Miss Melanie was an expert in the water, a fifty-something mom who could still slice from one edge of the pond to the other with a stroke so powerful and technically impressive, she seemed better suited to teach lessons than the pimply lifeguards who lined the beach. But Etsell flopped in the waves, inelegant and leaden, working to master the dog paddle after three years of instruction.

"Just once," his mother urged him when the shadow of another school year loomed long over their tranquil summer. "Imagine what the boys at school will say."

Etsell's eyes went soft as he told the story, and it was

obvious that in his mind at least Melanie's prompting was tender, affectionate; born of a deep-seated belief in her son and his abilities instead of a desire to push him to succeed. She encouraged him gently, and then even showed him how to do it, parting the water with her hands and scissoring out to the platform herself.

Melanie's hair was turning gray, but in the sun and at that distance it shone silver in the moment before she stepped to the end of the board. One knee lifted nearly to her chest, the aluminum plank bowed, and in one graceful movement she had sprung from the very end, arms tucked tight against her ears and toes pointed. When she split the water with her fingertips and was swallowed whole by the pool of azure, there was hardly a splash.

Five minutes before the final whistle was scheduled to blow, Etsell swam out to the diving platform with his mother. The sun was already starting to duck behind the trees, and the breeze on the water was cool enough to hint of the autumn to come. Ell had chosen his time carefully, waiting until the beach had started to empty and the only people who remained were mothers gathering up very small children and a handful of construction workers who had popped in for a quick dip at the end of the day.

The platform was empty, and when Ell climbed to the concrete staging ground, he was surprised to realize that Melanie had not followed him.

"I'll wait here," she called from the water. Her legs were pumping slow circles beneath her, and her face was kissed by the last rays of sun and a sprinkling of tiny age spots that Etsell mistook for freckles. "I want to watch you."

Etsell laughed as he told me that his legs had never shaken quite so hard as they did on that endless climb. He said he counted the rungs, sure that the board could not rise higher than ten. When his fingers found the tenth rung, and he realized that there were more to go, he almost backed down. But she was there below him, treading water at the point where his trajectory would drop him like a cannonball.

"Come on!" She laughed, the sound rippling over the water.

The rest of the climb was more an act of love than a matter of pride, something he forced himself to do because he couldn't stand the thought of disappointing her. When he was at the apex, and when he had to take the unsteady walk to the very end of the board, he thought he would collapse from sheer terror.

"I can't do it!" he said, looking down at her from an unfathomable height. "I'll fall!"

"That's the point." Melanie grinned.

"But I don't want to fall."

"I'm here." She raised her arms out of the water, droplets trickling from her forearms like tiny, glittering jewels. "I'll catch you."

Etsell knew she couldn't catch him. That it would kill her if she tried. But he closed his eyes anyway, wrestled the drumbeat of his heart to a somewhat steady rhythm, and jumped.

It was a free fall, a spinning descent, a moment ripped from time when he was lighter than air and at the mercy of an unforgiving gravity all at once. It was over in an instant. The only thing he knew from the second his feet slapped the water was a sense of drowning, of being sucked under by something so immense and unfathomable, he knew that there was no possible way up.

But then he felt her fingers brush his, the beat of butterfly wings against his palms. Melanie's hands grasped his wrists, and then slipped under his arms and dragged him higher and higher through the blue-green tunnel of the lake until she could catch him about the waist. Etsell broke the surface of the water with a shout, a choking gasp that could have been a sob or a laugh. Maybe both.

But Melanie was laughing, hugging his little-boy body to her, holding them both up with each strong kick of her legs. "You did it!" she whispered against the slick skin of his neck. "I'm so proud of you! You did it!"

"I want to do it again," he said.

The truth was, he was desperate to do it again. To fly for less than a second as he slipped through the warm summer air. And, best of all, to feel her fingers when he fell, drawing him from the depths, helping him rise.

14

Still

The rain marched through Blackhawk like a soldier: quick and determined, with the final sweep of a black cape that wiped the sky clean in one swift movement. Behind the bank of dark clouds the horizon shimmered and danced, sunlight making prisms of every drop of water and slanting the world in a kaleidoscope, a fairy tale glimpsed through a lens of cut glass.

Dani didn't notice the rainbow puddles on her drive home or the light breeze that lifted the leaves above her and shivered a million tiny crystals over her car. She only felt the sharp corners of the paper she had crumpled in her hand, and the yawning cavern of the hole at her center where everything she believed in had been stripped away.

Her house was empty when she stepped through the front door; she could feel Kat's absence in the still, stuffy rooms. A part of Dani ached to pop one of Char's sleeping pills and crawl into bed, where she could tuck herself deep beneath the covers and pretend for a few hours at least that she hadn't fallen off the edge of her life. But she was too practical for that. Her hands weren't used to inactivity, and she found herself moving through the house categorically, opening windows to catch the breath of unseasonably cool wind, rearranging pillows on the couch, straightening the pairs of shoes that Kat had kicked off by the door.

Dani realized with a start that it was Monday, and re-membered that her day was booked full at the salon. She glanced at the clock on the sofa table and saw that it was seven thirty. Only an hour had passed since she set out to find Samantha.

Just the contours of that woman's name made Dani's palms go hot, but she couldn't go there. Not now. She pushed the thought from her mind with a desperate heave and headed for the shower. A sleepless night, a soul on fire . . . But what recompense was there for all she had en-dured? Etsell was gone, and the only thing he left behind was a paper begging for absolution.

And a baby that wasn't hers.

Anything—even smiling through ten matching conversa-tions about the unexpected morning storm—was better than being alone with herself.

Dani's first appointment was at eight o'clock, and by the time she opened the front door of her salon and hit play on the soundtrack of the day, she had fixed a smile on her face like an accessory. It had been difficult to find one that fit, a gentleness in her lips that didn't look like a grimace, but she had managed. And in the moment before her first appoint-ment hurried through the door, Dani peeked at herself in the mirror and decided that no one would ever know what was happening behind her eyes. Maybe she could exist like that forever—hard and cool as marble, carved, playing a part. Maybe no one would ever know.

The facade worked fine until her last appointment of the day. Dani knew that Natalie was scheduled in the final slot, and she spent the entire afternoon preparing herself for her sister's questions, the inevitable confrontation. Natalie was far too down-to-earth to indulge what she would undoubtedly consider Dani's selfish antics of the night before. There would be a calm interrogation, and a litany espousing the many ways that Dani could, and should improve her social habits. Never mind that they were family—that they should be allowed to fall to pieces in front of each other. Never mind that Dani had just lost her husband.

But it wasn't Natalie who showed up at the end of the day. It was Char.

"What are you doing here?" Dani asked, too surprised to be polite.

Char glanced around the shop as if she hadn't seen it in ages. And the truth was, she hadn't. "I forgot how nice it was in here," she said. "A little prissy, but nice. You need something black. Isn't that a design rule? Every room needs a touch of black?"

Dani repressed an urge to roll her eyes. Design advice from the woman who wore jeans better suited to an eighteen-year-old and bought her drapes mass-produced from Walmart? She might have been amused if she wasn't so raw. "Where's Natalie?" Dani asked, trying a different tack. "I promised to cut her hair before she went back to New York."

"She changed her mind," Char said. "Had some last-minute things she wanted to do in Blackhawk before she left."

It was a terrible attempt at a lie and they both knew it. Char tilted her chin a little and smoothed her tank top—a pink confection proclaiming that she was a Victoria's Secret Bombshell—over her hips. The weepy woman who had cried at Dani's table was long gone, and in her place was the mother that Dani knew so well. Char was her confident, remarkable self, a woman so content in her own skin, it didn't matter what anyone else thought. And for some reason, she had personally come to deliver the news that Natalie wouldn't be showing up for her haircut.

Dani felt a prick of disquiet, but she bent an arm to rub the twinge in her shoulder and stifled a weary yawn. "That's fine," she said. "I wouldn't mind getting off a bit early today."

"You're not getting off early." Char laughed. "I'm taking her place. I'm your next appointment."

For a moment, Dani didn't know what to say. She had been nagging her mother for this chance for years, but now that Char stood in La Rue in all her gaudy glory, Dani wondered why she had ever wanted the opportunity to remake her mother in the first place. But before she could worry too much, Char laid down the ground rules.

"Don't get too excited," she warned. "I want to be blond. Just like this." She fished a box from her purse and held it up for Dani to see. Gaping from the carton was a photo of a pouty-lipped woman with hair the color of champagne, and a big red X through the price tag assured Dani the highlight kit had been a clearance buy.

A thread of disapproval puckered Dani's mouth. "It won't look very natural on you—"

"I don't care," Char interrupted. "Either you do it like I want or I'll do it myself."

It took Dani a few seconds to decide. "Fine."

"Good. And I don't want you to cut it. I'm growing it out."

"How about a trim? Just to clean up the ends?"

Char pulled a couple of pins from the messy French knot that held her thin hair against her head. Taking a few strands between her thumb and forefinger, she studied the processed locks. "Okay. A bit off the end. But just a smidge." She showed Dani a half inch with her fingers and Dani mimicked the measurement, nodding her head solemnly.

At first Char let Dani work in peace, closing her eyes

when her daughter shampooed her hair and even allowing Dani to spin the chair around so that she couldn't see what was happening until everything was done. But Dani's strange disappearance the night before was a cloud between them, a thick and suffocating presence that slowly pressed them further and further apart. The opposite ends of a magnet.

Dani was exhausted, and unwilling to breathe even a word about what had happened, but she could feel her mother tensing beneath her capable ministrations. Even before Char cleared her throat, Dani knew what was coming—questions littered the air like silent ghosts.

"About last night . . ."

"I don't want to talk about last night," Dani said.

"Neither do I," Char complained. "Do you think I want to rehash all this? Do you think I like dissecting our feelings or trying to figure out if I need to replace your cutlery with plastic sporks?"

Dani snorted in spite of herself. "What is it with you people? You can't possibly think I'm suicidal."

"We don't. But we've never seen you like this before, Danica. For all we know, your warning signs are listening to Michael Bolton and forgetting to put on makeup. Both of which you're doing, by the way."

"I don't listen to Michael Bolton."

"Then what's this?" Char swept her arms to encompass the room, her hands pale and bony as they peeked from beneath the edge of the cape.

"It's John Coltrane. It's jazz. And I am wearing makeup. It's subtle." She almost added, cruelly, *But you wouldn't understand that.*

"Well, whatever. You know what I mean. You're acting strange, and we don't know what to do about it."

"You don't have to do anything about it."

"Easy for you to say. You're not the one who will have to find you if you decide to . . . you know."

"Excuse me?"

"It's messy." Char shivered. "I've heard."

Dani gave her mother's hair an unnecessarily hard tug and folded the foil she was working with into a too-tight rectangle. Against Char's wishes, she was weaving twilights into the platinum blond, darker tones of amber and honey that would mitigate some of the shock of her soon-to-be-yellow hair. But against the backdrop of their conversation, Dani was gripped with a desire to give her mother exactly what she wanted, to turn her into a Marilyn Monroe wannabe, a silly caricature.

"It's complicated," Dani finally said, reaching for her tail comb.

"Honey, life is complicated. Period."

Dani huffed, and was horrified to feel grief rise in her chest like warm steam. Her eyes watered. "You have no idea," she whispered around the thickness in her throat.

"Is that what you think?" Char put one heeled foot on the floor and spun the chair so she could face Dani. Her eyes sparked and her brow cut an uncharacteristically severe line across her forehead, deepening the wrinkles that she tried so hard to hide. "You think I don't understand complicated? Sweetheart, I wrote the book."

"You chose your life," Dani spat back. "I didn't ask for this!"

Char thrust herself out of the chair so that mother and daughter were standing toe-to-toe. For a moment Dani wondered if the older woman was going to slap her, but Char kept her fists balled and her posture rigid. "We all make choices, Dani, and I'm not going to excuse mine. But we play the hand that we're dealt. Do you think I wanted this? That

I wanted to be a single mom, just scraping by, the butt end of my grown daughters' jokes?"

"Char—"

"No," she interrupted, holding her hand palm up as if to ward off Dani's words. "You listen to me. Life really sucks sometimes. It sucks that Ell is gone. More than that—it's awful and unfair and wrong. It makes me want to break things and scream like bloody hell."

Dani didn't realize she was crying until she put her palms to her cheeks and felt the wetness there. "Please don't," she said. "I can't do this right now. I can't listen to a pep talk."

"This isn't a pep talk." Char reached for her daughter, caught her wrist for just a moment. Released. "I just want you to know that we get it. All of us. We don't know what it's like to lose a husband, but we know what it's like to hurt. Natalie came home, and Kat is standing on her head trying to be a good sister to you. And I'm here. I know that doesn't mean much, that I haven't exactly earned your confidence over the years, but we love you. You know that, don't you? I love you. That's got to mean something. It's got to ease *something.*"

Kat had said those very words, but they sounded different coming from Char. Maybe it was because she wasn't one for overt displays of affection—hugs and kisses, little touches that communicated more than an eloquent speech. And she didn't often tell her girls that she loved them. They knew it, and she said it just enough to keep them believing it, but it wasn't a sentiment that was tossed around in their family without weight.

Dani knew that she should say it back. That she should go to her mother and wrap her arms around the woman, cape and foils and all. But when she opened her mouth, she wasn't prepared for what came out. "I'm a widow." It was the first time she had admitted it, the first time she had spoken the word.

"I know, Danica."

"I should be old and gray. I should have the consolation of a lifetime behind me. Children and grandchildren . . ." Dani's chest was heaving, her breaths were ragged, ripped from the air. "It's not fair!"

"It's not fair," Char agreed, catching Dani by the wrists and holding tight. "But think of what you did have. Ten years, sweet girl. Ten years of the sort of love most of us will never know."

"Etsell cheated on me." It sounded so impossible, so surreal, that for a moment Dani was sure her mother wouldn't even be able to understand the words.

"What?" Char's indignant expression was muddied with confusion.

Something inside of Dani collapsed and crumbled to dust. She felt as if she were being sifted, every atom separated through a sieve that left her without form or boundary or purpose. She held her breath, afraid that if she so much as exhaled, the devastation would be complete. "In Alaska." Her voice was barely audible. "With that woman from the Midnight Sun."

"I don't understand."

"She showed up at my door last night. She told me what happened between them."

Char's mouth hardened into a furious line. "That little bitch. Why? Why would she—"

"It's my fault," Dani interrupted, yanking her arms from her mother's stranglehold. "I did this to him. I did this to us. And now he's gone and he can never forgive me for what I've done, and I can never forgive him. . . ."

"Dani—"

"Marriage is so hard," she whispered. "I mean, we loved each other, we really did, but nobody told me that years would go by and in the end we wouldn't be the same people as we were when we began."

Char reached for Dani's hands again and took them in her own, plaiting their fingers together like they were little girls. "Shhh," she said, pulling her closer, holding her gaze. "Don't do that. You loved each other. You said so yourself. That's the best anyone can do."

"But it wasn't enough, was it? He left me."

"He went to Alaska, and he got lost. He didn't leave you."

"He slept with her."

"It was a mistake." Char squeezed her daughter's hands so tight it hurt. "You know that, right? That it was a mistake?"

"She's having his baby."

Dani watched Char blink, a rapid-fire reaction that matched the flutter of her mouth. "What?" she finally managed, a question so tiny, so quiet, Dani would never have heard it if she wasn't standing less than a foot away.

"They fought," Dani continued. "He regretted it, and he wanted to tell me, but Sam tried to convince him that I didn't need to know. And then he took off. No destination. No flight plan."

"He disappeared," Char finished. She pressed her eyes closed as if making a wish, as if the harder she hoped, the more likely it was that her dreams would come true. "And you believe her? You believe that she's telling the truth?"

"I didn't want to, but why would she lie? Why would she fly all the way across the continent to torture me? It doesn't make any sense."

Char nodded, past the point of shock, obviously trying to process everything her daughter was throwing at her. "What about Ell? Did he know about . . . ?"

"The baby? I can't imagine that he did. He was only in Alaska for three weeks. I got the impression . . . I got the impression it only happened once."

"Murphy's law."

Dani pulled away from her mother and took a few steps back. She glanced at the door longingly, wondered what would happen if she ran for it and didn't stop. If she did something almost frighteningly out of character. If she just let go. But instead of fleeing, she made a pass at the tears that had already dried on her cheeks. "What do you mean?"

"Nothing." Char sank back into the chair and stared at herself in the mirror over the sink. They stayed like that for a moment, mother and daughter framed by the gilt edge of the mirror Dani had picked out with Ell, a tableau of loss. In the second before Dani turned her around again, Char caught her daughter's eye. "He loved you, Danica."

"Still." It was all Dani could bring herself to say, and it seemed to hold everything in the breath of that one little sigh. *Nevertheless, even now, yet.* Regardless of time and love and promises. We were one, and still . . .

"What are you going to do?" Char asked.

"What do you mean?"

But Char didn't answer. Instead, she asked, "That's why she came, isn't it? To give you a choice?"

Dani had purposefully kept that part of the conversation from her mom, but in spite of her numerous flaws and shortcomings, Char could be frustratingly perceptive when it came to people. Especially when she could relate to the person in question. Dani wondered, briefly, if Char had ever considered getting rid of her own inconveniences—the three girls who had pushed her meager income to the limit and assured that her life would be little more than one trial after another. She tried to picture her mother in a Planned

Parenthood clinic or sitting in a frayed office chair at an adoption agency. The scene wouldn't come into focus.

"Why did you keep us?" Dani surprised herself by voicing an impossible question.

"For the same reason that girl came to you." Char said, completely unfazed. She lifted one hand to push a weeping foil off her forehead, then pressed her fingertips against the corner of her eye as if to pat her makeup into place. "Because I couldn't imagine it any other way."

Danica

I thought about writing a letter. A letter that I would never send—could never send—and that he would never read. But there were words on my tongue, things I longed to say that stuck to the roof of my mouth for lack of an audience to hear them. They made me feel trapped and breathless, sick with the knowledge that I was full of things I could never release, an illness that threatened to consume me. And when my jaw ached from holding it all inside, I found my fingers itched, tense with the need to let it out somewhere. Anywhere. Even if it was on page after page of paper that I would then rip to tiny shreds, the refuse of a life undone.

What did I imagine would happen if I took a pen to paper? That my scribbled confessions would mirror the plea he scrawled over and over on the note that I still carried in my pocket? That we would find a way in the reflection to touch? To let it all go? I loved my husband and hated him in equal measure. I blamed him and I blamed myself.

In the weeks after Samantha appeared on my doorstep, summer quietly doled out the last remaining warm days and slipped away like a thief. Natalie went back to New York at the beginning of September, leaving me with nothing but a look that smacked of pity, and a quick, fierce hug that belied her final words, "Chin up, Danica Reese." She sounded almost chipper, but she feared for me. I caught it in the glance she threw over her shoulder, the way she held my gaze a second longer than necessary, searching for something that she didn't find.

After my conversation with Char in the salon, I expected Etsell's betrayal to be front-page news in Blackhawk. My mother was not one to keep confidences, but for some reason my personal hell proved to be the linchpin that finally sealed her mouth tight. She didn't breathe a word of any of it to Natalie or even Kat, and when Char stepped out of La Rue with a headful of soft, tawny waves, she gave me a wicked wink and said, "Not bad." One flick of her new 'do and it was as if the moment we shared had slipped away with the water down the drain.

I spun in a vacuum of my own design with no one to talk to and no way out. So I wrote. When the measure of my days was even, dull with the steady tedium of work and the motions of a hollow life, I bought a notebook and began to pen letters to my dead husband. One word at a time, one page at a time. And when all the lines were full, I'd rip the sheet from top to bottom and make confetti of my scattered thoughts.

In the beginning I tried to pretend that Sam had never come, that the chasm torn between me and the memory of Ell didn't exist. But I tripped into it at the most unexpected of times, fell headlong into my reality and landed so hard I eventually learned to hold her—and her baby—beside me. I could control them there. I could watch them out of the corner of my eye so that they weren't able to sneak up on me when I was least prepared for their unwelcome appearance.

It was a careful balance.

I was learning to survive in a place between, an existence where, if I breathed shallowly and clutched my secrets close, I could pass the hours like prayer beads between my fingers. One and another, a few more before I had to begin again. A careful repetition. A state of counterfeit peace. But when I woke up on September 10, my heart was fumbling for purchase, spinning and racing and stalling, and I knew my wary construction was little more than a house of sand.

It took me most of the day to realize why I was so out of sorts. And when I remembered, it was all in a rush, an onslaught of emotion that left me struggling for air.

Ten years. It was ten years to the day since Ell and I had gone on our very first date, the night that cemented our future and started us on the journey that led me, alone, to this moment. I could hardly picture us back then—children, really, with no way of knowing all that was to come. There was something melancholy in the air, a bittersweet note that hung over me as I flashed through those first encounters like slides that had gone fuzzy around the edges.

I remembered the box just as the sun started to set, and realized with a dark thrill that Kat wouldn't be back from work for hours. Whipping on a jacket, I stuck my feet in a pair of Mary Janes and hurried out to the shed. The faltering twilight was cool and dusty, dulled by the dirt kicked up from the first few combines that marked the very beginning of harvest. It had been a hot summer, and autumn would produce record crops. All the experts said so. Usually I loved this time of year, the way the air turned brittle according to the forecast and the leaves began to change. The yield of the fertile earth never ceased to make me pause, but now the breeze seemed somehow ominous as I threw open the shed door, sneezing and displacing weeks of grime.

The spade was lying across the floor, despondent, where I

had thrown it after planting those few bushes that Benjamin had gifted me. There were clumps of dry, ashy soil still clinging to the tip, and as I made my way to the willow, I tried to beat them off against the ground.

We had buried the capsule in the exact place where a knot in the tree seemed to point a gnarled finger at a dip in the grass. It was Etsell's idea, a notion that I cheerfully embraced when he came home from a flight to Minneapolis with a diminutive carved chest, hewn from a wood I couldn't identify, something swirled with an equal mix of dark and light that had been varnished to a gloss as hard and shiny as polished stone. Ell said it came from a tree that grew only in West Africa. He had found it in a little shop along a forgotten alley, a place that he was drawn to because of the scent of fresh tobacco and an unfamiliar spice that for some reason reminded him of his mother.

"It's precious," he said, his eyes twinkling. "Just think of how far it came. Just think of what we could put in it."

I ran my fingers up the line of buttons on his shirt and grabbed him by the collar. Pulled him close for a kiss. "It's a time capsule. You're making it sound like something far more mysterious. A treasure."

"It *is* a treasure!" Ell feigned a hurt expression, but he was too excited to keep it up.

"Only crazy people make time capsules out of wood. It'll rot."

"Not this wood." Etsell smirked. "The guy I bought it from said it's hard as a rock. Indestructible. Besides"—he tapped the top with his fingertips—"nothing is getting through this gloss. Come on, we'll fill it with secrets, and then dig it up when we're old and gray. Remember that movie? The one where the old lady gets Alzheimer's and can't remember her own husband? When you're all wrinkled and confused and wearing Depends, I'll use it to remind you of who you are. Of who we are."

"How romantic." I laughed, rolling my eyes.

Etsell lifted me off the ground for a moment and buried his face in my neck. "I adore you," he whispered against my warm skin. "You complete me."

"Thanks, Jerry Maguire."

"You make me want to be a better man."

"Jack Nicholson?" I guessed.

"La vita è bella; la vita è amore."

"Oh, now you're just showing off." I punched him in the arm and wiggled out of his grip, but he had already cast his spell—in my mind I was considering and rejecting the things I would tuck in his little Pandora's box.

We were young, and in the end we weren't very creative. There was a photo from our wedding, a candid shot of Etsell smearing a bite of French vanilla cake laced with raspberry cream across my cheek. Before the reception I had made him promise that he wouldn't do that, but at the last minute he changed his mind and dragged the frosting from the corner of my mouth to my ear like a stripe of war paint. I would have been angry except that he walked me to the bathroom under the guise of helping me clean up and then licked up every last trace with his warm tongue.

And we used a recipe card to write down a list of our favorites: favorite movies and books, television shows and dinners we made together. Etsell slipped in a CD that he had burned for us, a mix of Coltrane and Nat King Cole and Ella Fitzgerald that was still strange to me. Strange and discordant and jarringly lovely, but worth every unexpected note because, for some reason that I didn't yet understand, it spoke beauty over my husband.

I couldn't really remember what else we crammed in that

box, and when I finally saw the edge of it peeking from the hole I had dug at the base of our weeping willow, I felt a jolt of electricity rush through me. Tossing the spade aside, I knelt at the edge of the shallow trench and finished the excavation with my hands.

We had wrapped our package in an old burlap bag, and as I carefully peeled the covering back, I was relieved to see that time hadn't aged the chest much. Its sleek sides were still smooth as glass, and the simple latch still glimmered in the final glow of sunlight. It was heavy in my arms, weighted with the vows that our younger selves had so blithely made, and all the hope that we had crammed inside.

I fell back on my haunches and rested the box on my thighs, holding it gently with my palms flat against the high sides, trying with every ounce of my being to resist the urge to fling it against the tree. To watch the wood splinter. Or maybe I wanted to hold it close, to hug the sharp corners against my chest where I could pretend, if only for a minute, that everything was unbroken.

Lies, I thought. Lies and deception and broken promises and a life of loss like water through my hands. But before I knew what I was doing, my fingers were tracing the line of the lid, caressing it almost as I remembered doing the afternoon we put it in the ground. The dirt we threw over it a handful at a time, as if we were burying our dreams in a place where they had no choice but to grow.

"I can't wait to dig it up with you someday," Etsell had said.

"Do you think we'll be different?"

"Undoubtedly." Ell caught my hand. Squeezed. "What could be more exciting?"

I don't know how long I stayed beneath the tree like that: my head bent over a forgotten box, my hands cupping the sides gentle as a wish. But when I finally flicked the edge of the latch free with my thumbnail, my legs were numb and it was far too dark to see the contents of the small treasure chest. I had the impression of paper and a slim CD case, the muted shine of a photograph, and a few dark shapes I couldn't identify. It didn't matter. I didn't particularly want to pull anything out, to lay it across my kitchen table and dissect it as if I could unearth a vein of misfortune, of the tragedy that was to come in the flicker of our innocence.

Instead, I reached inside and felt blindly for the one last thing that I knew inhabited the depths. It was there, I found it almost instantly: a cold ring of woven metal that Ell had made for me after we had been together for one year. It was braided from the narrow thread of a wire that he twisted and then soldered together. A homemade gift. A promise of sorts.

"Every single time I take off I have to do a preflight check," he told me. "I have to make sure all the flaps are working and test the weights and double-check the tension of every little wire. That's where this came from." He held up the slender ring.

"Don't you need that wire?" I cocked an eyebrow at him playfully.

Etsell ignored me. Reached for my hand and slid the ring onto my finger. It was a bit big, but it caught just below my knuckle and stayed. "Without this tiny piece I'd crash. It's indispensable. Absolutely necessary. I wouldn't survive without it." He trailed off, incapable of articulating exactly what he was trying to say. Or maybe he wanted to let me fill in the blanks, draw my own conclusions about the boy I already claimed I loved. But though he seemed at a loss for words, he bent his head to kiss the ring on my finger, as solemn as a blessing.

He replaced that homemade piece of jewelry when he

proposed just over a year later. And the truth was, I was grateful. The wire cut, and the jagged edge where he hadn't soldered it properly snagged my sweaters. But I kept it in a small, beaded bag tucked deep in my underwear drawer, and when Ell came up with the idea for our time capsule, I happily resurrected it for inclusion in our project. It belonged with the mementos of our relationship.

The wind was starting to nip at my ears when I tried the ring on for the first time in nearly eight years. I was surprised to find that it slid easily past my knuckles. But it was too loose; the ring threatened to fall off and get lost in the gray-brown grass below my knees. So I put Etsell's creation between my lips, and eased off the platinum band that hadn't left my hand since the day we said, "I do." The skin beneath felt cool and exposed, naked in the autumn dusk. I quickly shoved the wire ring on and replaced my wedding band as a seal above it. The entire ensemble felt strange and bulky, but the discomfort was almost welcome. A reminder.

I started to close the box, ready to release it back to the ground from which it came. But the air around me seemed to hum with displeasure. I couldn't take the ring without leaving something else in its place. It felt wrong. Like I was looting a grave. Taking something that didn't belong to me. Not anymore.

Touching my neck, my wrists, my hands, I searched for a sacrifice that I was willing to make. But my skin was bare save my wedding ring and the ransom I had taken from the dark corner of the box. There was only one offering I could give.

I set the coffer on the ground so that I could reach into my pockets, to dig up scant handfuls of my most recent attempt at communication. Scraps that told bits and pieces of my story, fragments that fell from my fingers and caught the light like the tiny foil hearts that had glittered from our wedding table. That held all the things I couldn't bring myself to say. I stuffed them in the box, whispering the jagged slips down to settle into all the empty places.

To scatter their message over our shared history.

To rewrite it.

15

In Empty Places

A month had passed since Samantha's unexpected journey to Blackhawk, and still Dani made no attempt to acknowledge what had happened. The only things that marked the dissolution of Dani's world was a ring on her finger that hadn't been there before—a dull, grimy knot of rusting wire that rubbed her skin raw—and a creased note that she transferred from pocket to pocket. The paper was soft as fabric from being folded and unfolded, pressed flat and then crumpled up. But although she tried to throw it away on a dozen different occasions, Dani couldn't bring herself to do it. She kept digging the letter out of the garbage can, smoothing out the wrinkles with the heel of her hand, caressing the quick lines of his plea with her fingertips and avoiding the numbers that were inscribed at the bottom.

One day Kat came home with the metal frame of a twin bed in the trunk of her car. She hadn't asked Dani if she could move in, but it seemed so natural, Dani didn't think to question it. It hardly seemed like her decision to make. Instead of discussing it, the sisters carried the unwieldy rails into the spare room and set up the bed in the corner underneath the window. Dani made up the bed with sheets from her childhood, cotton so thin it felt like satin, printed with faded flowers the size of dinner plates.

"I remember those." Kat smiled. She was reclining in the office chair, cupped in the luxury of the deep seat with her legs thrown over one sturdy, leather arm and crossed neatly at the ankles. "How'd you end up with my old sheets?"

"These are my old sheets," Dani said.

"No, they're not. I distinctly remember sleeping on them."

Dani just shrugged, wondering if Kat would think of the nights they spent curled up together. If they were as important to Kat as they were to her.

"Either way, those froufrou sheets don't exactly match the decor." Kat swiveled her head to survey her surroundings. "I need a cigar. A cigar and one of those gangster suits with the pinstripes. No—a linen suit and a Tommy Bahama hat. The cigar works either way."

"I designed this room for Ell," Dani said, snapping the spare coverlet across the taut sheets with a flick of her wrists.

His name lingered in the air for a moment, a fine tremor between them. Dani didn't talk about Etsell often these days, and everyone else followed her lead. There were so many questions, so many things left unanswered, but after the night she left the house and drifted like a lost soul toward the river, it seemed best to let her set the pace. Hazel stopped pestering her about the trestle table. Her sisters tried to keep things buoyant, on the surface. And though Benjamin continued to take care of her lawn, he didn't knock on the door anymore. He didn't invite her to join him in the labor of digging dirt and planting, of forgetting. Sometimes the grass was freshly cut when she came home from work. And sometimes he worked in the evening and she watched him through the window above the sink and wondered if she should bring him a drink. Say thank you at least. But she couldn't quite bring herself to.

"I thought maybe if Ell had a room that made him feel like a world traveler, he wouldn't be so anxious to become one." Dani's voice was clear and strong, but her hand skidded off the end of the bed as she made the final tuck.

"Did it work?" Kat asked, studying the tip of a manicured fingernail.

Dani gave her a harsh look. "What do you think?"

"Well"—Kat swung her legs off the arm of the chair and stood with a flourish—"I think it's perfect. I feel like I'm checking into some exotic getaway—a Caribbean plantation. I can almost smell the frangipani."

"As if you know what frangipani smells like."

"I do!" Kat gasped. "I have a perfume that contains undertones of plumeria. Same thing, right?"

Dani shrugged. "How in the world would I know? I defer to your tropical flower expertise." She put her hands on her hips and made a show of studying her sister's new bedroom. The desk had been set askew in the very middle of the original hardwood floor, but they moved it to one wall to make space for the bed. Beyond that, it wasn't much changed, and yet just the knowledge that Kat was a more permanent fixture made everything feel downright foreign. The sheeted bed sent a little tremor through Dani, a shiver that acknowledged nothing would ever be the same.

Kat must have seen the transformation, because she stepped toward her sister, laid a hand against her pale cheek for the span of a heartbeat. "Just for a while," she said. "I thought you wouldn't want to be . . ."

"I don't," Dani choked. "It's just . . . I feel trapped. I don't know what to do." She considered telling Kat everything, about Sam and Etsell's secret and the baby that should have never been. That probably never would be. It had been four weeks since Sam left Blackhawk. For all Dani knew, she had aborted the baby.

The sudden idea stabbed through her like a knife. She tried to skirt around thoughts of what Etsell had done and the consequences that he had left her to deal with. But whether she liked to acknowledge it or not, she knew without pause that Sam was nineteen weeks along. That she was due at the end of January or maybe the beginning of February. A winter baby.

Dani knew Kat couldn't begin to suspect what was going on in her mind. That her sister would be horrified if she knew. Furious. For a minute she indulged an impossible daydream, one in which Kat met Sam and learned of what the vile woman had done. Dani had longed to slap Samantha, but she knew her sister would have no qualms about actually doing it. A faint smile creased Dani's lips.

Kat's eyes widened a bit. Seemingly encouraged by Dani's smile, she gave her a quick, hard hug and pulled back to hold her at arm's length. "Don't hate me," Kat said in a rush, "But I think I know one thing you should do."

"You do?"

"How long has Ell been gone?" Kat asked the question gently, but it still fell like a gauntlet.

"Four and a half months. Eighteen weeks."

"That long? Has it been that long already?" Kat looked genuinely distraught. She shook her head as if to clear it. "Dani, I want to remember him," she said, squeezing her sister's arms, pleading. "I know we can't have a funeral, not really, but don't you want to honor him anyway? To talk about his life and who he was and how much we loved him? It might help. It might be good for all of us. You know, help us—help you—move on."

"I don't know if I can do that," Dani said.

"Why not? You could ask Benjamin. He'd do it for you."

"I know, but—"

"He loves you, you know," Kat cut in. "Benjamin, I mean. I don't know if he's *in* love with you, but all you have to do is see the way he looks at you to know that—"

"What?" Dani choked out, her voice so ragged it stopped her sister cold.

"Well, don't make a big deal out of it. I was just saying."

Dani lifted her shoulders a little, one arched higher than the other, as if to mirror the confusion she felt. "My life is a mess. I don't want to hear that right now."

"Anyway, I don't want to talk about Ben. I want to talk about a memorial for Ell. Don't you want that?"

"I don't know what I want," Dani said helplessly.

"Maybe it's not about what you want. It's about what you need."

"And you know what I need? I have no idea where I'm going. And even if I did, I wouldn't know how to get there from here."

"That's the problem." Kat pressed her lips together in frustration and let her arms drop to her sides. "There's no map for this sort of thing, Dani. You act like there should be a handbook. Like if you search hard enough you'll discover a Twelve-step program. But it doesn't work like that. You fumble through the only way you know how. It's not a matter of doing it right or getting it wrong. It's a matter of putting one foot in front of the other, even when you don't want to."

"Isn't that exactly what I'm doing?" Dani made a noise of indignation in the back of her throat and snatched a pillow from the floor. Stuffing it into a flowered pillowcase with more force than necessary, she said, "I have done everything in my power to pick up the pieces. I know I moped in the beginning, but I got over that. I'm putting in crazy hours at the salon, I've spent days on Hazel's table, I even help Benjamin with the yard work. What more do you want from me?"

"I want you to be more than a paper doll."

"What in the world is that supposed to mean?" Dani growled.

"It means you should stop using the salon and the table and yard work"—Kat grabbed the pillow from Dani—"and pillows as an excuse. That's not life. That's a to-do list."

Dani glared at her sister for a moment, then she spun on her heel and stormed out of the room, slamming the door behind her. It felt so good, she wrenched open the door and did it again, smashing the heavy, single pane of warped wood closed with all her might. The frame shook. Her hands trembled. But she felt strangely satisfied. Exhilarated.

It had been days—weeks?—since Dani had touched the trestle table, but after her fight with Kat, all she wanted to do was hide in the garage. The sun was setting and the air was cool when Dani stepped from the house, but she zipped up her fleece in one determined movement and jogged across the front yard. She slipped through the side door, feeling for the light switches and flicking them all on. When the fluorescent bulbs were humming in the dimness, she slammed the door behind her for good measure. Then she locked it, struggling with the rusty dead bolt for a few seconds before the heavy latch finally gave and slid home.

Dani heaved a weighted sigh and closed her eyes, taking in the silence, the cold nip of the evening air. She counted her heartbeats, lost track, and started again. Mostly she tried to forget what Kat had said. Words laden with all the things she should do. All the things she couldn't.

When she could breathe again, Dani put her hands on her hips and considered the table before her. It was stripped completely bare, the wood vulnerable to the elements, as naked and fragile as her own soft skin. She had bought a can of honey stain, a warm, soothing color that she had matched perfectly to the original finish. It was going to be a gorgeous table, a golden goddess spread out in invitation to come, to sit, to rest.

But for some reason, as Dani reached for the can of creamy stain, she paused. It felt wrong somehow to try to restore the table to what it had been. After all the antique trestle had been through—the life it had seen, the road it had traveled—a redemption in replica seemed like a cheap cop-out. It would never be what it had been. It couldn't. And as she ran her hand over the pocked surface, Dani realized that she didn't want it to be.

Tucked on the bottom shelf behind Etsell's metal toolbox, Dani found an old can of wiping stain in russet cherry. She gave the can a few hard shakes, then popped the top off with a screwdriver. It wasn't as old as she had imagined; hardly any separation had taken place. Certainly nothing a good stir wouldn't fix.

In a matter of minutes she was poised over the table, frayed rag clutched in hand, the flushed stain soaking the cloth like melted rubies, like the last fringe of sunset, like blood. Her own blood was pumping hot and fast, and her palms were clammy at the prospect of smudging the wood with the dark stain. Everything in her rebelled against the idea of ruining the heirloom before her. To mar it with anything other than the original color was nothing less than an act of destruction—she was no better than the misguided soul who had painted it blue.

As Dani stared at the soft pattern of the wood grain, she realized that she didn't care. It would be red. Spilled wine. An offering.

The first few strokes were shocking. The dark stain bled into the old wood, seeping into invisible crevices and ensuring that whoever inherited Dani's table would work their hands to the bone erasing the damage she had done. But she thought it was beautiful. Beautiful and terrible all at once—irreversible.

Forever changed.

Danica

It took two weeks for me to finish the table. Two weeks of spending every spare minute holed up in the cold garage with a rag clutched in one hand and a can of stain at my side. I could have done it much faster with a paintbrush, but I wanted to feel the wood beneath my fingertips, to smooth the color on in patterns that only my hands could expose. It was a labor of love, I suppose, but there was a bitter edge to my work—the understanding that I was taking something of great value and selfishly, greedily making it mine.

When the last corner of the farthest leg had been varnished and sealed, I let the table set for three straight days. I didn't peek at it once, didn't admire my handiwork in the uncompromising sheen of autumn daylight, even though I longed to. Instead, I locked the garage doors as if ashamed of what I had done. I hid from my own creation. And then, when I couldn't stand it another second, I called Hazel.

"I want to show you something," I said.

She didn't question me. She just came.

It was a Saturday afternoon and the sky was so blue, I couldn't bring myself to look at it. White clouds dotted the garage windows in an imperfect reflection, a work of art in white, and the sun so brilliant and bright, I had to squint. Hazel was wearing sunglasses, and I could see myself in them: my own wide, unblinking gaze, the slight part in my lips, as if life had taken me by complete surprise. I closed my mouth, erasing the evidence of my shock. Cleared my throat.

"I finished the table," I said without preamble.

Hazel's eyes were hidden behind her sunglasses, but her mouth tightened, a look that I had come to learn was her personal version of a half smile. "Took you long enough."

Rather than defend myself, I pushed the button on the garage door. The small motor choked to life, dragging the heavy panels up with a sort of feeble drama. I would have laughed but for the wind—it swept around the corner of the house and lifted my hair, breathed a hint of winter down my neck.

I had pulled the table into the very middle of the garage, and it seemed to take up the entire space. It shone in the sudden sunlight that poured through the open door, sleek and larger than life, glowing red as the ring of a distant harvest moon.

"I thought you were going to restore it—stain it gold. Puritan pine or something like that." Hazel walked into the garage and peeled off her sunglasses. She raised a hand above the top of the table as if she was going to lay her palm against the surface. Changed her mind. Put a fist on her hip instead.

"I decided I liked this better."

She gave a jagged nod, the sort of gesture that could have been interpreted a dozen different ways from appreciation to disapproval. "It's dramatic," she said.

I shrugged.

For all I knew she was disappointed in me. Maybe she had wanted me to restore the table and sell it, use the money to do something special in honor of Etsell. Erect a statue at the airport, a pilot fashioned from bronze with an epitaph that people would ignore. Or maybe she just disliked my bold act of defiance, of the way that I defaced something as stunning as the antique trestle table.

"I love it," I said, more to myself than to her.

"I do too."

She sounded sincere, but when I caught her eye, she looked so serious, I took a tiny step back.

"Look, Dani, I know who came to your house that night."

I didn't have to ask her what she meant, there were only two nights that seemed to matter in my life: the night I got the call from Alaska, and the night that Alaska came to me. "How?" I asked.

"Who else could make you look like that? Like you had come face-to-face with a ghost." Hazel sighed and hooked the arm of her sunglasses through her belt loop, where they dangled like a pair of discarded eyes. I had the impression that she wanted to see me from a different perspective. "I think I knew in Alaska. Or, at least, I guessed."

"You did?" I was too stunned to be upset.

"It was in the way that girl looked at you."

"Hatred?" I guessed.

"More like jealousy. Fear."

"Jealousy?"

Hazel brought her hand to her forehead and rubbed her temples between her thumb and forefinger. "Fill in the blanks for me," she said. "He had some sort of a fling with her and hated himself for it. Am I right so far?"

It took all my willpower to force one tiny nod.

"Was it . . . did he . . . ?" She made an effort to collect herself. "Did Etsell go missing on purpose?"

"I don't think so," I said. "I think he was angry. Distraught."

"Accidents happen," Hazel said, so softly I had to strain to catch it. She exhaled hard and then raised her head to pierce me with a pointed gaze. "I'm guessing Sam didn't come all the way to Iowa to break your heart."

"She's pregnant." I watched the effect those words had on Hazel, the way they made her eyes go flat, and took a small measure of consolation from the fact that I could tell, beneath her stony expression, she was livid.

"Stupid, stupid boy," she hissed. For a moment I thought that was all she was going to say, but all at once something shifted in her expression and I saw that she had come to a conclusion. "I'm going to tell you something," she began. "You're probably going to hate me, but I think you need to hear it all the same."

"Excuse me?"

"Just sit down and listen." She spun around and grabbed the Queen Anne chair that she had brought me all those weeks ago and set it down in the center of the garage with a bang. "No interrupting."

I sank to the ratty velvet with a feeling of foreboding, a sense that my world was about to shift on its axis yet again. "I don't think I want to hear what you have to say," I muttered, starting to rise the moment I felt the seat beneath me. "Please leave, Hazel."

"No." She put her hands on my shoulders and shoved me back against the chair. "I'm going to say what I came to say. And then, if you never want to see me again, I won't blame you. I'll leave you alone."

"It might be too late."

"It might," she agreed. "But I'm going to have to take that chance." Hazel turned her back to me and paced to the other side of the table, collecting her thoughts, marshaling her words before she dared to open her mouth. "Do you remember that day I saw you in the hardware store with that guy?"

That guy. Of course there was only one person she could possibly mean. It was so long ago, so innocent now that I knew what Etsell had been capable of, that I felt almost indignant. "Are you kidding me? You're going to bring that up when you know what happened between Ell and Samantha?"

But Hazel ignored me. "I told him," she said.

At first I didn't know what she meant, but as realization dawned on me, I found I was too angry even to respond.

"I told Etsell about what I saw, and what I suspected. I know you probably think that I was trying to break the two of you up, but that's not the case. It's true, I've always thought you and Ell were a strange match—and I probably wouldn't have picked you for him if I could have been the one to choose—but I didn't want to ruin your marriage. I just wanted him to know."

"Know what?" I spat out. I was clutching the arms of the seat, my fingers white-knuckled and my chest heaving. For a second I indulged an impossible fantasy—one where I flung myself up, slapped Hazel across her weathered cheek. "What did you want him to know? That he was ignoring me and that some stranger made me feel pretty?"

"Exactly."

Anger whooshed out of me in a hot rush. "What?"

"I wanted him to know that he was screwing up his marriage. That relationships are a tenuous thing—fragile as crystal. He wasn't being careful with you. He needed to know that."

Astonishment made me unsteady, and I slouched into the chair, my spine curved dolefully against the stiff back. "He must have been so angry," I breathed.

"He was," Hazel said. "He was angry at himself."

"But—"

"Oh, he was pretty pissed at you too. But mostly he blamed himself."

We were silent for a few moments, surveying each other with what I first believed was mutual distrust. But we had come a long way since Ell's disappearance, and there was something in Hazel's face that I wasn't prepared for. Affection? No, it was more than that. I understood with a quick and devastating conviction that her heart was breaking for me. And yet, that knowledge didn't change the implications of what she had just said.

"What are you trying to say?" I asked, because the question needed to be voiced. "That it's my fault Ell had an affair? That I should blame myself for what happened between him and Sam?"

Hazel slipped her sunglasses from where they were hooked on her belt loop. She put them on, her chin set in a straight, stoic line, then turned her mirrored eyes toward me. "I'm just telling you what happened. It's up to you to draw conclusions."

I felt rooted to the chair as I watched Hazel walk to her truck. It struck me for one of the very first times that she was old, that her spine was beginning to bend her head toward the earth. And she seemed just the tiniest bit unsteady on her feet; there was a quiver in her step. I thought about calling after her—I wasn't even sure why—but before I could make my mouth form the words, the door of her truck slammed shut. The engine caught and the truck backed out of my driveway.

It wasn't until after she was gone that I realized why she put on her sunglasses.

Hazel had started to cry.

I was sixteen years old when I first met Hazel.

Etsell and I had been dating for just a couple of months, but it was already serious. Or as serious as a relationship can be when you're too young even to know what a relationship truly is. He picked me up one afternoon under the guise of taking me to a movie, but instead of driving toward Sioux Falls and the theaters, he took off in the opposite direction, toward the airport.

Hazel had been asking about me, he said. She wanted to meet the girl that had him tripping over his own two feet and showing up late for scheduled flight times—something he had never done before.

I won't lie. I was downright terrified to meet Ell's surrogate mom. She was notorious in Blackhawk, a stern-faced workhorse of a woman who farmed beside her husband and raised a pair of sons in relative anonymity until Mr. Jansen got sick and died a slow and agonizing death. His illness left its mark on her, too, and when she was finally able to lay him to rest, she spun her life around with the reckless abandon of someone who didn't seem to care anymore. Of someone who had completely forgotten who she was and should be.

First, Hazel sold the farm. Then she started taking classes at the local tech school, introduction to mechanics, metal engineering, and even CAD. Soon she had enrolled in flight class, something she swore she had wanted to do ever since she was a little girl.

Hazel's sons went out of state for college, and never came back. Rumor had it they resented her for taking the small fortune that Mr. Jansen had left to languish in the bank and investing it in the stock market. It didn't help that their mother was a fifty-something college student, and more concerned with airplane mechanics than doing her boys' laundry or fixing the sort of roast-and-mashed-potato meals that they had grown up enjoying on the farm. It was as if in the twilight of her life Hazel had decided that she was going to start from scratch. And everything conveniently fell away to accommodate her new dreams: her husband, the farm, her kids.

When eight-year-old Etsell started hanging around the airport, they were ripe for each other. He was longing for someone to fill the hole that Melanie left behind, and Hazel took him under her wing before she could stop to wonder what she was doing and why. Behind her back people said that it was a second chance at motherhood, an opportunity for her to make things right, but even then I knew that Hazel loved Etsell for who he was—not because of who she wished he would be.

My hands trembled as Ell walked me into the hangar that day. I laced my fingers through his to hide the evidence of my anxiety, and stuffed the other fist in the pocket of my coat. Hazel's back was turned to us when we slipped through the side door, and her cheek was pressed against the side of a small plane, a rusty old thing that matched the color of her stained overalls almost perfectly. Though our footsteps echoed off the concrete floor and rang in the metal rafters of the cavernous building, she didn't acknowledge our presence. My tension mounted.

She would hate me, I was sure of it. Surely she knew who my mother was. Everyone did. Surely I wouldn't be good enough for Etsell, for the boy that she was pouring her heart and soul into, the young man she was resurrecting.

The child who, I understood in a rush, had saved her too.

I licked my lips, erasing the smear of my pink lipstick with my tongue, and wished that I had worn something less pretty. I felt out of place in the drafty hangar, and even more absurd in comparison to the harsh lines of her steel-toed work boots and wild mop of unkempt hair. My own red-blond tresses were elaborately braided, a twisted, intricate up-do that suddenly made me feel like something out of a storybook—a fair maiden, the sort of fainting girl who didn't stand a chance against the evil stepmother.

Hazel ignored us up until the moment that Etsell reached out to her. He laid his hand against her shoulder, a touch so gentle that I wondered if she would even feel it. But she brushed a dusty rag against the side of the plane, smoothing it over the rivets, places where the rust had eaten away the paint, and then tucked the frayed piece of cloth in the front pocket of her coverall.

"Hey, sweetie," she said, finally turning toward him. He was still holding my hand, but she didn't acknowledge me. Instead, she grazed her lips against his forehead, eyes closed as if she was feeling for a temperature. They stayed that way for a long moment before she pulled away and sighed. I felt her eyes fall on me.

"So," she murmured. "She's the one."

Something surged through me, an emotion that I couldn't identify at the time and was scared to examine later. I should have been deferential, shy, but instead of cowering beneath her scrutiny, I threw back my shoulders. Looked her full in the face.

"Yes. I'm the one."

16

Because Everything Has

There was a warm streak the second week of October, a brief Indian summer that descended on Blackhawk like a sudden blessing. Though Dani opened all her windows and resurrected a few forgotten T-shirts that she had stored on an unused shelf in her closet, she rolled her eyes when Kat spread a beach towel on the front lawn and arranged herself on top of it in nothing but a string bikini. All the same, Dani couldn't help but turn her face toward the sunshine, closing her eyes and arching toward the light like a cat about to stretch and purr.

On Sunday the warm front hit its zenith, and favored the autumn afternoon with a fresh and whisper-still eighty degrees.

"Let's go to the lake," Kat suggested. "Or maybe for a hike. We have to do something."

"I thought maybe you'd lay out in front of the house again," Dani said, only half teasing. "A living lawn ornament. Apparently you're decorative."

"Not enough people come by this corner." Kat smirked. "That's why I want to go somewhere else."

"Take off," Dani said, convinced that her sister was sticking around only to make sure that she didn't mope the day away. "I want to get some things done around here."

"Such as?"

"The table should have one more light sanding."

"Are you ever going to be done with that table?"

"Almost." Dani smiled almost shyly. "I'm almost done."

Kat threw up her hands. "Fine. I'm going to call some friends and head to the lake. Join us later?"

"Maybe."

But Dani had no intention of going to the lake. She planned on sanding the table, just like she said. And winterizing a few of the plants. Maybe, just maybe, she'd take a walk to the river.

Dani threw open all the garage doors while she worked, and reveled in the crisp harvest scent of the unseasonably warm air. It seemed laced with apples and earth, just a hint of smoke, as if someone had decided it was the perfect day for a bonfire. And it was. A perfect day for evening bonfires and reading a book in the shade and inhaling every moment of the last reprieve before the weather did a one-eighty and draped Iowa in a shimmering gown of snow and ice.

As she moved around the table, Dani tried to make her mind blank, to exist in the fragile heart of the day as carefully as the last few leaves clung to brittle stems. She was succeeding, until she caught a glimpse of something out of the corner of her eye and came to peer through the window overlooking her backyard.

Benjamin was standing at the very edge of her lawn, one hand on a railroad tie that stood beside him like a staff. His dark head was bent and he seemed to be considering the ground before him. He scuffed it with the toe of his tennis shoe, then dropped his shoulders and looked up at the sky, considering the sun, the way that it would slant.

As Dani watched him from the frame of her garage window, she couldn't help but think about what Kat had said. The truth was, she was too numb to feel much of anything, to allow herself even to dwell on the implications of her neighbor's goodwill and all the ways he had reached out to her since Etsell's disappearance. But he had been there. That should count for something. And though Dani contemplated leaving him there, pretending that she had never seen him at all, there was something about the serious way he worried his bottom lip that made an unexpected smile tug at the corner of her mouth. At the very least she could offer him a little direction.

Abandoning her sandpaper, Dani stepped out of the garage and into the full splendor of the sun. She shaded her eyes with her hand and made her way to Benjamin, waving her fingers a little when he looked up and saw her coming.

"Are you allowed to work on Sunday?" she asked, indicating the wooden beam with a tilt of her chin.

"Are you kidding?" Benjamin gave her a droll grin. "I work every Sunday. Twice. This is for fun."

"Studying my brown grass is fun? I thought you'd have had enough of it after all the mowing you did this summer."

"Oh, I'm done with your grass," Benjamin said. "I've decided that today would be a good day to start on that strawberry patch you wanted. I'm not much of a gardener, but I do know that we'd be well served to get a couple loads of manure worked into the soil before the first frost."

"I had kind of forgotten about it," Dani admitted. She regretted it immediately, hoped she hadn't hurt his feelings.

But Benjamin seemed undeterred. "It takes a few years for a strawberry patch to really produce," he said. "If you'd like fruit before you're too old to enjoy it, I'd better get started."

Dani struggled for a second, wondering if she should

excuse herself and let him work in peace. But whether it was the sunshine or the fact that Benjamin had done so much for her, she couldn't bring herself to disappear back into the garage and leave him to labor alone. "I'll help you," she said.

He looked at her quickly. "You don't have to."

"I want to."

Benjamin shrugged good-naturedly. "I won't talk you out of it. Maybe we can get it done before I have to shower up for the evening service."

They measured out a large bed, Benjamin walking off the dimensions and marking the spot with landscaping ties that he set up at the perimeter. Then it was a matter of pulling up the sod, a task that was made all the more difficult by the fact that the ground was dry and hard, and that Dani was woefully inept at using the spade as a blade to hew hunks of grass from the dusty soil.

"If I'd have known I'd get sweaty," Dani said, passing her wrist over her forehead, "I wouldn't have offered to help."

"It's not too late to back out," Benjamin joked. But they both knew that Dani wasn't going anywhere.

It wasn't until Benjamin was drilling holes for the stakes that Dani worked up the courage to ask him the question that had been plaguing her since she first caught sight of him from the garage window. "I know we don't—I don't—go to your church, but I was wondering if . . . I was hoping that maybe you'd be willing to do a memorial for Etsell."

The drill went silent, but Benjamin's head stayed bowed over the splintered wood. For a second, Dani wondered if he had heard her at all, or if her request had fallen on deaf ears. She swallowed hard.

But then Benjamin looked up, and his eyes were so soft and earnest, it made her breath catch. "I'd be honored," he said. "Truly, I would. Etsell was an amazing man."

"He was," she echoed, surprised to find that it was suddenly hard to speak. "We . . ." her voice broke.

"I can't imagine how hard this must be for you," Benjamin said.

Dani wanted to make light of it, to break the spell of her need and his compassion, but it was too late to dissemble, to go back to the work before them as if nothing had ever happened. She had just admitted that Etsell was gone. That she was ready to let go.

Benjamin must have seen the anguish in her face. "You're very brave," he told her.

"No, I'm not."

"Of course you are."

She shook her head quickly, denying it. "I don't really know how to do this. What a service would look like."

"I'll help you figure it out."

"I don't even know where to begin."

"I think it's important that we remember Etsell," Benjamin said. "But it's also important that we acknowledge what you've lost. Honor your relationship."

Dani looked at the ground because she didn't want to look at Benjamin. "I used to think we were holy," she said. "I mean, I thought our marriage was holy. You know, holy matrimony and all that. That must sound so silly to you."

"Marriage *is* holy." Benjamin used one hand to push himself up. He stood before Danica with the drill dangling from one hand and a faint smile on his lips.

"I don't really even know what that means."

"It means set apart. Purposeful." He lifted one shoulder as if in apology. "I actually think most relationships are worth much more than we give them credit for. They mean something—God wants to use them for something. But we fall short. We mess it up."

Dani bit her lip. Wondered if Benjamin suspected more than he let on. And wondered why he wasn't going on—why he wasn't evangelizing, asking her to repent, or at the very least encouraging her to join him at the evening church service.

"You let me know when you're ready," Benjamin said, and for just a moment he laid his hand over hers where it rested on the handle of the spade. Then he glanced at the quickly setting sun, his watch. "I'd better get going or I'll be late. I'll wrap this up tomorrow, okay? Get a few loads of manure, finish staking the borders . . . I promise I'll have it ready for spring before the first snow flies."

Dani nodded. She just stood there as he kicked the last railroad tie into place and left the stakes in a neat pile in the dirt. Then he gave her a close-lipped smile and tipped an imaginary hat.

"Tomorrow," he said, taking off across the grass.

When he was sheltered beneath the shade of their shared apple trees, she called out to him. "Why haven't you ever talked about him before? God, I mean. We've lived by each other for years, and you've never so much as mentioned his name."

Benjamin turned toward her for just a moment. "I have," he said, his eyes bright and burnished by the faintest of smiles. "In lots of different ways."

And then he was gone.

〜

Dani pulled the paper from her pocket and flattened it against the kitchen table with her palms. She was poised on the very edge of one of the chairs, back pin-straight and toes pointed against the floor as if she was about to change her mind. As if she might flee at any moment. But the phone was on the table beside her, and before she could lose her nerve, she grabbed it and punched in the numbers.

Samantha answered on the first ring. "Hello?"

"Sam?" Dani asked, breathless. She swallowed, tried again. "Hi, Sam, it's Danica Greene."

"Oh."

"Please don't hang up."

"I wasn't going to."

It was an impossible conversation, and they both knew it. Danica could tell by the way Sam's voice echoed high and taut, stretched like a tightrope about to snap.

"I don't know how to do this," Dani admitted after an awkward moment. "This is much harder than I thought it would be."

Sam didn't say anything.

"It's just . . . I know that he's gone, that he's not coming back," Dani said, haltingly. "I've accepted it, I guess. And, honestly, I can hardly stand the thought of you, but if there's a part of him that is still . . . I mean . . . I just want to do the right thing."

"That's why I came to Blackhawk," Sam broke in. "I was trying to do the right thing. God knows I've done enough things wrong."

Dani almost smiled. Almost.

"My brother flies for United. It was easy enough to hop on standby. . . . But it was stupid." Sam sighed on the other end of the line. "I thought that maybe, if you knew, you would—"

Would what? Dani wondered. Adopt her husband's baby? A child that wasn't hers? And yet, somehow she knew that this would never be over—that she would never be able to leave Ell behind—if she didn't let Sam go too.

"I'm glad I know." Even though Dani said it, the statement surprised her. But she lingered in it for a second, came to the conclusion that she meant it. "I am. It changes everything, but I can't wish it away."

Silence.

Dani gathered herself, mustering the courage to ask what was plaguing her. Her blood pounded in her ears as she struggled to form the words. "You said you couldn't keep the baby. Is there . . . ? I mean, did you . . . . ?"

But Sam didn't answer. Instead, she said, "If you want to pretend that nothing ever happened, I'm fine with that. We can hang up the phone and just let it all go. . . ."

Pretend that nothing ever happened. It was a tempting thought, an idea as thick and comforting as wool, the sort of daydream that Dani longed to wrap around herself. She'd close her eyes, tuck those secret hopes in tight, and make believe that everything was as it should be. That Ell was home. That he hadn't failed and fallen short and broken her heart. That she hadn't done the same. Or maybe she didn't have to construct so lofty a facade. Maybe it was enough simply to forget what she already knew.

But as she clutched the telephone that suddenly felt agonizingly heavy, Dani knew that pretending was exactly the problem. It was where everything began to unravel. In the white lies they told each other. The big ones they told themselves. Promises they didn't plan to keep, differences that they made valiant attempts to dull, to push aside as they shifted and tried and then tried again. It was too much. It wasn't enough.

"No," Dani told Sam. "I don't want to live like nothing ever happened. I want to live because everything has."

Danica

The day of Etsell's memorial dawned clear and bright. The air was sharp with cold, and a thick layer of frost robed the earth in a gown of shimmering white. Each blade of grass, each twisted tree branch was finely wrought, fragments of handmade lace that shone against a landscape of blown glass.

It reminded me of our wedding somehow, the winter morning just a few days before Christmas when Etsell and I said, "I do." We had planned to take outdoor pictures, but the temperature was well below freezing and my lips turned blue after just a couple of shots. In the end, the only photo worth salvaging from our icy adventure was the very last one. I was shaking from the cold, and rather than let me pick my way back to the car through the snow, Etsell wrapped his suit coat around my shoulders and swept me into his arms.

The photographer zoomed in and snapped a quick close-up, capturing the split second when I reached up and kissed Ell's neck before tucking my chin into his heavy coat. In the photo, my lips are slightly parted, and they just graze the place where Etsell's pulse throbbed steady and warm beneath his skin. Afterward, I didn't remember kissing him, but when I flipped to the picture in our wedding album on the day of my husband's memorial, I could feel the brush of the fine hairs on his neck. I could taste him. Tracing the photo with my fingertips, I told the girl in Ell's arms to savor the moment. To press her face into the firm curve of his shoulder. But it was too late.

"You ready?" Kat popped her head into my bedroom and found me staring at the wedding picture. We both jumped a little and looked away, persuaded by the surprise of the moment that she had caught me in the act of doing something shamefully intimate. "Take your time," Kat backtracked, forgoing her usual boldness. She ducked her head almost timidly. "I'll be waiting in the kitchen."

"No need. I'm coming." I shut the photo album with definitive slap and bent to slide it under my bed. "I can't be late. They'll talk."

"Who'll talk?"

"They."

"Ah," Kat nodded. "The ubiquitous they. Bastards."

I tucked my lip between my teeth, nibbling back the sort of dangerous smile that would undoubtedly be a prelude to tears. Although I thought I had progressed to the point where I could leave that sort of messy sentiment behind me, the fact that we were finally doing this—that I was saying good-bye in such a conclusive, permanent way—left me fragile. Off-balance. One unexpected memory away from losing my tenuous hold on the aura of cool composure I worked so hard to cultivate.

"Hey." Kat caught me beneath the elbow and squeezed. "You all right?"

"Fine," I lied.

Kat arched an eyebrow at me.

"Terrible," I amended. "Is that what you want to hear? That I'm not okay?"

My sister studied me for a long moment, then bent toward me and touched her lips to my forehead. "You are okay," she said, backing away. "You've made it this far, haven't you?"

Six months. That's what she meant. I had lived in this new life, this hollow, husbandless life for almost exactly six months. Twenty-six weeks. Half a year. A lifetime. And in many ways, Kat was right. I had made it this far. There were times I longed for Etsell with an intensity that still made me weak in the knees, but there were days when he was nothing more than a soft ache. Something familiar and bittersweet, the source of a manageable and not altogether unwelcome pain.

"I'm okay," I said, as if saying it was enough to make it true.

"Hell yeah." Kat winked at me. "You've got this memorial thing in the bag." She sounded confident, but her voice wavered just a bit. Enough to assure me that she was having a hard time saying good-bye too.

I glanced at the clock on my bedside stand. "We'd better get going."

"It takes what? Five minutes to get to the hangar? We need to hit the kitchen first. I have something for you."

Although Kat was not the gift-giving type, I half expected some sort of memento to commemorate the day. A card at least. Something that tried to express what my sister couldn't bring herself to say. But what awaited me in the kitchen was a bottle of booze and a shot glass.

"You want to get me drunk before the memorial?" I choked.

"No! Of course not." Kat clipped across the kitchen in her heels and took the delicate, faceted bottle in her hand. "It's just . . . libations?" She tilted the bottle back and forth, a cheesy smile on her face. It faded. "Look, it's something

I do. At work. When people are sad or . . . you know. It's stupid." She hastily deposited the bottle on the counter and spun to face me with a look of false enthusiasm. But she seemed to realize that enthusiasm wasn't quite the right note to hit. Kat bit her lower lip, crossed her arms, and then put her balled-up fists on her hips for an apparent lack of a better place to put them. She sighed. "Oh, forget it. Let's just go."

I wasn't used to seeing my sister so flustered. She didn't know what to do with herself, and as I watched she raised a hand to her mouth and tucked a fingernail between her teeth. It was an unconscious move, something she hadn't done in a very long time.

"What do you do when people are sad?" I asked gently.

"It's stupid."

I rolled my eyes. "Tell me. Please."

"No, I—"

"Katrina." I scowled at her. "We're not leaving this house until you tell me."

"Fine," she huffed. "Sit down."

I took a seat at the table and Kat lowered herself into a chair across from me, smoothing her wool skirt against the back of her legs so it wouldn't wrinkle. She peeked up at me from beneath her eyelashes, and cleared her throat. I could tell she didn't quite know how to start. "When someone comes into the bar," she began haltingly, "and I can tell they're really upset—not the 'I just got a speeding ticket' sort of upset, but really, bone-crushingly hurt—I take this bottle out from under the bar." Kat patted the patterned glass as if it was an old and trusted friend.

"What's in it?"

"My own concoction. Brandy and crazy-strong black tea, some lemon sour, and a few other things. The alcohol content is pretty low, but it doesn't taste that way. It's sharp, you know?"

I didn't know, but I nodded anyway.

"People want to drown their sorrows, but I know from experience that doesn't work. Everything is only harder, messier, when you sober up." Kat fingered the drop pearl of her earring and cast a furtive look over her shoulder as if she half expected to find someone sneaking up behind her.

"Kat, I—"

"Let me finish." She gave her head a clarifying toss and then took the shot glass in her hand. Pouring it three-quarters full of the murky liquid from her mysterious bottle, she placed it directly in front of me. "Here's what I do: I tell them I'm going to pour them three drinks. Just three—no more, no less. And when those drinks are gone, they have to go out and face whatever it is that drove them to drinking in the first place."

"Nothing drove me to drinking," I argued.

But Kat acted as if I hadn't spoken at all. "Danica, I'm going to pour you three drinks, and when they're gone, you have to go out and face this."

"I am facing this."

"Chin up, shoulders back, strong and confident and capable. You face this, and then you move on."

"I don't—"

"You move on, honey. No buts."

"But—"

"No buts." Kat tapped the rim of the shot glass with her fingernail. "One drink to get you through," she said with an emphatic sense of ceremony.

I would have fought her, but Kat looked so earnest in that moment, so much like the responsible older sister instead of the flaky, would-be best friend that I obediently raised the glass to my lips and tipped it back in one, long swallow. It burned going down.

Kat poured again. "One drink to remember." She nodded at me.

I drank.

"And"—Kat filled my glass a third time—"one drink to forget."

The alcohol was cool-warm against my tongue, spicy and caustic just as Kat had promised. Her last words hit me in the second before I swallowed. *One drink to forget.* Everything in me rebelled against her proclamation, and I think I would have spit the drink out onto the table if I could, but it was too late. The liquid was seeping down my throat, and before I knew it, half of the elixir was gone.

But I coughed, and the rest of the draft swirled back into the shot glass. I slammed it onto the table half full, leaving the faintest mark that would forever bear witness to the place that I took my stand—that I refused to forget entirely about my husband. A few drops sloshed from the rim, staining my hands and rimming the table with a dark smear.

Kat smiled at me, nodded. "It's enough," she said. "I think it's just enough."

The memorial was a very casual affair. We congregated at the airport hangar outside Blackhawk and talked about Etsell as if he had merely stepped from the room and would be back at any moment. But we all knew that wasn't true. He wasn't coming back, and we didn't need the black box from his airplane to prove it.

Benjamin facilitated everything, passing around the microphone that we had hooked up to remote speakers the morning before the actual ceremony took place. Having Pastor

Miller there lent an undeniable weight to everything, but I was grateful for the laughter of Ell's friends. For the stories they told and the irreverent way they chose to remember my husband. We laughed until we cried, and then we cried until the only thing we could possibly do was laugh at ourselves. At the depth of our emotion and at the way we could—after all this time—conjure the memory of Etsell Greene with the devotion and tenacity of those who had loved him best.

As I listened to each carefully chosen tribute, the moments that pieced together the life of a man that I believed I held as dear as my own breath, I realized that my husband was a soul in limbo. A man chained to this town, to a father who couldn't love him the way that he deserved and a mother who had left too soon. Shackled to the earth when he wanted to fly. Bound to me. I had held him just like he now held me. But didn't we all do that? Hold each other close when what we wanted was to be free?

When Benjamin finally decided to end the memorial with a time of prayer, I stiffened. We hadn't rehearsed this, and I had no idea what he would say—or try to say—through an institution that I both secretly admired and couldn't begin to comprehend. There was something inside me that gravitated toward Benjamin's words like a compass points north, but the skeptic in me worried about what everyone else would think.

I needn't have worried.

"Thank you," someone said when our heads were bowed and our eyes were shut tight. Just that: "Thank you." As if Etsell's life was a gift. And, I suppose, it was. The most beautiful, undeserved gift.

"Be with Dani."

"Be with us."

"Help us understand."

Oh, God. I wanted that more than anything. To understand why. Why did we allow ourselves to drift apart? Why did he leave? Why did he ruin everything by permitting himself to love her, if only for one lonely night? But in that moment of longing I knew that nothing was as simple as that. I would never know why. And it didn't matter. *Why* meant nothing at all. *What* mattered. The one thing that counted for everything from this day forward was: What?

What now?

It was as if Benjamin could read my mind. "Grant us grace," he prayed as he concluded the service. "The grace to know where to go from here."

17

Right Here

Natalie came for the memorial, and for a few days Danica's life was as neat and tidy as the four square corners of a well-sealed box. Char and Natalie and Kat and Hazel hemmed her in, pressing her inside their haphazard haven with the sort of attentiveness that they had somehow neglected in the days immediately following Etsell's disappearance. It was as if everything finally made sense, the story had come full circle, and all at once the reality of what had happened echoed with a solemn finality.

But their story was no bleak tragedy. They played cards and dusted off old memories of Etsell, homespun treasures that they offered up one precious experience at a time. Dani tucked each anecdote carefully away, smoothing every layer of Ell's life one on top of the other until his narrative was a complete, unbroken whole. A piece of handmade art that was both painfully beautiful and brilliantly flawed.

There was food from friends and neighbors, casseroles and soups and pot roasts, and this time, Danica ate it. In fact, they all ate it, gathered around the little round table in her kitchen. More often than not they simply grabbed a handful of random cutlery and dug in, twirling strings of gooey cheese from the tines of their forks and scraping the last few morsels from the pan with their fingertips. They licked off creams and bits of shredded chicken and hot gravies that made them feel warm and satiated. Dani gained five pounds in a week and her jeans stopped slipping off her narrow hips.

"You look fantastic," Natalie said the day before she left for New York again.

"I do?" Dani smoothed her hands down her sides, shocked that she no longer had to stick her fingers in the waistband of her pants and hike them up. "I'm fat!" she gasped. "When did that happen?"

"Oh, for heaven's sake, you're not fat. You're on your way to *normal*." Natalie pinched Dani's midriff through her shirt and flashed an uncharacteristically mischievous grin. "I told you: you look fantastic."

Dani threw her arms around her sister and forced Natalie to endure a rare sisterly hug. "You look pretty great yourself." She lowered her voice, whispered in Natalie's ear: "Promise me you won't make me wait so long to see your sweet face again."

"I hardly have a sweet face," Natalie complained, pushing out of Dani's embrace and pursing her lips as if to affect an appropriately sour expression.

"It's sweet to me."

Natalie took a step back and gave Dani a calculating look. "Tell me this: Will there be a specific reason for me to come home?"

Dani could have feigned naïveté, but she knew exactly what Natalie was talking about. A few days after the memorial, late one night when the wind howled outside and the first few winter snowflakes began to whip against the windows of her little house, Dani had broken down and told her sisters about Ell's infidelity—and the consequences thereof.

"What are you going to do?" Kat's reaction was visceral and immediate. She leaned almost desperately over the table and clutched at Dani's hands as Char and Hazel looked on. But while Kat's emotions boiled, the two older women remained unyielding as ice. They were thin-lipped and silent, and Dani could tell that they both wished Dani had kept her mouth shut.

"I don't know," Dani said slowly. Her eyes flicked around the circle, trying to gauge everyone's reaction at once.

"What do you mean you don't know?" Char and Hazel spoke at exactly the same time.

"It's a pretty life-changing decision, don't you think?" Dani couldn't help feeling defensive. "Sam is giving the baby up for adoption no matter what. Either I take the baby or some stranger does."

"*You're* some stranger," Char reminded her. "You are no more connected to this child than some random housewife from Anytown, USA."

Dani could feel her jaw slacken. She snapped her mouth shut and swallowed hard. "But . . . but it's Ell's baby," she said, struggling to articulate how she felt. "We may not be flesh and blood, but *still*."

"How could you move on? How could you ever heal if you have to deal every single day with the living reminder of what happened?" Hazel's skepticism was even harder to take than Char's.

"I thought you of all people would understand." Dani shook her head in disbelief. "This baby is like your grand-child."

Hazel recoiled as if she had been struck. "No," she said firmly. "Someday, when this is far behind us and you have learned to love again, *your* baby will be like my grandchild. I look forward to that, Danica. To building a family again. But this child . . ."

When Hazel trailed off, Kat dove in. "This child is unwanted? Is that what you're saying? That he or she was an accident?"

"Of course not." Hazel exhaled sharply as if she could blow the very notion away. She seemed to struggle for words, then cast an oddly despairing look in Char's direction.

"That's not what she's saying." Char leaned forward in her seat and tried to pick up the conversational slack. "It's just that you're in a very vulnerable place right now, Dani. You have more than enough to deal with without throwing the child of your husband's one-night stand into the mix."

"I was the child of a one-night stand," Dani muttered.

Char rolled her eyes. "No, you weren't. But even if you were, it's apples and oranges. You were *my* baby." She softened, the lines around her mouth disappearing as she gave Dani a faint, sad smile. "You *are* my baby. And you've got a long way to go. A long life ahead of you. I don't want you to be chained to this. I don't want you to wake up five years from now with a preschooler who looks like your dead husband and like a woman you hate, and think: 'What happened to me?'"

"You're so young," Hazel said. "A strong, lovely young woman with the entire world spread out before you. You'll have a baby of your own. Someday."

It was obvious to Dani that Kat disagreed, but her sister didn't say anything further. Natalie remained conspicuously silent, her face angled toward the window over the kitchen sink, where a cardinal had taken up residence in one of Dani's naked trees. Of course, in the middle of a growing storm, the vivid bird was nowhere to be seen, but they had all learned in a week's worth of communing at random times in Danica's kitchen that he would be back eventually. He seemed to like watching them as much as they enjoyed catching the merest glimpse of him.

"Well." Dani put both her palms on the table and pushed herself up. She bustled around the chairs set at crooked angles, trying to hide the tremor in her voice by clanking plates and glasses together as she swept them into her arms. "Nothing has been decided yet. But when I do decide . . . I hope that . . . I'm going to need you all to be . . ."

"Danica." Natalie finally spoke, and when she did, the room seemed to go still. "We're here for you. All of us. Come what may."

And a few days later, standing in almost the same spot in the kitchen as she said good-bye again, Natalie repeated those words. "*You* are my specific reason to come home," she told Dani, waving away her earlier question. "I shouldn't have asked you that. And don't worry, I'll keep coming back. Come what may."

"Even if I decide . . . ?"

"Whatever you decide," Natalie assured her.

"I don't know what I want," Dani said. "A part of me wants to start over. I deserve that, don't I? A chance at love? At life? Maybe even a baby of my own instead of the child he gave to someone else." Dani's throat tightened and she had to fight to get the last few words out. "Sometimes I want to tear out the pages of this chapter in my life and make a clean break."

"Is there such a thing as a clean break?"

"Of course not. And even if there was, how could I entertain such a thought? This is *Ell* we're talking about. I just want to do the right thing."

Natalie seemed to think about that for a few seconds. "I

don't think you can do the wrong thing, Dani. I would never dare to presume that I know what is going to be healing for you. And once you make that decision, it's done. Your life takes the shape of the choices you've made. No matter what, it's going to be hard. Life is never easy."

"Tell me about it." Dani's laugh was dry and brittle, short-lived. "I want to just walk away, but I don't know if I can bear the thought that there's going to be a piece of him out there somewhere. I feel like I'd spend the rest of my life looking, waiting for the moment when some little boy would run past me in an airport and give me a one-dimpled smile. Etsell's smile."

Natalie shrugged. "There's something poetic about that."

Dani tilted her head and regarded her sister. "Since when are you a romantic?"

"I didn't say romantic, I said poetic. You have to admit that there is something incalculably fitting about Ell's child wandering the big, wide world."

"Ell's child wandering," Dani repeated, her words carried on a ragged breath. "Ell wandering. His *wife* wandering."

"You're not wandering," Natalie said.

Dani nodded. "You're right," she agreed. "I'm not."

❦

The day Natalie left for New York was the same day that life went back to normal for Dani. Hazel and Char stopped spending so much time at the house, and Kat picked up some extra shifts at the gentlemen's club to make up for the time that she had missed.

"I thought you were going to look for a new job," Dani said as Kat crouched on the floor, lacing up a pair of suede, high-heeled boots. They were riveted from toe to knee and hugged her slender calves like a second skin.

"I'm looking."

"You are?" Dani could hardly contain the excitement in her voice.

Kat gave her sister an arch look and brushed her long bangs back behind her ear. The Audrey Hepburn cut was growing out, and Dani guessed that by Christmas Kat's hair would graze her shoulders. Of course, Kat was gorgeous as always, but there was something about her that suggested she was caught in a moment between. A place where her past and future met at a crossroads. Dani could relate.

"Anything look promising?" Dani couldn't stop herself from probing.

"Lots of things look promising," Kat said. "But the illusion of promise and the reality of it are not always the same thing."

"Oh, don't be like that." Dani lightly nudged her sister's arm with a pointed toe. "I'm just taking an interest in your life."

"My life is not very interesting."

Dani lifted one shoulder noncommittally and then held out her hands to help Kat stand. They gripped wrists and Dani pulled until Kat was teetering before her, looking beautiful and tired, and not at all excited to head to work.

"I'll help you if you'd like. Look for a new job, I mean."

"*I'll* help *you* if you'd like," Kat parroted, but she didn't explain how she intended to do so. Did she want to help Dani cope? Help her change diapers if she decided to raise Ell's baby and encourage her to leave the past behind if not? Maybe it didn't matter. Maybe it was enough that they were willing to take each other by the wrist. Help each other stand.

The house seemed empty with everyone gone, and since she hadn't booked any appointments at the salon for one more day, Dani wandered the halls aimlessly. Everything could have used a good cleaning, but she wasn't in the mood, and instead of scrubbing toilets or running the vacuum in the living room, Dani decided she needed a breath of fresh air. She ended up slipping her feet into a pair of snow boots and stepping outside without a coat.

It was still snowing, but the wind that had raged the night before had decided to sleep away the day, and there wasn't even the slightest hint of a breeze. The flakes fell straight and true, delicate slivers of shaved frost that clung to the dark sleeves of her sweater and alighted in her eyelashes.

Dani didn't really have a destination in mind, and when she found herself standing at Benjamin's back door, she woke as if from a trance. She really had no idea how she had gotten there or what she hoped to accomplish by waylaying her neighbor in the middle of the day. Surely he was at the church office working on his sermon or whatever pastors did in the middle of the week. She could go back home and pretend that she had never come at all. But when Dani turned around, her footprints marked a straight line in the snow from her back door to his. Evidence of her unanticipated visit. Dani had never knocked on Benjamin's door before. Not once.

And, as it turned out, there was no reason to knock now. The door creaked open and a warm gust of air greeted Dani at the same moment that Benjamin said her name. "Is everything okay?" he asked, concern evident in his voice.

She whipped around, blinking at her neighbor through a lacy curtain of new fallen snow. "Fine," Dani said just a little too quickly. "I'm fine, Benjamin. I just wanted to get out of the house and . . ."

"Why don't you come in?" He stepped back and held open the door, revealing a kitchen much larger than her own.

The countertop was overflowing with thick books and loose-leaf paper, and an austere, wooden stool stood bellied up to the chaos. At least Dani knew how he had discovered her presence at his door. Benjamin had watched her come.

"Oh," she demurred. "No. I don't want to intrude. I just wanted to say thank you. For the service, I mean."

Benjamin gave his head a sad, little shake. "It's never enough, you know?"

"No," Dani interrupted before he could go on. "It was enough. It was perfect."

They stood there for a few seconds with the door open, Benjamin in his stocking feet and Dani collecting snowflakes in her hair like diamonds. She didn't even realize she was cold until she shivered violently, an unexpected quiver that sent a shower of snow drifting from her shoulders.

"You're cold!" Benjamin said. The discovery seemed to startle him. "You're not wearing a coat. Let me get you a coat or—"

"I'm fine," Dani cut in, clutching her arms tight to her chest. "I'm just fine." But her teeth had begun to chatter, and though it was partly due to the snow and the way the winter air nipped through the loose weave of her sweater, there was an earthquake of emotion just below the surface. All at once, it bubbled up and out of her, spreading hairline cracks through the very foundation of her being and making her shudder uncontrollably.

Dani didn't know where to turn, or what to do with herself, but before she could give it much thought, Benjamin stepped from the golden halo of light that spilled from his kitchen and took her into his arms. She gasped, shocked at his touch, and he immediately pulled away.

But Dani's arms were already around him, her forehead pressed to the place where the collar of his shirt hung crooked against his neck. She clutched at his back, her eyes squeezed tightly shut, and savored the faint thrum of his heartbeat beneath her skin. Benjamin was exotic, foreign, and the fit of their tangled arms, their heads bowed together, was lopsided and imperfect. But Dani didn't care. Everything about the way they held each other was unfamiliar, but it didn't feel wrong.

Benjamin's breath was cool against her cheek and somehow, impossibly, it seemed, laced with the scent of fresh cucumbers. Clean and sharp, as if she could taste the cold snick of the knife as it sliced a perfect white-green disk. It was a surprise, the fresh caress of his exhalation, and as his mouth found the hollow beneath her ear, Dani stifled a cry.

He didn't kiss her, not really, but his lips hovered against the taut line of her skin, daring here and there to press closer, to light upon her cheek, her neck, her collarbone as if he was checking for the warm pulse of Dani's blood beneath his timid exploration.

For some reason, she was grateful that he didn't smell of peppermints. Sermon candy. She could picture an entire glass jar of the lozenges on his desk at church, a subtle charity for everyone who sat in the faded leather chairs that surely flanked his desk like tired old friends. Dani would have pushed him away if he reeked of Sunday. Or stale coffee. The tea-colored Beech-Nut blend that congregants sipped in the fellowship hall after a quiet service. She couldn't have handled that.

But Benjamin smelled new. New and unexpected and completely different from what Dani always imagined a pastor should smell like. Completely different from anything that she had ever known. She drank him in. And then, because she forgot that he was Ben—or maybe because she knew *exactly* that he was Ben—Dani touched the line of his jaw, tilted it toward her face. She couldn't see him, but it didn't matter. His lips found hers, and the tenderness of his gentle ministrations was suddenly, irrevocably gone. There was an urgency in his mouth that startled her. That left her gasping for more.

Benjamin Miller kissed Dani long and hard, and when he finally pulled away they fell back from each other as if they had been stung. They stood apart, panting, astonished, and Dani raised her finger to her lips, searching for proof of what had happened between them. She found the place where his tongue had smoothed away all the tremors that shook her.

"*Danica.*" His voice cracked on her name like it was a powerful incantation, something he hardly dared to utter. "Dani, I'm so sorry, I'm so, *so* sorry."

"Don't be sorry," she whispered. "Please. Don't be sorry. I'm not sorry."

"But—"

"Not now," Dani said. And as the words fell away, she could see the crossroads of her life mapped out before her. It was a wheelhouse of choices, a future that contained so many possibilities, so many chances at redemption that the very fullness of it all was dizzying. She thought of her first date with Ell, their childish kiss behind the hangar. The subsequent years that had knit them together, the moments she believed they were made for each other, and the times when she could hardly stand to look at him she was so angry. So fed up with trying to make it all work. But it was exquisite, Dani decided. Worth every single minute. All of it. And maybe, just maybe, the best was yet to come.

"When . . ." Benjamin stopped himself. Started again. "If . . ." He released a jagged breath and ran both of his hands through his hair. His dark waves were instantly mussed; they stood on end in the most endearing way. "I'm here," he finally said simply. "I just want you to know that I'm right here. I'm not going anywhere."

Dani smiled, turned her face to the soft cloudburst of snow. "Me either."

Epilogue

Danica

The breeze was less than a breath, but it drifted across the patio all the same, carrying the mingled scents of Russian sage and garlic from the potatoes that were just starting to brown on the grill. I put my hands on my hips and surveyed the table, spread from end to end with plates and neat little clusters of silverware, a centerpiece of green hydrangeas, wineglasses that caught the final rays of sunshine and cast it back against the cherry-colored wood in bursts of crooked rainbows. There were Christmas lights in the lilac bushes, and Chinese lanterns hung from a crisscross of fine wire that arched over the patio in a haphazard pattern.

Over the winter, Hazel had helped me make a bench for one side of the trestle table, and I indulged myself by trailing my fingertips over the high gloss of the seat. It was a seamless plank of black walnut that swirled and eddied in waves of coffee and cream, a masterpiece; an extravagant creation that was perfectly mismatched with the table that already bore the scars of an abundant life.

But I rarely sat on the bench. My seat was the Queen Anne, the claw-footed relic that I refinished in one frenzied afternoon. The seat was re-covered in sprout green, the wood painted a brown as deep and dark as bitter chocolate. As rich as earth. It was my place to sit and think, slouched low with my feet curled beneath me and my head tipped against the backrest, tilted toward the sky.

I liked my feet on the ground, but I couldn't stop myself from looking at the heavens. Following the arc of stray clouds as they scudded across a sea of blue so endless it seemed full of possibility. I slept with my eyes open sometimes, or rather, I dreamed. And every daydream ended the same: with a flicker at the corner of my vision, at the place where my conscious began to blur every edge. The flash of a Cessna on the horizon, the merest hint of red-and-white.

But today I didn't have time for turning my face toward the sun. They would be here soon, all of them, and the thought made my heart trip over itself. I was little more than an excited child, I decided, and laid my palms against the smooth tabletop, focusing on my to-do list, making sure that it was complete. It was.

When Benjamin came walking across the grass, I could see that there was something in his hands. They were cupped in front of him, held out in offering as if he came bearing gifts. And in a way, he did.

"We'll have enough this year for jam," he said when I was close enough to hear his proclamation. His bare feet padded on the smooth stones of the patio. "Jam and pies and tarts and sauce for ice cream . . ."

"And fresh eating." I smiled. I plucked a strawberry from the deep bowl of his hands, popped it in my mouth whole. Warm from the sun. Sweet on my tongue.

"Of course," he said. "Fresh eating. As much as you want." His eyes searched mine, and then he leaned forward, pressed his lips to the spot where my tongue had caught a drop of juice only a moment before. "They'll bloom again. And if they don't, I'll plant more."

I reached for the berries, intending to take them inside, rinse them in cold water, and put them on the table in a colander so they would stay fresh all night. But just then I heard the first car in the driveway. The slam of a door, the sound of laughter. And at the same moment there came a cry from the house.

The baby was awake, and he would want me. He would be waiting, fists pumping, cheeks turning pink before they darkened to rose, eyes flinting from blue to gray to charcoal if I took too long. He was too little to be patient.

"Go," Ben said, winking at me. "I've got this covered."

I touched his cheek for just a second before I spun on my heel and disappeared behind the screen door. Through the kitchen and down the hall, and then I was tiptoeing across the hardwood and bending over his crib. Trying not to laugh at the sight of his bare feet, the darling rolls of his chubby legs. He was crying, so I lifted him from beneath the mobile, the fleet of paper airplanes that flew over him in his sleep. I pressed my lips to his cheek, whispered against his sleep-soft skin, "Hush. It's going to be all right."

Acknowledgments

Thank you, thank you to an ever-growing list of amazing people. I would love nothing more than to express my sincere gratitude with a home-cooked meal and a bottle (or two) of fine wine, but Iowa is hardly a vacation destination. I may have to settle for offering a simpler token of my enduring thanks—and the assurance that my door (and my kitchen) is always open.

A huge thank-you (and an even huger hug) to Josh and Jessica Louwerse for taking care of Aaron and me when we were in Anchorage. From breakfast at Snow City to a last-minute trip to Seward, you unknowingly set the stage for this entire book. Thank you especially for introducing us to a host of people who helped me better understand all that is Alaska. Every conversation counted.

I am indebted to Ken Moll and Blair Rorabaugh for sharing their knowledge of all things aeronautical. Thanks especially to Blair for taking me up in your plane over Resurrection Bay and not crashing when I was sure we were doomed. This book is richer for the experience and for your expertise. And, of course, any mistakes or inaccuracies in this book are all mine.

Big thanks to the lovely ladies who helped me navigate the stacks in the Alaska collection of the Loussac Library in Anchorage. Librarians rock.

To my patchwork of editors—from Todd Diakow (who has been with me from the very first draft of my very first book) all the way to new reader Katie Nice (who stepped in with encouraging words at exactly the right time), *thank you*. As for the rest of you, you know who you are. I would be lost without you.

I am beyond blessed to be represented by the amazing women of Browne & Miller Literary Associates. Thank you for your wisdom and advice, and for late-night brainstorming sessions fueled by cupcakes and wine. It still humbles me that you believe in me and my stories.

Forever and always, thank you to my family, for putting up with me when I'm scattered and distracted, and for letting me do this thing that I love. More than anything, thank you for continuing to remind me that the greatest story I'll ever tell is the one I live with you. Aaron, Isaac, Judah, and Matthias, I love you to the moon and back.

Reading Group Guide

TOPICS & QUESTIONS FOR DISCUSSION

1. Why do you think the author chose to include a Prologue from Danica's point of view about the first time Etsell took her flying? How did this opening set the tone for the rest of the novel?

2. The author uses an interesting point-of-view technique, alternating chapters from Danica's first-person point of view with those from a more limited third-person point of view. What effect did this have on your reading experience?

3. Danica feels betrayed and upset when Etsell tells her about his three-week trip to Alaska. She accuses him of making an important decision they should have made together. He in turn accuses her of making all their decisions. Explain Danica's reaction. Do you feel that she is justified? How accurate is Etsell's complaint? Use examples from the novel to support your opinion.

4. On page 47, Benjamin tells Danica, "Never do what you should do, Dani. Do what you have to do." What do you think he means by this? Do you agree or disagree?

5. Danica and Etsell may not have had much in common, but they both grew up with untraditional parenting. Compare and contrast the relationship Etsell has with Hazel (his "surrogate mother") with the relationship between Danica and Charlene. Did Danica have a "surrogate mother"?

6. Danica describes her oldest sister as somewhat detached and cold. Natalie doesn't come to visit Danica until Etsell has been missing for two months. Yet Danica is "convinced of her sister's love, even if Natalie couldn't bring herself to say it and didn't know how to show it." Do you think Danica understands her loved ones and forgives them for their faults, or does she just have a lifelong history of making excuses for everyone around her? Explain your opinion.

7. Who did you suspect was at the door on page 235? Were you surprised at Sam's news? Why or why not?

8. Danica asks her neighbor Ben—a pastor—why in all his visits he's never mentioned God. "I have," he says. "In lots of different ways" (page 312). What do you think he means? Identify and discuss what some of these "different ways" might be.

9. Danica's older sister Natalie tells Danica, "We fail each other. Every day in a million different ways" (page 224). Does Danica agree? Do you? Why or why not?

10. When Danica finally tells her whole family about the baby, everyone seems divided on what she should do. Hazel and Char seem to think it would only hurt Danica in the long run to have such a reminder in her life, whereas Kat seems to feel the baby belongs more with Danica than with a stranger. What would you do in her shoes?

11. Unlike most widows, Danica is never delivered a body or even true confirmation of Etsell's death. Identify and discuss some of the ways in which she attempts to move on with her life. What finally marks a true shift for her toward healing? How does she find closure?

12. At the end of the book, Danica wrestles with whether or not she should adopt Etsell and Sam's child. In the Epilogue, she is definitely mothering an infant. Whose baby is it? Etsell and Sam's? Or Danica and Benjamin's? Use clues from the text and your own understanding of Dani's growth throughout the book to make a case for the scenario you believe is the most likely.

ENHANCE YOUR BOOK CLUB

1. Sam's unexpected visit interrupts a game of canasta between Danica, her sisters, their mother, Hazel, and Ben. Try learning to play this popular card game from the 1940s with members of your book club.

2. Danica and Etsell often hike to the river and enjoy lazing around, their feet in the water. Bring a little of their world to life by holding your next book club meeting beside a local river or lake.

3. In the novel, Kat decides to mark Etsell's passing from their lives in a very physical way, asking Danica to lop off her ponytail and give her a short new hairstyle. Many women mark major life changes by dramatically coloring or cutting their hair. If you're feeling brave, why not experience the difference such a change can make in your life by visiting your favorite beautician and trying a totally new look?

A CONVERSATION WITH NICOLE BAART

1. *You write a blog on your website, www.nicolebaart.com. What made you decide to start blogging, and how is it working for you?*

I started blogging shortly after I signed my first publishing contract because I thought it was part and parcel of the whole writing gig. At first I felt silly and inadequate as I tried to come up with witty, interesting posts. Now I just write about whatever is on my mind. Sometimes I blog about my publishing experiences, but more often than not my posts are a place for me to think out loud about life, family, relationships . . . I even post recipes or snippets of funny conversations I have with my kids. It's a pretty mixed bag, but I do love doing it. There's a fantastic online community that I never knew existed until I started to blog.

2. Far from Here *is your fifth novel. How has your writing process evolved since your first novel? What is the first thing you do when beginning a new book?*

The first thing I do when I begin a new book is buy a brand-new package of my favorite pens and six legal pads of paper. When the notebooks are full, the book is done. That's how I wrote my first book, and my process hasn't changed much since then. I still write longhand and then transfer the book chapter-by-chapter to my computer. I'd say the biggest thing that has changed about my writing process is my approach to plotting. I used to just let the book evolve, but I like to have a pretty detailed outline to work from these days. Of course, that doesn't mean I stick to it.

3. *You include a lot of specific details in your novel, lending authenticity to your settings and characters. In particular, your description of Danica's work in the salon and her restoration hobby, as well as her trip to faraway Alaska, come to mind. What kind of research did you do for this book?*

My mother restored furniture when I was a little girl, and it's something that has always interested me. I'm currently in the process of refinishing an old dining-room table for outdoor use by weatherproofing it and creating a mosaic tile pattern on the tabletop. It's fun, but a bit overwhelming.

As for Danica's experiences in Alaska, I knew I couldn't accurately capture that atmosphere without going there myself. So Aaron and I flew up to Anchorage for five days. It was a whirlwind trip but we had an amazing time. We have friends who live in the area and they were very gracious tour guides, ferrying us from the Loussac Library to Seward and through countless little airports and hangars. I was even able to go up in a Cessna over Resurrection Bay. It is an experience I will never forget, and one that hugely impacted the way I wrote *Far from Here*.

4. *Danica's situation is complicated from the beginning and only gets more complex as the novel progresses. What inspired you to write this story?*

They say life is stranger than fiction, and in this case it's true. My dad's best friend disappeared in a bush plane in northern Alaska and was never found. His story always haunted me, but as a grown woman I began to consider it from the perspective of the people left behind. How could you live not knowing? The unknown can be so scary, and I tried to imagine what it would be like to live with all the questions and what-ifs. Could a person find hope even in that? I'd like to think so.

5. *This novel is set in Blackhawk, Iowa, which is described as a tiny, out-of-the-way town that time (almost) forgot. Is this a real place, or based on one? What was it like writing about a small town like the one you grew up in?*

There is a little village not too far from my hometown that served as the inspiration for Blackhawk. It's tucked next to a small river in a valley that cuts between acres of rolling hills and farmland. I've always loved it—especially the big, white bridge that spans the river as you enter the town. However, I took some serious creative license as I dreamed up Blackhawk. The fictional town is bigger and more picturesque. A perfect Anytown, USA.

As for writing about small towns, it just feels natural to me. I've lived in the city and on a farm, but I'm a small-town girl at heart. There is a very unique sense of community in a small town, an unspoken understanding that we are all family—even quirky great-aunt Mildred and the guy who talks to himself next door. Everyone fits somewhere in a small town, and I wanted that sort of close-knit community for Dani.

6. *Though love is an important theme in this book, it's anything but a typical love story. Through your characters, you explore how love and marriage can change over time—how careful we must be as their caretakers. At one point, Natalie seeks to comfort Danica by telling her, "We fail each other. Every day in a million different ways" (page 224). Do you think this is true? What's the most important thing you've learned about marriage?*

I do think that we fail each other, but I believe even more strongly what Dani muses shortly thereafter: "Sometimes we come through for one another. Sometimes we forgive" (page 225). The truth is, we are all very selfish beings. We try to put others first, but even in the relationships that mean the most to us, we often default to elevating our own wants and perceived needs above those of the people we love. Love is a daily, sometimes hourly, choice. Even though we fail, we have to keep trying.

It breaks my heart when I hear a version of the sentiment: I love him, but I'm not *in love* with him anymore. What does that mean? To me, it's just a pretty way of saying: "I don't feel like trying anymore." That may sound harsh, but love is hard. It can be exhausting and frustrating and heartbreaking. But I'm a romantic at heart—I believe it is always worth fighting for. I tried to communicate that through the pages of *Far from Here*. In spite of their differences, and in spite of all that happened, Etsell and Dani kept fighting for each other. They forgave. And in the end, I think they both chose love, even though they stumbled and fell and could have spent the rest of their lives resenting each other. I think that is the single most important thing I've learned about marriage: Be gracious to one another. Always.

7. *The issue of adoption comes up at the end of the book. You also have adopted a child. How did that experience influence your inclusion of this plot twist in* Far from Here?

Adoption is very near and dear to my heart, even if it is a hot-button topic in the world today. Some people will argue that children should remain within their context at any cost, and though I agree that the preservation of identity within a particular culture or society (even the culture of a specific community within the same state or country) is important, I believe that in an ideal world every child should experience the love of a family. Sometimes that family isn't going to look like a "normal" family. Sometimes that family might live across the country or even across the globe. It probably sounds idealistic, but I think that love really does have the power to overcome seemingly insurmountable hardships. I wanted to address that belief with Dani's impossible question: Could she adopt the love child of her husband and a woman with whom he had a one-night stand? Could I? Could *you*? The answer is going to be different for everyone—and that's okay—but that doesn't change the fact that a living, breathing child is the result of Etsell and Sam's "mistake." A child who needs a home. Who needs the miracle of adoption.

8. *Tell us a little about One Body One Hope, the nonprofit you co-founded.*

One Body One Hope is a nonprofit organization that works alongside a church and orphanage in Monrovia, Liberia. My husband and I met the pastor of a Liberian congregation when we were in Ethiopia bringing home our son, and it was evident in the two weeks we spent together that we simply couldn't walk away and pretend that our lives could go on as normal. The people of Liberia had imprinted themselves on our hearts in that short time, and we left Ethiopia with the promise to do anything we could to support our new friend and his struggling community.

One Body One Hope began with basic relief work—distributing rice to starving families and providing a monthly sponsorship program for the fifty-some children in the church-run orphanage. But we've moved past those fledgling efforts and are passionately committed to rehabilitation and development in both the orphanage and the greater community. Liberia is still experiencing the devastating effects of a bloody civil war, and the economy is very fragile. Eighty-five percent of Liberians are unemployed. We'd like to see that change. It is our goal to walk beside our Liberian friends and offer whatever assistance and support we can to help them rebuild their country—one family, one person, one community at a time.